Roebuck

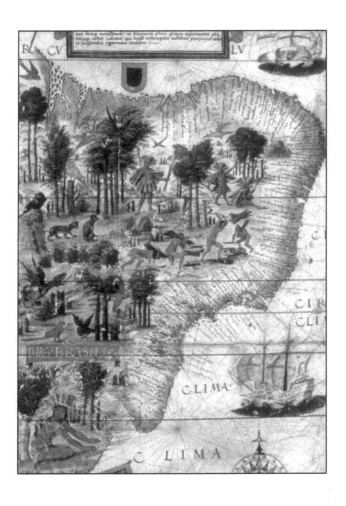

Roebuck

Tales of an Admirable Adventurer

By Luke Waterson

urbanepublications.com

First published in Great Britain in 2015
by Urbane Publications Ltd
Suite 3, Brown Europe House, 33/34 Gleamingwood Drive,
Chatham, Kent ME5 8RZ

ISBN 978-1910692387
EPUB 978-1910692042
MOBI 978-1910692059

Cover design by Julie Martin
Design and Typeset by The Invisible Man

Printed and bound by CPI Group (UK) Ltd, Croydon, CR0 4YY

urbanepublications.com

To my mother - the reason I first fell in love with writing.

ONE

"We lay seven and twentie dayes driving to and fro without puffe or winde"

Anthony Knivet, *Admirable Adventures and Strange Fortunes*

They hanged him in the hottest part of the afternoon and we stood on the deck and watched.

At first we watched out of duty, for our General was in such a foul mood we believed he would have strung us up there alongside the victim at the slightest provocation. But soon our curiosity kicked in. The General had instructed the noose to be tied in such a way strangulation would come, but slowly. As was customary, the man was dressed in full armour, so in this fierce sun his brain could cook before he would choke. And of course he had beer in a purse that his hands, though bound, could just reach; a tradition, like many King Hal had conjured up, aimed at eking out a wrongdoer's agony. So there was the possibility of a long, lingering death. But – and here was the devilish ingenuity – that purse contained one further item: a knife. If the man so chose he could cut himself free. But because of the position of the mizzen arm to which he was fastened he would fall like a stone to the sea, and drown.

"He'll choke," guessed Waldren, our boatman, while the General was out of earshot.

"He'll guzzle the beer, then cut himself loose and get to go to the grave slightly drunk," whispered Harris on my other side. "At least, that's what I would do."

"No" I said. "He is a Portugal. He will give us some speech on

1

how we will roast in our English hellfire of eternal damnation for what we have done to him. And if he does, it will most probably be an astute prediction."

"You were ever a cheery soul, Knivet."

The Portugal got one of his hands free fairly quickly. But the knots hampered him from freeing the other and he opted, rather than partaking of his beer, to clutch the mizzen arm to alleviate the pressure on his windpipe. For some minutes he held on, regaining breath, knife between teeth. He was bracing himself for the moment when he must again let the noose rip into his neck flesh, for, were he to prevail, he would need the one hand to liberate the other. He appeared to be deciding which part of his throat was least scarred to bear the rope's pressure, but from where we stood it all seemed mighty raw.

"Could he not... could the General not show some mercy?" ventured Barrawell, a young man of my own county for whom I confess I felt the closest thing to affection it was possible to feel on that ship.

Waldren and Harris laughed.

"Still so green, Barrawell? The General have a change of heart? He would sooner cut out his own than go back on his order! They say that on his last voyage, he beat a man to death for looking at him wrong." Waldren leaned close to emphasise his words. "For looking at him, lad, is like looking at the devil, and there ain't nowt there in them eyes of his save a devastating determination to do his will."

"His will?"

"Aye. To round that Cape of Horn a second time. And God knows he might, as a devil, for no man ever managed it."

The Portugal was tiring. His eyes bulged. He had both hands again at his disposal, but seemed reticent to cut that final rope from around his Adam's apple; thinking, perhaps, that there was nothing else between him and a nasty tumble should his arms fail. The day so was damnably still we heard each of his grunts.

"What is he doing?" Barrawell asked. "Why does he twist his head so?"

Then I saw I had misjudged the man's actions. What I had taken for writhes to keep the rope from throttling him were far from it. They were movements to a rhythm. The poor dog was singing. And, given a noose had been crushing his throat the preceding half hour, in a voice that was remarkably resonant.

"It is like angels," Barrawell said, transfixed. And it was.

"I can't understand what he's saying," Waldren complained. "What's he saying, Knivet?"

"I believe it to be a sonnet."

"I care nowt for his form of verse. What are his words?"

"Love," I translated, dully. "He sings of his sweetheart, and how she will be waiting for him, in his homeland across the seas."

"Live!" cried Barrawell, and pathetic as this sounded, it occurred to me it was a human tendency to express such an elevated hope only when its very antithesis was imminent. I will give you some food, you say to a starving beggar. All will be well, you say, after it has gone horribly, irrevocably wrong.

Then, where normally there was a rush of sound – of barked commands, of straining rigging, of winds foul and fair – there was no sound. Our five boats, becalmed, lashed together on a latitude we could only guess at, and all the eyes of the company[1] fixed in fascination on the man the General had deemed a traitor, and sentenced without trial.

"*Quão cedo de meus olhos te levou,*"[2] the Portugal was gasping. How soon from my eyes were you taken… Unseemly froth welled at his mouth. He forced it away, impatiently, with the air of a man set on orating. I still believed my prediction could prove correct,

---

[1] In this sense, all the men in the fleet: individuals bound together on an adventure.

[2] From the Luís de Camões sonnet *Alma Minha Gentil*

and that he would start regaling us with some Catholic rant about our Protestant sins. But he concluded merely with a dedication of his ditty, which was, I will own, anticlimactic compared to my own vision of his demise, in which his accusatory screams about God's wrath on English curs bombarded us along with a meteorite-like shower of brimstone and I stood in the middle of the deluge as everyone else fled, arms raised and laughing because the brimstone was glancing off me harmlessly. "To our General Don Cavendish," he croaked, now in almost impeccable English, "with all my heart, may God…"

We did not learn what the Portugal willed God to do or not do to us. The man cut the final rope, and his arms at long last gave up. At the aft end of the vessel alongside the General's, I was well positioned to gauge the expression on the man's face. It was a frown, as if he were confused about why he was being executed when so many of those we depended upon to man the ships were managing to die without any assistance at all. And, perhaps because of the couple of tentative inches he had hauled himself along the mizzen before letting go, perhaps because at that moment the wind at long last got up for the first time in a month, the Portugal fell not into the sea as had been intended, but onto the gunwale. Blood and bad beer exploded around the broken body, but no one dared move. Not even the General's boatswain, who, standing adjacent, had his smock spattered red from the discharge.

"Glad it ain't my job to mop up them brains," Waldren grunted.

Barrawell vomited.

The General's eyes swept over the company. 350 men, and we each shivered as though he could detect our innermost thoughts.

"What are you waiting for?" he screamed. The buttons on his dandy's doublet gleamed and I detested them but wanted them. "Clean that dog from my deck and get to work. This wind is for Brazil, and I do not mean to miss it on account of a heretic!"

The General's boatswain was still gawping at the expanding

patches of blood on what were probably his only clothes, but had the presence of mind to set two of his underlings to the task.

"The ninth circle," I said, half to myself, but Waldren heard me.

"I'd watch yourself, Knivet. You saw what just happened to the only other poet on this voyage."

Our supplies were nigh on gone, scurvy had already set in to some fifty of our company, we still had no idea how far we were from the coast of South America, and the boatswain's mate was on the sterncastle deck scrubbing off the remains of the Portugal pilot, the only man who had truly known the waters of the coast to which we were headed.

I wondered, then, for the first time, why I had so readily abandoned my green homeland for this pitching deck at the mercy of our General's increasingly evident madness, assailed by this sickly tropical air and the pit of hunger almost always in my belly. But the truth was that I had never had any choice, not from the very beginning.

TWO

It was a miracle my father managed to participate in the duel at all, given he had but one leg. His opponent was a hot-headed young dog from the neighbouring village whose reputation was already in such tatters that backing down, the gentlemanly thing to do as my father already occupied a position of considerable standing, would not have redeemed it. Besides, such knaves are motivated solely by how to advance their own social status, and not by any nobler principle. The venue, the wood that separated their respective parishes, was covered in mist that autumn morning, which no doubt influenced the outcome for my father's sight was already failing at that time. I arrived early, but the dog Moody and his retinue of followers were already there, with Moody boasting of his gunmanship and rights to our family's lands, which none but one who was inept with weapons, and in the wrong, would do. The appointed hour came and went. My father did not show until after a further forty-five minutes, during which time Moody screamed such obscenities against the Knivet name that I had a mind to emerge from my hiding place and finish him with my own hand. My father eventually appeared dressed in a ruff after the style of Drake himself, a fitting tribute to our family's connections, citing his need for a hot breakfast on this chilly day as the reason for his lateness. So when the seconds instructed them to go back-to-back and walk the ten paces, he most likely had indigestion too or, at least, an inhibiting bloatedness. The bailiff, my father's second, objected that given Moody's superior number of limbs, the paces should be called out by a mediator at a speed sufficiently slow to give my father time to manage them. Even as the older man, and on crutches, he was the very essence of good breeding beside his uncouth rival. At pace four he was still jovially reminding the bailiff of his dinner invitation that evening.

"Seven, eight, nine" shouted the mediator and before ten was called Moody turned and fired.

My father took the shot to the right of his heart and was pronounced dead by a doctor at the scene, although this person was an acquaintance of Moody's and transpired to be nothing more than a travelling quack. But the bailiff, observed movement in the corpse and Moody, as superstitious as he was impetuous, interpreted this as a sign that some things are ordained by the good Lord, and one of these was my father's rights to the estate over which they had fought. I will own it was amusing to see Moody come full circle from the cocky upstart to the pale, repentant figure who now, fearing that having shot at my father he had somehow gone against the Almighty's wishes, scuttled around scouting out the nearest dwelling at which my father could be attended.

Everyone, Moody's supporters and my father's, repaired to an obliging farmhouse not far distant. Only myself, the two village boys who had accompanied me to the duel, and the quack, were not permitted entry – the latter because the farmer remembered him as the peddler of ointments whose extortionately priced wares had brought his wife out in a rather sensitive rash some years before.

"Get gone, pests! Find me funny, eh?" the quack cried, as, picking himself up from where the farmer had thrown him, he heard my companion's laughter. With his purple French cloak, sequined shirt and elaborately tasselled shoes he did resemble the fool in a pack of tarot cards and I would have laughed too, had I felt so inclined. "I could hex you!" he hissed. "See how that farmer feared me, and he a grown man!"

My companions backed off, for when the man thus contorted his face he looked malevolent enough, but I stayed.

"What are you doing here boy? Who are you?"

"I am the son of that gentleman your friend shot in such base fashion."

"Ah," the quack said, stroking his beard in pretend earnestness. Then: "And I am the Queen's physician!" He broke into a guffaw that quickened as I clenched my fists to defend my family's good name. "I know for fact old Knivet has but two daughters."

"He's a bastard!" The cry came from behind the farmhouse wall. My two companions, regrettably not departed as distantly as I would have wished.

Quivering with rage, I looked from the quack to those village bigmouths, torn as to whom it would best advantage me to dispatch some select blows upon. I chose the two boys, and set to the pair of them, giving them a hiding that sent them wailing to their mothers. For they were the respective offspring of a rag-and-bone man and a farmhand, whilst the blood of the Lord of the Manor flowed through my veins and that it flowed courtesy of a surreptitious union with his cook did not trivialise the fact.

"Fought like a Knivet," the quack smiled. "And some would say better than a Knivet, since you succeeded where your father failed. Not bad given you are, what…twelve?"

"Thirteen," I lied, although I was but recently turned eleven. "But I would not flinch to take on two twice as old as them, nor twice as big!"

"That would still be rather small."

He must have seen me regarding him warily, yet beneath my boyish scowl I was concealing a sense of intrigue and, perhaps, a nugget of respect towards this strange man in jester's clothes, with an odour of clove water and strips of silk in his ears. People like this did not pass through my village every day.

"We should not quarrel. We are alike, you and I. You, like me, do not fit in. But we are destined to do great things."

"Great things?" My eyes narrowed.

"Aye. A new path of stars, like Copernicus. New lands, like Da Gama. New verse, like Dante. Anything is possible! Now tell me, do you know the gemshorn?"

I did not, of course, as I did not know much of anything he told me. It was a horn much like a goat's, hollowed, with small holes beginning near the base and continuing almost to the curved tip. When he put it to his lips it produced a sound similar to the flutes I had heard at village fairs, only with a more rudimentary and somehow more haunting sound.

"You summon all your breath into the first note," the quack explained, "until the sound is even. Then you are away, and can become its master. You see, boy, I am no musician, but I can play."

"You are no doctor, but you readily practice medicine."

The quack took this in good humour.

"True. I have been, in my life, different things at different times…"

He told me of how he had hunted bears in Russia, entertained at the Venetian court, traded cinnamon in Alexandria. He told me of his loves, a merchant's wife in Petersburg and, so he claimed, King Henry of France himself. He told me of vast red deserts in Africa where you could see nothing but sand, and still vaster Siberian plains where the snows never melted even in summer.

"And always," he said, "none but the wind determined my course."

The quack played me 'Come Over the Burn Bessie' and 'Scarborough Fair'. As he played me 'The Good Soldier' my father's screams rang out of the mist, and as he began 'By a bank as I lay' a buggy containing my father's wife and, as I supposed, my two half-sisters, pulled up. They entered the farmhouse and I saw that they, like me, had the strong Knivet nose and high Knivet forehead. And I supposed that, in a parallel universe, I might have been going in with them as their brother and equal, as the man of the house consoling them as they wept, and as the future heir of the estate receiving well-wishers with a manly demeanour. It grieved me sorely to see them permitted entry and me, despite possessing the best qualities of the line, obliged to wait outside, no better than an outcast. And I resented, by turns, my mother for seducing my father with her fleshy charms, and society for not permitting their legitimate union, for she was a very good cook.

But the quack's melodies did much to temper my sadness. Long after he had gone on his way I was sitting on the farmhouse wall, thinking about the world. And years later, when the boatswain's whistle ordered me this way and that on a ship on the other side of the globe, it would be the gemshorn that I recalled, and the oakwoods on the turn in the mist, and the melodies of the person who showed me more kindness than any other on this Earth, bar one.

I saw numerous important individuals come and go at the farmhouse over that month my father wrestled with death. The sheriff sent round the county's entire contingent of militia, for my father was responsible for their training. Members of parliament arrived, for my father was a revered politician. These included the Earl of Suffolk, Sir Thomas Howard, the latest thing at the Queen's court and most particular in his affections towards my half-sister. The Queen sent her physician, for my father was much remembered by her for his acts of bravery in the name of the Crown. On another occasion a fine whirlicote decorated in ostrich feathers drew up and who should alight but Secretary of State, Sir Francis Walsingham, who sent off the great Drake on his historic circumnavigation. He wore a sable satin travelling coat fastened at the neck with solid diamonds, but seemed exceedingly stiff in his attire, and I believed I could have carried off the same outfit with more dignity. My mother sent some comfrey pies, under the impression I would be admitted bearing such delights; but I elected, rather than suffer the humiliation of being again refused entry, to eat all of them myself. It was the least I deserved for my attentive vigil.

In that month I saw many things. I was shown how to hold and load a firearm by one of the militiamen, who preferred my company to the cramped and frankly awkward conditions inside the house. I saw Moody come out on several occasions and pray, promising the Lord anything and everything in return for my father's recovery. I witnessed Walsingham strike his deputy for suggesting England's fleet of fighting ships was inferior to Spain's, should it ever come to battle. I saw Sir Phillip Sidney striding the farmhouse garden turning words for a poem over in his head. I felt closer than ever to my father, whom I imagined, in the occasional screams that filtered down, to be calling for me, his only son, to recompense me for never being able to acknowledge my existence. I ate a veritable glut of comfrey pies that my mother, flushed with how favourably her first batch of baking was received by my father, continued to make for him. I dreamed of Russia, of Venice, of Alexandria. And I grew up.

My father, I thought, was a great man for having these great personages concerned for his wellbeing, and England was indeed a great country with such great personages at her helm to drive her to victory. But there was no greatness there for me, God damn it. There was no greatness there for me.

THREE

In the July of 1591 – my twenty-second year – my father sent for me for the first time. There was much debate as to whether I should use the entrance for gentry or the servant's entrance at the back. My father in his sensitivity for my predicament suggested the rear; my mother wrote back that her son was a Knivet however much he might wish to forget it, and would use the front entrance or none at all. The messenger returned promptly with ten shillings with which I was to find 'proper attire'. Ten shillings was then more money than most villagers made in a quarter and I set out in a bright doublet and hose red as a frigate bird's belly, a brown leather slash-jerkin and tapered shoes which, every time I glanced down and saw them keeping pace with my movements, made me think I had temporarily inhabited the body of some blundering exotic creature. I was sweltering, and somewhat ashamed that the villagers I passed on the way to the gates of the estate had that morning seen me glazing apricot tarts in my mother's bakery. Nevertheless, I looked nearly as fine as one of the Queen's courtiers, and was in fact exhibiting infinitely better taste, since my mother had kept six of the shillings back for what she grimly referred to as 'severance dues' and left me but four with which to deck myself out in a manner befitting of a gentleman.

"Anthony." My father seemed much as on our last encounter at the duel a decade before: crimson-faced, corpulent, and vague. It was hard to picture him as a man who had rallied troops against the French or been prepared to fight to the death for a principle, but my mother forewarned me this was his way; complacent in his familial relations but ruthless in his others. Stories circulated in the village of him smiling in a kindly, avuncular way as he pronounced sentences in his capacity as councillor, or personally clapping a just-evicted tenant on the back with an absent-minded 'dear fellow – I simply had no choice' whilst the poor man's cottage burned behind him.

"Do sit down. Would you care for some wine?"

I felt immediately I was being tested.

"A small glass, thank you father."

My father winced, and held up a hand. "No, boy – I appreciate your excitability but that really will not do… 'Sir Henry' will suffice. You do see that?"

It was a bright day outside but dark in the study where he received me. Only his eyes stood out. They did not even look at me, but had a most uncommon effect on me nevertheless. They were so glazed with indifference I wanted to startle them, to bring out some emotion, ideally admiration although I would have settled for anger, anything. I wanted to make my mark there.

"How was your walk up? Pleasant?"

"Very…"

"Good. Heh, heh. And your mother? Doing admirably with the bakery, is she not? I did always love her comfrey pies. Does she still make them? How is my wine? Apples from my estate, you know. How are my orchards coming along? Did you see if they cut that tree back on the avenue? It was ruining my prospect, you can imagine how that grieved me…"

He trailed on in this manner awhile, as if anxious to avoid a subject that would inevitably arise. I was hurt that that he did not refer to the Knivet lands with a more inclusive 'our'. Of course I knew the apples were ripening well. I walked among them almost daily, in full knowledge they produced one of the finest wines in the county, one I had for many years desired to sample and now had, casually, thrust before me in a gesture that meant nothing to him and everything to me. I knew the avenue too, better perhaps than the gardener himself. I had often imagined that as Lord I would perhaps extend the paths through the woods to show them off more beneficially to guests.

"You know that you cannot inherit?" he finally said, abruptly. My mother's parting words flashed before me: "when he mentions money, remain calm. Say you'll think over whatever he proposes." We had, of course, been assuming there would at least be some proposition and I wondered what my father had in mind.

"Education – good. Propensity for languages – good. Shooting – very good. We will need, heh heh, to get you some more practice." It was only at this point I realised he was summarising my life's achievements to date.

"Sir Henry?"

He gave me his pained smile. "There is a ship. Some say it is *the* ship. Its commander is planning to do for the second time what Magellan died doing and Drake could only manage accidentally…"

"'Sail round the world," I breathed. I had followed our country's heroic exploits at sea avidly these last few years, for they were better than the best of the chivalric romances. Hawkins capturing Iberian[1] treasure ships in the Caribbean, Raleigh

---

[1] After the Portuguese crisis of succession in 1580 King Phillip II of Spain took over Portugal (his claim to the Portuguese throne was murky but a union promised economic benefits for Portugal). For the following sixty years, Spain and Portugal became ostensibly united under one crown in what was known as the Iberian Union.

founding the colony in the wilderness at Roanoke and the great Drake – what style! – finishing his game of bowls on the Hoe before trouncing the Spaniards.

"Quite. So how about it? The fleet leaves Plymouth in mid-August. I know the man behind the expedition; he awaits you there. You shall need money for the journey down." He clanked down twenty further shillings out of an overflowing purse. "As for clothing and provisions for the voyage, heh, well they are available in the port. Someone with your upbringing will be far better finding out *where* than I would be."

I sipped my wine, appreciating it, showing it. I was a man of breeding and knew my good wines from my bad. It was a glorious year for wine. On the estate my father's apples grew to the size of coconuts and strained the very fibres of the trees. Outside the gates famine ravished the land and people dropped dead in the streets.

I had on the desk in front of me the passage out of my village I had dreamed of since the quack first told me about his travels in distant lands. But I was not at all sure I wanted it. Such far-flung adventures were but fantasies. My life was here. I was a Knivet. It was only a matter of time before my father would school me in the running of his estate. But then I realised: this was his great test for me. The Earl of Suffolk, that bright young thing whom I had seen kissing my oldest half-sister's ungloved hand all those years ago after the duel, and who had long since married her, might have been *named* my father's successor. Yet I saw this was only a temporary measure, pending my return from foreign climes. Of course I knew the 'man behind the expedition' was Cavendish, an ambitious captain who they did say would eclipse Drake in notoriety upon his return. Many young men amongst his crew came home from his first voyage rich beyond their wildest imaginations with Potosi silver and Venezuela pearls. How fine it would be to return a man of means with tales to tell, coming up the driveway in a carriage of dodo or quetzal feathers to make Walsingham's look no better than a common trap, adorned in clothes not sourced at a market town's cheapest half-decent cloth merchant, but woven by the very tailor Drake used! This was the way to claim an estate, and despite a certain uncertainty welling within me I silently congratulated my father for devising such a worthy initiation. I saw he was offering me the chance to win his respect.

"You do not seem happy, Anthony. Surely you weren't expecting something more?"

Toy soldiers. I would have liked you to play toy soldiers with me. It need not have been public, or official. It just needed to have been something.

"I did not come here expecting anything, Sir Henry."

"Good. Then give my regards to your mother. And do see my butler about the shooting lessons. My understanding is that on the voyage, heh, they will come in exceedingly useful."

I bowed; paused on my way out.

"Fa… Sir Henry?"

"Yes?"

"I will make you proud of me."

From the corner of the walled garden a path wound through thick oakwoods up onto open moor behind. The gamekeeper's cottage was there, and a fire still smouldered nearby. I stoked the embers, unbuttoned my jerkin, tossed it into the strongest flames, did the same with the ridiculous frigate bird doublet and was just beginning on the hose when I heard her:

"Baker's boy!"

I had told her before how vexed I was when she called me so lightly by so base a name. Had it been a man hailing me thus I would have advised him to retract his remarks swiftly or face my sword, but alas Kathy was the daughter of the village apothecary, and my betrothed – a union which promised my mother a generous portion of the apothecary's premises for her bakery, the apothecary a worthy match for his only child and the rest of us precious little.

"Cat got your tongue, baker's boy?"

"Kathy," I muttered, already furious with her, for it was difficult to assume Lord-of-the-Manor airs whilst half-naked. "Your hair…"

She took a strand of it, studying it with an ostensibly careless but certainly affected gesture. "Seems I do have hair."

She raised her skirts and negotiated the muddy path to cross to my side. What lady did that? I would have crossed to her, or thrown down my cloak for her had I been wearing one. Not that I thought of her as a lady of course. She was more a fearless spirit, sent to torment me. What was she even doing here, in my father's private woods? She had approached from the direction of the north gate. Hardly anyone dared take that route. It was the domain of Old Elias, the gamekeeper outside whose cottage we now found ourselves. Old Elias, with an eye lost from one brawl, scars from several others, and a particularly malevolent way of skinning rabbits that convinced you he would rather be honing his butchery skills on human victims. It did not even go anywhere, that route. You would not take it unless you were looking for trouble. Oh, Kathy, who astonished me on so many levels! "Does that surprise you, Anthony? My having hair?"

"It is so… loose."

Her hair was red and her gown was green. Red and green are colours that stand out for you when you are at sea on the other side of the world, looking back. Sea washes away colour and Kathy had so much colour.

"Ask me where I've been, Anthony. The fair at Crudswell! All night. The bailiff's son told me I was the most beautiful creature he'd ever seen. I danced with him. Felt his hands all over me. D'you want to know if I kissed him, Anthony? D'you think I'm the most beautiful creature you've seen?"

I doubted she needed me to tell her, and I did not, then, although there were times later I wished I had. Not because it were true, but because it felt good to say the thing that led to the next thing, like the domino that knocks the chain to make the shape and beholds, as it knocks into the second, the very last standing at the end waiting to fall.

"I see you're in your undergarments, Anthony. I confess I've the right to be the more surprised of the two of us."

Yes, there was that matter too. And to explain why I was burning the clothes I had made a fanfare of choosing and so proudly worn down the village street a few hours before.

"You find me indisposed... regrettable... it is perhaps not fitting..." I stumbled, hurrying on down the path. "My mother! I need to get back to help with her damson scones."

"I'll walk with you," she stepped nimbly in front of me, "seeing as we're bound the same way."

Ah, that walk. A golden light did seem to bathe it. The parasol mushrooms, the shapes of the chalk stones on the heath above the wood, my search for one flat enough to skim on the cow pond there, her impertinent questions, her mouth wide when she laughed in a mockery of my answers but her teeth of incredible condition.

"... you could keep a damson scone for me..."

They were the paths I always wandered, rehearsing the day I would step up to take over my father's lands. But I would have picked the best apples from his orchard, bagged a pheasant from his hedgerows even, had I known the walk that summer day would be my very last on our family's estate.

"Not got a taste for the high life this afternoon, baker's boy? Looked like a fine doublet on that fire..."

"We should not talk to each other like this. It is not right, Kathy."

"And how is it we should talk to each other... Anthony?"

"With... respect."

"How maddening!" She rolled her eyes. "The days of knights are over! We're promised to each other, can't we dispense with such formalities?"

"And the bailiff's son, he has a special way of talking to you?"

"At least he…"

"At least he what? At least he what?"

She pulled at my undershirt; a tug that pulled her face up to mine and mine down to hers.

"What d'you think of me, Anthony?"

I thought she confounded every one of my thoughts. I loved her because I knew I should and I hated her because I knew that I would.

"I want what is best for my family." And then, because I knew that was not enough of an answer, "My father… has a mission for me. Thomas Cavendish – the renowned explorer – he sails for the Cape of Horn next month. I have been selected as his right-hand man for the voyage."

"Where is this Cape?" she studied me with interest; I warmed to my theme.

"It is not on many maps, for it has not been properly discovered. But it is very far away, and the voyage there is very dangerous. I would be gone a year or two. But I would return with riches, Kathy, like the crew from this man's first voyage. I could bring you silk to tie in your hair! I could bring you pearls as white as full moons. Then we could build something, you and I."

"Will you really be this Cavendish's right-hand man? Or his dogsbody?"

"I will be no-one's anything when I come back. I will be my own man."

"When you'll inherit, of course," she said casually. I never knew when she was poking fun at me.

"Of course."

We were almost at the village; bells peeled for some newlyweds just out of the church. I always felt sadness at weddings, although perhaps it was more longing – not merely to be in union with a beautiful girl in a white dress, but to be standing at the front of that church with the entire village looking on, and to have a feast thrown in my honour, with roast peacock and French wine.

"And I will write every word of my exploits," I told her. "So my father will know."

"How will he know if you write the truth?"

An astute question, Kathy. How would anyone know? *I am doing something now, in our own days, that you will not believe, even if I was to tell you*[2]. A few months on from that afternoon, I would scarcely believe what I was doing myself.

"I don't give two figs for your words, baker's boy." She planted herself on the path ahead and would not let me pass. "I believe in actions. You want to go off to this Cape of Horn for years and leave me waiting? Then do something, right this minute! Marry me. Have me here in these tussocks. Do something! No? Thought not!"

I was primarily concerned with extricating myself to a safe distance: out of the immediacy of her eyes, away from her hot breath on my neck. And when I had:

"God, it is too easy, do you not see?"

She laughed, but this time it was abrupt, and I knew I had hurt her.

"Don't expect me to wait for you, baker's boy! Don't expect me to cry for you, don't expect me to pray for you!"

And although I would have liked it, I did not expect it.

* * *

---

[2] Habakkukk 1:5. Knivet prides himself in an extensive knowledge of the Bible, in spite of his own relationship with God which is rather more nuanced.

I pummelled butter into flour, I boiled up damsons, and dowsed them with sugars and spices.

"That batch done, little man? I could use another."

I stoked the fire, bonnetless Kathy with the curling red hair and green dress, dogsbody, dogsbody, I churned up cream. My mother came in as I was getting the second dozen in the oven.

"So how fared my little man up at the big house?" The sound of her hands rubbing on her apron was like water swashed across flagstones. "What did your father have to say?"

"He told me never to call him father."

"It's of no consequence what you're obliged to call him little man! What did he deliver?"

When I was young and needed comforting my mother's apron-clad girth, with her smell of lard and dried fruit, was a refuge. I would press my head against her immense bosoms and her floury hands would pet me; "there, there, little man, we won't let them stop us." But increasingly my mother had retracted that circle of intimacy, and I sensed I was part of what was stopping her…stopping her from getting her own back on the world for the perceived disservices it had inflicted upon her, which was the stance from which she habitually came at life. And when you were not in my mother's circle, then you saw her flip side – and it was indeed most fearsome.

"He wants me to undertake a voyage," I said it with as much self-importance as I could muster. "There is a land across the oceans called Brazil…"

"Where the nuts with the unpleasant waxy taste come from."

And my bravely prepared speech of the wild Cape of Horn, and of discovery, and of nobly battling untold dangers for the advancement of mankind, it wilted in my mouth before her disapproval.

"How dare he? After all these years I have waited…"

I cowered like a miserable dog before a beating.

"So he's sending you to sea? Out of sight, out of mind – like he did with me?"

"Do not talk about him like that."

"When I require your contribution, little man, I'll ask for it. You, a sailor, my eye! You'd last five minutes! Now I've comfrey pies to make, will you prepare the candied flowers?" she suddenly mellowed.

I marvelled at her ability to alternate so readily between tones of loathing and something that seemed like love. And I attributed it to the conflict between my mother's wish for what was best for her son and my father's understandable inability to help that wish into fruition.

"I know you love making candied flowers. Then take your mother to evening mass. What would you do without me, little man?"

Candied flowers are roses, and cowslips, and violets. You pluck them at the root and boil them in a caramel sauce. It is a most difficult operation for you have to immerse the flowers in the caramel quickly, before it hardens. Yet simultaneously you must ensure not to ruin them, for the point is that they will appear, when finished, as if fresh picked. The candied flowers were why our bakery was renowned across the county, and I was entrusted to make them because I could do so better than anyone.

Normally I was good; that evening I was exceptional. I covered each petal and leaf in the caramel. I sculpted them into shape. The flowers, frozen in their sugary frost, gleamed with purples and yellows and reds more radiant than any meadow. I positioned them just so on the shelf. I licked the caramel from my fingers. I unfastened my apron. I took ten of the just-baked damson scones, and a flagon of my mother's elderflower wine, and stuffed them into a small bag. Given the profession into which I was entering I had thought it prudent to take a pistol from my father's armoury. It was, after all, the family armoury and therefore a justifiable action. The bakery also possessed an admirable selection of knives and, finding that which my mother used for cutting pork meat to hang most comfortably from my belt, I added this to my belongings.

Out on the high street the sun was setting on the hamstone cottages. Nothing is more beguilingly English than sunset on hamstone cottages. Villagers were already strolling to church for the service. I wanted – I silently implored – one of them to exclaim, 'well, there goes Anthony Knivet!' But no one did, so I caught the overnight coach toward Plymouth.

FOUR

"...a Gentleman following a Gentleman...
unmatchable... for the rare adventures,
disadventures, and manifold successions of
miseries in those wilde countries..."

Samuel Purchas introducing Anthony Knivet's account of his adventures,
Purchas His Pilgrims

The village was on the shoulder of the moor, with a scant treeline protecting it from the bleakness above. The churchyard was overflowing with graves and the few houses stank. At the far end was a tavern; I went in.

"An ale."

"Most assuredly." A bleary-eyed man looked up from his hunched poise at the bar. "We have ale."

I shook the rain off me and spread my travelling cloak by the fire. The bleary-eyed man had not moved.

"Then kindly serve me one, sir. And tell me," I added jestingly, "what sorry plague lies upon these lands that this deluge across them never abates?"

"You are mighty talkative stranger." The proprietor's hose had a stain upon the thigh and his shirt was rumpled.

And when was conversation a crime, I thought angrily. Something in the ambience of this hostelry was making me clench my hand a little tighter around the handle of my knife.

"I have been travelling since daybreak and have not met a soul all day."

24

"The plague you speak of lies upon this whole country." The proprietor slammed down a tankard; the ale within slopped about like a puddle of mud. "And those that stop by, late at night, speaking in the voice of a gentleman yet wearing common folks' clothes... I might be forgiven for being wary of such types."

"Yet you would be appreciated for treating me with the courtesy due to any guest at your establishment." I particularly resented his comments about my attire.

There were none too many faces in that sorry place, but those there were regarding me with a mixture of suspicion and intrigue. They looked the sort to cheer at a hanging, or perhaps orchestrate one should the opportunity arise, and there were enough there to outnumber me in combat.

"Where I am from we welcome visitors." I kept the trace of a smile upon my countenance, for I was tired after my day of walking and in no mood for trouble. "We see to it they are given good food and board."

"Where is it you are from, stranger? For it is clearly far away."

"You can call me by my name, if it inspires your trust as it should. I am Anthony Knivet, from the good county of Wiltshire, and am journeying to the port of Plymouth to meet with a certain General there."

"The Knivets of Wiltshire?" the proprietor interrupted. "Do not speak to me of them. I have a history of some colour with Sir Henry, for he evicted me from my lands there not two summers gone. Left with nothing, we were, and the bastard..."

He did not get further with his grand speech, for a white rage seized me. I took him by his rumpled collar and acquainted my mother's kitchen knife with his Adam's apple.

"You will not," I said, "ever talk that way about my father."

Two of the other rogues at the bar were upon me in seconds. One tried to grab my arms and pin them behind my back. The other advanced on me with his weapon, which was a main-gauche, a coward's choice of blade for its primary use was in surreptitious thrusts rather than outright combat. The proprietor was too cowed from the tickling I had given him with my own knife to intervene, but the fatter of the two fellows had seized my blade arm and twisted it. I jerked backwards suddenly in realisation surprise was my only advantage, jolting the man against the wall and winding him, which loosened but did not free his grip. As the other came at me I dealt him a flying kick that sent his blade clattering to the floor and him reeling. Off-balance, I could do nothing but bring the fatter man down with me as I fell. Landing on top and with superior weight the impetus was with him; he had me squashed as a mouse beneath a bird of prey. My blade was again in his grasp and with solemn and farcical slow motion it was inched towards my heart. I was damned if I was going to be finished by my own mother's meat-carving knife and struggled violently, but to no avail. I was considering making my peace with the good Lord – for we had not always seen eye to eye based mainly on the fact He had never granted me what I wanted nor indeed shown a particular inclination to keep me from harm's way – when the much-rusted tip of a dagger appeared through my assailant's midriff.

"Harry Barrawell of Trowbridge," the man clasping the dagger stammered. "I think I have killed him, have I not?"

"Anthony Knivet of Charlton," I replied, heaving myself from under the deceased and trying to avoid the worst of the blood for I was wearing a white linen shirt of reasonable quality, "and yes you have."

"Should I twist the blade once or twice to be sure? I have heard that is the done thing."

Harry Barrawell did not look the sort to be knifing people through the midriff. He looked like he should be convalescing in bed with a hot beverage. His skin, which did not seem as though it normally saw much sun, was yet several shades whiter at that moment and his brow appeared feverish.

"It can do no harm," I agreed. It was the first corpse I had encountered at such close quarters, but was not about to reveal that to this youth who looked but a day out of school.

"Hmm… m…must have innards like iron." Barrawell winced at the effort of wrenching the dagger out. "Your shirt! I hope you have another!"

"Naturally."

I had one other, but this was my best - and the soiling of it did grieve me.. I saw the blood had stained the hem and something of the cuffs, which were akin to those Drake has in the portrait painted after his return from the first circumnavigation of the world. He has on a red cloak with velvet lining and a ruff like an angel's halo. The cuffs of his shirt are rounded and frilled and his hand rests upon a globe. I summoned the proprietor with my right hand, as this cuff was untarnished. He was still dabbing at his neck with a handkerchief, the fussy fellow: his wound was no worse than a shaving cut.

"Get this man a drink!" I cried. "And myself too - for we wish to drink the health of Wiltshire. It is a county we are most passionate about."

Barrawell was an earnest young man of seventeen: exactly as old as he seemed. In moments of emotion he rolled his 'r's' and dropped his vowels after the West Country fashion but nevertheless came across as learned and not only knew his letters but could recite an astounding number of bizarre remedies for various ailments from memory, with both the common and Latin names of the herbs involved, for his mother was a hypochondriac and his family resided near an abbey.

"I could not abide to see them tarry with you," he said around tentative sips of his ale, which from the way it caused his eyes to water I judged to be the poor boy's first. "Given as how we seem set to sail on the same ship. I could not help but conjecture the General you m…mentioned is the great Cavendish?"

"The very same. You have secured your place on board?"

"No." Barrawell was downcast. "I pray he will take me, for

my family sorely need the m…money the voyage promises."

He was the eldest of five sons by some way, and his widowed mother's only prospect of income for whom, given his frail disposition and the arduous mission Cavendish was planning, I felt no small amount of sympathy.

"Your prayers shall be answered. With my connections I shall ensure you are among the crew."

"You are m…most kind." Barrawell gushed gratitude. "Anthony Knivet! It is an honour to m…make the acquaintance of a gentleman!"

"Harry Barrawell, the honour is mutual since you saved my life – or at least assisted in the prolongation of it."

I shouted for more ale, and slammed a shilling down on the counter in lieu, which diminished my supply of coinage significantly but felt marvellous.

"How m..many days have you been on the road?" Barrawell appeared so delighted with our acquaintance I felt almost guilty.

"The coach dropped me in Exeter. I fancied the walk from there." I smiled, electing to conceal that the real reason was more a matter of saving money than of craving the exertion. "I started yesterday afternoon. They did warn me the way across this moor was yet more replete with bandits than the average in the country, which is already mighty high of late. But savagery is no deterrent for me. Indeed, I thought immersion in a portion of it might even prove good practice… for the voyage."

"Yes!" Barrawell was all admiration. "And did you see many bodies?"

"Bodies?"

"I m…mean human bodies. They do say they are so starved in some villages they are falling dead in the streets. The famine, you know."

"Oh, yes. In one case, I saw an entire congregation too hungry to stand at mass. The vicar was giving the sermon on the feeding of the 5,000, and they were so starved they were convulsing with the descriptions of the bread and the fish. And afterwards some thirty expired before my eyes whilst returning to their houses."

"God would never condone that!"

"His eye was probably turned elsewhere. He is mighty busy answering prayers and saving souls this summer."

"Then we m…must pray His eye is upon us!" cried Barrawell.

"We are Englishmen, and representatives of England's finest county. So come what may, we have good cause to believe we will prevail. We must prove ourselves not to God, but to our families." And fuelled by the bad ale I made a small incision in my wrist with the knife. "Blood brothers, Harry Barrawell?"

"A blood oath!" Barrawell's eyes shone. "I heard of this in old books! But I m…may not join you Anthony Knivet, for my m… mother tells me I have thin blood and it does not clot easily. M… may I take your hand and kiss it, and convey everything a pact m…might by the gesture?"

"You may."

"And can I ask why you carry a kitchen knife? I have no doubt," Barrawell continued eagerly, "there is some enthralling story attached to it."

"It is my mother's knife," I said, resisting the urge to tell the one or two enthralling stories that did at that moment come to my mind. "And I can tell you she has found it most effective in cutting meat."

* * *

We set out at daybreak in a foul drizzle. The unnatural cold upon this lonely moor persisted. Even down in the valleys the corn that usually ripened the land by this season was absent. Families sat outside their mean houses and stared at us dimly. About midday we came upon a village that was smoking in the aftermath of a fire.

"What happened here?" I asked a fellow rocking mindlessly

on his haunches outside the timbers of one building.

"The government – or the lackeys thereof," he told us hollowly. "They asked us to move, and we refused, for where could we go?" He stood up as we passed by, emaciation and despair in his face. "God save our Queen!" he shouted after us, and began laughing manically. "God save our good Queen!"

Barrawell refused to have his spirits dampened. He interpreted the devastating scenes, I believe, as proof of the necessity of our voyage. "Are you looking God?" he would cry in his half-broken voice, prancing about waving his arms at the grey skies.

I was born and raised in an age when they banned dancing within sight of a churchyard and ale on Sundays because it displeased our Lord. I was born and raised in an age where they counted the months between marriage and the birth of a first-born to try ruining newlywed's young lives with prosecution on grounds of premarital relations, in an age where the church owned our country's greenest lands yet offered none to the poor being banished from theirs, in an age where England could not prosper by commerce except for the kind that involved plundering and butchery – and our Lord smiled benevolently on just the same. Did I share my companion's belief in God as a guiding light? Not nearly so much as I believed in myself.

The cloud lifted, and below us was Plymouth.

FIVE

"We lie here in the most dangerous haven of England for so many ships"

Lord Admiral Thomas Howard on Plymouth

It was a street we quickly became acquainted with. The whores jeered at us from the windows above and the drunks leered up at us from the gutter. It was impossible to sleep after six in the morning due to the commotion of the sardine vendors; by seven the effluent was cascading down the cobbles outside and the stench was beyond bearable. We had a shared bed in a room on the topmost of four floors, a garret that leaked with the relentless West Country summer rain up a staircase so low we were obliged to crawl like dogs to return into our hole at night. Barrawell would sporadically thrust back the covers during our few allotted hours of slumber in a sort of waking dream and scream for his mother. Despite my assurances our crew-to-be would take most unkindly to his fits he seemed unable to temper them and I unable to return to sleep afterward. Thus I would stand, window-watching, seeing the sailors and the merchants and the clergymen take their turns in the bed of the whore across the way. The sailors had the most fun. For the merchants and the clergymen it was more an act of embarrassment, to be completed and forgotten about as soon as possible. The whore saw me watching her sometimes. Our gazes would lock across the street and there would be a moment of intimacy in which we understood one another utterly. Curiously it would always be her who looked away first. But sometimes I believed I was looking not at her, but through her almost, through her across the stinking port, but not to the world I had left nor the world I was about to go to. It was always to an idyll – me as a Roman Emperor reclining eating grapes; me as a Galahad or a Tristan sipping mead at a court. Always these idylls featured me imbibing some food or drink, and I suppose that was because we had so little sustenance in our daily lives.

Each morning we would breakfast on bread and barley gruel occasionally augmented by sardines from the irksome vendors, then pace the docks waiting for Cavendish to show or for the Minerva to open. When the first did not happen, the second inevitably did and it was to this tavern that we went to wait once more for tidings of our good General and when he would select his crew. We dispensed with luncheon, for of course we were spending our money on drink to eke out our time in the alehouse which, being the established haunt of seafaring types, would furnish us with Cavendish's movements before anywhere else. I would take off on long walks, leaving Barrawell to man our sorry corner table. I would observe the traders clad in foreign silks with their Italian beards and French perfume. I would observe the ladies with pearls in their braids, and pelts of mink, with the latest Farthingales that made them seem like they were not walking but floating on a cloud of finery. I would observe apprentices on errands with vials of peculiar potions, or correspondence from overseas, or opiates for the barber-surgeons, or spices for the gentry, or parchments for the mapmakers. I would take in the metallic odour of the chandlers and the waxy smell of the sail-makers; the tar from the caulkers and the sweat from the blacksmiths; the swagger of the naval officers and the scurry of the servants. I would take in coils of rope as thick as serpents with length enough to plumb the oceans, and pines as high as churches being planed and primed for masts of vessels that would voyage to the edge of the charted world and over it. Each walk I would finish the same. I would tarry outside the celebrated Jacka bakery, looking in at the crisp aprons of the workers, and the convivial blaze of the oven, and the aroma of powder sugar, and sometimes staring for hours at the trays of herb lattices, and venison pies, and lavender cakes, and cinnamon buns. In my old life I had taken them for granted: now they looked the epitome of exquisite cooking contrasted with the soup I could expect to be ladled out for my supper by a landlord with no grasp of seasoning.

In the clamour of mallets, and the grating of saws, and the hammering of tacks, in the haranguing of hawkers and the screams of sailors, in the grubbiness of dockhands faces and the sheen on officers epaulettes, in the stink of mackerel and the sweetness of ambergris, there was a certain something - a frenzy, a glamour; a hunger, an industriousness - which chimed with me. This was the port from which Lancaster had embarked for the East Indies and of which the great Drake was governor, and I liked that. I liked that a lot. But I hankered to be a part of it, and my store of money was fast dwindling. I was spending almost a shilling per day on board and food and drink and whilst I saw the workers swarming daily over Cavendish's flagship galleon, there was no sign of the General himself. They did say he had a thing for one of the Queen's ladies-in-waiting and was pleasuring himself in the Royal residence. They did also say he had a love of fine parties and was on his Devon estate hosting a debauch of Bordeaux wine and quail's eggs, or that he was attending the lavish celebrations at Cowdray, grandest residence in all the south-east, at which the Queen and every aristocrat deemed to be of significance was present. Others held that he was a gambler, and played for high stakes in the members' rooms of certain London taverns. But he was not here, and whilst he was not, the loyal men that would risk their lives for him as his crew in foreign climes boarded in damp hovels frittering away their hard-come-by pennies.

One afternoon I returned to the Minerva and found Barrawell in conversation with a woman. She had on a bright blue dress remarkably low around the neck and I had the nagging suspicion I knew her.

"You do not recognise me, perhaps, in such modest attire," said the whore with whom I had exchanged so many glances in the early hours from my lodging-house window.

"I am unaccustomed to seeing you at such close quarters."

Some nearby drinkers chose this moment to laugh coarsely and I would have ran each through with my knife had a lady not been present.

"Mr Barrawell has been singing your praises, Mr Knivet."

"He does heroise me, lady, and it is not wholly deserved," I said modestly.

"Partly, then, if not wholly?"

"I leave that to your good judgement."

"I judge it high time I took some air," she said. "Would you come with me?"

I motioned to Barrawell to man our table again.

"I did not expect to see you in a tavern of disreputables," I blurted, when we were outside.

"What type of tavern would you like to see me in?"

This seemed a reference to our wordless night-time exchanges and I was somewhat embarrassed.

"Perhaps I could… that is, the bakery do very good cinnamon buns."

We ate the buns, and I found it was most enjoyable to watch her eat. She did so voraciously, with the sugar freckling her cheeks.

"You are mariners?" she asked.

"Adventurers. We sail with Cavendish upon his voyage to the New World."

"Mr Barrawell told me. It must be hard, waiting. With so little money."

"We stay in those lodgings to fit in. I am assured of a good position amongst the crew."

"Fitting in? Is that what you were doing all those nights watching at the window, Mr Knivet? You disappoint me."

"I meant that we do not want for money."

"Of course. Your connections."

Barrawell had been most free with his mouth. This was the problem, I lamented, with drinking bad ale for protracted periods.

"It is the adventure, then, that appeals?" she continued.

"It is more a test."

"Of your mettle?"

"If you like."

"Now that I relate to. It is not dissimilar in my profession."

"You have something to prove to someone?"

"Oh yes. My mother. She left me when I was thirteen, when it appeared to her I had no inclination to follow in her footsteps."

"Her footsteps?"

"She was a whore."

"Whereabouts?"

"The whereabouts is not the issue." She frowned. "She left with a tailor, although he was better at ripping clothes off than stitching them up, as I recall. That is not the issue either... the issue is that she did not care for me. I look at you like this," she half-shut her eyes and slightly parted her lips in an expression of the most ardent desire, "or this," her eyes clouded, and her brow tautened, and her lip curled, "and that is something! But ambivalence is terrible... so much can be conveyed in a look, Mr Knivet. Much more than in any physical act, would you not agree?"

We took a turn round the harbour. Some men were bludgeoning fish in a recess, but not getting the hits accurate, for in the slime and blood the fish kept slipping. I felt curiously optimistic for those few furthest from the swipe of the club – as if the spiritedness to their flopping gave them hope they might yet evade their assailants. Up ahead on the bluff construction on the fort was progressing slowly. Queen Bess in her generosity was funding this most critical of defences in the port that launched England's finest voyages not with her own coffers but by leveeing tax on the town's fish merchants, which for the common man meant black market herring and sardines at cheap prices, although little for the safety of the realm. I chose cheap fish. I had to choose cheap fish, despite knowing the consequence was that this illustrious port was left open to attack by Spaniards or Portugals. It was not an easy time in which to have ideals. It was not an easy time in which to do good.

"She was wrong," I said hotly "to abandon you thus. Any mother should be thankful to have you as a daughter."

"Do not concern yourself, Mr Knivet." She studied me, perhaps with amusement. "I am the better now for having striven to attain her respect. I should simply never have striven on her account."

The boats of the harbour lay spread before us: French fishing boats and Dutch frigates, carvels and carracks, merchant ships and marauding ships, ships carrying bullion from the West Indies and ships bearing pepper from the East Indies.

"I have dreams too, Mr Knivet. A farmhouse, perhaps, out in the country away from this stink."

Overcome, I seized her hand. I daresay she expected me to pull off her gloves – which were sequined – and kiss her slender fingers like any port rogue but I did not.

"Take this!" I emptied the last of my shillings into her palm.

"What service can you want from me, Mr Knivet, at this price!"

"It is not that," I said quickly.

"What then?"

"Take it. For your farmhouse."

"You need it. You do not fool me and I know that you need it."

"I do not." I pointed to Cavendish's galleon in the water out beyond the gaggle of other boats. I had studied it each day since my arrival. And I could see the flag of St George, and the Royal colours, and above them the three stags' heads of the Cavendish coat of arms had been raised, which could mean but one thing. "The General has arrived."

* * *

We clustered round the dock, young hopefuls and old sceptics, out-of-work navy men, and famished farming men, and disenfranchised military men, and banished Low Country men: we that would make a living from the sea.

General Cavendish[1] minced among us, choosing carefully where he stepped with his slashed leather shoes and silk green hose amidst the fish carcases. With him was the navigator John Davis, who seemed to be accompanying us on this voyage in sufferance. He was Cavendish's polar opposite, built like a battering ram with a face as weathered as the General's was smooth and a despicable sense of dress. After the success of his first voyage the General fancied himself as something of a mariner, liking to choose his crew personally rather than delegating the responsibility, and he bid us fan out in a line as he went so he might converse with us individually.

"You are prepared to undertake a voyage to discover undiscovered lands and treasures, in the name of Queen Bess and of God? And why should I select you? You can shoot? Hph! You served under Raleigh? Hph!"

He had a fey and monotonous voice that would have rendered the most exhilarating of escapades more lacklustre than a mathematics lesson, and fingered his moustache, of which he was evidently proud, like he was engaged in one. But as he made his way towards Barrawell and myself I witnessed his infamous temper flare once or twice. "Drake," he screamed at an old tar who mistakenly mentioned he had gone on the first circumnavigation in 1577 "has no authority in this harbour at this moment! I am master, imbecile – as you will soon learn if you do not scrub the decks like I say, climb to the crow's nest when I say, and work and work although your old bones will be aching and your eyes half-blind with salt and sweat – for if you do not then so help me God

---

[1] He was not really a General, of course, in the official sense, but this was nevertheless a term even privateers used for the leaders of their fleets.

I will devise such ways to break you that you will wish the sea had broken you first…"

"He sounds lovely. Get him out in open sea and he may really blossom."

The speaker was a swarthy fellow, lean and taut as a length of rigging, with a Mediterranean accent that explained why none of the other would-be crew would stand near him.

"You sound like a Portugal sir."

"And you, *senhor*, do not sound a common crewman."

"This recruitment is a formality for me. My father knows the General."

"The General does not seem taken even with Drake. He must hold your father in singular regard. Especially to take a man on… on a voyage like this… with no experience."

"What do you know of my experience?"

The Portugal chuckled.

"The character of my family, sir," I said defiantly "counts for a great deal."

"He is a Knivet," Barrawell chimed in. "And I a Barrawell, which…" I nudged him to remain quiet.

"And your family sir?" I asked the Portugal.

"Very little for the telling."

"And what makes you think you will not be thrown into the nearest gaol, once it is known who you are?"

"*Por cima destas águas forte e firme,*" said the Portugal after some seconds. He was no longer looking at us, but off into the distance beyond the jaws of the harbour. "*Irei aonde os Fados o ordenárium, pois por cima de quantas derramáram*[2]. Because I am the only one who knows where in Hell we are going."

The General was standing before us.

"Why should I select you for the voyage?" he addressed the

---

[2] From the sonnet *Por cima destas águas forte e firme* by Luís de Camões, a poet this man apparently loved to quote.

Portugal.

"I am a pilot, and know the waters where we are headed from Pernambuco to the Straits."

"That is some claim. How?"

"I served in the port of Santos three years."

"And you could betray us to your kind the moment you return with us to those shores." It was an observation, not a question.

"I am my own kind. You want prosperity for this voyage. I want a share, like every man here. And I can guide us to where we shall find it."

"And your religion?" The General's voice was almost a whisper.

"I will serve he who commands the voyage."

"But you believe in purgatory, Catholic. You believe in prayer that will speed your admittance into Heaven... at the expense of God-fearing Englishman."

"We will all end up in Hell if we get dashed on the rocks of Brazil." The Portugal stood tall and serene. He seemed to me as untouchable as a ship's figurehead at that moment.

Cavendish stroked his moustache, and raised an eyebrow at Davis, who nodded. A pimply boy stepped forward with a roll of parchment and ink.

"Make your mark here."

The Portugal signed 'Nicolas Rodrigo'.

Barrawell was next.

"Why should I select you for the voyage?"

"I am a poor..." Barrawell began, but I intervened to save him. "He is with me, General."

Thomas Cavendish, noble explorer and circumnavigator of the world, turned to me for the first time and scanned me up and down.

"A fact that would advantage him, undoubtedly."

"Herbs," broke in Barrawell. "I know a considerable amount about herbs. I can m..make remedies... and poultices."

The General smiled in his superior manner.

"Are you a religious man?"

"By God's grace yes."

But the General spent rather longer gazing thoughtfully at me, I fancied.

"You have a gentleman's voice, and a poor man's clothes. You have a recommendation from a county sheriff and a companion that looks like a vagabond."

I felt exultant at his recollection of my connections.

"I am honoured, General..."

"Why should I select you for the voyage?"

I was taken aback to be addressed in the same detached tone as the others.

"I... can speak four languages, including Portugal."

"Linguistics," he said "will be less effective on this voyage than how ably you can engage your weapon."

"I can handle my piece as well as any militiaman, having been trained by some. And I can cook."

"Cook?" the General arched his eyebrow again.

"Buns and suchlike."

"Hph!" I never again saw the General laugh as he did then: a long string of sniffs as if he were dispelling something vile from his nostrils.

"And your religion?"

"I despise Catholics."

At least half of Cavendish's mind seemed elsewhere, as though he were imagining the fine wines flowing at his London gentleman's club. For a moment it seemed unclear if he would smile or scream. The lines upon the forehead of Davis expanded; contracted. They made me think of the clashing rocks Jason and his Argonauts must sail between.

"Sign them up," said the General. "They will have ample chance to prove their prowess is no lie. If they fail... my loathing of liars is not unknown..."

I was already wondering whether the foodstuffs the carters were unloading onto the ships would be sufficient to concoct a good fruit duff.

"And get some appropriate clothing. You are not landlubbers anymore."

The General concluded his interrogations, and the men dispersed, but Nicolas Rodrigo stood staring out at the harbour long after the others had left. His hand was shielding his eyes and he was sucking at something from a small clay pipe. After he sucked he breathed smoke back out of his mouth like a dragon. He offered us the pipe, and Barrawell declined mistrustfully, but I accepted. I inhaled, and coughed a little but not much, for the substance inside was strong.

"Not bad," Rodrigo said. "I see many who partake regularly splutter more."

"It is tobacco?"

"From the forests of Brazil. The Indians who live there take it for their health and strength. They drink the juice of fruits sweeter than we can comprehend. They anoint themselves in gold dust, and pay homage to many-jewelled kings. It is a land of opportunity where we are headed, Anthony Knivet."

"You kept your knowledge well secreted. How do you feel, being the only man who knows what awaits us at our destination? A Catholic, with several hundred Protestant souls in the palm of his hand."

"How do you feel, being the only man amongst our crew who understands the man with this knowledge?"

"I am... familiar with Camões."

"He speaks from the soul."

"I write myself."

"I admire he who can do so."

"I do not yet know how to describe what I am working on now... but it will be the most marvellous account of my adventures." I took a hit of the tobacco. These Indians, I fancied, must possess most discerning palates.

"Then God speed with your adventures." The Portugal took the pipe back and sucked methodically. Pernambuco. Santos. He reeled off these exotic names so calmly and I saw in that moment this must be the way to treat such a strange new world: by embracing it for what it was.

"God speed!" said Barrawell.

"Good speed," I said.

Something in the Portugal's manner assured me it really might not be so bad, this Brazil where we were bound. A month more, of course, and he would be dead.

* * *

We returned to the Minerva that evening different men. For we were clad in sailor's attire: cotton shirts and baggy hose. We had acquired sturdy leather jerkins for battle, and thick woollens for wild ocean winds. Barrawell had bought them for both of us, and was buying the ale too, and for the first time I noticed him slightly peeved.

"Good God Anthony, you gave everything to her."

"Sometimes you must do such things because they are right and honourable."

"But she is a whore you barely know!"

"Do not call her that!" I cried, although I was angrier about barely knowing her. "You know nothing of women, Barrawell."

I soon rued this remark as he had confided in me of his virginity, and despite being a man of experience in these matters, I could imagine how never having been with a woman could weigh heavy on one's mind before a long voyage. But then I was so speechless with rage I thought I would strike the boy if I remained a moment more in his presence. I stormed out of the Minerva passed the other mariners celebrating newfound employment with the General, right into the path of a man with a voluminous black cloak, cartwheel ruff, scarlet sash and extremely prominent cuffs.

"I beg your pardon," I stammered, for I knew immediately who it was.

The great Drake had a beard far more pointed than portraits suggested, and an expression infinitely more imperious. Or perhaps it was just inaccessible. Yes, a man who had done more good for England than any other, who had taken countless lives and treasures from Iberians in countless lands for the glory of the crown, yet who bore his status with a good-natured and weary acceptance rather than outright arrogance. The two men with him were the kind that dress without imagination despite having the means to attire themselves well, and although they chastised me for my clumsiness I paid them little attention.

"I am Anthony Knivet, sir, of Charlton. You and my father have the same tailor."

"Sir Knivet," Drake laughed, and his laugh was more pleasant than Cavendish's. "We are then, as you see, almost identical." His companions sniggered, as sycophants often do, without understanding whether something humorous or heartfelt has been said.

Then I glanced down aghast. I was of course no longer wearing my linen shirt with the stylised cuffs but my cotton sea clothes which, although I had delighted in them at first – they were my first clean change of garments in some days – I now found dismally plain, with the beige hose tied awkwardly at the knees, bulging above and too tight beneath in a manner reminiscent of duck's legs.

"Goodbye, Sir Knivet!" said Drake, and touched his hat, adorned in various bright feathers, towards me in a most respectful gesture.

"Goodbye!" I cried.

Their dark-cloaked shapes faded into the night, which stunk of sardines.

Like the General had observed, I was not a landlubber anymore. I thought of the Portugal, Rodrigo, and how effortless a mariner he had seemed. I would be like that, I thought, and murmured again those lines he had quoted down at the dock: *"Over these waters firm and strong I sail to whatever the fates desire Since I've managed, somehow, to survive."*

I laughed. I went laughing madly back to my lodgings and settled on the bed to await the appearance of the whore in the window opposite. I imagined she might have bought a necklace with my money, and would clutch the jewel and look into my eyes as another man writhed and thrusted behind her. But her window was dark. And the light did not come back on.

SIX

"I... was matched with the most abject-minded and mutinous company that was ever carried out of England by any man living."

Thomas Cavendish on the subject of his crew to Sir Tristram Gorges;
Purchas His Pilgrims edited by Samuel Purchas

Christopher, the Japanese, was not really called Christopher, of course. His given name was Katsu, although he did not tell me that himself, for he never gave a straight answer to anything. He was a survivor from the General's last voyage, and thought a talisman by the latter, having been a crewman aboard the treasure ship that gave Cavendish's first circumnavigation its finest takings: gold, and damask, and cinnamon, and incense so fragrant it took days after landing for the English winds to disperse the smell. He reminded me of a cat for the way he could slink up upon you like a shadow, and he was a sly and unscrupulous devil indeed.

I befriended him at watch one night not long after Rodrigo's hanging. Most of the rest of the crew aboard our ship the Roebuck were drunk. Davis had that day announced he had devised an invention that would revolutionise navigation by calculating the altitude of the sun or moon no matter what their position in the heavens, and our fleet was carousing to mark the occasion. Crews do not need much to spark their celebration just as they require little to facilitate their mutiny.

"He was a great gambler, your Portugal."

"He is not *my* Portugal," I snapped.

"He beat me many times, in Plymouth. Especially at dice."

"Are we not all gamblers on this voyage?"

"We do not all play for stakes like he did."

It was Christopher, we all knew, who had informed the General that Rodrigo, our recently executed pilot, had been a traitor. Rodrigo had stood accused of counselling Christopher and other non-Englishman amongst the crew to run away with him at Santos across country to the South Sea, where the plundering was riper. I did not believe a word of it, for along such a route there were hundreds of leagues of wilderness populated by hostile Indians, that only the foolish, recklessly brave or extremely knowledgeable would try to traverse. But the General had not needed many of Christopher's words in his ear to string Rodrigo up. The Japanese could concoct the most far-fetched stories and make them convincing. He knew how to fan the fire of the General's temper and blow it in the direction he chose. As to why he had chosen Rodrigo to be the victim of his schemes, that was a question I was not sure I wished to know the answer to.

"The General," said Christopher, "is most enamoured with you."

I knew that the General was most enamoured with Christopher, and entertained him in his cabin at night, and offered him Bordeaux wine which none of the rest of the crew saw. I paid attention - guardedly.

"Perhaps it is that you are an educated man, aboard a ship of imbeciles. Perhaps he respects you, or fears you, which can be the same as respect."

"What of it?"

"I... know the General," said Christopher carefully. "He has a good eye for people."

"I will allow he does," I said, recollecting how he had chosen me for the voyage. "Although he has picked a crew full of drunkards too."

"I need a man of intelligence," simpered Christopher "for a project I have. Rodrigo told me certain things in our gambling sessions. He knew Brazil's coast well."

"Precious good it will do our voyage now he has been hanged by your word."

"Yes." Christopher smiled. He said "yehhhhz" like a town crier. "Cavendish is a good leader, when the going is good. But can you guess what would ensue if the going was bad? Chaos!" He pronounced the word with too much relish. "And chaos, Knivet, creates a diversion. You understand?"

I shuddered to think that I might, but I did not reply, I did not even look at him because there was something unspeakably repulsive about this man. Something in his eyes, something Hellish; something that gave me a horrible thrill.

"My mission," I quavered, "is to endure. We are the General's men."

"Yehhhhz. Very honourable. Look around you and tell me where you see honour. We are privateers, Knivet! We think now, on board, of our *duties*. But when this rabble get to land, do you think there will be discipline – out there in the forests?" He shook his head. "It will be each man for himself. And what if I was to tell you what Rodrigo told me: that at the town of Santos, where we are bound when we reach Brazil because the General plans to loot it, there are stashed certain stores of treasure, such as only one who knows their locations could uncover? In the chaos to come, Knivet, a little presence of mind could go far. A little presence of mind could get us a large fortune." He held out his hand to me, whispering, "I know you want what I do."

I made sure I was not breathing too quickly; that my expression could not be betrayed. I was beginning to see why Rodrigo had died. I took Christopher's hand. It was as cold as a grave. And we shook on it.

"Good (gurrrrd, he said). I think we can profit very nicely

from this… venture of ours. Watch for my sign when we hit shore, Knivet."

I was not a rich man, but I knew etiquette. I was not naturally a sailor, but yet I sailed the seas. And nor was I religious, but I knew the Bible. And at the end of that Holy Book God takes John up into heaven, through a small door secreted beyond the sights even of Copernicus. And He says unto John 'Come hither, and I will show you the things that must be hereafter'. John goes up and he sees the scene of a throne, and of One who sits on the throne, daubed in jasper and rubies, and of other marvellous treasures in the vicinity. Does John fill his pockets and leave? Well he was not going to write that in his book now, was he? And if that scene was transplanted to some town on the edge of Brazil, and John was a sailor fortune had hitherto passed by? Vision. Vision is something for any man to imagine for himself.

August became September, and the watery sun under which we had departed Plymouth grew fiercer. About this time there came the most otherworldly light around dusk, indigo in colour, that crackled at the masts of the General's Galleon, and of our vice-admiral the Roebuck, and of our other ships the Desire and the Dainty and the Blacke Pinnace; it appeared to surround our fleet alone out of all the places on the oceans it could have shone. But I was aft at the time to get the Roebuck's bonaventure mizzen sail up and the light did most significantly gather around me. Our company seemed divided as to its portent: some were ecstatic; others terrified.

"You were like a spirit, Knivet! You glowed."

"Why did *he* glow?" countered the doom-mongers.

October became November, our fresh food was long gone, and there was gossiping in the crew that we were headed to Hell on account of the heat, and the disease spreading like wildfire through our company. Some blamed the lack of supplies, and cursed our victualler's inattentiveness. Some blamed the helmsmen and some blamed the General and none whatsoever blamed themselves. Each dawn delivered more cases of scurvy as surely as it delivered a sun that had us cooked before breakfast, and each Sunday saw more men with minds turned mad from a lack of sustenance than it did men turning to God for sign of respite. In the midst of it all there clustered about our ship a flock of birds with the greatest wings I have ever seen. As we were pitifully low on supplies several of us loaded our guns to shoot a few. I brought down six of the nine we dispatched, and found that when roasted with salt their taste was agreeable, if a little inky. Waldren told me it was not done to kill these birds, since they were mariners' friends, and indicated land was near.

"Then I am a mariner's enemy," I quipped. "But I am a starving man's friend, since I have conjured from air the best-tasting meal aboard this ship since we left England."

But I am not, unlike some of my time, one to brood over omens too much. Each man makes himself, and travels along his path until that path is destined to end.

In any case, Brazil was looming up to starboard.

I saw yellows, the fierce yellows of beaches, and greens, the greens of the trees behind. They were more intense than any yellows or greens I had ever glimpsed. Most shocking was the absence of settlement. In England even a remote tract of land has a certain closeted feel. Here there was nothing. Not a fort not a hut not one column of smoke.

"Beautiful, is it not?"

I turned round. The General. It was hard to know when he was addressing you directly, for he had a habit of gazing over your shoulder when he did so, as if he were more interested in whatever was there in the distance than he was in conversing with you.

"I have only known England, General. To me it seems very strange indeed."

"You will know Brazil soon enough. And as you will soon discover" he said, softly, matter-of-factly. "It is a nightmare."

There was a commotion across the company, then. We had spied a small ship. We had been adapted so long to the daily necessity of survival, that to suddenly be presented with the prospect of plunder was akin to waking early after a night of heavy drinking and forcing oneself to attend the morning church service when you knew full well the sermon would be on the evils of alcohol excess. But we of the Roebuck got enough of our men out of their sea stupor to engage the guns and the ship soon put up the white flag. It was overburdened with African slaves from Pernambuco, a bulbous headland to the northeast, and in no condition to put up a fight. It had few Portugals on board, and still less wealth, so we viewed it as practice for the better prizes to come, and captured just the pilot to guide us around the sandbars that plagued this coast. It was the Roebuck too that took on the few chests of loot we had won, and opening them in expectation of the ambergris travellers did say Pernambuco shores were littered with, we found a friar who had taken refuge there. The friar's death was already secured for being a vehicle of the Catholic Faith, but he had come aboard to preach to us of the errors of renouncing the Pope, and this inclination significantly worsened the means of his end for him. His pockets were loads with the heaviest, cheapest plunder his ship had carried, and we threw him into the sea.

"We do the converting around here," Cavendish said coldly, giving the execution order. "From soil to gold, and from heathen to Christian – but a Catholic is lower and meaner than the soil. A Catholic is a vessel of the deadly disease that strives to spread to Westminster, to Englishmen's hearts, and every corner of our Earth where it is not wanted, and the only good place for one is beneath the ground."

We closed into shore. In the shallower waters we began to see canoes, hollowed trees manned by one or sometimes two men of dark complexion and long hair. They were absolutely naked, and defiantly so, as though it were our clothes and pretensions toward civilisation that made us the savages. Sometimes they gawped at our ships but sometimes they seemed to see no one or nothing save themselves and their world as it had been before our arrival.

Our new pilot, whose name was Jorge, had been transferred to our boat so I might speak with him, and translate his directions as to the water depth and what lay beneath. He told me this place was called Cabo Frio, or cold cape, and its name was appropriate for it left me feeling cold despite the cloying heat. Cold - yet with a certain tingling. I had a sense of foreboding at these wild scenes, but at the same time something had snapped into place in my mind.

One such canoe we passed contained Portugals: a father, two sons, and the daughter, who was on her way to be married that afternoon. The General waved in the Dainty to get them, as her keel was shallowest. They were taken to the flagship, and I was taken to translate. The old man was thrown straight below deck, and the two sons with him following a beating within a hair's breadth of their lives by Stafford, who was a vicious brute of a soldier turned mercenary and much favoured by Cavendish. There remained just the girl quivering on the deck, badly bruised, and with her wedding dress ripped half off. She looked from one to the next of us and quickly away again, as if despairing instantly of finding any humanity in our eyes.

"Ask her where she was going," sighed the general.

"*Onde você vai?*" I knelt before her.

"*Por favor. Você não é como eles.*" You are not like them.

"*Agora, devo ser como eles.*" Now I must be like them. "*Onde você vai?*"

"Santos. My betrothed…"

"Forget your betrothed. Santos will be ours. How far off are we?"

"Continue like this and you will see it within three days." Her crown of hibiscus flowers had remained intact, but her hair was in disarray, and her eyes white and wide beneath the black strands.

I relayed this to the General, who sipped his afternoon wine in small sips, and ran his tongue along his moustache afterwards, as if that were some high and mighty way of imbibing good wine.

"Shall I tell her we will set her ashore?" I asked him.

"Take her below," he commanded. "But not *right* below, Captain Stafford."

Stafford did so. It was not long before the screams began. The General stood savouring his Bordeaux, regarding me wryly. I had the feeling he had singled me out for some horrible test, because gaining intelligence had clearly not been his intention with these Portugals, but rather wielding his power once more with me as a reluctant witness. Stafford emerged, fastening his hose, and sent the next man down.

"Captain Stafford," said the General. "Meet Anthony Knivet, our translator. He is a *gentleman*. Greet him, Captain, as one gentleman greets another."

Stafford extended his hand, brimming with the gleeful malice I would quickly learn was his trademark. I grasped it, and although I was not prone to seasickness I felt, for the first time upon that voyage, sick.

"Return Mr Knivet to his ship!" smiled the General, satisfied the scene had impressed upon my mind.

"Chaos," a voice whispered at my ear, as I climbed back over the gunwale of the Roebuck. "It's almost time, Knivet."

SEVEN

"Here we had such disorder amongst our selves, that if the Portugals had beene of any courage, they might have killed many of us"

Anthony Knivet, *Admirable Adventures and Strange Fortunes*

The sweats and ravings of scurvy; the smarting sores, chafed lips, gnawing pains, bloody swellings, the desperate dark hallucinations of starvation; the burn of tepid beer and malnutrition on the throat; the crunch of weevils and the malaise one quarter of a year at sea induces. It can be imagined what Ihla Grande, with its clear springs and fruit heavy on the boughs, signified to us that sticky December morning we moored on its coast to re-victual some thirty leagues shy of our destination.

But show me an Eden truly an Eden.

"Eat today," cried the General, slouching by his cabin with his carafe of Bordeaux as he waved us to shore. "Fight the Portugals tomorrow!"

He had assembled most other commanders of the company about him. John Cocke of our good Roebuck was there. The wine glass looked ridiculous in his large hands. Randolph Cotton of the Dainty was present, and did a better job than Cocke of laughing at the General's jests. Toby Master, the fat farmhand of a sailor who seemed to have gained control of our fleet's smallest vessel the Blacke Pinnace solely through his daredevil nature, said least, but keenly observed the words of the others as if waiting to gauge who spoke most sense. Only Davis was absent from the gathering, no doubt on his ship the Desire engaged in something of fundamental importance with his star-gazing equipment.

In an absence of real leadership amongst our shore-going party, Stafford, with the General's other precious captains Southwell and Barker, went in command.

Stafford gave orders: dividing us into foraging parties, stipulating how we should obtain provisions to replenish our empty holds, and by when we should return. But as he growled his oafish words I thought of him forcing the Portugal bride below deck, and then of her screams, and then of my empty belly. And I had eyes only for filling that, and became aware everyone there had eyes only for his own needs, for duty restrains a man on a boat because fulfilling that duty is tantamount to survival, but on land that same duty-bound sailor has his bonds severed by his animal needs: sex, where there are women but most of all food, where there is a chance of it. And the oranges fat on the beach-side trees, and the swollen potato roots in the jungle behind were worth more to us then than all the gold-dust those Indians could paint themselves with – and certainly more than our commanders' fine words.

"The fight starts here," growled Waldren, hacking a path through foliage back from the shore. "And here I am with a drunk, and a schoolboy, and a God damned poet!"

The drunk was Harris, and the schoolboy was Barrawell, and the poet was me, Anthony Knivet. And poets, they do say, are sensitive souls who can attune with remarkable alacrity to their environment, and whilst I disliked Waldren's coarseness I saw no better man to be with when the going got tough.

"God has shown us the path to a land of plenty!" Barrawell enthused. "Anthony, did you ever see such fruit as these?"

The estates of my family, I thought wistfully. They had such fruits.

"God may make us battle for the plenty," muttered Waldren.

From a clearing ahead came a horrible sound: a cross between the strangled cry a pig makes when slaughtered and a shriek of human agony. We hurried over. Five of our company were tussling with the largest hog I ever laid eyes on. The hog was charging about in circles and squealing. One heroic sailor straddled its back, with his fingers in its eyes, and another clinging on to its tail was being dragged along behind. Two more attempted to intercept the beast from the front with knives, but even encumbered by two brave men in fighting garb it out-manoeuvred them. A fifth was rebuilding a fire for the feast-to-be that the hog-and-man whirlwind had already blundered over and almost inadvertently extinguished.

"I will tell you three freely now," whispered Waldren, whilst we were still concealed from the hog hunters, "I don't mean to go back aboard without fresh meat."

"You m…mean to steal their hog?" asked Barrawell, aghast.

"Do they look the sort to share it, lad?"

"There are other hogs Waldren. And ones with less competition for their flesh." This from Harris.

"Aye?" Waldren retorted sarcastically. "How many have you seen thus far, you pox-ridden excuse of a mariner? And how many this near death? Even with the feckless thrusts from their blades it be on its last legs. As for the competition…"

The sailor clutching the hog's tail inched his grip up as if hauling in a bowline until his head was level with the rump, then with a pocket knife started gouging out a piece of flank. He drew blood but the flesh was tough; impatiently, he tried finishing the cut with his teeth. The hog bellowed, threw the other unwanted rider and promptly trampled him, only to collide hard with a tree. This stunned the beast but did not finish it. As the sailor with the pocket knife picked himself up and punched the air with delight at his perceived victory the hog backed round, charged once more, toppled him, and ran straight onto the knife of one of the other advancing men who, through coincidence rather than anticipation, conveniently had his blade extended at the correct angle to do irreparable damage.

"...even you might stand a chance of overcoming them Harris. What about you Knivet? Fancy getting your blade dirty, you young buck?"

I was never convinced what Waldren really thought of me, although, balding veteran seadog that he was, he must have seen countless similar young men, riding the oceans for the first time, high hopes and hot heads. Nor was I much more convinced what I thought of Waldren; I was not sure I would trust him much further than I would Harris to give up alcohol for Lent or Barrawell to bed a whore. But he appeared to have a plan, and I was heartily sick of month-old salted meat.

"I shall take the beast with one bullet," I vowed and stepping out despatched a shot from thirty yards I declare my father's best militiaman would have envied. I hit it between the temples and finally laid it to rest.

"Great Knivet. You killed an already dying pig."

"We Knivets are born with firearms in our cradles," I said proudly.

"The idea was to finish the beast with a knife, Knivet, you squid's entrail of an enterprise. If there be other foraging parties hereabouts they'll come running now at the sound of your shot."

"They're coming over," whispered Barrawell, indicating the three approaching hog hunters that had emerged from the escapade with fewest injuries.

"Have no fear. Let me talk to them," I said to Waldren, who looked sceptical.

""We are of the Roebuck," I greeted the men. "We saw you in difficulty."

"We are of the Desire. And I do not recall asking for your assistance," the man who had been tending the fire said, in ragged breaths.

"Aye, this is our meat," said a second man, who did not seem to have shaven since the equatorial line. "We worked for it."

"And almost lost your lives in the process," I reasoned.

"You may have had good intentions, sailor, for which we are grateful if so," the breathless man said. "Now go find your own hog."

"Be reasonable! I saved your companion's life! As you know meat of this quantity is hard to come by and harder to bring down. And here is enough for the nine of us."

"It would divide more kindly between five," said the second man. "I haven't tussled a half hour with a mad pig to share its flesh with John Cocke's crew."

"What have you against our commander?"

"Davis does say he is a simpleton, and holds no discipline in his ranks!"

"I hear your Davis spends his time below deck making maps," Harris grinned, "when for you and us both it would be better if he turned these parchments into food, and wine, and gold!"

The third man approached. Laboured speech, girth and an extra head of height: it was clear he preferred negotiating physically rather than verbally.

"Meat needs doing." He folded his arms; glowering at me, at Harris, then back to Waldren and Barrawell.

"They were just leaving," the breathless man said.

"Aye, we'll go!" said Waldren, who had remained silent during this exchange. "You'll be eating spoiled meat, anyways, if you don't get it on that fire right, and quick."

"What do you mean?"

"Carcass that size. Spoils mighty quick in this heat. Maggots and the like."

"He's lying," the bigger man growled.

"Lads, I were a butcher before I were a sailor."

"Wait," the breathless man said. With the rivulets of sweat on his face the heat did seem his most accursed enemy and he looked like he would believe it capable of any and every evil at that moment; Waldren had done well to mention it. "You say the whole hog will spoil?"

"The way you're going about it, aye."

"Very well. Come."

"Food!" Barrawell clapped his hands in jubilation, although thankfully behind the backs of our new hosts. Like most devout men he was easily swayed.

"Were you really a butcher?" I asked Waldren in a low voice.

"Spaniards and Portugals mostly, lad. Some Scottish too, in former years."

"So the way they're roasting the hog is in fact satisfactory?"

"We'll let them *think* our expertise was what saved them, eh Knivet?" Waldren winked. "Get that flame lower," he called ahead. "Raise that spit higher."

"And wrap the beast in leaves for the roasting," I added anxiously, "or there will be no flavour retained."

"Lads!" said Waldren. "I am your butcher but this man shall be your cook!"

Ah, the smell of strange wood sweetly crackling and the fizz of pork fat on embers! Ah, the rose-pink of a rump smoked soft just so, and the moistness of meat as it separates in your mouth, with the taste, I swear, of nuts and pepper and lemons. In these times that were for all us men slowly darkening and as the better paths our voyage might have gone down were one by one cut off from us, bountiful times like this would stick whimsically in my senses.

"How is the meat Knivet?" they asked me, hanging on my every word. "When in your opinion may we eat?"

I tried to make the meal a civil one, but with the two men injured in the hog chase so uncouthly frantic to get meat in their bellies it was not easy. Time and time again they fell upon the part-roasted pig with little regard as to whether they were eating raw flesh, and so I would pull them back and the breathless man would apologise for their behaviour.

"Marlowe," he introduced himself.

"Like the playwright," I smiled.

"And there is a Knivet in parliament, is there not?"

"In the Privy chamber," I said happily. "Only a handful in England have the honour. He is my uncle."

"Why are you at sea, then, and not in politics?"

"You know how it is with young men of our age. They want to tip the balance. They want to run full tilt at their adversary and somehow stay mounted. They want adventure. I am no exception. I may take up politics one day... but to do so without experience of Life, Marlowe! Those who enter offices tamely by inheritance alone win no respect from me."

"I would settle for any experience other than this," sighed Marlowe. "Biggs there," he indicated the big man, "and Russell," he indicated the bearded, "have served twenty years between them in the navy and with privateers, and this they say is the direst voyage they ever did sail on."

"The direst?" I asked, surprised.

"There is talk the General is the very devil incarnate. There is one Christopher – the Japanese fellow forever slipping between ships, you know him? –"

"Somewhat."

"– who says he is so obsessed with finding a safe trade route through the South Sea to China that he wrote a letter to his London lawyer saying he was not concerned how many men he lost in the process."

"That Japanese says many things."

"Our Davis does not care for the General, I think. And I trust Davis. He cares about the betterment of the world."

"We all have our agendas."

"There is more. The voyage here. Those strange purple lights, like God's own candles, above the sails as we crossed the equator. They are a portent! The old tars on our ship crossed themselves and swore nothing but bad fortune ever followed such lights!"

"That's true," interjected Waldren.

"But it is a general feeling," said Marlowe. "Badness. I do not care for this damned country. I do not like its heat, or its diseases, or its savages that roast human flesh on a whim."

"I understand," I said, "but there is opportunity here for the right men."

"*Over these waters firm and strong, I sail to whatever the fates desire…*" that had to be the way, I thought.

"And we heard there were some from your crew who brought down several albatrosses a week or so back."

"Aye," said Waldren. "Knivet bagged six himself, as I recall."

"What?" Marlowe's mouth dropped open.

"I knew it," Biggs growled. "Told you they were bad news."

"Come!" I said half-heartedly. "You are being superstitious!"

"You did great wrong, Knivet," Marlowe whispered, pale.

I looked for support from around the fire, but even Harris' normally innocuous face was turned uncomfortably to the ground.

"I am going to gather berries," I muttered. "Coming Barrawell?"

"I will stay here, Anthony. I am not inclined to walk."

Precious good it was being blood brothers, I thought, if your blood brother does not stand by you. Precious good it was killing a hog for some rogues whose gratitude was not as strong as their fear of a seabird being shot.

I felt much better when the clearing was out of sight and the trees closed around me. The leaves felt cool on my cheeks and smelt of a salad such as only my mother could make. There were one thousand things moving in that jungle. One thousand strange plants. One thousand strange animals. There were whistlings and moanings and trillings and croakings. There was a flower I witnessed suck insects as large as dinner plates into its mouth; there was a lizard as long as the Roebuck's shore boat with jaws that could accommodate a man whole. I craned my neck and saw the upper branches of the trees soaring so high, so thick, so intricate, that even the sky and the sea became part of another world. I fancied I was looking up instead at the roof of an immense cathedral where I, Anthony Knivet, was seated on a bough and they – the hog hunters, our company, the Portugals, all of them – came to pay homage to me. And Indians materialised to paint me in fine colours and bring me offerings, and I was very much respected and loved.

I got good store of a bulbous tuber called cassava that afternoon, and good berries. I gorged myself unrestrainedly and still had pockets that bulged with my foraging. But presently I felt bad for deserting Barrawell, and mindful of the hog that would soon be tender for the eating. I readied to return when I caught through the undergrowth the strains of a ballad – violins and accordions, and resonant voices engaged in the execution of it. As they were English voices, I followed the sounds. Around a kink in the path several of the General's musicians were dressing whelps for their dinner, singing as they went.

Not wishing to interrupt their melody I asked by gesture if I might join them, offering the cassava and berries as contribution to their meal.

"You play most exquisitely," I told them, and not without a tremble of emotion, for the way they touched their instruments conjured a welling of something within me I could not name but sensed was momentous.

"Thank you, sailor," one said. "I can tell your appreciation is heartfelt."

"There is too little dignity here. We lose sight of it, and when we do we are no better than animals."

"That is perhaps why the General wanted us. The jest aboard his Galleon is that he searched the length of England for musicians that met his standards, yet chose the first group of ruffians showing up at Plymouth dock for his crew."

"We mean no disrespect to you, sailor," another added quickly. "Truthfully in all the evenings we have played since setting sail we have not met another save the General who has your understanding of melody."

I accepted the compliment graciously.

"At times I have felt most isolated by the abundance of knaves amongst my companions, true."

"This very day we witnessed fights over as little as a plantain!"

"A man wresting a monkey from another's jaws."

"And that Stafford beating men for failing to return with food, yet pilfering the best of what came back for himself."

"A man wants to eat," I agreed.

"A man *needs* to eat."

"How can we sustain the General's good grace with music, if we have no energy to lift our bows?"

"Carnage. If we act thus to each other now what will happen when we encounter the actual enemy?"

On this sobering thought the musicians again took up their instruments. Like a wave the song spread from the fiddle of one to the flute of the next. The melody sounded like the end of something. It was hopeless and helpless. It picked you up then threw you down. It was as if the notes had been hanging somewhere in the Earth's atmosphere since the beginning of time and, now they had been found here in remotest Brazil, could play forever. I preserved a brave face until the players were done with playing, and I had whispered my thanks, but once I had taken my leave to return to the ship, I wept and did not know why.

On the shore plentiful supplies had been amassed: plantains and fish and fowl now being dried and salted, and cashew nuts, and cinnamon pods, and cassava roots. As I contemplated this banquet Stafford came and shouted at me to start shifting food to the boats, who did I think I was that I could stand idle whilst others worked? I would have begged him consider who he was that he could treat others like dogs when he was no better than a dog himself, and in fact less intelligent than many dogs I had encountered, when he added a comment that threw me into a frenzy.

The General had bid me appear at sundown in his cabin, which was in one hours' time. Sundown, as everyone in the company knew, was when the commanders of all five ships were meeting to determine how Santos was to be taken, for we planned to seize the town the day after tomorrow. Evidently they wanted me to be present at the discussion. I pondered on what this could mean. I hazarded that word of my shooting ability had reached the General, and that I must be selected to command one of the units to be deployed in the attack.

"Where did you get to, Knivet?" Harris asked me in the shallop[1] on the way back to the Roebuck. "We were waiting for your garnish of berries."

"I saved you some hog," said Barrawell, placatory as ever, "but it will be the less tasty for lacking your direction during cooking, no doubt."

"What did Stafford want with you, lad?" asked Waldren, gruff as ever.

But I remained tight-lipped and aloof for I saw they needed me more than I needed them.

---

[1] A small vessel for use in shallow waters; crucial for those early explorers from Europe who arrived on Brazil's sandbar-ridden coast with big, deep-keeled boats.

EIGHT
(The General)

"How gracious of you to accept my invitation" our General Sir Thomas Cavendish spoke with dreadful quietness, seated behind a table on which were an empty carafe of wine, some disorderly charts and a Coverdale Bible with particular Old Testament sections bookmarked. As I entered two of the musicians I had encountered earlier were finishing some ditty that presumably pleased him, for he laughed, hph, hph, and rubbed his long white hands together at particular passages. The musicians, previously so cordial, avoided my eyes as they left; the General continued the hand rubbing. He did so most gently, the middle finger of one hand beginning on the pulse of the wrist of the other, drifting up until his second hand's fingertips were stroking the prominent wrist veins of the first.

"We did well re-victualling the ship today," he said. "The holds are almost full."

I was breathless from the walk up to his cabin. The flagship of our fleet was twice the size of the Roebuck: a deck higher at least, with the aft-castle where the General was quartered soaring like a fortress above that – accessed by several sets of ladders as if with the intent that all should arrive at his cabin door at least slightly flustered. And I *was* flustered – what with his gambit about re-victualling – for I was entertaining the possibility that, far from

my promotion, it might be the actions of certain men of the
Roebuck on the island today he now wished to discuss.

"That is welcome news General."

"My thanks to you for the part you played."

"Not at all." My palms sweated. "We are here to serve you."

"There are those that would follow me and those that would
usurp me. I need, hph, to conduct my little inquisitions sometimes,
to ascertain who falls into which category."

He shifted position; his chair back was green velvet; he seemed
to exalt in the awkward length of the pause.

"At Plymouth you told me you could cook."

I nodded, relieved.

"Cocke, Cotton and Master are coming here soon to
dine. Davis too – should we be able to lure him away from his
instruments. You have two hours to prepare."

"My pleasure, General."

And as I turned to go:

"You want the stars, do you not?

"I beg your pardon General?"

"The stars. You believe you are entitled to them. There they
are." He pointed to the cabin ceiling. "Take them."

"Forgive me General, I do not know…"

"I colonised Roanoke[1]. I fought with tribes in the Magallanes
and Manilla. And do you think it is easy, to capture a 600-ton
treasure galleon in a 140-ton ship as I did?[2] When you see a ship
like that bearing up on you, you tremble. You have to stem your
own trembling and the trembling of your entire crew. You have

---

[1] An experimental colony founded in the 1580s in the wilds of North
America under Sir Walter Raleigh - and an ultimately doomed colony,
too.

[2] The incident, which took place off the coast of Northern Mexico,
was considered one of the crowning glories of Cavendish's first
circumnavigation.

many men's lives in the palm of your hand and you have to make them believe. You have to help them overcome fear as only God can do and so help me God, you become a God – their own little God upon the waves! Boys like you read about the clothes we made from the silk we took, how we seized enough damask to make our sails from the stuff for the return voyage. You heed nothing of what we had to endure to get there. Hunger. Battle. Death. Grown men emptying their bowels into their breeches with sheer fright. When you face those things, and come out on top, hph, then…" he held up his right arm "…you have a place at the right hand of this little God. But there is no hereditary respect on my ship. You might be a gentleman with an education. But I would sooner trust a brute who has proved himself. That is all."

When a brute gets put in charge, I thought, then maidens get violated and order becomes chaos – as evidenced this very day with Stafford giving orders. When a brute is in charge the world cannot become enriched. But I dearly desired to be at that right hand; I wanted to be raising my own right hand to others. So I meekly bowed, making my exit, thankful to have escaped without punishment.

"Oh, Knivet? Again, really well done on your execution of mine and Stafford's orders."

His hands were so white and smooth. He could not even grow a beard.

NINE

I chose guinea fowl, and cassava, and sweet purple berries that invigorated the senses remarkably. I had been allotted a place for preparation on the quarterdeck itself and - given the importance of the task - two sailors to do my bidding. But I trusted my hand alone to deliver, and returned to that cabin with fowl roasted to a fine degree of subtlety served in berry compote, with cassava puree as an accompaniment - a la Knivet, and a la Knivet alone.

The commanders were assembled, and in hot debate, with the point of contention the number of men to deploy in taking Santos. Cavendish favoured less; Davis more. Cocke saw Davis's point, but was anxious not to offend Cavendish. Master drummed his fleshy red hands on the table-top, and although I could better imagine him as a yeoman slurping cider atop a hay bale, the gossip was that he was not nearly so stupid as he looked, and merely weighing up who would be most advantageous to side with in an argument. Cotton sat and smiled and drank, which surprised me little for he was a Devonshire man and if there is one thing Devonshire breeds better than mariners it is drinkers.

I served each of them, thinking the aromas created from the herbs I had used praiseworthy, although Cocke alone thanked me. I waited for their opinions. The other commanders waited for their host. The General ran his nose lingeringly around the plate, then jerking upright knocked his lovingly prepared food on the cabin floor.

"How regrettable Knivet, would you clear it up and fetch some more?"

Mortified I stared as the compote seeping into the floorboards. There was no doubt his action had been intentional, but I rallied to the task, and came back within minutes with another portion. The General smiled his joyless smile, picked up his plate then again emptied the food at his feet.

"Knivet, would you clear it up and fetch some more?"

My cheeks burned with indignation. Had a lesser man acted thus against me he would already be regretting it, but I restrained myself, vowing then that my moment with him and with all these sailors who tried their superior airs on me would come. Cocke was blinking rapidly as he always did when uneasy and even Cotton was finding it hard to look entertained. But Davis was livid.

"I came here to discuss a strategy, General, not to watch pantomime." I heard his gravelly voice as I again cleaned cassava from under the table.

"What are you implying?" came the insidious reply.

"Let us proceed with the meeting," pleaded Cocke.

"...is that this is the mainstay of our plan you now risk jeopardising." Davis was arguing as I returned a third time, this time with the last available portion of supper. My eyes met the General's as I gave him the plate: they conveyed first surprise I should dare to meet them; afterwards amusement. For my part, whilst resenting he who purported to command our fleet I was yet more concerned to alter his opinion of me, which appeared most overtly and inexplicably negative. I wondered if it would be an appropriate time to make my input. Jorge, the recently-captured Portugal pilot, had informed me the optimum time to attack would be an hour after dawn on the day after tomorrow, the twenty-fourth of December, for that was when these Portugals celebrated Christmas, and all Santos would be in the church.

"...the necessity of preserving as many of my men in able-bodied state as possible for the Straits which we both know will be deadly." (Cavendish)

"...take Santos, and take it well, and keep it, and let the dividends be an engine for the remainder of the voyage." (Davis)

"With your good leave." I cleared my throat.

Five sets of eyes on me. Cocke's: nervous; Master's: intrigued; Cotton's: wine-befuddled; Davis': narrowed; the General's: nothing, nothing at all.

"You are certain?" breathed the General, when I had spoken.

"Indeed, General, my grasp of Portugal is good."

"Then my resolution is substantiated!" the commander of our fleet announced to the room. "We need but few men for this enterprise. Even the dumbest dogs among us should have no problem vanquishing Portugals as they are kneeling in prayer!"

"I urge you again," rasped Davis. "We do not know Santos. We do not know this coast. We do not know what it might throw at us. We should take extra men."

"You are forgetting the General has come this way before," said Cocke.

"That was different," said Davis, who looked like he needed no reminding of Cavendish's past accomplishments. "Portugal has fortified its coast since. It has shipped more armies from Lisbon to defend its shores, and more slaves to do its bidding."

"There is the issue of the men," said Cotton. "They are hungry for action, and it might be wise to let as many of them have it as we may."

"The men?" Cavendish screamed and then, collecting himself: "I am General, and the men will do my bidding or face my wrath. As to Portugal's defences, hph!" His gaze caught his Bible and a serene look fell across his countenance. "God is smiling on us.

Our path has been ordained by Him!"
But God, I thought, never smiles upon the devil.

TEN

The night before our attack a waning moon like a round of cheese filled the sky and I thought of Kathy, who used to tell me jestingly this was the moon to make spells by – if you were so inclined. Oh, she was an unmanageable girl, and took nothing seriously, and teased me until I felt wretched, but as we neared the place where we would do battle with the Portugals I thought of each curve of her body as I had observed them that last afternoon in my father's woods. She had bid me take her in the tussocks and I had declined. And now I might now be killed without having ever known a woman, or fulfilling my true calling in life, by which I mean fame as a man of means, and with tales to tell.

Fortunately for the General we had a healthy wind the whole day long, for he was now Hell-bent on taking Santos that next morning in accordance with my advice. Yet even at full tilt his plan had left but little room for error, and his crew at their wits' end. The timbers and the backs of every man had strained, and just after dusk we had gained the isles at the mouth of the estuary in which Santos sat.

We went into shore as close as we dared. Most was forest, but there was more cultivation than further north, and more heat, and an obnoxious biting fly that pestered us even out at sea and enhanced the general mood of agitation. We caught sight of the glimmering furnace of what Portugals call an *engenho*[1], or sugar mill, for, cruel masters that they are, they work their slaves through the night to maximise their production of sugar cane. Sporadic fires burned on the shoreline and we wondered what manner of people had lit them: friendly traders, or crazed missionaries, or Portugals plotting our demise, or cannibals anticipating our flesh.

The commotion began about ten. It became known the General wanted to launch just one boat for the attack, and of course there was not a man present who wanted to pass over this opportunity of plunder. There were such squabbles as we all justified our claims to a berth on the shore boat that a man listing reasons for his true love to wed him would have entreated less. But Cocke, who liked me very much and would have guaranteed my place, was a weak commander; the General screamed for order and made it known he would decide on the raiding party if no one else could. Hearing this, whilst attention was diverted I slipped under the seat of the shallop I knew to be reserved for Waldren, as the boatman bringing us in, and waited. It was a long wait. The shouting did not diminish that whole night, and I marvelled that all Brazil did not become aware of our presence. My legs had a crippling cramp on account of how I had twisted to fit in, and the damnable flies of Santos crawled across my face and feasted, but I dared not stretch, or even scratch, for fear of being discovered. Then I heard Jorge's voice urge '*agora*!' (now), and pairs of shore shoes clomping around me, and ropes being cut. The boat was lowered, but was grossly overloaded. It was not only Waldren's feet blocking the entrance to the hole I had crawled into, but many feet. So close were we down to the

---

[1] In the 1580s the Portuguese realised sugar production was their best chance for profit in Brazil. Many *engenhos* were built and, to man them, slaves from Portugal's African colonies (deemed better workers than Brazil's tribespeople) were shipped in.

waterline that each oar stroke splashed brackish water on my face. The discomfort was immense, then unbearable, for I was being slowly suffocated. Oh, Kathy in the soft moss of the field edge, I would give myself to you now if I knew your reaction to finding me thus might be something other than ridicule. Oh pearls, oh gold dust, oh ambergris! Oh God, you rogue, did you not turn water into blood, and bring about plagues of frogs, and flies, and locusts, and cast darkness across the land? You behold the irony, do you not, that here lies a man, trapped, craving only liberty, a man who would BE, a man...

"Knivet!" Waldren's head, round and rough as a coconut, appeared upside-down between his feet. The tropics had hard-boiled this old tar. "You want help getting out?"

No doubt he will make me beg, I thought, but Waldren prised back the boards and freed me without exacting any demands. But I knew as I rose up, spluttering, that I was beholden to him and that just as he saved my life, I would be duty-bound to one day save his. I read of such understandings in my boyhood books of chivalry: should it so happen, it was a matter of honour – a life spared for a life spared – that was all.

"Anthony!" gushed Barrawell. It was ever a juxtaposition to see his delicate countenance amongst the roughneck rabble of our crew.

"Harry Barrawell, volunteering for action?" I smiled weakly for breath was slow in returning to my body, adding into his ear: "My diary. I am keeping one of everything that passes upon this voyage. The truth, Barrawell! A precious jewel indeed amidst this perfidious crew."

"Why?" Barrawell looked confused. "If it is discovered you will be strung up like Rodrigo! I could not bear seeing you die, Anthony!"

"You will not." I seized him, perhaps too emotionally, for he flinched. "But if anything happens, you are the one I trust, for we are blood brothers, and..."

I whispered the location of the chest in which I had stowed these papers and made Barrawell promise to deliver them to none other than my father should something befall me, for the odds I placed at that moment upon my long-term survival were not high.

Our boat hit shore. Dawn was coming. The others alighted rapidly, stealing across the bay in the direction of the church tolling its doleful bell for Christmas mass, where we believed the Portugals to be gathered, oblivious. I was slower, massaging my crushed limbs and replenishing my starved lungs in the hot, sweet air. Portugals, I did hear, were ruthless fighters, and our ships looked like toy ships back out in the bay. Say a spell for me, Kathy, I implored, for I go to win you your pearls.

ELEVEN

"We continued two months at Santos, which was the overthrow of our voyage"

Anthony Knivet, *Admirable Adventures and Strange Fortunes*

The poor dogs stood no chance. They had eyes only for the bread of the sacrament the priest was holding the moment we entered the church, and had left their weapons outside. The General had put Cocke in command of our raiding party but it was Stafford who nonchalantly strolled down the aisle, once we had the exits sealed, singing the most tone-deaf strain of 'Greensleeves' I ever did hear and looking inappropriately at various female members of the congregation.

"Someone had better explain to these Catholic imbeciles who we are... *bom dia*, padre," he said mockingly, patting the priest on each cheek. "Anythin' in your Christmas rant about how there be Englishmen takin' your town today, and relievin' you of your gold?"

Something about Stafford made most Portugals there restrain themselves from retaliation. But one of their hot-headed captains with a "*mio deus*" sprang forward regardless to protest. Stafford was still faced away jibing the priest, but pivoted and let fly his dagger into the Portugal's belly in one movement – so fluid it seemed rehearsed. The man knelt immediately, and then lay still as Stafford put a boot to his face.

"Padre!" Stafford continued. "What part of Thou Shalt not Kill did you neglect to teach your flock?"

One thing we did not lack was rope. We began tying up prisoners, and Stafford marched amongst the womenfolk, marking out certain prettier girls to be set aside and giving each a good manhandle as he went. Even we his crewmen were not sure what his game was, and the Portugals must have feared the worst.

"*Senhor*," pleaded the priest, who spoke the best English amongst them. "We can help you with many things, but show mercy."

"Mercy, Padre?" chuckled Stafford. "Get Knivet here, don't he speak their tongue? Tell him the only thing I want his help with is findin' this town's finest young maid, for I've me a sweet tooth for Catholic lasses!" Stafford's henchmen found this funny, and consequently the rest of us felt obliged to laugh, but I did not for at that moment I felt ashamed to be an Englishman. Bending down, I revived the priest with a draught of communion wine, which he guzzled most gratefully.

"Fear not," I said in a voice just audible to the two of us. "No lady here shall be improperly treated whilst I draw breath."

He gazed at me, perturbed; confounded not by my words but by something in my appearance. I roughly snatched the wine from him, downing the remainder myself, and bid him speak, for I could not abide anyone to look at me too long.

"Your eyes," he said. "They betray you. You *care*." He switched to Portugal and clasped my hand in his wizened ones. "I know you will not let those brutes harm my people."

I looked around the congregation. I looked at the patches in the faded hose of the men, imagining their bold declarations to defend this makeshift nation made an ocean and a lifetime away. Without fighting attire they appeared as lost as lambs. I looked at the women, wearing their best dresses from the haberdasheries of Lisbon to bring a dash of civilisation to the rudimentary settlement their husbands had been posted to, now rumpled after several seasons in the Santos swamps. I looked at the children, shoeless and severe beyond their years, as if bearing an immense burden, and the burden of course was the jungle – that infinite sweaty prison – for there it was; there it was again; there was no escaping it. And the sentence for these poor colonists was years – years out here before the next ship relieved them. For years they were as trapped as the slaves that worked their sugar mills and the tribes they professed to have conquered, for they lived as all Portugals lived in Brazil: on a thin strip of coast in constant fear of the forest coiling behind. They were petrified of the very thing this land was more than any other: forest. They were petrified, here and now, of us Englishmen; they were petrified, week upon week, of other marauders, and of disease, and of starvation. But mostly they were petrified of IT, the dark unmentionable, the forest. For the forest represented something far worse than death. It represented the unknown. And that, to their carefully assembled lives, was most terrifying of all.

"The colours we sail under are not necessarily the colours of our hearts," I said to the priest.

"Your sail. One of us spied it, yesterday. But only one of us, and he was a known madman, so no attention was paid him. For who fights on Christmas Day?"

"For us it is not Christmas Day."

"The English are a contrary race."

"The Portugals are a doomed one."

"How so?"

"You are ruled by Spain. Your forces are weakened. The Spaniards have the territory with the best of the gold and silver, and have left you with the sugar. They control you, and even as they control you they laugh at you."

"Who is the greater fool?" the priest regarded me sorrowfully. "He who has little, or he that comes to plunder he who has little?"

Christopher the Japanese was watching us.

"It is necessary you tell me where you have hidden what treasure you have," I hissed to the priest. "It is me or him, or all of them." I indicated first Christopher, then Stafford and his henchmen.

"I will tell you, when the time comes," the old man nodded. "We have a deal?"

His face was white: the whiter for his black cassock. The colony has sucked him dry, I thought.

"Remember who you are, and who I am," I retorted. "You have a chance now to save your life and other lives. That is all."

"When you came," he said distantly "I saw it in the sky. Rain clouds: for the first time in months. A storm is brewing. That has to mean something."

"It means you will get wet, padre."

"Bonding with the local populace, Knivet?" Christopher circled. Ever since we had sight of Brazil he had been wearing an inappropriately frivolous piece of silk tied around his head, and I wondered where he could have got such a thing.

"Extracting information as I was bidden."

"Yehhhz… On what, I wonder?"

"Details relating to the taking of the town." I shot the priest a warning look.

"Gurrrrd. You recall our little project?"

"I remember."

"I suggest tomorrow, at midnight. It will be opportune. Our men will be drunk, for it is Christmas and they will imagine themselves victorious. You know the problem with this expedition, Knivet? It is a concept. The execution of it…" He shook his head and leaned closer. "Our General has passages from the bible scrawled on his charts. He calls our voyage the immaculate voyage." He touched my shoulder and I flinched from fear and excitement. "But I do not trust in God enough to believe that He will protect us on this voyage, and nor do you. What we will be doing is investing, Knivet." I thought of my carriage of quetzal feathers approaching my father's house. My house. I thought of villagers cheering; of how my Kathy would bow her head for me to place a necklace of fine stones around her neck. "Any man here would do what we will do if they possessed our foresight. It is no wrong, but our right."

I could no longer pretend I did not know exactly what Christopher intended: making off with the treasure from under the company's noses, which is the one thing guaranteed to get a group of marauders nursing a nasty grudge against you.

"Pull your weight, Knivet," snapped Stafford, suddenly. "I'm sick of catchin' you standin' about idle. I wanted that priest to tell you where my store of ripe Portugal maids lies, not convert you! If you've been doin' a spot of convertin', padre, it will be the worse for you! We've problems," he confided in lower tones. "Cotton's men ain't here."

There were 300 Portugals in the church that morning, and twenty of us, and we held them at bay solely because they imagined us more in number. But as the hours crept on and the heat increased, maintaining our perceived position of power became harder, for we were relying on Cotton's men in the other shore boat to secure the town. We were loath to dispatch anyone to discover what was hindering Cotton and loath to set any prisoners at liberty for fear of them alerting others. Our men had bound the hands of every man present, and beaten a fair few. The best of the girls had been herded to the altar, and those that possessed any sense had given up on screaming. The children were wailing. Someone had defecated, and one old wife had fainted, and there was a growing feeling no one knew what to do next. Oh, we were gallant sailors, to have conquered our enemies thus.

"We have sent a man with a message to the General." Cocke leaned on his arquebus, dejected. The lines on his face were wrongly placed for a commander: around the eyes, as on one who smiles too much, rather than about the mouth or upon the forehead, which would at least have indicated some gravity. The collar of his doublet was too high, almost about his ears; he better resembled a provincial government official than a mariner.

"A good hour too late," grumbled Stafford, who desired Cocke's position – fruitlessly – for he was not of noble birth and could not conduct himself accordingly. And such things matter, even amongst privateers on the other side of the ocean.

"What choice did I have?" appealed Cocke; his nervous tick accentuated.

"You did your best, master." I addressed him by his true title, to reassure him because he had been good to me, and to make a dig at Stafford, whom I had not and would not ever call by any title.

"You should consider," said Christopher slyly, "that every hour we tarry here we lose what the rest of Santos might have. We give them opportunity to conceal the very wealth we seek."

"Aye!" said Stafford. "And their lasses! What did that old priest say, Knivet?"

"That they have no treasure," I lied; already calculating a story that would keep Christopher off my back whilst my priest was showing me precisely where the loot lay. "That its existence was pure invention."

"Those dogs have treasure," Stafford growled. "There's hoards they're hidin' – I'd stake my mother on it!"

"I will not renege on the General's order," said Cocke. "We will wait, and hold the church."

"Wait!" ejaculated Stafford. "These men have done nowt but wait since Plymouth! I say if we wait the least we should do is take some choice lasses and have a little fun!"

I was prepared to say my piece, with my hand naturally sliding to the handle of my mother's pork cutting knife, when Cocke said quietly:

"This is a holy place. I am in command and I say we will not harm their women. And you will obey me, Stafford."

Stafford's mouth fell open, his features heavy as a bloodhound's.

"But the General allows it!"

"Maybe," said Cocke. "But I command the Roebuck, and it is the Roebuck's boat that brought you here. We on the Roebuck do things differently."

So we waited.

It stretched to noon; the sun beat down. The flies massed. The hardiest amongst us reeled from lack of water. As for the old wife that had fainted, some Portugals clamoured that she was dying, but still we held our positions. A boy of maybe twelve years of age broke free of his family, then, making a dash for liberty. He darted passed those guarding the doors aiming for the cover of the first houses some half a mile distant. But he was not as fast as Southwell, who gave chase, and came back some minutes later with the broken body slung over his shoulder.

"He would not stop hitting me, the dog," he explained.

The Portugals cursed us, and swore they would send us to Hell at the first opportunity; those who killed children deserved nothing less. Stafford and his henchmen went to dispatch the troublemakers, but I restrained them, reasoning it was natural they should be aggrieved at the death of a boy, whilst placating the Portugals. "*Para baixo,*" I said unto them. "*O tiempo para resolver esse não é agora.*" It had become clear to them that I was a man worth listening to, so they obeyed me.

The messenger returned.

"The General says to release the captives," he said, relishing his moment of importance unbecomingly. "Cotton's men have arrived and the town is ours."

"After all these hours he wants them released?" Cocke frowned. "Are you certain?"

"If you're lyin' I'll skin you over a hot flame, you dog," Stafford added.

"The General says to retain only seven or eight of the most prominent Portugals as prisoners, and release the remainder."

"That would seem unwise," said Cocke, and most of us there agreed, for a freed enemy was sure to raise the alarm.

"That would be wise," countered Christopher, and sometimes I was convinced causing mayhem was his sole motivation. "We are wasting our time here."

"He m… means here?" murmured Barrawell to me. "Or in this entire enterprise?"

We kept two Portugal captains, a sugar merchant, some village elders, the priest and the two girls Stafford deemed ripest, then marched down into town.

Santos looked like a gypsy encampment, only with the hovels laid out in lines. Dust blew down each wide street in nauseating gusts. Any voyage that relied on getting supplies here was a voyage I had little hope for. There were only a few buildings around the central square befitting of civilisation. One of these, the College of Jesus, was where most of our company were gathered, and by the sounds of things with ample jars of alcohol.

The College of Jesus was a striking edifice that, whilst it may not have rivalled my ancestral home in faraway Wiltshire, had an entrance of marble steps, and an interior as spacious as a modest English cathedral. There were two principle levels and a spiral staircase connecting them. The main room was a banquet hall that King Hal would have hankered after, and I did wonder that an establishment set up for studies in devotion to Christ should be centred around a place for feasting and the consumption of intoxicants. But just as it suited Holy Catholics it seemed to suit a party of jubilant privateers, and there they all were in the rapture of victory whilst we had been since morning without sustenance in the church.

"Cocke!" the General beckoned our party over. "What detained you?"

"Your orders, General," Cocke said stiffly. "And waiting for Cotton, as was agreed."

"I bid Cotton join me in a victory toast, as you see," the General said softly. Both he and Cotton had evidently consumed a fair few 'toasts' but even when shining with drunkenness the eyes of the commander of our fleet had an unnerving way of icily boring into us, as if searching for potential challenges to his word. "Today and tomorrow are for celebration. For it is Christmas night."

Several of us searched for Davis in that banquet hall rabble, as the obvious candidate for the challenger. Not finding him, no one said anything. But the foolhardiness of sanctioning a two-day debauch was obvious. Already there had been word of Portugals regrouping outside town, and not one of us knew the lie of the land now Rodrigo had been hanged, or the nature of the provisions Santos could offer. So we sat down in resigned silence and joined in the discussion – which was on nothing more meaningful than who should get a bed in the grand College of Jesus, and who should be accommodated in the town's other hovels – and passed around good store of a potent drink made from molasses. I observed Christopher pouring away his drink secretly. He noticed me doing the same.

There was space in the college only for those of high rank, but in an underground vault we discovered a small friar's cell, and Cocke saw to it that I was given this for my quarters, meaning I slept not with the lowlier members of the crew in mean wooden houses but with the General and other gallant young gentleman of the voyage.

The rain clouds mustered that night and the storm that had threatened broke. I chuckled to think of Waldren and the others in their leaking huts. I slept on a bed that did not move, and I was dry. Starting to write by candlelight, I realised the table on which I leant was hollow, and in actuality a chest. The wood was thick, but old, and gave when I kicked it. Out fell pile upon pile of *réis*. Did the deviousness of these Catholic friars know no limits? I examined each for sign of forgery, for good fortune was my most infrequent visitor. But they seemed genuine, with the Iberian King's ugly face scowling back at me, and numbered 1700, which was over 6000 shillings[1]. A Christmas gift from Brazil, I exalted, but then began panicking how I could conceal this find. My pulse hammered. I knew I could be a rich man with this, and spared the hardships the rest of the voyage might entail.

Next morning, with the others still glugging molasses liquor,

---

[1] This is the conversion Knivet makes in *Admirable Adventures and Strange Fortunes*.

I set off to find a hiding place for my loot, or a means of escape with it. I discovered why Santos stank; outside town the cleared land became fetid bog, and part-submersed forest, and round this again on each side curved the rivers that fed the estuary, which accounted for the presence of those loathsome flies. This also made Santos an island separated from the more fertile land across the river. The township might seem to sailors like a haven with its sheltered waters, but in fact it was Hell. I climbed to a low ridge with a view inland, over the muddy river to an emerald-green land that erupted in mountains then dipped into dense forest. There were trees that stretched away many times further in distance than all Wiltshire, or even England, all the way to Peru and the west coast: this was the way I would need to go with my loot to evade the General's men. These forests were still a wondrous new thing to me, and if I did not look upon them with dread, like many of our company, I still reserved for them some awe. To have any chance with my treasure I would have to first hide it, then later get across the river with it. And, I realised with a sinking feeling, to do this I would need Christopher.

I found him by the house on the very edge of town where he had stationed himself, making notches with a knife near the base of his dwelling. He looked furtive whatever he was doing, especially so now, and I wondered why he had chosen this place for his lodging, as if he had wanted a room in the College of Jesus he would certainly have been granted it.

"Knivet, I was about to come looking for you," he spoke sweetly.

"We had an agreement; I am not one to go back on it."

"Nor I on you."

We looked at each other like we believed we had the measure of the other.

"Gurrrd," he purred at length. "I was fortunate to find someone so trustworthy as yourself. How did you fare in your search?"

"How did you fare?"

"Gold, Knivet. *Réis*, candlesticks, some jewels. It seems some in Santos did very well for themselves… until now," he sniggered.

"I found *réis*," I said. "A chest of them."

"I suspected as much. I was watching you.'

I shivered.

"I thought we could make a go of it, as you implied we should. With two we would be faster. You and me. Across the estuary. We might befriend some Indians perhaps. They could help us across country. To Peru. To the South Sea."

Christopher suppressed a smile.

"Indians would eat us. And the season for such an enterprise is gone."

"Then what do you suggest?" I was riled at his patronising response.

"We bury all we have and save it for later. This very night. The rest are drunk; they will not heed us. Leave your treasure with me. Meet me later at the orange tree by the pier. I have a canoe. We can float our loot to a place beyond prying eyes."

The rain was cascading over the roof of the porch under which we were ducked: a wall of drops that rendered the space we shared far more intimate than it would otherwise have been. It was like Hell. Looking at him was like looking into Hell. It might have seemed surprising I did not question delivering my *réis* into his hands, but in the context it was not, for although we were both going along with our relationship just so far as it proved useful, I could never have guessed the game would be up as soon as it was.

I waited in the rain at that orange tree five hours and might have tarried all my life. Christopher did not show. At first I wept at my sorry predicament, at being wet, at how easily I had been cheated, at being a penniless nobody hundreds of leagues from my home and at the baked goose and plum frumenty my dear mother would be serving right now for Christmas dinner. Then no fellow sailor, but two *cariihos*, the tribe of Indians that dwelt nearest Santos, materialised. We exchanged no words, and they exchanged precious few between each other. They squatted at some distance, regarding me, smoking a pipe I guessed to contain tobacco. They seemingly cared not for the deluge or for the insects that plagued us mariners or for any other thing save existence. They were as much a part of the landscape as a tree or a flower. And after they left something stirred within me – not just anger at Christopher's betrayal but something wilder. I will call it the Thing. It began with me ripping oranges from the tree boughs and flinging them far out into the sea. Then I opened those oranges and rubbed their juicy flesh upon my face in an imitation of the markings the *cariihos* wore on theirs. Presently I had leapt to my feet and I was dancing, not the court dances of our day but savage steps to a beat that was the rain on the mud, wind in trees, waves on shore. As I danced I laughed – in spite of everything. I laughed because I knew I could not be stopped. Then I checked myself, and went to get riotously drunk. It was, after all, Christmas.

I awoke feeling terrible, and harbouring the same terrible anger towards Christopher.

I smelt burning. Men under Stafford's direction were setting fire to huge swathes of that part of the town by the shore, right along to Saint Vincents at the other end of the island, which was where many of the poorest inhabitants lived. In spite of myself I cried out that this was wrong. They told me the Portugals still remaining had raised a false alarm in attempts to divert us out of Santos so they might retake it with their forces that had been mustering across the river, and that this was their punishment for so doing. I thought it equally a punishment against us, for this order came from the same General who had sent parties to gather materials for a new boat capable of plying shallow estuary waters, and badly needed all the wood he could clap hands on. My own orders were to join the men securing the town perimeter, which I willingly obeyed, as I wanted to hunt for Christopher there. The perimeter was impossible to erect effectively due to the lack of stone or metal in the vicinity, and we used cobbled-together wood that might better have served for our boats' construction, and would in any case provide scant protection against a Portugal attack. Not seeing that villainous Japanese I found means of deploying myself to the party searching for treasure. A significant hoard was accruing, even though Christopher had creamed off the best for himself. The plan became that Cotton would return with this stash to England in the Dainty after we reached the Río de la Plata. Plata means silver in Spaniard speak and the General knew previous explorers had found wealth along that river, and deeply desired it to be said by the historians that he, Thomas Cavendish, had outdone other explorers. Davis disagreed, saying the loss of our fastest boat could only hinder us, but perhaps the General was thinking of the debts on his estates, for he would not be swayed. But I cared little for this disharmony. The image that smarted against my pupils was of my knuckles on Christopher's cheekbone, and I longed to convert this into a reality. I got leave to join those fetching timber in the nearby forest, thinking he might be making himself as scarce as possible. This operation too was proving to be a shambles, with trees of insufficient girth being felled, and I envisaged how I would have supervised matters better. These sailors stumbled about like fools in a mummer's play, in various states of lethargy. It entertained me to imagine each with his own ulterior mission, gold or women or mutiny, and that they were playing the General just as he was playing them, but the sad truth was that they probably lacked such vision. After that I volunteered to take supplies back out to our ships, but Christopher was not aboard any of them. My fury grew. I had now partaken of each of our company's labours, working twice as hard as anyone in the process – and all to no avail, for my quarry eluded me.

It was dusk when I returned to shore. It had rained a second day straight. My clothes were soaked through. I could hear our crew's far-off merry-making, but, too distracted to participate, I took a walk around the back edge of town to collect myself. I passed Christopher's hut, ascending to the bluff from which I had surveyed the interior the previous morning, and then I spied him. He was down by the river edge, conversing with some *cariihos* in canoes – two of which I fancied were the pair who had been watching me last night by the orange tree.

Without ceremony I went to meet them, nodded to the *cariihos* and as Christopher opened his mouth to speak I dealt him a meticulous blow across the jaw for I did not believe a word that came from his mouth. He fell into the shallows but was up immediately, pouncing upon me like a wildcat. The *cariihos* stepped back, curious, being themselves a placid people. Christopher was not so frail as he appeared. He went for scratching eyes and biting ears, a blackguardly way of fighting, but sprang up as often as I knocked him down. The mud weighed heavy on us. Soon it was an effort even to sidestep or throw a punch. Once we both fell back, spent as two half-beached whales, and glared at the other. His eyes smouldered indignation at having been unmasked. But in this lull he merely hissed and readied to launch himself at me once more, and still he did not say the thing he knew I wanted to know, which was where he had squirrelled my stash. We went at it again, and I was the thirstier, with righteousness on my side, and when I found his midriff with the full force of my fist he collapsed moaning in the mud: an eye for an eye, one hit, tooth for tooth, another hit. White prisms of light flashed before my eyes, cold river silt plastered my skin, my cotton shirt felt cumbersome and I tore it off, ha, the Thing was back with me.

"He has done me wrong," I explained to the waiting *cariihos*. The eyes of the savage are most humbling: like the eyes of deer. They implore you to justify your actions, and I never had a problem justifying mine; here they are all set down for the world to see and I would not record them if they were in any way unbefitting.

A third hit and his blood spattered my knuckles. "Anthony!" I dispatched a fourth hit and Christopher's head was thrown back; his precious strip of silk dirtied. "Anthony!" It was Barrawell.

"What in God's name are you doing?"

"God's name!" I paused, bare-chested and blood-smeared. "I do nothing in God's name!"

"Stop it Anthony! Sweet Jesus, you look awful, like… like…"

"Like one of them?" I indicated the *cariihos*.

"Who is he?" Barrawell peered down.

"One who would cross me."

"Sweet Jesus. What have you done, Anthony?"

"Sweet Jesus this! In God's Name that! Did you not swear to be my blood brother? To stand by me in all that might befall us? But you stood against me when we were roasting the hog, eh, Barrawell?"

"I came to say that you should come instantly to the beach," he said, tightly, and at that moment he looked the fully-grown man and I the stammering youth.

"I am busy. What is it?"

"I have never seen the like."

Now that I listened those distant sounds of high-spiritedness had grown frenzied. I had no wish to miss any action. I gave the prostrate Christopher one last pummelling that forced the whereabouts of my treasure from his lips. His bone went crunch, squelch; like a jump on frozen puddles in wintertime. Then I nodded to the most senior of the *cariihos*.

"He is yours," I said. "But I do not recommend doing business with him."

* * *

I doubt if any sailor amongst us had ever seen the like of what was happening at the beach. Around a fire squatted a wide circle of *cariiho* men, as naked as the others I had encountered with nothing but plumes of feathers covering their genitals. They were banging drums and shaking instruments wrought from hollowed gourds, with stones sealed inside that made a dramatic rattling. Within the circle many of our company were dancing with the *cariiho* girls, and these girls were absolutely naked. Along the sand more sailors were sharing molasses liquor with the girls, and spilling the liquid over their pendulous breasts and bodies, and licking it off with much gaiety. Further along they had broken into smaller groups, one girl to every one or two sailors as there were more of us than them, and were fornicating like rabbits. I saw one old tar waving to some comrades as a girl young enough to be his granddaughter futilely sucked at his flaccid member to spark it into life. I saw one of the cabin boys lying facing his *cariiho* and tenderly feed her pieces of pineapple. As her mouth closed around his fingers he closed his eyes and sighed, like one who, in a deep sleep, thinks they have found paradise, and this from a lad I had seen do nothing but scowl since leaving Plymouth.

"What is this?" I whispered.

Some more of our men were sitting outside the circle of revelry, clapping or tapping feet to the *cariihos* rhythm. From this group Waldren waved at us frantically.

"The rains came, Knivet," he drunkenly slurred.

"What of it?"

"The water of life! They hadn't had no rain, these three months gone. Now it comes just as we arrive. To them we're the bringers of water. We're Gods!"

"That is blasphemous," mumbled Barrawell, but he was staring transfixed at a group of nubile *cariiho* girls as yet unattached, and they were smiling playfully back.

"I do not understand." I shook Waldren roughly.

'Don't question it, Knivet! Partake! Give one your best shot, you young buck…" So saying he slumped into a stupor with an idiot's smile on his leathery face.

"We are Gods, Anthony Knivet baker and translator."

It was the General speaking, and I had not noticed him there in the firelight, smoking tobacco with a hide of some worth draped over his shoulders.

One of the *cariiho* girls approached; spread her arms in an inviting embrace. Her hair was long and straight and black as the night and the ends tickled her nipples, each of which was pierced with a piece of chalcedony. This was a stone that much excited me, for, being versed in the accounts of the early explorers, I knew it to be highly prized. But even with the pulse quickening in my loins it was Barrawell she extended her hand to, and he succumbed, and let himself be led away.

"What better way to give thanks to a God?" observed the General.

I did not answer, but attempted to quell my mounting erection. I saw Barrawell start to say something, and the girl put her magenta lips on his opened ones. She placed his trembling hand on her nipple. His thumb and forefinger felt first the stone and then tentatively the hardened pink flesh. The *cariihos* increased the speed of the music. The girl pulled Barrawell out of the circle of dancers, beyond the light of the fire, and pushed his head down to the pale orbs of her breasts shining wet with fresh fat raindrops, then down again over her belly to the darkness between her legs. Like a giddy, greedy lamb at the teat, Barrawell indulged. Then they misplaced their footing; tumbling over each other; giggling; becoming part of the beach of thrusting, moaning, blind-drunk sailors receiving their thanks for making the rain come.

"We are all Gods tonight," said the General again, softly.

"Excuse me," I mumbled, and walked rapidly in the direction I least anticipated encountering any more *cariiho* maids, for they were a sore temptation and I knew not how many more I could resist. I sensed a pressing wildness everywhere: the wildness with which these tribal women gave themselves unrestrainedly to their chosen lovers; the ease with which our men abandoned all order and gave themselves to orgy, with not one pair of eyes on where Portugals might be nor a care about how long they might dally in this fleapit town whilst the mild weather for rounding the Cape of Horn ebbed away. I was conscious of how the wildness affected me, too. I fought it. But I knew what I was becoming.

I washed Christopher's blood off my hands; retreating deep into the forest where everything was cooler and taking off my remaining clothes, which I folded very neatly and put to one side. I found some of the same purple berries I knew from previous foraging missions, and made a poultice of them. Then I anointed my face; across the forehead, down each cheek. I lay back in the leaves, and pleasured myself. My fantasy began with Kathy, but her red hair and freckles soon metamorphosed into a shadowy goddess with chalcedony stones piercing her nipples, and soon again into an apparition, part woman, part many-toothed reptile, part albatross, and the reptile was chasing me, and the albatross was reprimanding me for shooting at it, and the woman was lifting me up the vast length of her painted body, which was as high as a jungle tree, up to the canopy then placing my mouth upon her breast and allowing me to see the view across the treetops, all of it – which stretched very far indeed.

TWELVE

"Such flights of snow, and extremities of frosts, as in all the time of my life, I never saw any to be compared with them."

Thomas Cavendish to Sir Tristram Gorges, *Purchas His Pilgrims* edited by
Samuel Purchas

The General slid his bishop to take Davis's uncovered rook; check;
the cabin boy told one of the General's musicians who shouted
it rather theatrically across the decks. I had been transferred
to the flagship for the purpose of conversing further with our
Portugal prisoners, and was pleased with a promotion that freed
me from the more mundane duties I had considered beneath me.
At long last, I thought, my value was being realised – and I admit
I allowed myself, with a fresh and favourable wind blowing at
our backs, a moment of happiness. As was the pattern when the
going was good, for we were flying southward towards the Río
de la Plata, the General had invited all captains and commanders
of the fleet aboard for a celebration. This time the theme was a
tournament of chess, which the General liked very well indeed.
The last two remaining in the competition were Cavendish and
Davis. Davis moved quickly and decisively, blocking with his
queen but leaving her beyond the protection of his pawns, and it
was almost certain he was carrying out a calculated defeat, a likely
attempt at pacification for Cavendish and he had been openly at
loggerheads of late. Cavendish, after deliberation, slid his bishop

across to make the obvious checkmate. And at the moment he uttered the word the storm broke.

We had idled at Santos two months, and within our bellies full of two months' worth of meat and liquor we felt the lurch as the wind whipped the waves into menacing peaks. Davis, Cocke, Cotton, Master and the other captains barely had time to return safely to their ships. With the General indisposed – and it was little secret a carafe of wine too much was the cause – his right-hand captain Barker gave the order to batten down the hatches with his customary dry efficiency. I had nothing against Barker, and know any negative remarks I make here will be construed as jealousy at the influence he held, but I do think a leader of men should be strikingly dressed, and Barker, a notorious puritan, wore black, and certainly practiced self-flagellation, which tempted me to conclude he found his position a strain. I saw in the faces of the old hands as they hurried to take in the sails that this was no ordinary storm. The sea rose up like a demented grey monster and within seconds waves the height of church towers lashed across our decks, sweeping away many things not yet stowed. One wave knocked Barker, who clutched a rail to steady himself, but with a flailing arm he hit Cavendish, who had been preening his moustache in a handheld mirror having finally emerged from his quarters. The mirror shattered.

We all heard the glass break, and knew who it was, for the General with his mirror and the stash of wine in his cabin was the only one aboard who had glass. In that wild sea with all the droning of wind and groaning of timbers a palpable hush fell amongst us. Thomas Cavendish, it seemed, had used up his store of good fortune.

It was not until the General screamed to get our superstitious brains and lazy hindquarters below decks if we were not doing anything useful that anyone moved, and then it was with fear for our lives that we did so. In the blinking of an eye a squall had descended so black that we could not see the rest of our fleet, although they were but a musket shot distant. A wind had got up with the strength of a cavalry of charging bulls and the deck was treacherous wet – at near right angles to the water.

I found myself in the hold with the Portugal prisoners not yet executed, which were the priest and one of the captains; the latter had survived only because he claimed to be a cousin of the Spaniard explorer Sarmiento de Gamboa, and the General had not had time or inclination to work out the truth of this. Whilst these Catholics bred like mice I thought the story highly unlikely, and might have told the General as much if I thought he would heed common sense. But if the Portugal could spin such a far-fetched yarn he probably deserved mercy for his quick wits alone, for our company possessed precious little wit even amongst the commanding officers collectively.

"*Mais uma vez, nos encontrarmos,*" said the priest, whose bound hands clasped a hook used for the hanging of ropes when they were not, as now, in action holding our ship together.

"Indeed. We meet again," I spoke in Portugal for the benefit of the captain, who, because of his noble bearing, I thought it prudent to impress. "I own I preferred our last encounter, padre, were I forced to choose between the two."

"You benefited from it, did you not?"

"Your descriptions of where the valuables were located was accurate," I said. "Although you neglected to mention there was ten times as much located in a chest beneath the College of Jesus."

The priest paled. I suspected he must have been aware of the stash in my Santos quarters, but still expected him to protest his innocence. He did not, and maybe it is indicative of a man of God that he tells the truth when it does not service him whatsoever yet devotes his life to spouting lies about salvation.

"Have mercy on an old man for desiring to keep some back for himself."

"You are requesting significant amounts of mercy of late, padre."

"I would show it, were our positions reversed."

"Would you? And you, *senhor*, would you show it?"

The captain, who was a devilish good-looking rogue with hair as curly as Queen Bess' own wig, looked up.

"I would."

"Well know that if I show it, it is from knowledge that even if you Portugals are almighty curs, and abuse your Indians, and would likely knife your own mothers if you sensed you could pocket a *real* from the task, I have my doubts as to whether the English aboard this vessel are very much superior."

"From an Englishman," said the captain, "I will take that as a compliment."

"As well you should. The next compliment you receive might be a noose around your neck. Such is the mercy our General dispenses, for his judgement is as final as it is wrong, and unfortunately takes precedence over mine at this time."

"That is a shame, Englishman." The captain managed a ghost of a smile. "Were you in command this voyage might just be more pleasurable for us all."

The ship was pitching so violently from starboard to larboard, then, that all our energy became channelled into securing ourselves in a way that spared us from being flung the length of the hold. The smell of stagnant seawater from the bilges mingled with excrement, and it was clear some sailors, the dirty dogs, had been defecating down here. How easily we abandon etiquette, I thought. How easily we let ourselves go. Aside from the clattering of dislodged chests and tools, the other thing that caught my ears was of someone praying to the Lord for safe deliverance, and seeing the priest green in the face from seasickness looking quite the most fallible human being I ever did see made me angry suddenly.

"What is your answer to their prayers, padre? That God is upset with us, and has bid us all die in this storm? That is too easy, old man! That does not make what you preach any less of a lie, just that you found ways to dress it up! You think there is some sublime entity, controlling everything, according to how much we have pleased or offended Him? It does not get more sublime than you and me in this hold in the shit, padre! Some of us might be dealt a hand of aces, and some of us twos and threes, but you can still make something of yourself with a hand of twos and threes!"

I paused. The priest looked very ill, and was whimpering. I remembered he was a rather old man, and felt remorseful.

"I am frightened," the priest moaned. "I cannot swim."

"Content to give newborns a dunking in water, yet scared of it yourself!" I muttered. Then, thinking it might be a ruse to show the priest some of the very valuables he had tried to secrete from me, I recalled the chest I had sneaked aboard stuffed with treasure was still on deck, and, excusing myself, hastened to remedy the matter.

It was difficult enough getting to the ladder such was the violent motion of the vessel, and as I climbed out of the hatch a wave churned over me so powerful that I was almost thrown overboard, saved only by some unsecured rigging. There were few men on deck. Cavendish was busy shouting obscenities at the helmsman, but neither the commander of the ship nor he who steered it could do anything against the sea in its current mood. The wind made a sucking sound as if, not content with knocking us about, it wanted to consume us in its greedy black lips. As I watched one of the *cariihos* who had come aboard at Santos, having pleaded with the General to deliver his people from their misery under the Portugals, suffered the fate I nearly had and was washed into the water. Several men threw him ropes but within seconds he had disappeared. As for the chests that had been on deck, all, including mine, were gone.

"Were any chests saved?" I seized one clueless fellow after the next, and they shrugged or shook their heads, for they were more concerned with the drowned man.

Gone, Kathy, all that I went to win for you – gold coins, and rare silks, and the means to put pearls around your white neck. I smote the deck in rage, not heeding the shouts to get below, and stood at the bow cursing God, whilst rain drenched me and the gale tore at me and neither of the two of them could conspire to drown me.

"Your precious treasure is no more," I said dully to the priest upon going below again. "Swept out to sea, every piece."

"Perhaps it is a good thing. It never brought me much fortune, and given you find yourself in one of the foulest storms God ever brewed, you neither."

"Think of Atahualpa," interjected the Portugal captain helpfully. "Two rooms full of gold he offered Pizarro for his freedom, and they executed him nonetheless."

The ship gave an almighty jolt, and some barrels of beer became dislodged and hurtled towards us. I flung myself out of their path towards the captain but the priest, whose hands were bound, could not move.

"Back against the wall, padre!" I cried, but it was futile. The barrels looked to have crushed just his legs, but when I came to his aid his midriff was stuck fast as a mouse in a trap against one corner of a keg.

"Do not die!" I strained to force the barrel free, but it was wedged between beams and the eyes of the priest were already rolling in his head.

"He has gone," said the Portugal captain.

"No," I whispered, and continued heaving against the slimy edge of the keg, despite knowing it could not budge and my priest could not be saved.

"Why do you care so much about him, Englishman? He was a Portugal."

"He was a vestige of good aboard this ship. Now that vestige is gone."

"Free me," said the Portugal urgently. "Do not leave me trussed to die like him… it is not as if I can jump ship in this storm."

I hesitated. I had not forgotten my responsibilities as regarded this man.

"I was sent aboard this ship to get information from you."

"Ask me anything. Only cut my bonds. I will make it worth your while" he added slyly.

From a fold of a well-worn but well-embroidered chocolate-brown peascod doublet that exactly matched the colour of his eyes, the Portugal drew a gold ring embedded with an emerald, and engraved with the initials 'S.C de Sá'.

"A token of my appreciation. Be assured it is genuine, for Salvador Correia de Sá, Governor of the chief city of Brazil, gave this to me himself."

"How many Indians had to die in the mines of Portugals and Spaniards for this to be fashioned? At least we English only plunder the plunderers!"

"Yet you will accept it – yes?" the Portugal grinned.

"I could oust that ring from you by force," I growled. "And still keep you tied up like a dog."

"You would not do that. We are better than that."

I cut the rope. The Portugal was right. The best men hold on to some values, even as the world collapses about their ears.

"I will tell you one thing freely," said the captain, massaging his wrists and ankles where the bonds had lacerated into his flesh. "From what I gather your ships are bound for the Cape of Horn. And this winter has come early, Englishman. If there are storms this fierce at a latitude of thirty-three degrees in March, imagine what weather will be like down at fifty-three in a month or two. Your voyage is a doomed one."

I turned the ring over in my hands. The gold bore the mark of the Potosi smiths – the finest mark in all the Americas. A sigh escaped me as I looked upon it.

"S.C de Sá," I mused, "must be very wealthy."

"Our governor is the most measured man I know. His shrewdness is why our colony prospers. He is the epitome of elegance, and a model to us all."

There was water in the hold; I suppose I hoped it was

originating from waves washing over the deck rather than from a rent in the keel. But as I observed some other sailors panicking and busying themselves with buckets, ridiculous ants, I felt the now-familiar stirring, akin to a spell of dizziness but also to the soaring in your stomach excitement or fear induces, and knew that this was not my time. What with the priest's death, the thought hung heavy for a moment: had his treasure been cursed? But if that curse had been transferred to me, I would dearly love to know who was in control of it, and who believed they had any power to wield over me, magical or otherwise. The ancients? Ha! Atahualpa? Ha! God? Ha, ha, ha! I recalled Barrawell, scampering over the moors above Plymouth, shouting to the sky, 'are you looking, God?' Well, Lord, look: your wrath is nothing to me.

I cradled the ring, and imagined this S.C de Sá, in a nice white house with many abysmally-treated indigenous slaves serving him, his so-called shrewd and elegant face looking out over his lands, smoking some tobacco his slaves had dried for him and partaking of some fruits they had picked for him and thinking 'all that I can see is mine'.

"Knivet!" the General's scream jarred me awake two mornings later. The storm had abated, but the wind was still strong enough to prevent us from resuming our course.

I followed the screams down to the hold.

"Were you not in charge of our prisoners?" the General cried. "Can you explain how one is dead and one vanished?"

"Impossible…" I muttered. But it was true. The Portugal captain was nowhere to be found, and nor was one of the Galleon's shore boats.

"If I did not need every able-bodied man aboard this ship, Knivet, I would flay you dead for your remissness!"

I bowed stiffly and made my exit. Whilst my actions in freeing the Portugal had been justifiable, there was no point in giving excuses based on reasons of humanity to Thomas Cavendish, for they fell upon stony ground.

It was calculated we were several days' sail off the coast, whereas we would normally keep it within a horizon width. Murmurings of discontent rifled through the crew, for the Roebuck, which carried our fleet physician and most supplies, had separated from us in the storm and several of our men were sick from the unnatural cold turn of the weather. The General roused us by promising twenty English pounds to the first who spied land. He further said that he had instructed the other commanders to wait two weeks at Port Desire, the next hospitable harbour down this unruly coast, should bad weather divide our ships, and only then to continue with the voyage in our Queen's name and in God's. I guessed he added these last two for motivation, and whilst that tactic held little sway with me – my dear father, I considered our family's name superior to either –it worked with the rest of the crew. Heartened first by hopes of sustenance, close second by money and third by the prospect of gaining God's grace, we reached the port in ten days' sailing, relieved to rendezvous with the Desire and the Blacke Pinnace and the badly-beaten Roebuck, by a slim margin within the two week period set. The Dainty, however, never made it, and we could only assume she had been lost in those tempestuous seas. As is customary amongst fickle souls such as many of those that sailed in our fleet, the very men that had spent the last months whining about Cotton's ineptitude now professed to rue his absence most. Oh, was he not a brave sailor? Oh, how selfless, to have come this extra distance to explore the inland rivers at the General's entreaty! As for myself, I was accustomed to people with base motivations and did not discount the possibility that he had used the storm to desert and return to fairer shores.

Port Desire was not so called for inspiring any feelings of lust. The General had anchored there during his first voyage of circumnavigation, when his flagship was the very same Desire Davis now commanded, and the sorry spot was named accordingly. In truth it did not inspire any emotion whatsoever save perhaps dread. Maybe this qualified as an anchorage, but only because this was a mean-spirited coast that yielded nothing better. We had left tropical waters behind us, along with the food and women they had offered. Gone was the forest; in its place a sombre windswept plain which dropped precipitously to a grey sea and left in its wake just the few houses of Port Desire near the shoreline. Some traders, the kind that choose to leave their country behind them most probably because of a dark past they wish veiled, lived here in uneasy peace with the tribes that inhabited the interior, but such was the reputation of these tribes that the Spaniards who ruled the region posted no soldiers in the vicinity nor attempted to found any settlement.

I was one of the few that volunteered to be in the landing party. A savage wind sung through the timbers of the miserable abodes we came across, whereupon they emitted a baleful creak similar to that of the gibbets that swing by our English crossroads. A French sealskin merchant emerged from one hut gibbering how there was nothing left for us to take. He and his family had the scurvy, he said, and bared his ulcerated gums to prove it. They had found no fruit or vegetables for weeks because of the onset of winter, and had survived on penguin meat alone. We asked what penguins and he indicated along to where the cliff subsided into stone ledges just above the waves. At least, I guessed it was stone, as it was difficult to see any ground beneath the mass of bloated black and white bodies. Our eyes were not our only sense to get assailed. These penguins squawked with more clamour than any English seabird and let off a stink many times worse. The way they stood reminded me of overfed priests in their cassocks, delivering sermons and caring less about whether the congregation was listening than about the sound of their own voices. Being sailors who will eat most things if they so much as move, we took 20,000, and were much applauded in the fleet, for this was the best food forage in many days.

"And what of the tribes in these parts?" I asked the sealskin merchant.

"Very awful," came the reply. "We live in daily fear of our lives."

"Can there be anything worse than the people of Brazil, who eat human flesh?" I wondered.

"There can be. And the *patagones*[1] are that thing. In Brazil there is other food. Here where there is nothing the people are more desperate.."

This was one conversation I chose not to translate to the rest of the crew.

We saw them three days later, perhaps a hundred standing in a long line along a cliff top, with nothing but hides across their loins as protection against the bitter weather, and bows and arrows at the ready.

"We will go in," said the General. "We could trade with them."

"What I understand," I volunteered, "is that they are not the sort who care to trade."

I saw the General was divided between punishing me for freeing the Portugal prisoner and entreating me to go to communicate with this people. We both knew he could easily do both, too, but his popularity among us sailors also hung in the balance. Commanders of ships fear mutiny more than they relish exacting cruelty; even him.

"It is your chance to redeem yourself, Anthony Knivet. You have a way with languages. Time to try your hand at another. Say we come in good faith, and desire to trade with them, weapons in return for food. Take twenty men. Captain Stafford will go with

---

[1] *Patagones* was the name given by early explorers to the *tehuelche* people which inhabited much of the southern extremities of South America at the time (the wilderness of Patagonia, in modern-day Argentina and Chile, traces its etymology to the *patagones*). The *tehuelche* were depicted by explorers as being incredibly tall, and with big feet (in 16th-century Portuguese *patagão* is thought to have meant big-foot). But European explorers would have been significantly shorter on average than travellers today (and could get away with telling taller tales), so the *tehuelche* were probably not that large.

you."

"And who will be in charge of the shore party? Myself or Stafford?"

The General raised an eyebrow.

"Both of you; Stafford of organising the men, you of negotiations."

I stood at the bow of the boat we went in on, not without pride, for I was able to forget about the General's past abuses now he was elevating me to a position of importance once more. I kept my hands at my sides loosely, with my weapon hidden so as not to frighten these savage people. I thought about how best to parlay; unsure whether the fact they held back from direct contact, at the top end of the precipitous path rising up from the shore we were aiming for, was a good omen or a bad.

Aside from Stafford, who was as tough-talking a little terrier as ever, our men were tense. A sailor of our times knows instinctively when he comes within a weapon shot of a potential foe, and their expressions betrayed an uneasiness I prayed these savages could not discern, for it could be misconstrued as hostility. Of course, in none of the accounts of the early explorers is the viewpoint of the savage once considered. Spying such unkempt, invariably odious white men emerging from boats as large as jungle villages, wielding deadly devices that made fire at one click and claiming land as casually as one might take seconds at dinner must have caused them considerable consternation. And we carried on, surprised that they objected to such invasions, and documented them as aggressive! But I, ever a whipping boy at the hands of white men, identified with these wild peoples' plight, and in this sense I was quite the born negotiator.

I recalled the few words of the *cariihos* I had learnt, and also that these tribes had a love of our English blades as they were wrought of metals Indians had no knowledge of. Just before where the ground sheered steeply up from the beach, I bid our party lay down all arms so as they might be seen, and ordered retreat to a respectable distance. Looking up at the Indians now, I saw plainly that they were giants. The shortest of their women reached six feet and the tallest of their men seven or eight, and all kept firm grip on their bows. Our men, now weaponless, quailed and would have fled were it not for my presence of mind. I demonstrated by gesture that we came in peace – opening my arms, then placing my hands on my heart to symbolise that peace, an ingenious improvisation I do think and inspired by the statue of an angel I had seen at the good church of Malmesbury in Wiltshire – and only desired food in exchange for these blades.

The group above us on the cliff top pushed a few of their number towards the front. They were women; it seemed the women of this tribe were in command. A girl clad in a guanaco hide that barely covered her genitals and left nothing else to the imagination whatsoever led her people towards us. I was conscious of our men imbibing her breasts and thighs and, were they too modest to look there, her feet which even in relation to her lofty height were huge. Had any one let loose their bows we would have stood like dozy leverets and taken each shot, as we were transfixed, and it occurred to me Queen Bess should use such brazenly naked women in her military campaigns if this was the havoc they could wreak.

The baleful eyes of this warrioress sat unnaturally large in a countenance the weather had hewn hard; she was certainly very young but the lines of labour made her seem old. She filled me with dismalness. I was struck again by how savages reminded me of the deer on my father's estate. Nothing is sadder on this Earth than the deer. I recollected hiding there as a child, in woods tinted autumn red, and scanning the foliage for the buck, with its coat the exact same shade; my father and his select gentlemen, guns cocked, were patrolling the paths below doing the same. But I had keen sight; I often saw the buck first. Then it would be just him and me; for an exquisite, tragic moment he was *there* – majestic – before his features separated from the landscape and he became

the huntsmen's target, or bounded away and became lost forever.
My father's deer were less creatures than moments; you could
not reach out and touch them, because by the time you did they
would be gone. But even free, they were half trapped; a clock
ticking against their freedom. They were on a leash, and I saw
the same leash around the necks of the people of this far-flung
continent. There was no telling when the tug would come, or
from whom, but it would come. And just like the wild deer, these
people advanced upon us cautiously, and would not come beyond
a certain distance.

"*No ten-e-mos*," said the warrioress, in faltering Spaniard speak.

"*Por favor*," I implored, kneeling. The others, dwarfed by
these giants, quickly followed my lead and even Stafford, left
temporarily as the only Englishman standing, had a rare moment
of enlightenment and elected to do the same rather than pursue
his own whirlwind of a path. "*Tenemos hambre.*"

The girl, having halted some two ships' widths from us, looked
at me blankly, and I rubbed my stomach in circles to illustrate
hunger. "*Hambre.*"

"*No ten-emos alimentos*," she replied.

"We could kill every last one of you if you don't give us what
we want," smiled Stafford sweetly. His attempt to arrange his
mouth into an expression of charm was more loathsome than
most men's scowls.

"*Vayase.*" The girl spoke more firmly. Go away.

"*Espere!*" I tried again, and pointed at the blades, broad-swords
and backswords, cutlasses and daggers, riding swords and rapiers,
lying at my command in a heap that were befitting of trade
anywhere on this Earth for they were manufactured with English
steel. "*Regalos.*"

The girl cast her eye across these offerings, and picked up
Stafford's ruby-encrusted dagger. I nodded encouragingly,
thinking she meant to examine it for defects, but could not have
anticipated her next action, which was to lift up her guanaco hide
and insert the hilt slowly into her vagina.

"*Muy frio,*" she said, having kept it there some seconds. Our men were lost for words but I somehow managed to respond that yes, it was cold, and indeed of a superior quality to any other blades I knew. She conferred with another women at the front of the group, who also tried Stafford's dagger in the same manner.

"Dear Lord, do I hope she gives that back to me now!" murmured Stafford.

After some debate, of which I understood not a word for their language was far thicker than that of the *cariihos* and had been conducted guardedly, they appeared to accept and gathered our collection of blades. Not wishing to come closer, they then pushed forward a bundle by means of a long pole, which rolled down to land at my feet. A successful trade negotiated by Anthony Knivet, I thought; so linguistics were less important than an ability to engage my weapon, were they General? Ha! I opened the bundle. Inside were feathers; azure feathers with yellow tips, and green feathers flanked by mauve, and the scarlet-and-black feathers that the tribe favoured above all others for their dress, and nothing else.

"*Ahora,*" the girl said. "*Vayase.*" Her words were backed up, this time, by bows being pulled taut in our direction, loaded with arrows headed by acute-angled flints.

"Avast!" growled Stafford. "Where be our vittles, you whore?"

He made to draw his musket but an arrow had lodged itself in his belly before he got so far as halfway. Before Stafford's enraged bellow had faded, Edward Stubbes of the Desire, the most docile and inoffensive sailor you ever would see, took one of these giants' shafts through the heart. To my mind this concluded negotiations.

The men fled. With the words of parlay withering on my lips I got the collapsed Stafford by the armpits and did the same, although not before I had stuffed a handful of those fine feathers into my hose.

Nine of us did not make it back. Somehow, despite being at the rear of the group, and dragging Stafford as well, all the

Indian's arrows missed me, or perhaps my entreaties to them had persuaded them to spare my life, although within a day I would be wishing they had taken it. The rest of the party had already taken off in the shore boat, and I had to splash out to join them in a sea not a degree above freezing. Stafford was heavy for a small man, yet despite the inconveniences I had suffered on his account his words, when they were coherent through the bellows, were all curses against me and of my incompetence.

The General was grimly waiting for us upon our return and by his side, seen for the first time since the pummelling I had given him at Santos, was Christopher the Japanese. Whether it was Stafford's accusations or Christopher's treacherous influence I cannot say, but it was evident I was to be blamed for this failure. I sat shivering on a rotten chest and absorbed the insults the General unleashed like I was the mud on his boots. At several points I pleaded for a hide such as those the commander of our fleet had draped about his shoulders, for all my spare clothes had been washed overboard in the storm, but no sailor ventured to aid the subject of the General's wrath. As a gentleman it was most unpleasant to hear a so-called other of my class mistreating one who had done their utmost to do good for the company, and been thwarted through no fault of his own. Nonetheless I went to sleep that night with abuses such as 'bastard' and 'knave' and 'pansy' coursing through my ears. The next morning, dawning stark and cold, I was so numbed that I could not move my legs, and pulling off my stockings, my toes came with them, and all my feet were as black as soot, and I had no feeling in them. Then I was not able to stir for many days.

THIRTEEN

When I awoke it was to the wails of men being thrown overboard, and I was in the queue to join them. Two sailors held me fast by the arms, and were dragging me towards the gunwale.

I was too weakened to fend them off but begged them to desist. They replied that I was unfit to do any useful work aboard ship and a danger to those that were, and so must be cast off. The General, having brought his crew to these squall-ridden latitudes at a time of year he had been repeatedly advised was merciless, was sick and tired of his sick and tired men, who were beginning the morning able-bodied yet ending the nights frozen to death. So the dead and dying were being thrown directly to the sea, and the unfit set on shore, a place that, being so bleak, was sure to become a mass grave for all abandoned there. I reasoned to these men that I was not dead and, knowing them to be devout, added that God would deny them a place in Heaven should they cast me into the sea before I was. The men concurred and, electing to capitalise on their amenable nature, I begged them fetch me a portion of salted penguin meat, so that I might have strength to man the ship with them. They told me there was no meat. The continual rain had lashed not only into the marrows of our bones, but into the depths of our driest holds, inducing a loathsome worm that had spoiled all our provisions. I asked then what there was to eat and they told me: one handful of cassava meal daily, to be reduced by half in three days should we spy no land yielding sustenance.

I slipped back into unconsciousness, and dreamed.

I was riding a white steed through the sunny chalk hills of Wiltshire; it was intricately decorated with barding forged from Combe Martin silver, just like the Crown Jewels of Queen Bess and commoners stood to one side to let me pass and tipped their hats at me. A heavy rain began, and as I rode across a valley bottom I saw my father seated alone at a banquet table in a field. I asked him why he was not at home and he pointed at the river, which was rising fast towards where he sat; I asked why then did he not leave that place and he pointed to me. The water level swelled, and swept him up, and I saw him no more.

Everything was covered with water, and smelt of seaweed, and faeces, and rodents, and through the swimming grey I discerned a face.

"Christopher," I said faintly. "Where are we?"

"Where we are not is in the river at Santos, Knivet." He gazed right through me as if I was a mere step on the way toward his ulterior aim. One eye was still swollen from its encounter with my knuckles. "How the tables have turned, eh?"

"You deserved your beating."

"No," Christopher said abstractedly. "You carried on hitting me long after you needed. You went too far. That is... understandable," he smiled, and winced with the effort. "I am going to go too far with you now, too. Yehhhhz. You will dearly wish those Indian's arrows had finished you! Have some more cassava meal. I want to eke out your sorry existence long enough that you witness the end I intend for you."

I reclined miserably on my rotting chest. I had lost three toes of my right foot and one of my left, and had no feeling of any kind below the ankles. Listlessness came upon me; if I could not walk then how could I ever survive these South American shores? Rather than fight my malady I slumped into its mire – a mire in which I imagined Christopher forgot his ominous promise to me, although I knew he was not the kind to ever forget. So violently were we pitching that I needed to tie myself down to prevent being lost in that cauldron of a sea seething around the Straits. It seldom got properly light anymore, and if it did I could not discern which part was my waking life and which my nightmares. The rush of the sea was in my ears; the motion of the sea was in my bones; I could not extract the damned sounds from my skull. I broke out in clammy sweats, and went from shivering cold to suffocating hot in a matter of minutes. I was convinced the sweating sickness had claimed me; after months voyaging with the devil, the time for my descent into the inferno had surely come, just as it had for four score other sorry souls of the 350 we left Plymouth with.

It was a strange and deplorable state, this semi-death, but as your senses shut down, those that remain become heightened and oh, do you see some things! It is a crystallisation. As you slip away from yourself to wherever the angels or the demons or the maggots have conspired to send you, you see what you are leaving behind for what it is. I saw our best artilleryman clawing frenziedly with a makeshift fishing net at a sea in full storm and, in a desperate stretch, driven overboard along with the man who had been steadying him. Some other hunger-maddened unfortunates resolved to eat the contaminated penguin meat, and within the hour were convulsing on the deck, banging heads and limbs until they were bloody and broken in an attempt to rid themselves of the bouts of pain, which eventually caused them to expire. I watched as one of our riggers, unfurling the foresail, let slip the rope on his part-frozen hand, whereupon it burned through his fingers and severed them. I beheld two young gentleman adventurers playing dice on the chest of a just-deceased comrade; the stakes they played for were their shares in the voyage's plunder and I wanted to shout to them that they were playing for a share in Hell. Even the fit members of our crew whimpered for a return to Santos, but none too loudly; the General was acting increasingly irrationally, and all feared him. For his part, he sensed he was disliked. He hid from us in his cabin; when he did appear he had his nose buried in his Bible as if using it as a barrier between himself and us, and the canny Christopher was at his side sowing further lies in his ears.

When I had lain perhaps ten days like this, a day came when there was a lull in the weather. We were well into the straits by a fair green isle; across the water on the north side ice-topped mountains rose from the sea in brutal blacks and greys, yet where we were it was green. Somehow our ships were still together. Our General went to confer with the other commanders to determine the state of his fleet, and I was much heartened to discover it was Waldren of my old vessel the Roebuck rowing him back.

"On death's door again, Knivet?"

It seemed even our fleet's plight could not quash this indefatigable tar and he forced a glimmer of a smile from my lips. You never forget the crew of the first ship you sail with. And whilst Waldren with his coarseness, and Harris with his buffoonery, and Barrawell with his fool's faith in God, might represent traits in a man I would stay clear of in England, we were at sea, and do what we must. And the Roebuck under the good Cocke was my home at sea.

"If you're bound for death, you can take solace from the fact you'll be in ample company. The Roebuck has sixty living men aboard, and that be without dumping any in the sea like the General has. Then there be the matter of a mast, which we don't have, as it snapped in them storms like a sapling. The Desire looks pretty bad hit despite Davis' mighty airs, and as for that Toby Master in the Pinnace it's a case of name not being anything like nature, I have no doubt."

"Waldren." I mustered energy to speak for the first time in days. "How fare Harris and Barrawell?"

"Like you care! Harris lost his nose as he went to blow it, but he'll live."

"And Barrawell lost his faith?"

"No, he has it in abundance yet. Says we should all pray harder."

"*Cuius religio, eius religio.*"

"What?"

"It means that whatever the monarch of our country believes, so must we its subjects believe. What do you think, Waldren? Should we be Protestants because our Queen is? Should we risk our lives on the other side of the world to keep Her treasury topped up with plunder?

"I ain't a man of education like you, Knivet, but I'll tell you something. We spend a sight too much time on this ship harking on about God whilst them." He jabbed a finger inland. "They do just fine worshipping a few spirits."

'Waldren?"

"What is it, Knivet, there's work to be done and I'd sooner occupy my mind with the doing of it."

"When we were running from the savages... not one of their arrows hit me, although they hit precious near everyone else in our party."

"You lead a charmed life."

"It is not that. It was not my time. There was a reason why I was spared."

"You're ranting again, Knivet. What reason could there be?"

"I do not know yet."

The General's temper had been souring that whole afternoon. "Ungrateful dullard!" he shouted at one ailing sailor. "Hph, I could have left you in Plymouth like the beggar you are and if you do not pull your weight on that rope by God's grace I will whip such lines into you that the furrows I saved you from ploughing in your inbred family's fields will not have a fraction of the depth!" To another: "Keep the water out of those bilges, rodent, or what the Romans did to our Lord Jesus Christ will seem like nothing compared to how I will nail you against those crosstrees!"

I somehow found the energy to get to my feet, or rather what was left of them, although this in itself was a miracle as I was still in near delirium. When I heard the crack I was convinced the mainmast was toppling the sound was so loud. Then I caught sight of the commander of our fleet with a look to him like a rabid dog, and I realised his sanity had utterly deserted him, gripped as he was by a rage Waldren seemed to have caused, for he was wielding a rope as thick as my arm upon Waldren's bony body. Now, we Knivets were born to defend the defenceless and until I drew my dying breath, which I envisaged would occur reasonably soon, I aimed to do just that. But to strike a commanding officer was a sure way to hasten my end as it was a crime punishable by death, especially given our General's proclivity for ordering bloody executions. My only recourse was to shuffle, steadying myself by ropes, and get myself between the General and Waldren, who was already slumped across the gunwale from the zealousness of the strokes.

I took blow after blow from that knotted rope, until the General's green silk doublet was spotted with my blood. Even after Waldren had crumpled on the deck the great Thomas Cavendish happily swung back to gain momentum for more hits, as if exercising discipline was less the thing for him than the act, regardless of the target. I caught his gaze as his strokes lacerated my flesh. His eyes had a sheen to them; that mouth was as cruelly curled as ever it was, but with the difference that his tongue lolled out a little as the whip smote down. It ran the length of his full lips, as I had often observed it did when he was swilling his French wine, and had missed a few drops in his guzzling.

At some point the strokes stopped. I had slipped into a sort of stupor, and could not have evaded the whip myself, but the General snapped out of his tantrum as inexplicably as he had snapped into it. Suddenly he appeared unable to bear the horror his temper had caused, for he screamed at two men to row him over to the Desire, because he could not endure another moment with such imbeciles as this crew fate had dealt him, and besides, we were dying so rapidly we might as well be abandoned. I was crawling to where Waldren lay still with his head at an unnatural angle. I was shaking him. I was blowing the little air in my lungs into his. I was pleading with him to speak from that ugly mug of his, anything would do, even one of his bawdy shanties I so hated. But the Roebuck's boatman had no sarcastic retort in readiness. The General's whip had brought the base of the gunwale deep into his skull, and he was dead.

I lay on top of Waldren and dumbly observed blood, mine and his mingled, expanding around us. The General climbed daintily into the shore boat, vexed by a patch of my blood on his ruff, which he vainly tried brushing away. And the damned weather kept undoing whatever we did; beating us back where we would have gone forward, snuffing us out where we would have had hope.

We made it into the harbour of Port Famine at the seventh attempt on the twenty-first of April; I made marks with my mother's meat-carving knife on a plank in the orlop[1] deck, where the sick and wounded had been moved, for the passing days. For three days straight we had been occupied with the doubling of Cape Froward, so-called by Cavendish on his first circumnavigation for its perverse nature, and remaining as true to its name; now we were anchored the attention of those in command could turn to other matters. Now, the General had been acting like God Almighty for some time, or at least like a demigod who expected sacrifices in his name without question, and I wondered if he had bookmarked the chapter of his New Testament where Paul calls upon the Corinthians to examine themselves to see if they had the faith. I had little doubt that if the men in our fleet still blessed with beating hearts had looked deep into them they would have a shred of faith remaining in he who commanded us. The Galleon had a hundred men; the Desire and the Roebuck no more than another hundred between them and the Blacke Pinnace under two score. Of those, most were gentleman adventurers, or soldiers,

---

[1] The lowest deck of a ship, usually sitting below the waterline.

or tradesmen; the sailors who had done the tough work in the storms had also died quickest and only a fraction of those left able to stand above hatches had any idea how to manage a vessel. There were no sails but those now bent, and no spare cordage, and still less food. The wind was against us; temperatures were against us; many of us seemed against ourselves.

Davis, the only one amongst us with experience of sailing in such bitter climes having voyaged many times in the Far North, thought the snow could not last, and that we should hold out, then make for the South Sea, which was now a mere forty leagues distant. Cavendish, accustomed on his previous voyage to accruing wealth and reputation with ease, now erred towards sailing for the Cape of Good Hope. I saw his thinking, as the pickings there would be easier, and the chances for commanders to distinguish themselves still high, but his motives contrasted with what was feasible more than ever before. The men signed a petition against this plan, favouring Davis' strategy of waiting for a window in the weather to press onward for the South Sea.

But that window did not come; it closed in and made a mockery of us for considering we had options regarding our future. Our only refuge from the storms was a port even the fabled Sarmiento de Gamboa had failed to colonise[2]. In Spain the artists at King Phillip's court made engravings of the magical *Magallenes*: these very Straits, depicted with pretty forests, with proud ships sailing by, with the sort of Spaniard courtiers that would not last a day in these waters generously planting flags on these native peoples' soil and holding out hands to them as if saving them from drowning. But the men Sarmiento de Gamboa had posted at this uttermost

---

[2] Pedro Sarmiento de Gamboa named the settlement he established in 1583 Rey Don Felipe. When Cavendish's first voyage of circumnavigation passed by in 1587, they picked up one survivor. The rest of the 300-odd colonists had perished, most likely through starvation, and Cavendish gave the place a more appropriate name: Port Famine.

end of the Earth had died. They had starved or frozen to death and Port Famine was strewn with their bones. Each day we were anchored there some of us fought our way ashore to forage, and came back with little save stories of how this town of 300 souls had perished; of agonised messages carved on the derelict buildings in writing driven unintelligible by the madness that sets in before such manners of death. If trees existed on this barren coast, they were stunted; if ships passed by, they were wretched ones. Port Famine became a metaphorical barrier for us: we saw no way through to the respite that must lie on its other side. Now the men, that it is fair to say had fancied the South Sea for the sun and women and gold it might hold rather than attaining new heights in navigation, began pining for Brazil as the surest course to getting their wants. And somehow that became the plan. Having endured so much – having come so near completing the most perilous part of our voyage – we were retreating.

The General came back among us with a veritable prance in his step; we would take Santos again, and the other ports at the River of January and Spirito Santo, and better equip ourselves for a second run at the Straits. To this end he wanted to rid himself of his bad apples, and put Christopher in charge of setting on shore all who were infirm.

The Japanese obligingly shook me awake before nominating ten of the most hopeless cases to be brought above deck for throwing in the shallop, and gave me to understand I was tenth up.

The air, like a set of icy knives, stabs you. The already-weakened body shuts down as it becomes exposed to these elements; it is like a paralysis but at the same time like a wound ripped open. Then there is the view of men you know; good men; lying in a shallop oblivious, and in the positions they had been thrown, having gone to sleep in good faith their shipmates might help them through their sickness and yet about to be murdered by those same shipmates. Christopher ensured I saw all this horror before he cast me off to join them. I did not resist. I was sick of words, or at least of the kind that held sway with these men. And as I was dangled over the edge, and certain of my death, only then did I hear him say: "Not him, not yet."

I was pulled back, and set on deck, and saw the shallop with nine crew members scarcely able to stir, cast loose into a violent sea skilled oarsmen could scarce have negotiated. Several men prayed for them. It might as well have been their funeral.

The next day, and again the day after, Christopher gave his touch of death first to twenty, and then twenty more. Again I was on the list; those driven sick by cold and starvation were carried passed me, the sons of men delivered into the hands of sinners. Twice more I was spared at the last. I was sure Christopher had increased my rations deliberately, by enough to keep me conscious during this sanctioned slaughter. He changed my allotted sickbed, too. I woke up that third time at the end of the orlop foul sailors used for their toilet when too lazy to go above deck; rats crawled on my legs and cockroaches five times the size of the English variety on my face. I was allotted a sheet to protect myself from the cold but it was the thinnest, most pox-ridden sheet any man had to cover him ever. I saw what the Japanese was doing: giving me the most protracted passage to death possible.

"Why are you doing this?" I asked as he walked among us, for it was not enough for him to inflict misery; he had to observe the suffering. I was like him; I had schemes like him; the only thing setting us apart was that he was a knave; why should he be the General's man?

"Do you recall how many times you set your knuckles into my jaw at Santos?" he replied.

"Let us end this," I begged him. "You have had your vengeance. Finish me. Bleed me from the throat, or twist a knife in my heart, but finish me, for I swear upon all I hold sacred I do not deserve this suffering."

"Getting what I want, Knivet, is the only thing I hold sacred."

I again flitted between the waking world and the world of dreams. As we limped north the cold abated, and with it some strength returned to my body. But if we had expecting some paradise awaiting us back in Brazil we had poor memories. Almost two weeks after we left the Straits the hatch opened and some forty men, badly if not mortally wounded, were shoved unceremoniously in with us on an orlop already cramped with the infirm. The crux of our General's tattered plan hinged on being able to capture one of Brazil's wealthy ports or all of us were doomed; this we had tried at Spirito Santo but in our weakened state we were not half the Englishmen we had been, and the Portugals had got the better of us. We had lost eighty men of the 120 in the landing party.

One wretched sailor from this attack told me the particulars with his dying breath. We had been deceived about the depth of the harbour by our pilot Jorge who had presumably wanted to help his countrymen thwart our attack. One shore boat had gone to ground on rocks and the crew had been picked off like pheasants in the woods as they floundered in the water and drowned. The other boat had landed and despite being outnumbered these men had driven the Portugals out of the town's fort, but then been surprised by a group of *tomomynos* Indians who had been bribed by the Portugals into fighting for them.

"*Lovas eyave pomombana,*" the unfortunate sailor whispered and I wondered what he could mean. He told me the *tomomynos* were the most vicious fighters he ever had seen and I believed him, for this was coming from one who had fought with the English in the campaigns against the Scots, and witnessed his share of brutality. They paint themselves head to foot in black tar, with the blood of their victims on top of that, said the sailor, then set fire to many-feathered hoops that they hurl at their enemy, howling *lovas eyave pomombana*; just like this shall you be consumed.

"Oh!" the sailor winced "how they consumed us!"

"Tell me how!" I seized him.

The sailor quivered, babbling that he could not, but I discerned some coherent phrases; 'pleaded for mercy', 'cut into pieces'; and that was enough to make me glad the General had beat a hasty retreat.

I desired to know more about these Indians, but regrettably the man had lost much blood, and expired. I was not surprised: he did not have the Thing. To prevail out here you need the Thing.

With Brazil's more clement weather restoring life to my bones once more I strove to stand, thinking even sailors' labours would aid my recovery more than remaining a patient in this filthy floating hospital. But I regretted my return above deck almost instantly. We had not lost eighty men, I found out, but closer to 180. The Desire and the Blacke Pinnace had deserted us after the Straits. This left our two ships combined with under 100, and perhaps three score in a state to man them. With heavy heart I wondered what the General's resolution could be now we were reduced to such a lowly state.

"Saint Vincents," came the reply. "We are to take the town, then with the proceeds ready ourselves for another go at the Straits."

"Like we took Santos before? Like we took Spirito Santo? Are we to flit this way and that along this coast at the General's whim forever? Going again for the Straits is madness with so few men, and taking Saint Vincents is but a little less foolhardy, given we spent last Christmas burning the best part of it to the ground!"

I am normally a gentleman well versed in the art of discretion, but on this occasion, what with my dismay at learning of such catastrophic events and of such a flawed course of action, I concede I spoke without heed of who was directly behind me. And the persons behind me were the General and Christopher. A flush appeared on the General's cheeks and for one so fair he gave me a glower of the ugliest blackness. I later heard that for several days straight he had been uttering such a tirade of complaints against all the circumstances he thought to have conspired against him – the Queen for not seeing us off in Plymouth; the winds for not blowing, and then for blowing; his lamentable commanders; his lazy crew; the Portugals, the savages, his pilots and above all Davis, that turncoat in whom he had wrongly placed his trust and who might very well now be sailing through the Straits towards glory – that all feared he might strike them dead as soon as look at them. Had I known this I might have spoken with more censure. As it was, the pink spots on the General's cheeks came out like angry rosebuds and he croaked 'take him below' which Christopher did with several cold movements, knocking me down the ladder with the hatch locked shut after me in such a way that I almost broke my neck, saved by the same speedy reflexes that had got Knivets out of danger on many an occasion in many a generation.

To a man barely back on his feet after illness, you can imagine, Kathy, that any state of wellbeing spiralled once more out of my reach. I was back on the orlop deck with the other diseased and dying, with the dark, with the damp and – most unendurably – with reduced rations.

I longed for those early days of the voyage when our eyes sparkled with what might be, when I could stand in the Roebuck's prow and bask in the equatorial sun, full of beer and biscuits. I longed for my blood brother Harry Barrawell's earnest gaze; Waldren's jibes; Harris's foolish grin.

But I might have better hankered after a place at God's right hand in Heaven. Some few days later the Roebuck, still under John Cocke, ran away from us in the night, along with many of our able-bodied men, our surgeons and almost all our supplies. The General's senseless barbarity had got too much even for Cocke his most loyal servant. And more than the General's servant, Cocke had been my sole protector. On the day of the winter solstice, at an island off the coast from the town of Saint Sebastian northwest of Saint Vincents, myself and twenty other wretches were piled into the Galleon's last shore boat; to be abandoned on inhospitable shores we stood no hope of surviving upon in our condition. Two oarsmen brought us in; these grim Charons would not look at us as they did so, for they well knew the fate to which they ferried us.

"Cocke is not here to entreat for you now, Knivet," Christopher had said, as he flung me in himself.

The Roebuck is not a ship like any other. Its men did things differently. They treated each other as men should. Now I saw it, dearer and clearer to me than ever: sails puffed out as on a dream sea; wind straight; sun high. It was a beautiful boat. It glided through that water, not ungainly like a Galleon or unstable like a pinnace; it glided like a condensation of all that was beautiful. That was how I first knew the seas! The commander gave his cry to the men and we did his bidding, for we were gentlemen, and adventurers, and bound for gallant adventures.

I had not had such a bad life, I decided, collapsed in that shore boat, half-dead and outcast by my own countrymen and without a penny or a pie to my name. I had seen such things. To most men – those that pace only the confines of the horizon within which they came into this world – my adventures would seem like a fairy tale.

We touched shore. I lay down destitute in the sand, like one lying down in his own grave, and wished most fervently for the end. But I would not give God the satisfaction of praying for it.

FOURTEEN

"I came to my selfe, as a man awaked from sleepe; and I saw them that were set on shore with me, lye dead and a-dying round about me..."

Anthony Knivet, *Admirable Adventures and Strange Fortunes*

I pulled up my visor, dismounted my steed and waded up the avenue that led to my father's house, where the water was already deep and fast rising. My chainmail glistened, and looked very well. From the upstairs windows came screams. There in a line were the quack who once played the gemshorn for me, and my mother, holding a tray of just-baked damson scones and shaking her head disapprovingly, and Barrawell and the General, who had been invited for some unknown reason, with their arms linked in prayer. All were being offered apple wine by my father's butler Goodman, which was a nice gesture on his part for even in such trying times one needs to maintain a semblance of etiquette. Christopher the Japanese was loitering by the well at the side of our property, drawing bucket after bucket of water and throwing each at the flood to make it rise all the faster. You, Kathy, you were there too, in-between my mother and the General. And they were all screaming, one distorted incessant sound like a banshee's wail.

"Father's dead," I said. "Drowned."

And they said: "we know."

And I said: "what now?"

And they said: "now we must die."

And I said: "why?"

And they told me: "because our master is dead, so the Knivets are dead, and what is the beast without the head?"

And I said: "do not fear, I am here now."

I went to embrace each of them by turn, as the water rose about our hips and chests. But the tighter I embraced them, the more unearthly were their screams.

It was the twenty other unfortunates abandoned alongside me on this wild isle by their ship that were screaming. In desperate hunger they had eaten of a venomous pease that grew in abundance on these shores. It had made every part of their bodies from their bellies to their tongues swell to many times the normal size, and was crushing the life from them. Before I had properly come to my senses, the last one was expiring before my eyes.

The cosy reader thinks many things. They do not know about phenomena like the giants at large on this continent; they do not comprehend the daunting scale of these forests or what it is to stare at the sea searching for a sign of salvation so long it makes you mad; they do not see the many ways in which the end can arrive out here, nor what a scant chance there is of anything good arriving ever. And thus my reaction to my shipmates' deaths was not what might be expected. It was not sadness at their passing; nor repugnance at the manner of it. It was pure jealousy that I was not joining them. I cursed my hard fortune; that death itself did refuse to terminate my tormented and most miserable life. I saw nothing to eat but these pease, and if I did eat them I was sure of death; if I did not I saw no remedy but to starve.

At that time the sun had not beat its rays fully through my body. The continual threat of a watery grave in the ship of Thomas Cavendish had sucked the Thing out of me. I did not then have it, and without it in this jungle you have no fire inside you.

But presently I realised, as I lay upon that beach, that I was no worse off than I had been aboard ship. I had no more and no less food, and without the waves or Christopher's cruelty to erode me I felt somewhat improved. And here at least I knew plainly my enemies were Portugals, rather than speculating which of my supposed comrades might stab me in the back next. As for the tribes of this strange land, I saw no reason why we should be enemies, for with the majority of them I had in common a hatred of the Portugals. And, Portugals or Indians, perhaps there was a way of working with them – a role I could fill – for I saw no hope of survival without dealing with ample quantities of both. The Portugal colonists, and the English privateers and the French traders had, for all their differences, arrived on these lands with the same attitude: "I come to do my thing." Well I had seen little evidence of that working. Better to say, with open arms, to any I encountered: "I am Anthony Knivet and I come – and that is all."

Kathy, your father had a love of dominoes; I used to spy on him through his workshop window. Amongst those bubbling apothecary potions he had a table set up with a pack of them, in formation so that if you knocked the first, the rest would tumble and make some shape in the process. My life now resembles those dominoes. Were it not for the lamentable situation regarding my inheritance setting in motion my journey, were it not for my prowess as baker and translator knocking me in then out of favour with the General, were it not for the tile with Christopher on it setting in motion this tile with me abandoned on a Godforsaken island, then... But even your father sometimes misjudged the space between dominoes as he built his formations. Then they fell into place only so far, and stopped, with the shape half-finished. This is the thing: out here I do not know the gap between the dominoes. I do not know what shape they might make. And Kathy, with your loose curls skipping through the woods, I was not going to that workshop to catch a glimpse of you as you might have thought. I should confess that. I was going to see your father turning metals into gold. In went bronze, and lead, and saltpetre, through phials, through presses. It was like baking: it transformed substances into other substances. I thought I might do very well at it myself, as I could work wonders with dough. How different things might have been if I had not needed to travel these seas to win my fortune! But I do not think your father ever succeeded – with the gold, I mean. He would not be so fixed on our union – one that promised him but modest financial gain – if he had. What could we have if our families joined forces? Cakes made of fool's gold? My hands trace the movements in this hot heavy air that they would if untying your corset, and clasping what must lie beneath. Oh I crave what lies beneath! But in reality would you not laugh, would my hands not fumble? That would be our life; you laughing and me fumbling and not feeling at all what the chivalric romances suggested I might towards you. Well. The dominoes will fall and we shall see. But I do not see any pearls here. I cannot place seashells around your neck, for then not just you but all Wiltshire would laugh at me. And neither your father nor my mother would be nearly so enthused over our marriage as formerly, which does raise the question of whether it is worth any of us holding out a hope for.

Weighing up these things I scanned the horizon for a sail, any sail; the Roebuck's sail, Barrawell crying "Anthony!" Who would have guessed I would miss that boy, with next to no experience of the world and his conviction God would deliver us from all evil? But he was a man of my own county, and my blood brother for better or worse. And his domino had knocked into mine.

No sail came. I got up, limped through the corpses and went to search for food.

Things were stirring by the seaside. The ebbing tide had left crabs in small holes in the wet sand, and I filled my stockings with them as I went. I had thought to eat them raw, and was hungry enough, but rounding a headland I saw the embers of a fire back up by the treeline behind the beach. They were scrawny shellfish, but sweeter to me then than my own mother's lavender cake, and to my shame I partook without pausing to search for any sort of herbs to enhance their flavour. Only after I had gorged did I think about the implications of those embers. Someone had been here, and recently. The isle I had guessed deserted was very much inhabited.

I returned to the beach where my dead comrades lay, intending to bury them as men rather than letting birds peck their flesh. Yet the stench was too much, and I could not, electing rather to continue walking around the isle. Presently I found a place with fresh water and seclusion within the trees if so desired. I would have made camp there, for that is how the tribes here did it: they became at one with the land. But a commotion arose and a creature like a huge serpent shot out of that water with many rows of fangs bared straight at me. It would have taken off my leg or worse had I not kicked sand in its eyes, and escaped as it thrashed about in rage. I began to entertain the notion I might be the plaything of a sorcerer, for on that same stretch of shore black demons, something like monkeys only infinitely larger, launched themselves at me from the trees (I evaded them) while out at sea mermaids frolicked and seemed to suggest I should join them in the waves (I did not succumb).

I walked on. I worried that this isle contained little possibility for survival, and that undeserved as my companions' ends were, my allotted fate – this dangling above the precipice of death with the rope supporting me fraying fibre by fibre – seemed infinitely crueller. The mouthfuls of crabs had barely sustained me, the fruit on the trees did not look well, and I was wary after my companions' deaths from the pease. So my belly and the filling of it occupied most of my thoughts – that and the fire. Those who had made it would return. It was one thing to face Portugals or cannibals with firearms and a crew, but it was another entirely to face them alone, and with nothing in this world save your mother's kitchen knife.

Then I sighted something huge lying on the sand where it tapered to a point at the north of the isle. It was a whale, and but freshly beached! I did marvel, for the season for them was over;

they were gone south, as every good sailor knows, and made a better job of so doing than Cavendish ever managed. But not this one. I swear it was as long as the hull of an English carrack, and I was two minutes just walking around the circumference of its body. I touched its meaty walls with quavering hands to check this was no hallucination. My head told me this was but another dangling over death's jowls, and would merely eke out my misery, but my heart beat fast and my belly growled in anticipation. I fetched deadwood from the forest, got me a fire going there on the open sand and had a feast such as I had not enjoyed in months.

I ate senselessly. The passing of days I began gauging by the roasting of blubber. The whale had a natural oil which enabled me to cook the meat most tenderly. At different meal times I indulged in different parts: near the gums was good for a breakfast and belly worked better at dinner. It was no easy task carving up a beast so big. I toiled those first few hours to get as much cooked as possible for fear of putrefaction, and wrapped what I could not eat in jungle leaves. There was an art to it. Too small an incision, and you could not gain leverage to extract the meat; too large and the smell attracted vicious birds, which I saw off with no small amount of abusive language. "Winged knaves!" I danced about and waved my knife, maddened by their audacity. "Phoenixes!" I presently found stuffing certain plants into the holes I bored within the beast not only reduced predators but added piquancy to my food. In all Europe, I thought, there could not be a book with recipes from these shores and I was better qualified than any other to write one; I could have one chapter dedicated exclusively to whales. All households might then have a copy, much as they might a bible. When the saltiness of the whale got unbearable I returned to fetch fresh water; otherwise I moved little distance from the carcase. One side of my beast I kept in tact, and here I made a shelter, near the tail end where the stink was least. The sand here was compact, too, and became a blank page as surely as my finger became a pen. Sustenance and words, words and sustenance: I was quite content. But a terror was kindling in my soul – the black terror of AW, or after the whale. After the whale was nothing. After the whale I would starve, or capitulate in my weakened state to whoever or whatever might attack me. I became angry. Much of the account of my voyage was lost at sea and the part that was not was etched in sand the sea would ultimately sweep away. I shuddered to conceive of this beach, months from now, with the whale's bones, and my bones, and the sand all smoothed again where I had written in it, and nothing of mine indelible upon the world. I made rash charts to calculate how long my whale would last. My calculations did not satisfy me. I made others, based on lower rates of consumption and then days of eating nothing. I began to deceive myself about my calculations. Then I would lose my temper entirely, and cook up more blubber. And AW would creep closer.

One day I glanced up from my whale to see a shallop much like the Roebuck's pulling into an inlet a few bays down. I gazed at it woodenly for some moments. Then I washed the fish blood from my blade, sharpened it on a stone and secreted it in my hose. Whether that boat promised plunder, or danger, or good old-fashioned human contact, I resolved to meet it. Sun and the consumption of fish had made me as strong as ever I had been since departing Plymouth, the seawater had healed my feet and as any Wiltshire militiaman will confirm I was capable of sparring with the best of them – particularly with surprise on my side. Besides, I did not see what any enemy could take from me save my life, and who would want that?

It could not be, and yet it was. I watched the men in the boat pull in, then ran to meet them with open arms. For sure as I was a Knivet, the crew were the Roebuck's! My joy was upon reflection misplaced, for if a shallop was here that could only mean its men had been deemed too close to death to bother encumbering the decks with. Indeed most of them fell upon the sand like sacks of stone upon landing. Others could walk up and down only weakly. And amidst this latter group – yes – there was a face as soft and white as a girl's, and a figure as slender, making a sign of the cross in that air that stunk of dead men when it did not stink of dead fish.

"What news?" I cried, and went to embrace my blood brother. I might have kissed him too, had it not been for the presence of others.

"Is it really you, Anthony?" Barrawell wriggled free, blushing at the intensity of my grip. "You have more lives than a cat, for I keep hearing you are dead!"

"I would show equal surprise at your presence here were it not that nothing surprises me any more – not after what I have seen this continent conjure up. The word was that the Roebuck deserted Cavendish."

"I believe there were some amongst us strongly persuading him that course of action was best. It was widely held Cavendish had lost his mind, and any command he gave would spell doom for us all."

"Barrawell, I spy but twenty men landed from this sorry shallop, and not a sight of the Roebuck's sail. Can it be Cocke has turned as cruel and addled in the head as the General, casting out his men?"

Barrawell shook his head tiredly.

"We got lost. We had no pilot. Our food dwindled. Our hope dwindled. It was Hell. Cocke summoned us and said we had a choice. We could stay with him, and risk death, or we could take the last shallop, and scout for land, and risk death."

"It seems we jumped ship at the right time," I said ruefully. "The Galleon can have precious few able to man her. Waldren is gone, Barrawell. Our good Cavendish beat the life from him. If he is prepared to do that to his best man then what would have been the use of standing by him? What is the point of any of it?"

But I looked on these leaderless men, ten too frail to move and the other ten sorely needing direction in their current predicament, I saw there was perhaps a point. My breath came quicker. My eyes must have taken on some otherworldly shine, too, for Barrawell noticed.

"Are you feeling better Anthony? In Santos you were… somewhat troubled."

He called the hitting of a man that had wronged you, and the removal of one's cumbersome clothes in this relentless heat, and the painting of your body with mud and with the juices of fruit… he called those things troubled!

"You never joined us when the *cariiho* girls came to pleasure us. You spent nearly all the time we tarried there by yourself in the forest. I – we – were worried."

"Have you not heard of a thing called restraint, Barrawell? If you give yourself freely to any tribal maid with chalcedony piercings in her nipples, do you think you are any better than a common whore? You have to hold on to some nobler principle. For the sake of your dignity…" My voice faltered. "For *their* dignity. You take advantage of their innocence when you let them… love you like that. It is a form of abuse."

Barrawell peered at me concernedly.

"Do you miss her Anthony?"

"Who?"

"Kathy."

"What?"

"Anthony, I thought you were dead, so there was no harm… I read your diaries."

"How much?"

"This much." He reached into his hose and pulled out a slightly dampened wad of paper, with the account of my admirable adventures as I had penned them aboard the Roebuck intact, despite where the words had lapsed into scribbles from the up-down thrust of the waves. I was angry and embarrassed and grateful all at once.

"I feel I am supposed to miss her," I said.

I missed field hedges. I missed the root systems of oak trees. I missed hamstone. I missed fresh-cut grass on my father's lawns and my mother's scones rising on the stove. And in my mind they had fused into one unified image. I suppose you could call it family.

"It was the only thing I thought to take with me." Barrawell referenced the journal. He regarded me keenly in that damned compassionate Christian way, like they are already saved and you are out there somewhere, lost.

"I thank you," I said, not without emotion. I felt naked before him. There were things I had said in those writings that were unfinished. Scribbled in passion. Raw. What must he now think of the Knivet name now? There were mentions in there of inappropriate feelings, treachery, worse – what if… But my words were saved. And therefore in a sense I was. Let Barrawell and the world judge if I was fit to be my father's heir, and deserving of respect.

We had walked to the end of the bay where the Roebuck's boat had landed. Ahead, the ground rose up in shelves of rock and the forest came down, forming a fortuitous screen for I recollected that just beyond was where the men I had come ashore with lay rotting. Behind us were men that might soon suffer the same fate. It became apparent what I should do.

"Did you ever play dominoes, Barrawell?"

"I never had opportunity."

"If you stand them all on their thinnest end in lines you can arrange it so that when you knock the first, they all fall, and create some sort of shape."

"I have not thought about it. What shape?"

"Any shape you wish."

"I do not know what you mean."

"I know you sense the blackness, Barrawell. Let me tell you as one who has been a fortnight on this isle that it gets worse. I am dead for sure, you think; how can I possibly live? You can toy with the blackness, we all do sometimes, but we cannot give in to it."

"Anthony," he grasped my shoulders, "you are not making sense. If I did not know you I would say you sound more like a savage of late than you do a sailor."

"We are twenty-one." I made a quick tally of the men behind us. "Let us say fifteen, given some look certainties to expire. For all we know we are the last survivors of the second voyage of Thomas Cavendish[1] and we can lie here whimpering about it or we can seize the gauntlet and go to meet that blackness head on."

Sometimes the odds are stacked so terribly against you that you feel you may never topple them in your favour. But sometimes things happen, one after the other, outlasting a lethal shower of arrows, and fatal spells of cold, and poisoning, and creatures seemingly conjured up with the sole intent of ending your days upon this Earth and then – the feather in the cap – for the account you had kept as proof of your exploits to show your dear father to wash up in tact alongside you! And then the odds do not seem quite so insurmountable.

I was accepted as leader more or less unanimously; no man there protested. They would have been ill advised to do so, as most were in advanced stages of delirium or worse and none had my knowledge of this wild territory. I believe we agreed on the title of captain but I was not one to insist on it. Five of my group expired that day as I predicted. Of the remainder I sent two parties in clockwise and anti-clockwise directions around the shore to scout out whatever – Portugals, Indians or sorcery – might be on the other side of the isle. I got another two fishing for anything we might eat, two more repairing the boat into seaworthy condition and the rest working on a makeshift shelter hidden within the trees. It all ran smoothly until the scouting party returned saying how they had found nothing on the far coast save the recently burned carcase of a whale on the northern point, and how it was a pity a people so stupid as to set fire to a creature without utilising

---

[1] Unwittingly prophetic words, for within two months Cavendish would indeed die at sea (cursing his crew to the last). Only some twenty of the men that set sail with him from Plymouth eventually made it back to England.

its meat might, by depriving us of the one food source this isle appeared to have, be our party's undoing.

I recollected how in my eagerness to meet their boat I had left my old campfire unattended, but deemed it prudent not to mention this. What we needed now was not to quarrel, but pull oars in unison and pull hard.

Under my direction many fish were caught, the repairs of the shallop neared completion and our camp became quite as becoming as any Indian's. But sailors, it is known, have mighty short patience for men engaged on some of humanity's most protracted endeavours ever. We were all questioning in our hearts the big IF: the blackness and what that meant for us. How long could fifteen sailors – when the only way they knew was marauding – survive when they lacked resources to attack? Discontent simmered, and a man named Merryweather excelled at stirring it. The most noticeable thing about him were his beefy forearms, with blue markings in the form of coiled snakes. He had acquired them in the Far East on one of Lancaster's voyages and his chief pleasure was to exhibit them by folding them in a stance of all-knowing defiance.

On the fourth or fifth day around dusk I was awaiting the return of my scouts from the far side of the isle. I had deployed a party of three, reasoning that if something should befall one of them, there were was still one face to look forward and one backward. Perhaps they were looking so keenly in these directions they neglected to check left and right. Only one of the three returned, much maimed and gasping out how they had been ambushed by the biggest group of Portugals he had ever seen. They had killed the other two, he said, he had only eluded them by fleeing into the high forests in the middle of the isle. I pressed to squeeze sense out of this man and further quantified Portugal numbers as "fifty, but with many savages flanking them." Still, we were fifteen minus two, and even I agreed with the superstitiously inclined that thirteen was a mighty unlucky integer if it referred to men outnumbered at least four to one by their enemies.

"We must go with a flag of truce to meet them," I said, and removed my own shirt for the purpose. "It is our one hope."

"Truce?" scoffed that afore-mentioned rascal Merryweather. "I am not surrendering to a Portugal."

"They could be just here a-foraging," argued another amongst us. "Why risk a meeting with them if we can avoid it?"

"I know Portugals," I countered, "and they are feisty hunters once they sniff blood. If they killed two Englishmen here they will be scouring this isle for more."

But my men did not make their ears attentive to my wisdom. And soon it was high tide and impossible to execute my plan. Thus we remained where we were; easy pickings; hemmed in by the sea on three sides and the forest behind. Apprehensively we hid and kept lookout. To make everyone of good cheer I instructed we drink the final beer from the shallop, and eat the turtle we had caught; a last supper – ha – if ever there was one. I took first watch. I did above and beyond my stint and called on Merryweather to step up given his protestations had forced us to this course of action.

"Tut, tis a lie!" he shouted, and as he did so the first of the Portugals came upon us from behind, having been guided through the forest by their Indians.

They were *wayanasses* from Ihla Grande, that island of thick jungle south of the River of January where we of the Roebuck had formerly run into the scrape with the hog; these Indians were not half the warriors some tribes had but were perhaps most dangerous of all, for they could be easily bribed and were unpredictable as the wind. In the skirmish, such as it was, the Portugals let the *wayanasses* do the work. They were squat fellows, but heavy, which made them hard to wrestle with: one got me by the legs and crushed the circulation from them with his arms, which were thicker than my thighs and equal to all of my kicks. Down we skipped to the seaside, one or two *wayanasses* dragging each of us. They threw us in the surf; their cheeks bulged with the wads of tobacco they chewed and smirking, chewing, smirking, chewing, they wielded cudgels about their heads and when the speed was right brought them down hard on our heads, splintering the skulls of my men like they were barley stalks.

"*Você deve parar!*" I pleaded, when my turn came: stop!

I kissed the feet of the Indian whose lot it was to despatch me, which was easy, as he had already dealt me two blows to leave me grounded. As far as final pairs of feet upon which to look in this life go, these were intriguing ones: mighty broad but with blunted, even stunted toes. I sensed I had achieved the window of time I needed for he was paused mid-blow in genuine puzzlement stemming no doubt from the fact that Englishman were not known for entreating and even when engaged in a combat they could never win stayed obstinately fighting just the same. How this next idea occurred to me in the seconds available I cannot say but the best in our line are blessed with hereditary quick-wittedness and maybe it was that: I cupped some seawater in my hands and set to washing the Indian's feet, from the shins right down in-between those stumpy toes. It is difficult to find it in you to kill a man who washes your feet and I sensed some twinges – pleasure or an attempt to contain it – that suggested the way I moved my hands was not altogether repugnant to him. Well, he managed an '*aqui, aqui*', and one of the Portugals, the lazy cowards, who had come to inspect how the butchering of us Englishmen was progressing, saw what I was doing.

"What are you hoping to achieve, Englishman?"

"I am showing allegiance to my master, *senhor*." I kept my eyes firmly on the Indian's feet.

"And your master is a savage, you English dog?"

"This man is the slave of a Portugal and through him I kiss the feet of every Portugal and all my Catholic brothers."

"What are you, a disciple?"

"A follower, *senhor*."

"And who do you follow?"

"He who would lead."

"An Englishman with Catholic brothers!" The Portugal spat in the sand. "Your nation are about as Godly as gargoyles since your King made you stray from Pope Pablo, and a Catholic would only have a God-fearing man as an ally." He turned to the Indian. "Finish him, and quick, for I dislike the way his mouth moves."

"I can prove the truth of what I say," I shouted, as the Indian drew back his cudgel for the final swipe. "I am not only a Catholic, but a good friend of your Governor, and I will follow you, and go wherever you go if you spare me!"

I held up the finger with the ring. Gold, set with an emerald, given to me by the prisoner aboard Thomas Cavendish's flagship not three months previous.

The Portugal turned white, then red; seized the Indian's cudgel; threw it into the surf.

"Make ready!" he snapped at his men. "We are going to Manoel!" He lifted my face quite gently so that my eyes met his. "Rise. If all is as you say, Englishman, it will be well for you."

I had no conception of who Manoel was but I understood he might well have the power to save my life and was the reason, there and then, that I dangled alive and well over death's precipice, with just some few more fibres of the rope frayed.

The butchery of the others was continuing in the surf now foaming red from their blood.

"There is one more thing. Tell your Indians to save the boy."

"He with the girlish face?"

"The same. He is my blood brother."

"Is he now?" the Portugal regarded me quizzically. "Very well."

I was hoisted aboard the Indian's shoulders, and Barrawell on another's. Half-senseless we were carried around bays, and over boulders. Sometimes they swam with us and sometimes they ran with us. At one point we were closed together scaling a bluff, whereupon I reached out my hand to touch Barrawell's. He lacked the strength to speak, for his Indian had badly beaten him, but he smiled at me and I let him know by the look I returned him that I would see to it we were saved.

FIFTEEN

As the next day's sun arose we came to a great cliff, so high it cast a shadow across the preceding beach many canon shots in distance. My Indian whistled. Another answered him from the top of the cliff. Then five or six Portugals came to the cliff edge and beckoned us and we ascended to meet them.

"Manoel," my Indian kept saying, pointing up at the Portugals.

The early sun was fierce I could not make out the Portugals on the clifftop until Barrawell and myself had been set down before them, where we lay awhile rubbing our eyes and our wounds.

"You have something I want back," said the man I presumed was Manoel, coming forward into my vision. "You took it from me, I believe, not so long ago."

I squinted up. A man with long hair curling over a chocolate-brown doublet looked back at me, amiably munching on a helping of bread and marmalade. Much had happened since our last night together in the hold of Thomas Cavendish's ship during the storm but I would know that face, grinning with somewhat dashing lop-sidedness in the wake of seemingly any adversity, from whatever shore I looked at it from – and for as long as I lived. I cursed my bad luck. For here stood the one man who knew the story I had just given to save myself was a lie.

"Our positions are reversed," I said.

"They are."

"How did you do it?"

"How did I escape? In the General's shore boat, of course. Your General's cushioned seat I found particularly soft, I must say, after being trussed up in that hold!"

"But in a storm… and singlehandedly…"

"Always you Englishmen make the same mistake." Manoel squatted beside me. "You assume you know the seas. I made a calculated guess where the shore was. After all I am trained as a pilot: something of a novelty to the English race, no?"

"A calculated risk and a big one," I found it hard to keep the admiration from my voice, "for death surely awaited you had you judged wrong."

"Death seems to avoid us both, Englishman," Manoel said, chewing. "I wonder why? We watched your crewmen in their death throes from the poisonous pease, yet you survived. A fire on the north shore alerted us that more of you were come so I sent my most ruthless *wayanasses* to slaughter you. Yet here you are again."

"Take the ring," I said flatly, removing it from my fingers.

"Wrought by Potosi goldsmiths," he sighed. "Beautiful craftsmanship, no? But I read something further into it. I see it as a symbol of all that is great about colonisation of these barbarous lands. This ring represents Portugal's mission here."

"And what is that?"

"Power," said Manoel happily. "The acquisition of it."

"Yet that same ring when last we met symbolised the demise of Portugal influences here, and the rising dawn of the English. You were captive on an English ship that had raided your port and was bound for great things. So do not tell me you read your happy tale of power in your ring then."

Manoel put an index finger in front of me and turned it up first one way then the other in a seesaw motion.

"There is another thing I require of you; news, Englishman.

You must have knowledge of who is where on this coast at present, and now you are in my hands your knowledge is mine."

"I am hungry. Give me meat and I will tell you all the news that I can."

With that all the Portugals broke out in laughter.

"He wants meat! When our captain himself eats bread and marmalade!"

But they must have harboured no paltry amount of respect for my audacious nature, because they provided me with meat pies and with fish and with some of the captain's very own marmalade spread on some bread. I must say that whatever has been said about these Iberians' cuisine is an exaggeration because I found what they gave me to want so much for taste that a Devonshire tavern could do better – and as for their pastry it is a travesty. Still, I ate voraciously, and whilst I ate I told them every piece of English intelligence I could.

The English, I feel, are all for 'do' or 'die' without ever opting for the middle ground – which some call compromise – between the two. But compromise has its merits, not least of which is a significantly increased chance of longevity. In my defence I altered coordinates cunningly and provided these Portugals with detail tweaked into an ingenious falsehood for now I was in this lowly state I saw most lucidly the path to the top and vowed to devise a scheme, right there as the Portugals interrogated me, to win back greatness for myself; for my family name; for Wiltshire and for England. And if the fact I write this is not proof of my honest intent - for I faced most certain death at the hands of the Portugals if these last sentences became uncovered – then subsequent events in my narrative are. So judge me on this story in its entirety, dear father, only the entirety, because I really do not see how I could be blamed for what happened, and in fact I should be applauded.

Manoel nodded; motioned to the two *wayanasses* that had delivered us.

"So much for a Portugal's justice!" I cried, seeing those Indians standing over me with their weapons readied once more. "After the services I have offered you!"

"My good, good friend of the Governor," Manoel smiled, feasting again on his precious bread and marmalade. "Whatever do you mean? You promised to serve us, your masters, did you not? I am giving you the opportunity to realise that pledge. These savages are taking you on a trip to Salvador Correia de Sá!"

Kathy, when you looked at me you saw the twinkle of gold your father failed to make through his experiments. When I looked at you I imagined everything my mother told me I should do and never had space to imagine what I wanted for myself. A respectable woman once told me the look is many times more meaningful than the physical act. So let us just have the look. Yours as I declined you that evening in my woods; mine as I long for you now I know I can never have you. For you may recall the sermon we once had delivered to us at church in Charlton; I think it was the time after we were formally promised to each other, and my mother smiled from one side of the aisle and your father smiled from the other and we did not smile at all. It was about the man who once stood at the side of the road to Calvary as Christ passed by and taunted Him. Christ in his agony turned to him and cursed him: "Go on forever, until I return". I am him, Kathy. I am that Wandering Jew. All my control over my fate is gone, for I am gone – gone into the hands of an Englishman's worst and most volatile enemies. And Christ does not look to be returning any time soon.

SIXTEEN

Salvador Correia de Sá sat and wrote; what he wrote few knew; what all knew was that his word was *the* word and would determine the destiny of Brazil. He wrote permissions for exploration of the interior, he wrote grants for land ownership. He wrote demands for new plantations, and commissions for *engenhos* to fill them, and requests to Angola for slaves to work them. He conducted surveys of sites for potential monasteries to stand out as beacons of Catholicism and enlighten the regrettably high number of heathens residing within his domain. He made out tallies of goods that arrived in the ports under his jurisdiction and he made out cases against practitioners of the Jewish Faith – particularly if they were prominent in the sugar business. When he wrote, anyone happening to be in the same place was silent, for he could only dedicate himself absolutely to a thing and whilst dealing with it could abide no distractions. The scratch of his quill upon parchment was the most formidable sound I ever heard. As I was led into the assembly room where he did his writing that first time he wore black and nothing but black and I never saw him wear another colour. His choice of dress left his face looking pale; had Europe's gaudiest painter painted him they would have found no colour on which to seize when rendering his likeness; they would have needed to fabricate it and Salvador Correia de Sá could abide fabrication still less than distraction.

Unlike most captives I was not led before him in chains for Manoel saw how that would demean me. But I had to tarry an intolerably long time in that sepulchre of a room nonetheless. It was a room he had designed himself. It was dark and cold because the man disliked light and heat and it had as the sole ornamentation portraits of his predecessors in the governorship, because the predecessors were his family and he liked what they and he represented: order. The portraits had more life than him; he sat statuesquely still save for the motion of his writing hand. By contrast this was speedy indeed, and as for his signature I never saw such an elaborate flourish; it was the one free and easy movement he allowed himself. The only other people in the room with us were Manoel, who stood a little in front of me and from what I could infer looked uncharacteristically apprehensive, and, in a corner, an old hunchbacked monk, sitting with his head bowed and looking utterly miserable. From neither could I guess how long we might be obliged to wait.

"You like my uncle?" Salvador Correia de Sá indicated the painting on his right, setting down his quill with a sigh. People, it appeared, were a disappointment to the Governor of Brazil's principal captaincy after his papers; perhaps amidst his neat documents it really did seem Brazil was one great country whilst people reminded him of how it was tens of countries, and all of them at war.

I had to check then if he was addressing me or not; he did not look at me but more how an actor looks at an audience, at the room in general.

"You have his best features, *senhor*," I replied politely, albeit stiffly, for I was unimpressed with my treatment so far in this colony's nascent capital. It was not only how I had been kept waiting as if watching the Governor write was my life's only pleasure; it also smarted how unfittingly I had been delivered here – with many derisive comments at my expense.

The Governor inclined his head, as if he expected my compliment.

"My uncle paved the road to my making this country prosper. To do so he knew he had to have the Jesuits on his side. Do you know why you need the Jesuits on your side?"

"I would dearly like to know."

"Because then you have the savages on your side. Never underestimate whom you might need on your side. Would you not say, Anchieta?"

The monk glanced up bleakly. He had a face like a bird of prey's: a sunburnt nose like a hawk's beak and wildly staring eyes that resembled one who has witnessed the most horrific vision of the apocalypse.

"He is my equal," de Sá continued. "He has earned that right. He has devotion, which I prize highly. He helped turn many savages towards the Catholic light. We prize those who see the light. Those who work with us. That is the only way this country can function: by adherence to faith. He speaks the savage tongue so fluidly he recounts chants in the language in his sleep. Say some Tupi, Anchieta!"

"*Karaíba, karaíba. Abo aba-im, taba-uasù y aba-uasú, taba-im,*" said the monk, glaring at me with his bird's stare. "*Abape pe?*"

This translates thus: that there is the small man in the big village, and the big man in the small village – which are you, foreigner? I had no idea what he meant. He was clearly senile.

Well, this monk did not seem to care for me much, and I also doubted his attempts to pacify these tribes had been so successful as he imagined using a religion incomprehensible to people who preferred trees to altars. Then again, this de Sá spoke of rights when his own 'rights' to talk as condescendingly as he did were far from evident. I saw little merit in either of them, but much to be gained from both, and this business seemed to me to be about holding your tongue as much as anything.

"What concerns me with you," the Governor frowned, hands clasped as if in fervent prayer, "is whether you have, as an

Englishman, that faith."

"Show me a good man," I said, choosing my words carefully, "and I will show you faith in that man."

"You make a mistake. You speak to me as if you were a man. You are not a man. You are my man. You owe me your life. You must call me 'master'. And I will call you 'son'.'"

"That does not seem an equal relationship, master."

"My son. Do not misunderstand. You are very dear to me. Manoel has told me of the guile of your tongue. Portugal, English…"

"The tongues of the Spaniards and Frenchmen too," I added, forgetting I was interrupting one of the most important men in Brazil. "And more and more the tongue of the Indians." I flashed the monk a defiant look.

"Quite. With Anchieta too I will be quite the celebrated polygot. With language, son, comes unity, and you will be very dear to me indeed. But first and foremost… you will be mine."

Here he was – a man whose word travelled further than the word of most kings, from the Pernambuco sugar plantations down to the swamps of the Rio de la Plata – offering me a part in his domain.

I recollected that time almost exactly one year previous when I had stood before you, father and had needed to prove myself as now.

"I accept, master," I said.

The Governor of the River of January inclined his head again, sombrely. Behind me, I was conscious of Manoel barely succeeding in suppressing his laughter.

"So be it my son."

As a temporary measure I was to be transferred into the care of Manoel, a man the Governor respected, with the understanding that he would send for me soon.

We made our exits, Manoel and myself, and the view outside was of the four grand green hills of the River of January, the seat of power of the land, hewn out of the forest. There were the large, white-walled, red-roofed houses of the sugar barons and biggest by far, the Governor's retreat, out on the island in a bay that gleamed like pearls; there was the sun-drenched farmland in-between with the bananas, the manioc, the cows, the *engenhos* that gave them their wealth; there was the crumbled fort at the bay mouth where the Governor's uncle had trounced the French Huguenots[1] that tried settling there and proclaimed to all comers that this land was Portugal, now and for all time Portugal; there was potential!

Manoel could no longer control himself, but burst into a bellow of laughter that I wished he would desist in because others might have heard.

"You *accept*, do you, my good good friend of the Governor? Oh my! We are fortunate – all Brazil is fortunate indeed – to have you on our side!"

---

[1] In the 1550s, Nicolas Durand de Villegaignon led several hundred French Huguenots (Protestants escaping persecution in Catholic France) to Baía da Guanabara (Guanabara Bay) on Brazil's coast, one of several destinations in the New World to which they fled. In 1560 the Portuguese destroyed Fort Coligny, the colony the French founded in the bay. But many Huguenot colonists escaped and continued to live on Brazil's coast – needless to say, with a generally anti-Portuguese sentiment.

SEVENTEEN

"Hey, Englishman, what are you digging for?"

It was the same jesting fellows who made heckling remarks at my expense when I had first entered town, only now they were significantly more drunk.

"Digging your way back to England?"

"You'll have to hit Hell first!"

"Yes, hit Hell and keep going straight down!"

There were three of them but I bit my lip and kept silent. I was capable of taking them on in hand-to-hand combat, but they were armed and I was not. I also knew men like Manoel and the Governor were exceptions in this colony and the majority of those who came here from Portugal were knaves the kingdom was glad to rid itself of. Such types would likely not heed the Governor's orders that I was to be kept unharmed, and give me a drubbing with their swords should I show insubordination.

"Not very well-dressed, you Englishmen, are you? I say, look at that shirt! He's gone the wrong way through a mangle!"

Oh, I would dearly love to see one of them endure half the miseries I had and come out with a better set of clothes! I would have loved to see them come to Charlton and compete in elegance with any Knivet! We Knivets used the best tailors; the great Drake was our... but of course I could not mention that name here. Ha, they probably had comrades we had dispatched in the Armada! There were many things I could not mention here. I had to watch myself; stay a step ahead; stay strong.

"He more resembles a savage than a man of Europe!"

"Do tell me, is there a difference between the savages and the English? In the advancement of their brains I have observed little!"

"I say, let's have some fun with him. He's only a savage – a little white savage!"

They had been a happy few days for me, so of course they were numbered. I had slept in Manoel's house on the *Morro do Castelo*; that is, the Hill of the Castle – where the town had its noblest buildings. It was a fine white house with a terracotta roof like those of the wealthiest within the colony, for Manoel was much admired by the Governor. I had cooked Manoel his supper and he had complemented me on my cooking; I had been permitted to dine with him and even sleep in the same room as him on a hanging net he compelled one of his *wayanasses* to fetch me. The Portugals preferred beds and linens imported from Spain but the Indians used nets; these nets did give the peculiar but agreeable sensation you were sleeping on a big jungle leaf and were part of the jungle rather than a man surrounded by it. Manoel did not know about the crabs that lived in the holes in the sand and was amazed when I brought him some; he bid me bring him such crabs every day and it was my honour to do so. It was this digging for crabs that I was engaged in now and I was concerned these villains would meddle in my task – was it so very difficult for them to lend their minds to something of similar usefulness?

"I say, let's dress him up!"

"I have my wife's dress here; she uses it for drudging but it would suffice for our young friend!"

Hearing this I made to return home with my crabs, but they anticipating this bounded after me; I could only have eluded them by running and that might have enticed them to shoot.

"Here my pretty, put this on!"

One seized my hands and the others thrust the dirty dress over my head. It was black like these religious zealots often wear, and dismal plain. This done they pulled me towards the boat they had arrived in; my hands were impeded by the tight dress and I could not resist.

"Let us take a jaunt, my pretty!"

We put out to sea. It seemed they wanted to show off their sport to as many as possible for they paddled round the bay yelling "look at our prize, is he not fair?" I grew alarmed. The tide was strong. In the midst of their most ardent bragging I forced all my weight against he who was closest to me and bundled him overboard, succeeded in freeing my arms from the dress and dived into the water, striking for shore. I was a strong swimmer but the waves and my outfit were against me. Already this performance had a small crowd assembled on the beach and as I spluttered and splashed a woman saw fit to send out her slaves to aid me.

"You are an oasis of kindness, *senhora*. I would be a dead man but for you."

"Take my dress off, Englishman," she replied, tight-lipped. "That was all I had a care to save!"

I had the humiliation of taking off this woman's dress as she waited, in front of a crowd so surprised they scarce knew whether to laugh or stare in slack-jowled wonder. Meanwhile word had already alerted the Governor's men that I had pushed a Portugal into the sea, although of course none of the rest of the story whatsoever got related. It was in this state, the dress just stripped off me and smeared in crab juice, that I was unceremoniously dumped before the Governor for the second time.

* * *

Salvador Correia de Sá could not abide distraction as I have said and I could discern from how tightly he wrung his hands just how immense his displeasure was.

"I had not called for you, my son."

"Master, these villains…"

The Governor raised a hand; he was not a man who needed to utter the word 'silence' to achieve it.

"What makes a great country?" His brevity made each of his words bang into you like nails in that tomb of an assembly room.

"Faith," I remembered.

"Not simply *faith*. Devotion. Dedication to that devotion. I do not approve of theatre, my son, unless it illustrates some aspect of morality."

"Master, if I might explain…"

"You had a… a lady's dress removed from you at the beach. You attempted to… drown one of my men. These actions are not those of someone who exhibits faith, or devotion, or dedication!" At 'dedication' he rapped his quill on his marble-topped table; this small action was as far as I ever saw him personally stray down the path toward physical violence, and I was dismayed how much I had offended him. *I fear thee because thou art an austere man. Thou takest up that thou layedst not down, thou reapest that thou didst not sow…*[1]

"Master, I am but a poor ship boy who would serve you unflinchingly."

"Anthony!" a voice chimed from across the hall; I had no idea until then that the Governor's appointment I had interrupted was with none other than my blood brother.

"Anthony, whatever do you m…mean to say so to the Governor? You are a m…man of noble birth!"

"I am nothing but what I say…" I began, but Barrawell's remark had etched a rigid and terrible line to the mouth of

---

[1] Luke 19:21

Salvador Correia de Sá.

"Such behaviour in one of lowly origins I might excuse," he said, "but in a gentleman! In one in whom I had shown faith, to himself exhibit such an absence of it! Well son, you hasten my summoning you. It was my intention, conceived this very morning, to show you something of how my Brazil works. We have, commencing this week, the *safra*, the harvest of our most prized product. You know to what I refer?"

"You can only mean Brazil sugar, master, for its quality is known across the globe," I said meekly, aiming for flattery that would redeem me in his eyes. But as I dared to look up I saw it was too late for redemption.

"I do," said the Governor gravely.

"The ship from Angola is in." Anchieta, seated alongside the Governor as ever he seemed to be, spoke up. "Several hundred slaves eager to get out cutting cane."

The Governor nodded.

"Deliver him to the *engenho*!" he pronounced.

Before I could further protest two *wayanasses* had their hands clamped firmly on my shoulders, and were leading me away – not through the main entrance but through a dingy side door. This time, there were manacles on my wrists and ankles; these Indians delighted in tugging them viciously. Spasms from old wounds tore through me once more. I cried my innocence for all to hear, but I had already become invisible to everyone in that room; everyone save the old monk Anchieta who took it upon himself to hiss in an aside just intended for my ears:

"*Lovas eyave pomombana.*"

"Just like this shall you be consumed."

EIGHTEEN

"Hee did pittie my hard fortune to come to so bad an end as I was like to come"

Martin de Sá's opinion of Anthony Knivet's prospects in Brazil, as recorded by Anthony Knivet, *Admirable Adventures and Strange Fortunes*

The Governor's *engenho* stood on Governor's Island not far from the Governor's house; a small tamed section of an untamed forest. Salvador Correia de Sá my master had debated calling all three after himself but decided "Governor" was sufficient because after all he was the first Governor, the first true Governor of the River of January and in years to come after his death, he believed, 'Governor' would still evoke images of *him*, his pallid authority, his presence. The *engenho* was the pride and joy of the River of January captaincy: at least amongst those who cared about sugar. Pernambuco and Bahia might possess more sugar mills but there was no denying this was the greatest. It was so great enthusiastic townspeople would seize bewildered strangers newly arrived in the port and offer to escort them along the coast to where the best views of this marvel could be had. It was so great many referred to it as 'Cidade do Governador' for it was a city – with a schoolhouse and a chapel and a carpenter's house and a forge and a ring of huts for the slaves that worked within; the mill itself had a cane house and a boiling house and a purging house and a distilling house for the processing of cachaça – a drink made with sugarcane juice that everyone in this land consumed copiously. Then there were two huge grinding wheels, powered by water and by beasts and by Angolans with muscles the equal of the Titan Atlas, and my master had a man working on a new grinder which he did claim would revolutionise the sugar business not just within the colony but across the world.

Manoel accompanied me on the boat out. He seemed regretful about all that had happened, especially as I was sent here only through desiring to furnish him with a plate of crabs for his supper. I bid him be of good cheer, for I was certain to enjoy my new responsibilities here too; he gave me an odd look and embraced me as we said goodbye.

The factor liked to be called *senhor de engenho*, but was suffering from some inflated sense of importance for all this mere sugar mill manager did was spread his generous behind in an intricately carved chair imported from Madrid that strained under his bulk, putting ticks in boxes and collecting a salary exceeding nearly all others in the captaincy for this strenuous task. He disliked the English race and sneered when I told him who I was which made me develop a similar repugnance for him rather rapidly. As he wrote my name in his book and alongside it a number – thirty-one – he saw fit to grin at me and I mustered some sort of smile in return, although to a neutral graced with keen powers of observation it was evident we were simply adept at constructing walls around our true thoughts.

"*Massape.*"

"What?"

It was as if he were saying the English words 'must pay' and I wondered with what: perhaps he imagined my being brought before him trussed in bonds was insufficient penalty and only my life would be payment enough for my perceived crimes.

He motioned to a guard in the doorway.

"Lovely hands. Very soft." The handcuffs clamped on me upon arriving here were unlocked. My hands were forced to the table. I shuddered as he fondled each of my fingers. "Very, very soft." A moment later there was a flash and this fat factor with his easy, heavy movements had whipped out a dagger and slammed it down, impaling my right hand palm down to the wood. "What, señ-horrrrrr," he whispered, his syrupy voice hot in my ear through my bellows of shock. "What, señ-horrrrrr."

I managed to mouth the desired title a few times and he wrenched the blade back out, a gesture that, quite intentionally, caused me more pain than hitherto but left him looking somehow benevolent.

"It is accustomed to a position of influence, yes?" He regarded me lazily from under heavy lids. "I see that in its hands. They are not rough like worker's hands. It is of noble birth, yes?"

I nodded.

"I hate nobility." He grinned; beckoned me close. "And I detest English nobility. They think they can go anywhere; do what they please. I have here, for example, a letter to the Queen of your heathen isle – it was intercepted by our men, no doubt from one of your vagabond captains who roam the world under the guise of an explorer – "to serve God and defeat Catholics!" He read the words in English, sounding like a spoiled child as he did so. "Well not in Brazil! How does it expect me to treat it, hailing from a nation propagating such slander against the Catholic race?"

"As to that I plead not guilty. For I serve myself and my family and God not at all."

He shook his fat head in a show of fake pity.

"I'll wager it was, what – a captain?"

"I was."

"Thinking it could come here and usurp me?"

"No!" His question threw me. "It is merely that the Governor said I was to have a tour of your *engenho* here, in order that I might better understand…"

"Understand?" His grin broadened; it seemed to grow in proportion to his anger and a trail of spittle snaked out like a spider advancing across a web. "The Governor has informed me of everything I need to know! It will understand, have no fear!

It will have years to understand! Show thirty-one to the tailors to dress its wound, the forge to get the shackles on it and then... *massape*!"

The *massape* was the fields where the sugar was grown, and being sent there was a fate so desperate even the other *engenho* slaves, whose lives were wretched by almost every standard, gave you pitying looks. The cane itself was swamped by the advent of the rainy season, begun in earnest. Access by land was impossible. I set forth each morning whilst it was still dark in a canoe overloaded with West Africans who muttered chants to their deities until the supervisor whipped them into silence. Giving our bodies and our lives to these Portugals was not enough: we had to give them our spirits too. These sombre intonations were some sort of awful prelude to our sorry days' labour. We began just after first light and worked until sundown. The sugar canes in the Cidade do Governador were fabled throughout Brazil for their height and girth; they towered taller than many a jungle tree and we strove to cut them with blades blunter than my mother's meat carving knife, which had itself been cruelly confiscated by the factor. Ten pairs of slaves to a row and 500 canes per pair we worked. We stood in water up to our waists: slimy monsters below the surface sucked our blood and Catholic monsters above the surface beat us to greater endeavours and the sun beat down on us until we reeled. My partner was a hulk of a man named Quarasips Juca; he was half Angolan and half of the *tamoyes*, an itinerant tribe hereabouts that hated the Portugals and loved the French. When he did speak, which was seldom, he lamented that by his blood he was the Portugals' ultimate enemy and could therefore only be destined for a life of utmost misery regardless of what he did; I consoled him that I doubted I was far behind him in either respect. Conversation was limited between us, for he did not wish to speak of his past and looked at me like I was mad for entertaining thoughts of the future. We toiled in twos; a man to cut the canes and a woman to tie them in sheaves. Our boat was short on women so I took the woman's position. This inspired jibes from the supervisor but I defy anyone who claims my lot was easier. The pressure was on the cutter at the beginning of the day but on the binder at the end; as the binder all your hands and arms became lacerated whereas the cutter accrued chafing only on his knife hand and also got allotted more breaks because of the supposed back-breaking nature of the work. Fifteen canes made a sheaf; ten sheaves before we got sustenance; twice that number again before we could breathe easy that we would not be punished for laziness that day. The factor liked to dispense punishment himself. As a fat man he had a hefty blow and I saw him flog a couple of men with more meat on them than me until they dropped dead. Death in fact seemed the only way out. If you did not focus on your work like Quarasips Juca then death was all you could occupy your mind with: what a relief your own might be or how sweet the death of the factor would be. I imagined forcing his head into a bubbling kettle of cane juice; I imagined coating him in cachaça – the inferior sort of course – and impaling him to a path in front of a legion of soldier ants; I imagined grinding him bone by bone from the bottom up in the mill until his body was a pulp and his face was squealing like a pig's. Aside from these thoughts I grew careless what I did. I forgot what the taste of meat was like. All we ate was cassava meal; it was often crawling with insects and had a bland earthy flavour that to me became the flavour of the impending grave. As for my Englishman's clothes, they were in tatters around me and I was soon so dirty and tanned I was scarce discernible from my African and Indian brothers.

One morning I was planning my usual demise of the factor when I heard a trumpet. The sound came from a gaudy canoe bedecked with fancy cushions, with two smiling waving figures within that seemed so ridiculous in the festering Hell of the *massape* that I would have laughed had my throat been less swollen through being denied water.

"Quarasips?" I lacked energy to say his full name. "You recognise the boat?"

"Yah." My partner felled another cane with a particularly vicious swipe.

"Who is it, Quarasips?"

"The priest. He come to bless us; convince us we all be working in the good Lord's name."

"I know who the man in the cassock is. Who is that in the boat with him?" I indicated the young man with the wispy beard and the tall capotain hat tipped at a carefree angle.

"The Governor's son, yah. Just back from Europe. Got some fine notions in his head about how he gonna change this nation."

Change, I pondered. Fine notions. I splashed some water on my face and smartened myself as best I could. As the boat approached, I bent the cane into sheaves with extra vigour.

"We beg of You, in Your mercy, to bless our harvest," said the priest in the squeaky, overly-enthusiastic tones of one on his first posting. Again, it was enough to induce laughter and again, only my terrible thirst and perhaps the cocked musket of the supervisor prevented me. The priest squeaked more words about fruitfulness and faith and dipped his finger into a vial to anoint the head of Quarasips Juca. Holy water! It was too much. I snorted involuntarily.

"A blessing!" I said. "Would that we could take that water in our mouths rather than waste it on our foreheads!"

"He speaks against God!" the priest squeaked, most likely imagining his increased status with the inquisition judges for delivering them one so vociferously indignant against Portugal cruelty as me, and a transfer to somewhere slightly less Godforsaken to deliver his sermons.

"Easy," the Governor's son said. He scrutinised me, thumb and third finger gripping his chin and his second finger tapping the side of his nose. "You are not a savage."

"I am no more and no less since we are all abused here in equal measure."

"He is an English pirate!" the supervisor cried. "He has

committed numerous offences along this coast against your father, *senhor*."

"The man is more than capable of speaking for himself. Speak," the Governor's son entreated me. "Is what this moron says true?"

"I am an Englishman, and that is where the truth of it ends! I meant to serve your father, *senhor*, and serve him well, but a misunderstanding…"

"My father and I… we do not always see eye to eye. God knows he is so pious!" He took off his hat, which had a peacock's feather in the brim, and twirled it about. Oh, he looked quite the man who would inherit, and had styled himself accordingly – daring mauve hues in his jerkin, ribbons to match on his shoes – with that ease the rich have. His hat-twirling was less a gesture to impress than something that amused him, and I watched him flick it and flip it and catch him behind him without looking several times. The slaves stared at him from beneath their grime. "Tell me freely what you think of your work here."

"Our main grievance lies with the factor. I may be no expert in economics, but Brazil trades in sugar, and if you desire your enterprise to flourish *senhor*, then know your factor's abuses are impeding that aim. He lames and maims so many with his violence we are not half the workforce we could be."

"Hmm." The Governor's son tapped his nose with deep absorption. At length he squatted down in his boat so that our eyes were on the same level. "I shall see to it the factor will trouble you no more." He hesitated. "I am recently returned from Europe. I admire your country. In England you help your poor. Here we do not know how to help our poor. My father thinks of raising new churches, but I am more concerned with schools and hospitals, commerce and defence. I want our nation to be great, like Europe. I would welcome your thoughts on our *engenho* here. Are the conditions otherwise satisfactory? And the hours? Do you think they are perhaps on the long side?"

This speech was so marvellous to me that I confess I was lost for a reply.

"There is… potential for improvement."

He nodded seriously, then relaxed into a grin which better suited his face.

"Incidentally my name is Martin. Martin de Sá. Come, padre. We have done enough blessing for one day."

Later I watched the circles of sweat expanding under the luxuriant jerkin of the factor as he slouched back on his bespoke Madrid-made chair. The jerkin was a poor fit – his bloated body denied him those close-cut versions the latest young gentlemen wear. I might have guessed that after Martin de Sá had shown me favour he would be riled, and knowing how unexpectedly he could explode I kept my eyes lowered to minimise offense I might cause.

"I have seen plenty come, these six years I have been in charge," he said. His feet were up on the table, bared and wiggling. "Some show resilience. Particularly blackamores. Resilience is in their blood. But to look at them after a few years here!" his grin was cavernous "Mio Deus, they are broken little mice!" Ponderously, down came those big white feet and he hauled himself up with a cane. "They tell me it has more lives than a cat. Perhaps we could test the truth of that. I could engineer an accident for it. The Governor's son would never know. A limb lost in a grinder, then irreversible blood loss… it happens all the time."

I waited for a beating that did not come. From a man quite content to be brutal, the fact he did not lay a finger upon me that night disturbed me, for it was certain he was searching for a way to end my life. I again sensed that rope fraying, and that precipice beckoning, and whilst a part of me deeply wished for an ending the majority smarted that this fat factor should be the instrument. I comforted myself that I had the son of the Governor of Brazil's most esteemed captaincy on my side; I had a calling in this wilderness! But Martin de Sá did not come for me – that week or the next. Oh, my mind seized upon his final 'hm' to me! I saw the path out of my hardship to a master that would use me appropriately – perhaps to cook for him, or document his exploits, or communicate to him the will of the Indians, or fight at his side. But why did he not send for me when he knew I was here, toiling in *massape* that broke a man like Quarasips who was twice my size and strength? And after abandoning me here, did the Portugals deserve my help? Should they in fact count themselves fortunate if they avoided my wrath? Such meditations as these circled my mind as our party worked its way down the sticky, rows of sugar.

Now, the supervisor was a lustful fellow, and I observed him making eyes at one Angolan maid especially well-endowed in her figure. He showered her with small favours: errands that kept her from the toughest tasks and on one occasion when he thought none of us were looking, time alone with him on a separate row conveniently screened from us other slaves. But I was looking and had developed a manner of so doing so which fooled them all into thinking I was not. Towards the end of the row we worked, and at the end was the jungle. The irony was that the shackles the Portugals took such trouble to fasten on us allowed enough leeway for movement that escape was feasible. Our captors relied on our thinking that there was nowhere to escape to as sufficient deterrent. It was a fair assumption. Beyond the *massape* was forest full of those most vicious of cannibals the *tomomynos*, who were allied with the Portugals and were sure to eat me in no pleasant manner should they discover me. Complementing the *tomomynos* were the little less vicious *tamoyes* who, even if they had as their sworn enemies the *tomomynos* and the Portugals both, would be unlikely to object to dispatching me to my maker. For what else could a white man on their island be but their foe, and if I did manage to convey to them the marvellous events leading to my current predicament, would they believe me? I might swim to shore if I could loosen my chains but would end up riddled with Portugal bullets or cannibal arrows. Yet the Portugals had under-estimated me. I was Anthony Knivet. I did not fear such dangers. As the supervisor fornicated in the next row with his

Angolan conquest I gave the lot of them the slip, and in a few
steps vanished into the trees.

NINETEEN

"If nothing would satisfie him but my life..."

Anthony Knivet, *Admirable Adventures and Strange Fortunes*

My plan was to remain concealed until I had gauged the lie of the land and observed the tribes therein; their numbers and their tendencies. On my second morning of freedom I became acquainted with both.

Some *tomomynos* were gathered on a steep-shelving beach on the northeast side of the island, which the Portugals left to the Indians because they were afraid to set foot there. The waves were high, for the September storms were come, and pairs of *tomomynos* took turns to hold three captive *tamoyes* upside-down in the surf, slowly drowning them.

There was no struggle. There was barely any sound at all. Every so often the victims were raised back above the surface, allowing them a couple of ragged breaths before they were submerged again.

The rest of the *tomomynos* were nursing a fire and painting each other's faces in their customary tar. The painters took some time getting their artwork just right; perfecting it with blood from careful incisions on the *tamoyes'* bodies to render them the essence of devils incarnate. Then the almost-dead men were transferred from their watery grave to a fiery one. The first was laid straight across the flames whilst the other two were set hard by; hung by their feet and rubbed in a creamy fat like they were butcher's carcases. Herbs were added but I could not ascertain which. One of the *tomomynos* had the honour of being master preparer. He was decorated finer than the rest, and as the batch of meat heated up he began dancing. He chanted words I could not make out. The chant spanned as many octaves as an entire group of musicians and their instruments, shrill and deep, rich and raw. It built to a crescendo, and I saw the need for this as it masked the screams of the man on the fire. It was not done to show your pain amongst these peoples; the soon-to-be-roasted man was weak.

I could look no more. I fled to a safe distance; vomited; then gathered myself.

I had seen a manner of death that was foreign to me, but I daresay it was one that had been practiced centuries. The bird hunts the worm and the fox hunts the bird, but all three belong in the wood and not the hunter who comes with his gun for the fox. These Portugals who came and imagined they could dictate were like hunters who did not do so much as eat what they killed... their atrocities were worse. Out in this wilderness, I reasoned, I still might dangle unscathed over death's precipice a while longer than if I gave myself up to the Portugals, who punished runaways by notoriously prompt execution. And I was not prepared to surrender my fight for fortune just yet. You see how I fight, Kathy? Should you ever find an opportunity to tell my father how I fought, please do so.

Yet when all you have to do is fight for your life, it is quite dull. I grew listless. With listlessness comes a desire to throw yourself at danger. I stood on the shore and spread my arms to the rain, challenging it to give me some illness. It did not, although down the length of Brazil people died in thousands through maladies brought about by the wet. I sought out the lairs of the island's most dangerous beasts and taunted them: lizards the length of a galley slave's oar and lions with more teeth than a pincushion has pins. But they showed no inclination to finish me either.

I began wearing the hides of the beasts I killed, for they were more comfortable than my rain-rotted sailors' clothes. For a face paint I chose the green of a giant jungle fern, which I called the Great Fern because not only was it large in size but it also aided me greatly. I used it for the roof of a small shelter I constructed, and for protection from the fierce sun. But first and foremost it yielded the dye that kept me better hidden from my foes when I so chose than any Indian. I came upon parties of *tomomynos* and *tamoyes* but did not make myself known to any. Oh, I brought myself to the edge, many a time, but on the cusp of the actual encounter held back, relishing it, yet denying it to myself.

My impression was that the *tomomynos* were almost as vile to each other as they were to their enemies but the *tamoyes* seemed a people that did not quite warrant their formidable reputation. They did not eat each other like the *tomomynos* did and built better villages. They seemed to live for life's pleasures as well as war whereas the *tomomynos* were fighters whose only thoughts were for acquisition: for the scalps of *tamoyes* and for shiny things. *Tomomynos* were the most effective fighting force the Portugals had but they were being played for fools. They launched themselves at any group of Indians the Portugals cared to name and got largely valueless trinkets in return that they stashed proudly in holes in the ground. Of course, the *tomomynos* and the *tamoyes* were once one. Their leaders had quarrelled bitterly over who should be better rewarded by Vasco de Gama and since then, despite being more similar in looks and language than any other Indians, they each embarked on a campaign of extermination against the other which the Portugals – the callous dogs – saw how to exploit for their own ends.

One of the many ways *tomomynos* and *tamoyes* were still the same was in their preference to be by the water. It was a particularly dangerous preference for the *tamoyes* since the gravest danger they had of encountering Portugals was on the shore and, since the *tomomynos* were shore-lovers too, clashes between tribes were frequent. But this suited me well. I could depend with some certainty that the small caves within the inland hills were rarely visited by anyone, and here I made my home.

I nevertheless visited the sea often, despite the risk of encountering one or more of my steadily accumulating number of sworn enemies. It was not just to fish. I went to dream. One feels the need to dream most strongly when reduced to one's basest state. And across the oceans I would sometimes see you, my father; the estates I would inherit; how you would take me by the hand and say with tears in your eyes that all that was yours was mine.

There was always solace in the crashing of the sea during these months. The noise was therapeutic to me. I took pebbles of various sizes, and seeds, and hollowed-out gourds that grew in secret places I had discovered. Once dried the gourd shell emitted a sharp reverberating when struck, like a woodpecker on a tree, and when I inserted combinations of pebbles and seeds it was like a chorus of woodpeckers. But it was the sound of the ocean hitting the beach that I developed a desire to recreate with these rattles. For this it was clear I required different grades of both seeds and stones. The seeds would act as the mounting hiss of approaching waves. The shaking of stones would be the waves hitting, breaking, and dragging back. Mud helped. It muffled the acuteness of the other components when they shook and blended the overall sound of the instrument into a fluid melody. Preparation was the key. If I hollowed a gourd too eagerly, or dried one too thoroughly, the shaking sound was brittle on the ears. Leave too much of the softer flesh in the shell during drying and the game was up: you might shake the thing with the sharpest stones and hear but a dull thud. Adding a handle gave critical leverage, so my models soon had them too.

I arranged my wares in order of sound precision. In England there were knaves in travelling shows who demanded a penny to let gullible fools listen to the sound of the sea in a shell, and it was unquestionable I had already eclipsed their paltry services with these gourd rattles. I reckoned I could charge a groat for *my* sound of the sea, and still have crowds queuing, particularly in inland areas.

Thus motivated I began to play on the gourds several times daily: before going hunting, before eating, and once to celebrate sunrise, which was when I always entertained the possibility of an English sail appearing on the horizon. But this was little beyond a fantasy. In reality I never really expected to be anywhere else again.

* * *

There was a boy behind me. After so many days of concealment it was strange to see another human being observing me so keenly and I was instantly defensive. In truth I was just returned with my morning's fish and supply of a pear-shaped seed I was eager to try out in my gourds; his timing was incredibly inconvenient. He was placid enough, so I guessed him to be of the *tamoyes*. The war-like nature of the *tomomynos* affected the appearance of even their young, and they made warriors of their children as soon as they could hold a bow and arrow. This one was maybe eleven or twelve but did yet not have the pierced lip the *tamoyes* gave their sons around this age. His gaze was impudent, although *tamoyes* also adopted a similar expression when worshipping their Gods so the look could, I own, have been reverence.

I picked the most recently finished gourd and began to play. I captured the cadence of both approaching and breaking waves more astutely that session than I ever had previously, and when I augmented this with some low, intense tapping on a makeshift drum I had fashioned from stretching lizard hide over a hollowed circle of wood, it was evident I had him transfixed.

"A*iba*," I said. The sea. "Is that not the exact sound of the sea?" It was as if my words had broken a spell I had over him.

"*Y kûá*." The boy gawped and, with a look of terror, fled.

Y kûá – ha – the shore! He had compared my playing to the sound of the sea hitting shore!

The boy came back next day. By this time I had experimented with the pear-shaped seeds and had a new gourd filled with five or six of the things, along with some far smaller seeds and several shells. The sea sounds like this far out – vrsh-vrrrrsssshhhh – and seeds and shells can quite easily mimic that in the hands of a talented shaker. Yet despite the breaking waves having been my most constant companion these many months I was undecided on whether they were more a 'cush' or a 'kra-rrrrk'. With the pear-shaped seeds I knew I had come closest to getting it right. You started with soft shakes and then, eighth or ninth time around, flicked your wrists a little more. The seeds and shells continued the undertones of approaching waves. But the sharp impact of the pear-shaped seeds against the gourd grew out of that sound and into the very essence of storm-induced white horses; welling as white horses welled and with the same malevolence, crashing – as if reminding those at sea they would have to fight if they wanted to land and those who were marooned that they must strive, strive, strive again if they entertained any hope of escape.

"Ma-rahhh!" the boy cried, as I finished playing. "Ma-rahh, ma-ra"hhh!"

And that was it! Not a cush or a kra-rrrrk but a "ma-rahhh!"

I would have lifted the boy above my shoulders with a whoop but I remembered where I was and what I was just in time. It was gentle perseverance that had won the French and Dutch traders the trust of these tribes and I was not about to blow that away like a brutish Portugal. I invited him to sit at my fire instead; making it clear I wished to talk with him. He was reticent, but I soon saw this was because he was embarrassed. He was hiding something from me. I entreated him to hold out his hands and there on his spread palms was a rattle, fashioned from a small gourd.

"Ma-rrrrah," he mumbled, sheepishly. "Ma-rrrah y kûá."

I initially believed he had made it himself since yesterday, but it appeared his people had many such rattles. Indeed, they had made them for generations for use in rituals and yet this boy looked up to mine as the superior instruments. It was true his rattle was of rudimentary quality: it looked likely to disintegrate after a vigorous shake.

"Do not be disheartened," I told him. "Here, I give you my finest Ma-rrrah y kûá. Take it to your people."

The boy declined.

"Take it. It is a gift."

"*Abápe endé?*" Who are you? And the questions continued in a rush, as if he was angry he had not thought of them before: "what is your tribe?", "who is your leader?" and "why are you here?"

"I have no leader. I am my own man. As to why I am here, tell your people I desire to trade."

He fixed me with his intent look again and although I was tall and white and he small and swarthy, I from a land of cathedrals and he from a land of huts, there was not so very much separating us at that moment. We both had animal hides for clothes, we both had a passion for rattles that could recreate the sound of the sea, and we both had to make it, against the odds, in this damnable yet beguiling Brazil.

At first light four lusty naked men appeared at my cave mouth, with animal markings on their faces and feathers more brilliant than any jungle bird I had yet glimpsed on their heads. More to the point, they were armed with spears, bows and arrows, and looked strong. The little trickster has betrayed me, I thought, and chastised myself for not having envisioned a scenario where Ubi got the *tamoyes* to send men to kill me. Then, scurrying through the forest behind, came a clutch more of them dumping in my clearing a fresh-roasted pig, a mountain of cassava and baskets laden with berries. Mmm. Offerings. The four with the feathers took the liberty of squatting around the embers of my fire. One took a wooden pipe as long as a man's forearm packed with green weeds, lit one end and handed it to me.

"Tobacco," he smiled.

I inhaled. Comparing what I smoked that morning with what

Rodrigo had given me on Plymouth dock was like comparing a lion with a lamb.

"Good," I replied in Tupi, which initially confused them, then made them chuckle.

"We need twenty," said the one who had handed me the pipe, pointing at my gourd rattles. "Twenty Ma-rrrah y kûá."

"You shall have them!" I saw the others were not taking such deep inhalations as me. I blinked. My father kept denying me; Thomas Cavendish had denied me; it seemed the Governor and his son may well have denied me too: everyone, in short, save these naked feathered men. I wondered what other herbs were mixed in with that tobacco, for the four *tamoyes* had become about twice their original size, sprouting wings like parrots and faces like bears. They flew around me, looping and crisscrossing then soaring off through the treetops. Other shapes coiled out of nowhere: trees that stooped down, picked me up in their branches and catapulted me into the stars; rivers that turned into treasure; animals that spoke to me. I knew that I was still squatting outside my cave but I knew too that I was travelling the universe and seeing all that had ever been created or could be created. They had given me what they ingest to commune with their Gods, I realised; this is how it is to be a God!

The four *tamoyes* were gone, but I was back; enough, at least, to know I must begin. That day I hollowed gourds, and dried gourds, and sealed them with mud and decorated them with dyes like I never would again. As for the seeds and stones I selected for the beat, the like was never witnessed in that forest before. It was as if I had been born to do this. By dusk that day, I had outdone even myself, and twenty Ma-rrrah y kûá coated in the decadent hues of Brazil – the pink of brasilwood, the purple of acai, the mottled yellow of jungle clay and the green of the Great Fern – lay before me.

Trade flourished. Roast meat arrived at my cave regularly. The *tamoyes* knew a few things about seasoning: they coated their meat in a yellowish, gingery root called *guizador*, and sprinkled a powder as fiery as my betrothed's hair in their marinades. The meat came with diversely coloured fruits, and unleavened breads that crumbled wonderfully in your mouth, and pitcher upon pitcher of a brew of fermented cassava which was a veritable ambrosia to these people, and very much venerated.

Their offerings to me were clearly the best they had and yet no attempt was made to further incorporate me into their community. I was never invited to their village, wherever that was; they sent people to see me on business alone. However I often glanced beyond the clearing in front of my cave and heard whispers, or saw branches quivering, as if there was always someone watching me. And so even if I grew as close to contentment as I ever could, with the *tamoyes* looking up to me and my belly always full, in the core of my soul there was the old feeling that rooted itself whenever something good happened to me: the feeling that it could not last.

My one true friend was Ubi, the boy who had first watched me playing my rattles. I soon believed he preferred my company to his own kin. We fished together, we ate together, I improved my Tupi with him and taught him some of the English language in return. His name meant "lord of the woods" in his tongue and I asked him what mine would be. He hesitated, then told me: 'Jaci'; the moon, because I was white and powerful but also gentle, because he had thought me bad, at first, but knew now that I was good. He wanted to know what the jungle was like in my land and I told him we had only woods, albeit beautiful ones, and of course I thought of you, Kathy, and our walks there. He asked about my family and wives too, but on that score I said little. Up in the air, Kathy, is how I would have described it. I recall you saying you would not wait for me and I could never fathom whether you were joking, or if you really would make a cuckold of me with the bailiff's son from Crudswell.

It was a dark time for the *tamoyes* on the island, Ubi said. They were grossly outnumbered by the *tomomynos*, who had massacred more of them than was normal these last few moons. Moreover the *tomomynos* were constantly persuading the Portugals to join them in cleansing the island of *tamoyes* for good. I asked him if the *tamoyes* had no other lands to which they might go and he said yes, he thought so, but they were far away in the interior, and the way there was long and perilous.

One afternoon we were playing *peteca*, a game the *tamoyes* had great love for. The idea was to hit a ball bedecked in feathers over a creeper raised to about one and a half times the height of a man above the ground. Ubi adored *peteca* and hit aggressively. I saw no reason to dominate our rallies for I did not want him returning to his people discontented in defeat, but on this particular occasion he told me everyone in his village was aware he had beaten me and that this had caused much hilarity. Therefore on this afternoon I was trying my utmost. The winner was the first to ten points – a point being determined by hitting the ball into your opponent's court in such a manner as it could not be returned – and I was scurrying back across the clearing we were playing in with the entirety of my being devoted to returning Ubi's fierce shot. My heel caught a root and I sprawled backwards, landing stunned having struck my head on a stump.

The world spun, and when it settled there was a girl's face, regarding me from a few inches away.

"I have come for my brother."

I had not been at such close quarters to a woman in some time and to suddenly be addressed by such a comely one made me – well, in fairness I was still in a daze – struggle to find words to respond.

"Ubirajara!" she called urgently. And then, to me in passable Portugal: "I am sorry. It is time."

She had more hair than I ever saw on another human being; it cascaded down the entire top half of her body so that her breasts and belly button, although otherwise uncovered, were hidden. It had the quality of the hair in the paintings the Italian masters are now doing; it had the timelessness of a nymph or a muse or a Venus; it flowed beyond her into her surroundings. I still did not move. I exalted in not moving; the tops of the trees in my clearing and the lurid sky itself were flecked with her ubiquitous hair. Several strands went in my mouth but I fought the urge to cough for that would have compromised the moment.

"Why do you stare at me?" She glanced at me coyly. This stretched the markings on her face, which were the red of annatto seed paste rather than the red of human blood the *tomomynos* favoured, and in lines like a cat's whiskers. Unlike the markings of the menfolk of her tribe these were less obtrusive. They made her face seem kind. I decided she was kind; it could also no longer be denied she was arrestingly beautiful. And I had been long starved of kindness or beauty.

"I..." To trace the maze of your tresses, I wished to say, to swim in the green of your eyes. "I may be experiencing concussion."

"Con-cussion?" She frowned.

"Forgive me. When you get a blow to your head and cannot think coherently."

She gave me a severe look.

"When we *tamoyes* give a blow, or receive one, it is to kill or be killed."

I sat up.

"Then, lady, I count myself fortunate to be your people's friend."

"I should not be here." She frowned again. "It is not done for a woman to associate with a God."

"A God?" I laughed, secretly pleased. "Come, I am no God."

"A God will never admit he is a God." She hesitated, as if unwilling to divulge something which might be a burden to me. "Now Ubirajara must come with me and never return."

"I do not want to leave!" Ubi protested. "I like it here with the Englishman!"

"'Never', lady, is a strong word. Your brother likes my company as you see and I have become attached to him. And in the making of the Ma-rrrah y kûá he is useful to me. Why not let him return?"

"Ubirajara must become a man." She levelled her eyes at me from under her brow; they were as green and dancing as the jungle night. "It is a time of crisis for us. His tribe needs him. He must protect us from the *tomomynos* who would eat us and the white men with the big beards who would kill us all then not even eat us."

"Why do you not leave this place?" I seized her hand in both of mine despite myself and she pulled back, although I could tell she did not find my touch disagreeable. "Why do your people not go to join the rest of the *tamoyes* in the interior? I would gladly go with you," I added in a rush. "Would you not let me come, as your people's friend and guardian?"

"I advise you to look after yourself." She smiled a sad smile. "There is talk amongst our elders about whether you are a God or not."

"I told you already that I am not."

"If you are not a God," she said, "they will almost certainly want to eat you."

She had taken Ubi's hand and was leading him away as fast as she could drag him. He was resisting: "No, Katawa!"

And thus, by fortune, I learned the name that would one day save me – no, far more than save me – elevate me.

"The trees!" I called. "I have seen them moving; I have had them whispering. Was it your people, watching me?"

"Farewell, maker of the Ma-rrrah y kûá."

So they thought they could spy on me, did they? They thought they could stand concealed in the trees waiting for me to exhibit some *fallibility*; something ungodly in my behaviour? I heard the chattering beyond the fringe of the clearing more than before; I imagined my cave compromised: was there not wood on the fire I had not placed there; was my stash of sailor's things – my journal, which I had kept concealed from the factor at the *engenho*, and my few réis – not tampered with? I would show them. I stripped away my hide and rolled in the dust. Paints stick better to a rough service. And with the green of the Great Fern and the yellow of jungle clay and the purple of acai and the pink of brasilwood, with all the gaudy hues with which I had decorated my rattles, in a mélange of colour never before beheld by Indians I decorated myself. And seizing my bow and arrow I ran from that clearing and must have run for hours. Fleet-footed as a deer I ran and no movement – not the chirrup of a poison frog or the auburn flash of a tamarin – eluded me. My arrows found them all and I returned to my cave with a jaguar and a brace of lizards and a long-tongued kinkajou and a toucan. I stoked the fire high. I skinned those animals and adorned their skins, except for the toucan whose feathers I arranged in my hair. I took my two favourite rattles and started to shake them and the sound of the sea emulated from them. I danced, round and around, and if that does not sound like me Kathy it was because I was not me; it was not that I had lost that modicum of reserve that becomes a Gentlemen but there was no place for it here; I was a new version of myself; I was pulsating with the Thing. And I bayed. An unchained sound. Louder yet than the wailing of the *tomomynos* as they cooked their victims. I showed them that night that I could be a God; the God of the Ma-rrrah y kûá.

Kat-a-wa, I thought as I collapsed, spent, hours later as night subsided into dawn. It would occupy three out of ten syllables in a line of a sonnet.

TWENTY

The rattles were broken. I saw that first. My camp was a sea of squashed gourds. I crawled out of my cave and was set upon immediately; some fellows kicked me quite brutally and sent me sprawling before a pair of slashed escaffignons with fancy mauve ribbons, Venetian hose, a doublet with butterfly piccadills and a capotain hat festooned with a peacock's feather.

"You must have known we would come for you sooner or later," said Martin de Sá. "My father has been asking after you."

* * *

Salvador Correia de Sá ushered me in directly that afternoon.

"My son! I rue the day I let you out of my sight." He embraced me in that peculiar Portugal fashion and despite smelling like the sour end of a pig after my stint in the wilderness I judged it prudent to embrace him back. "My son and heir told me of the low condition to which you have sunk. Living with savages? Painting yourself? Going... naked?" It was evidently disgusting to him even to utter that last word.

"I traded with Indians, master, true: in order to survive." I skirted the issues of painting and nakedness. "In fact I found the *tamoyes* your current enemies most agreeable... there is potential for you to forge peace with them, and save your colony from much bloodshed."

I was risking much by admitting to association with sworn foes of the Portugals but I saw too that I must demonstrate my usefulness to the Governor if I wanted any future in this Brazil.

"Peace." Salvador Correia de Sá swilled the word around his mouth. "The *tamoyes* have killed more Portugals since I have been in the Governorship than any other savages."

"Portugals have killed more of them than any other tribe too, master," I observed.

His frown carved his entire forehead.

"Moreover they are sworn enemies of the *tomomynos*, who are our allies."

"Perhaps, master, with a negotiator..."

The double doors to the assembly rooms swung open. Anchieta, that glum monk I had already had the displeasure of meeting, hobbled in, coughing profusely.

"Anchieta, back from the interior! How did you fare converting those lost souls? You must remember Anthony Knivet."

Anchieta snorted exactly as I would have liked to react to his entrance, and took his customary seat like a cacodemon on the periphery of my master's vision; his good deeds did not fool me for I knew he had been instrumental in having me sent to the sugar mill. My prowess with languages threatened him. *Mi habilidad con los idiomas lo amenazó.* Ha! M*es compétences avec les langues l'a menace.*

"I had twenty *wayanasses* this very morning sitting about me like lambs uttering the Lord's Prayer," cawed Anchieta.

"I begged Anchieta to come out of retirement," explained de Sá. "A nation needs a unified religion, my son, and Anchieta is my most effective tool in this. He uses no violence; no bribery. Savages come to him of their own will."

Just a few good old-fashioned Catholic lies, I thought, and he has a flock.

"The *wayanasses* are your allies already. Try converting the *pories* who inhabit to the west or the *tamoyes* in the interior and you might find them less receptive. With my own considerable experience of their tongue I have found the Indians wholly open to negotiation, provided it is done on civil terms. Trade with them; treat them as men. Padre Anchieta's approach – bawling God's words until they acquiesce – is precarious."

"Padre Anchieta's approach has been proven over more decades than you have lived in total, my son," the Governor said sharply.

"Exactly what, de Sá, is your purpose with this Englishman?" Anchieta's lip trembled.

"I speak only as I find," I said.

"Leave us a while, would you Anchieta?"

"The world," said the Governor as the monk, grumbling about his poor bones being unnecessarily tested, departed, "is run by old men who are rigid in their ways. Anchieta has known Brazil since the early days. He sees conversion to Catholicism here as non-negotiable, with which I concur. He sees himself as the best vehicle to do this, which he is, and yet..." his hands wrung together "...old men must hand the baton to the young, and young men have ideas. My son - by which of course I mean my son and heir - speaks to me of changes that need to be made, of increasing our mining efforts like the Spaniards and further fortifying our coast. It is a position shared by De Sousa[1] to whose authority I must ultimately bow. But I do not apologise for believing in sanctity."

He looked at me and saw, what, my youthful curls of fair hair, my chancer's grey eyes, the lines of determination I noticed were always there now whenever I caught my reflection. He must have seen others like me in his time yet he chose me to confide in, and

---

[1] Dom Francisco de Sousa, seventh Governor-General of Brazil. The position of Governor-General was the foremost in the colony, with the Governors of the captaincies immediately below this.

I like to think what he saw in me were values, values in a land where values got cast by the wayside. "My son and heir thinks I believe in sanctity too much - to the detriment of our country."

It was a question – I knew.

"In my brief acquaintance with your son I have found him to be a man of grand ideas." I hoped that might be enough but he urged me on. "One who appears almost... impatient to achieve everything today, rather than tomorrow."

The Governor's hair was oiled back so that every iota of sternness in his brow was visible. He inclined his head, as if I had condoned the fervency with which he ruled, when all I had done was imply I could be a better son to him than the one he had by blood - and a better heir too.

"Thank you my son. I know I rule with a firm hand. That is necessary, in these turbulent times. But never let it be said I am not benevolent when benevolence is warranted. Sending you to my *engenho* was an overreaction and therefore I forgive you your association with the *tamoyes* and the heathen lifestyle you have led of late. Come. Let us forget the past and embrace, and find you more fitting employment."

The second-most powerful man in Brazil wanted to hug me again and I could hardly refuse. But I did not erase my months in the wilderness from my mind. It was the last thing I wished to do.

"And tell me truthfully, my son, before Anchieta returns. Am I wrong to prioritise religion? Should I concentrate more on mineral extraction and fortification, as my son urges?"

"Churches," I said, "are built with jewels of the earth and plunder from the seas. But you do not require miners or fortifiers for this, master. You need a born treasure seeker and privateer. And in both respects I would be happy to volunteer my services."

* * *

After that I was sent to the Governor's *engenho* again. My master emphasised this was a temporary measure, and different to before as I would be in command of the sugar boat that ferried supplies, a position superior to supervisor in many respects for there was but one boat. But the factor used me worse than ever. He persisted in calling me by the third person or, worse yet, number thirty-one, which was the number I had as a slave. Although he now knew he would be unwise to lay a finger upon me he nevertheless goaded me, abusing me with words. He would even blame me for the most preposterous things such as, on one occasion, the lack of copper for the kettles in the boiling house. During these most trying of trials, I handled myself – and my temper – admirably. I even proposed he should consider developing relations with the Swedes for I knew them to have lucrative copper mines and – check the history books if you will – Brazil would proceed to forge ties with that very nation.

It was the year the world's greatest scribe died; 1593; I heard the news from a stuttering French trader who could not utter a fluid sentence unless he was quoting passages from Chrétien de Troyes, which he could do most evocatively. Another autumn – which was spring, of course, in this upside-down place – had passed me by without fortune and I was exactly where I had been the previous September: in the filthy mire of the *massape* of Brazil's most notorious sugar plantation at the mercy of the factor, Brazil's most odious man.

Often it was my lot to transport slaves out to the *massape* for the same day's labours I had once undergone. The faces were new, due to the high turnover brought about by death. But I spied one brawny figure I recognised.

"Quarasips!" I got him alone.

"Well, if that don't be Anthony Knivet, God strike me down!"

"God will not strike you, for it is me."

"What did I tell you, yah? Things go in circles. Here you are again. A man try to get out and make something of himself, and

Brazil she bring him right back down."

"You were a true friend to me before, Quarasips. I swear I will get us both out of here."

"Yah? Where, Anthony Knivet? Your fine house in England, or the moon?"

"Do not be disheartened. I know the answer now. The answer is not the coast. There are too many Portugals and too much trouble. We have to make it to the interior; to your people, Quarasips."

In my mind was a vast clearing, like where I had lived in the cave only bigger and surrounded by thicker trees through which no Portugal could pass. I reclined there in a head dress of feathers bright as a rainbow, and there were gold necklaces around my neck, and *tamoyes* fed me roast hog ready-cut in mouth-sized morsels, and...

"I cut me some cane, some more cane grow. We'd die in the interior, Anthony Knivet, just like we'll die here. It just a question of what come first, yah."

I cut me some cane, some more cane grow. Quarasips Juca did not speak much, but the words he did say were weighty. It might seem to you, Kathy, that I really did not have so very tough a time, stuck as you are in England's mud whilst I gallivant about the tropics. But the coconuts and naked damsels (poor things) and the young men that return with their thousands made from sugar or spice or silver or somesuch – all those stories that filter back from Brazil to Plymouth and Plymouth to Charlton about life here, becoming more fantastical each league they travel – they represent a fraction of what the reality is. For most it is drudgery. It is the stink of the swamp, it is the sting of the factor's whip, it is the few hours of sleep you can fight for in the fetid night before it all begins again. And you would roll your eyes at me, for you never much cared for literature, but the star in the sky of scribes was dead, Marlowe was dead, and a little bit more of the little meaning that was left was gone. But on I toiled, Faustus of the forest. I cut me some cane, some more cane grow.

I daresay these words will reach England before I do. And if we can trust in the reliability of our coachmen, which we should be able to do at least as much as I can trust the storms of the Straits or the rapids of jungle rivers or the whims of my master Salvador Correia de Sá to deliver me to where I am destined to go, then they should reach you, Kathy, in Charlton. However many other pages of it you use on the fire, be sure to find a pretext to communicate this next part to my father. I believe he has a soft spot for you. Well, you are my betrothed, and the apothecary's daughter – and even the mighty need cures. Take him that balm for the leg that he lacks, and stop by my mother's house for some comfrey pies, and say that you have news of me. And if at first he shows disinterest, persist, and tell him this: that opportunity to journey into the interior came sooner than I expected. *He* sent for me. The son of the Governor of the principal captaincy in Brazil sent for me. He had a mission upon which the future of the nation depended, he said, and only I could be trusted with it.

TWENTY-ONE

*"This Caniball came through the house where
I was, with a woodden sword, in his hand,
and as hee came hee spake very loud, and
looked as though hee had beene mad, striking
his hand on his breast, and on his thighs...
After this... he stroke me on the head, and bad
mee welcome."*

Anthony Knivet, *Admirable Adventures and Strange Fortunes*

"The problem," cried Martin de Sá above the rush of the river
and the grunts of the *wayanasses* rowing us, "is that our slaves are
dying, ha ha, faster than we can replace them. The towns we once
traded with are empty of men and the women are only good on
the *engenhos* for fucking and sheaf-bending."

I coloured; I had been a sheaf-bender.

"What we need is daring, Anthony Knivet. We need to voyage
further into the interior to where the savages called *pories* live.
You will take hatchets, and knives – those savages are obsessed
with metal. In return we need fifty young men. Pick them ripe:
twelve up to about twenty-five. Over that age, they succumb to
disease."

I knew it was not just the Portugals who did it; Spaniards had started it even earlier. England was getting better at it and Dutchmen would do it more if they could. And of course slavery was as old as civilisation, but what the Iberian Union excelled at was trapping the most exotic peoples to use most brutally for their own ends. There is something particularly poignant in that: the caged bird is sadder to behold than the caged rodent. I often thought during my time at the sugar mill about my brothers – Angolans who had been kings or Indians who had been tribal chiefs – being the captives of dogs who were, likely as not, the rejects of their own kingdom. Perhaps only one who has been caged as long as me sees the tragedy of that; how the beautiful is locked up by the horrible; how the good ones are locked up by villains.

"Do not worry," said Martin de Sá. "They were once friendly with us, and we believe they can be won over with luck... although," he laughed gaily, "things could equally turn ugly."

It was an arduous journey upriver. We passed the furthest trading outposts; the river narrowed; the *wayanasses* strained at the oars to keep us battling against the mounting current and I had to help them when they tired.

"We go to their town," said Marin de Sá. "After that you are on your own. The town of the *pories* is several days beyond that. None of us can remember how many. It is years since any Portugal went there."

"Do they eat people; these p*ories*?"

"Do boats float?" he laughed.

"And what do I get in return?"

He looked at me thoughtfully, grasping his chin and tapping his nose with his index finger.

"How about one of them? One of the slaves you catch for me, for your own."

I was not sure I would like that, but a slave did give you status. Martin de Sá had an entourage of ten and even Portugals like

Manoel or the factor had two or three. Besides, I could choose to treat my slave as my brother once he was mine.

"We Englishmen," I offered him my hand, "have never feared to tread where others will not."

We began to pass tribesmen in other vessels that the *wayanasses* in our canoe hailed as their own. These men were squat like our *wayanasses* but more formidable to behold, being painted in ochre and with their hair long and wild at the sides but shaved on top like Franciscan friars. This rendered their already ugly appearance still uglier, and yet these short, fat, naked, ochre-painted people stared at us white men like we were the strange-looking ones. Even the normally exuberant Martin de Sá grew quiet as we drew near the town, and I guess this was because he saw how we were outnumbered, and how things could turn badly quickly.

"Are you married, Anthony Knivet?"

"I am not."

"You should marry. Those who do not marry here are spurred on to greater and greater heights until they do not know where the edge is, and then they fall."

"And you, *senhor*? Do you have a wife?"

"I keep two women. My father reprimands me, of course, but I need both. My sweet, meek Maria, my wife, and my wild Lourdes... she is Indian and has few inhibitions, unlike our corseted ladies of Europe..." he lamented. "You might call them my good side and my bad side. I am a white man, but I have a black side to me too. I let it run away with me sometimes." He emitted a curious abrupt laugh. "When I grow bored of being good."

I pondered which could be bigger: the black side of the white man, or the white side of the Indian. I asked the *wayanasses* sitting in front of me for a wad of their tobacco, and chewed it. It tasted green; damnably green.

At the last trading post Martin de Sá turned back. I was given eight *wayanasses* for guides, although they were limited use as they had ventured little nearer to the town of the *pories* than the Portugals and only then by mistake. Two years in Brazil, and I had never been so far inland. The interior smelt thicker, sweeter, richer. But it was a smell that choked you too, if you inhaled too deeply.

We paddled up a tributary so narrow branches brushed us either side and the *wayanasses* gave whimpering intonations to their deities for safe passage. This worked better than any Christian prayer I have heard for despite us traversing terrain replete with man-eaters in both the human and animal forms we arrived without incident several days later in the domain of the *pories*. As we neared the village a naked adolescent boy with remarkably smooth skin came to me and informed me that I was expected. We had approached like church mice in our vessel and yet these *pories* had been acquainted with our every move.

Their chief settlement was scattered haphazardly above some swamp where the forest had thinned; it was as if their huts had been built on the first available space for some were big and blocked the light of the others whilst some hogged the riverside and deprived the rest of access. I was ushered to the principle dwelling and bidden to lie on a swinging net and wait, which I was loathe to do as, being in a land of unpredictable, cannibalistic Indians, I felt a little tense. But I did not wait long. Many women painted in ochre, blue, black and green presently entered; each was as naked as Katawa, the *tamoyes* lady I had encountered, but none had her modesty or grace and they danced before me, wailing and offering me either their hair to stroke or their breasts to hold. But if I had consented I would for sure have done it wrong; I could imagine their tinkles of laughter and my mortification. I determined to lie still until they were done but this was difficult: they pulled at my new clothes given me by the Governor's son as if they desired them or desired to see me without them. When these seductresses had spent some time performing for my pleasure they realised I would not show favour to any one of them. They withdrew to one end of the dwelling and another, clearly more senior figure entered. The latest arrival was an old man, but a sprightly one. He danced before me a while, a blur of red and black, twisting his body in precarious positions for one of such advanced years and striking his hand on his chest in imitation of a drum; a ceremony I knew by now to be the customary introduction the menfolk of these tribes gave to strangers. Then he produced a short wooden sword and with an action similar to how the Queen knights a gentleman, he tapped me with his blade on each shoulder, then the forehead.

"Welcome!" he cried. "Yet why do you refuse my gift – these same fine ladies – to you?"

"I am an Englishman and it is not our custom to take women outside of our own country. I desire to make you rich, not to take your women."

The old man found this amusing. He had never in all his long life known a white man refuse a girl when she was offered to him. I told him many of my kind were weak but that I was strong and that he should know that regardless of anything else that might come to pass. He nodded craftily; clicking his fingers and summoning the most buxom of the dancing seductresses to serve me with food. This blue-painted lady fed me fruits direct into my mouth and ran her hands lingeringly across my body; her extraordinary nipples adorned with glowing stones were never further than a hand's breadth from my lips. Yet I held out; the old man perceived I could not be compromised, and the woman retreated. I had passed the first test of the slave trader: never to accept the first offer that was made.

We squatted down together. He bid me be at ease for his people were not cannibals; they had other ways to show their greatness than by eating each other and besides, he had tried human flesh and found it disagreeable to the digestion.

"I am King of the *pories*," he told me. "People fear us because of our wealth. We are mightier than other tribes because our lands sparkle with jewels. We have more than we can adorn ourselves with." He indicated the green stones that pierced his cheeks, so heavy they slurred his speech, and those on the breasts of the women. "I have never told a stranger about our riches, for the Portugals that came thought our village was simple and that we were poor. Yet I will share with you where these riches lie. And let us hope you have something I desire in return, white man!"

That next night was a wild festival. The whole day, the *pories* women chewed cassava root in their mouths, then spat the juice into ornamental urns, whereupon it fermented and served us for drink. This cassava brew was strong, and I took plenty. Again many women danced up to me, Kathy, but I resisted. The fire of the brew played havoc with my senses and perhaps I fell asleep because I dreamed, or at least became entangled in a memory that had the hazy quality of a dream and the bite of reality all at once.

It was the first time I entered your father's shop. The only natural light came from grills high above the over-piled shelves; it sent surreal shadows careening around the room. It looked how an apothecary's should perhaps look: slightly not of this world. I walked towards the counter; the castrated boar and the scent sacs of beaver; jars of leeches for bloodletting and vials of mercury for venereal complaints, crumbled cayenne for wound swabbing and heaps of hops for curing worms. Your bodice was not done up right. I saw that even in the darkness.

"My mother sent me."

"Then you did not come of your own will?"

"We are promised to each other."

"You make it sound like a death warrant."

"It is what our families want."

"And what is it you want? Do you want me Anthony? I should hate to be betrothed to a man who did not want me."

"I do not know..." I began. "Who is that?"

That is when I first saw Stephen, which you pronounced 'Stephan', buttoning up his doublet speedily and looking flushed. 'One of our suppliers' was how you introduced him, hardly able to contain your laughter.

The rest of my sentence, Kathy, would have been that I did

not know how to take you, even if I did want you. I was never myself with you. You never allowed me to be myself. Stephan changed a few times, did he not? He was the only one I saw but I bet there were others you could not resist; others with fancier clothes and more debonair airs; men who were born into their father's professions and were obliged only to think of life's pleasures, without a thought of its pains.

I was back in my hammock and the finest young warrior of the *pories* had invited himself into my quarters. He was armed and very angry. Of course I had to endure his showmanship before I could ascertain what was vexing him; he danced before me very prettily using two of the women that had entertained me the day before as part of his act. With a hand on each of their necks he wove in and out of them; they were painted blue and he was a brilliant scarlet and the spectacle would have been entertaining had it not become apparent he wanted to kill me.

"Do you see these women, fiend? You rejected them when they offered themselves to you. By my valour I got their loves; now their desire I am sworn to fulfil, which is to avenge the humiliation you caused them and see you killed as I have killed many more." He made a demonstrative swipe at his head in the way we in more civilised lands top boiled eggs, and it required little imagination to get his meaning.

My right hand trembled to teach him some manners but I held back; these days I was a diplomat and knew the value of adhering to diplomacy. And if there was to be a scuffle, I needed more time to recover from that night's intoxication.

"I come not as an enemy, but as your friend who brings you many things I am assured you want."

"What things?" he demanded. "For I have watched the King treat you like one of his own and we have seen nothing for it."

Villain, I thought. There are better Indians than you not so many leagues distant who view me as a God!

"Blades of the finest metal that you can cut with and kill with as you see fit."

This made him pause as I had guessed it might.

"What do you desire in return?"

I could hardly tell him my business before discussing it with the King and told him so.

"Liar! You come to sell our people to the Portugals!" He sprang to where I had stashed my possessions and began handing out my trading goods to his concubines. "Here is what you think we are worth; these few knives. What were your orders, fiend, one of us for each blade?"

I hated Martin de Sá then for forcing me to stand against my friends the Indians; my only true friends in Brazil save Quarasips Juca who was half Indian anyway and Barrawell who might have been dead for all I knew. But I did not like this man capering threateningly before me either; I did not need it after the quantity of cassava brew I had drunk. I hauled myself up; commanding him to stay away. As soon as I was on my feet he ran at me and the force of the lunge knocked me right back onto the hammock. My head ached and the room swam, but I was damned if I would let this upstart believe it was because of his fisticuffs.

"If nothing will satisfy you but my life, take it if you are able. But know your whole tribe will pay for it."

This angered him and you must never use your anger in a fight unless you know how to channel it; when he attacked me again he was thinking of strength not accuracy and I turned so that his blow inconvenienced him more than me. As he shook from the pain I smote him on the jaw with the flat of my sword; he tumbled back into the arms of his heckling concubines.

"I would wager," I breathed, "that I have had more attempts on my life than you have scalps. Have you looked your own death in the face yet, villain, eh? I thought not!" He looked utterly baffled; wiped the blood from his nose and barked at one of the women who supplied him with a small dagger. He came at me a third time. We sparred and he was firmer in his thrusts, but the greatest warrior of the pories was sweating; a torrent was pouring over his shiny pate and I waited for him to blink it away then made my move. At the very moment I brought him to his knees it was my good fortune that the King, alerted by the commotion, came in.

It could have gone either way. I hastened to get my word in before my assailant could draw breath. But I need not have worried. The brave warrior was still spitting blood and must have had a brain still feebler than his body for he could not construct a tale to save himself.

"You insult me on two counts," said the King, coldly. "You do me the discredit of meddling with a friend of mine, and the greater discredit of failing to kill him when that was what your empty mouth boasted you would do. You are not fit to represent me on the battlefield, and if you were anyone other than my foremost warrior I would see you killed for your treachery. As matters stand I will give you a fate far worse: banishment from my lands with return at your peril, and the knowledge that this white man now takes your place at my side."

As events transpired, it was far worse for everyone. The disgraced warrior, whose name was Waynembuth, used his exile to rally neighbouring peoples against the King and myself and the rest of the *pories*. So we all went to war.

Near the village was an area of swampy open ground; nearly all battles were fought here as it was the one place where there was ample room to swing a sword. Doing the utmost to brave my throbbing headache, I went at the right hand of the King. Leading an army was an honour, I did see that, but it did also expose you to an intimidating array of weaponry, and as we readied to ride out I made a calculation of how many lives I had used up thus far in this Brazil, and how many I might have left. But when we emerged on the field our sheer numbers intimidated the men Waynembuth had raised and they craved succour of us, saying how they came in good faith to trade, and not for violent purposes. As a token of their intent they presented me with toucan feathers; I put one in my hair and it suited me very well. The King invited them to his village for a great festival, greater even than the one he had held two days previous, but instructed me to do with Waynembuth as I saw fit.

"Come to gloat, fiend?" Waynembuth's cheeks bulged with tobacco but he did not seem enamoured with the taste. He crouched alone on the field; his allies were gone.

"I have no need. The King's favour in me speaks for itself. He is a wise man and has chosen wisely; I am his right hand man now."

"You are on top today, fiend, but tomorrow you may again be outcast. The King is fickle. You think he deigns to give you us his people as slaves because he likes your white face? He sniffs prosperity on you and when the scent is gone..." He tipped his hand one way, then the other.

"Your immediate concern is today," I said sharply, "and I consign you to worse than the death you will be wishing, on future days, that I had offered you. And that is to wander, Waynembuth: to roam without people to call your own, without ever fitting in, without purpose."

He chomped on that tobacco like a demoralised young bullock.

"Maybe, fiend, we will meet again upon the field." His eyes shone with malice.

"Your paint is thinning, Waynembuth." I repositioned the toucan feathers in my hair, and turned my back upon him.

The King was watching me attentively.

"You did not kill him."

"He will trouble us no more, sire. Death is not always the worst fate." I knelt before him, but from the corner of my eye continued observing him for perhaps it was true that the King could turn against me as quickly as he had welcomed me. Then he entreated me to rise. I was his equal, he said, and not one to bow like a servant. I thanked him for his faith in me and confided that if I had my way, I would trade with him and never with the Portugals, for again and again I saw his wisdom contrast strikingly with their ineptitude.

"Then let us drink to our friendship!" he cried.

I begged leave to postpone the toast. I was very much the worse for wear from the last instalment of his cassava brew, and needed sleep.

The alcohol of the *pories* had another use besides inebriating them. It was an effective polisher of metal. Later when I, having abstained from more drink, showed the drunken King my newly gleaming merchandise he was well pleased. He gave me seventy slaves – twenty more than Martin de Sá had imagined I could get – and 300 bowmen to get me safe passage to the first of the trading posts.

"And let me show you," said he, "why we *pories* command the interior."

We walked away from camp for several hours up a narrow tributary culminating in a steep-sided col. A slope of black earth reared above us. The King knelt and scraped back some of it. I gasped. There were flecks of gold, there again rubies and there again emeralds as fat as fists. Everything I had dreamed of attaining in Brazil was here. One domino bangs into the next and I entertained thoughts of all of it: my carriage of dodo feathers, my travelling cloak – sable or magenta would be best – and my dear father hobbling to the front door in his eagerness to see me approaching; his son. Father, Sir Francis Drake shared a jest with me; kings shared with me their fortunes and Brazil's most esteemed Governor did call me his son but I am returned to you and ready to serve you here as indeed I served you unflinchingly all the while from the other side of the world.

"And you thought Potosi was the mountain of wealth?" The King's eyes glittered and I understood there and then the relationship he kept most constant was with this hill of riches. "In Potosi they are obliged to dig for it. Here I stroke back this soil, and have more than I know what to do with."

"And the Portugals know nothing of this?" I whispered.

"Nothing."

"Perhaps we should keep it that way."

The King smiled cunningly; then he was chortling; then we

both were.

I fell to my knees, filling my pockets; I calculated the rates of exchange as they stood with the most honest merchants in the year I left England. In a half hour I had me a modest fortune and the King of the *pories* gleefully assisted me in accruing it. "Take it, white man!" He tossed me jewel upon jewel. "Take all you can!"

TWENTY-TWO

Martin de Sá was waiting at the dock as my laden boat drew into the River of January some days later.

"Anthony Knivet! I was about to send men to search for you."

"I bring you seventy slaves, *senhor*, and the compliments of the King of the *pories*, with whom we may now trade readily."

"Excellent," he beamed. "Now I must ask your advice. I have plans drawn for a school here in the city. Not just any school! I intend it to be a centre of learning, like the College of Santo Tomás the Spaniards have in Bogota. And you, Anthony Knivet," he grasped my cheeks in both hands and shook them, "shall, with your knowledge of languages, be a teacher! You shall have a paid position, and prospects!"

The scheme was a noble one but hare-brained. Bogota, as I understood, had scores of learned monks behind its university, and the River of January had but a handful of ignorant ones. Yet I elected to bide my time until a ship bound for Europe arrived in which I might hasten away with my new-found treasure, and indulge in Martin de Sá's whim. We gathered in his residence on the *Morro do Castelo*; me, a couple of priests, a stonemason and a man known to build boats but never a building that stayed in any one place. It did not seem a likely combination of individuals to create a beacon of learning in the southern hemisphere but the enthusiasm of the Governor's son was infectious. He demonstrated how the building might look when glimpsed from sea; he confided in me how he wanted the township to be great like London and Paris; great in size; great in wealth; great in culture. We talked of the architecture of Europe somewhat and whilst it was pleasant to discuss Oxford's colleges and the basilica the Emperor Constantine had built, it whetted my appetite for home, which was the only prospect I cared for. I contributed input of sufficient astuteness to stave off attracting attention, but far from Martin de Sá's project I was rather thinking of whether to risk a return trip to the *pories*. I had nothing to trade with them, for they now had more hatchets than inhabitants, yet there was several times more wealth within their lands than what I had already secreted at a cove north of the town. I decided it was too dangerous. I had the treasure now to make something of myself, and I was tired of putting my life on the line for whims.

"What did you say, Anthony Knivet?"

We were some days into the plans. Like a child that clamours for a present, Martin de Sá had got others involved in his scheme, although from the quality of the individuals recruited I would deem our fine school suitable only for teaching guile, and zealotry, and perhaps something of bloodthirsty combat.

"My slave," I repeated. "You promised me a slave of my own."

"Of course! When you return from your next trip to the interior. I needed to put those others to work. When you return next time you shall have two slaves, and you can begin your teaching post. But I must have you fetch another hundred savages, for how can we seriously consider constructing the university without them?"

Here I was, having spent weeks in hostile territories procuring slaves to fuel his *engenhos*, having helped him mould plans for his grand university and he thought he could sit there casually telling me that I was granted nothing for my pains!

"I cannot go." I rapidly thought of excuses why that must

be, for going again would mean I missed the Dutch ship I had ascertained was due in any day. "I am ill."

"Then rest! Go in a few days!" said Martin de Sá jocularly. "But I must have you as our man, Anthony Knivet, you know, ha ha, how indispensable you are to us."

"But I see nothing for it!" I cried. "Not even the slave you promised me!"

"You are forgetting who and what you are. I am the Governor's son, and you will do as I please."

But I had not forgotten who I was; nor would I ever. I was Anthony Knivet.

"If you need me so much then come and find me!" I sprung to my feet. "For I will rather deliver myself to your father, and to the *engenho* again, than jeopardise my life for you without recompense!"

Whilst everyone's mouths hung open in shock that I would speak so to the son of the Governor of the captaincy I stormed out. And wisely none there tried to stop me.

* * *

My master Salvador Correia de Sá seemed pleased with my return. He was about to take a walk, which his physician had recommended for improving his complexion. I was permitted to accompany him; imparting to him an edited version of what had passed between his son and myself and expressing my desire to remain close to him in the town as my first loyalty was to him. He was on poor terms with his son at that moment and so was contented with my having refused the junior de Sá in order to oblige the senior. When it was just us two, and Anchieta was not there to poison his character, things were good between us.

"My son, we must all get our hands dirty in this Brazil. Sugar is our lifeblood and the work to squeeze it out is not sweet."

Well-acquainted with him as I was I knew this was his apology – as close to one as a man of his noble bearing could bring himself when addressing he who served him – for sending me to the *engenho*. I readily forgave him. I always had felt closer to the Governor than to his son. If he had reared me I would not have been nearly so frivolous as his son either. Running Brazil was a serious business. It was not a place for childish whims.

"I preferred this hill by its old name," said the Governor. "The Hill of Rest. It sounded more spiritual. Nowadays we concern ourselves with fortifications" he shuddered as he said these words. "And we risk losing that which is most sacred: our faith. But what do we have to defend? What do we have to offer others? Take my staff, my son. Point out the most beautiful building you see."

We were on the ramparts of the fort of San Sebastian. Below were the other edifices that crowned the River of January, Brazil's grandest town: the assembly rooms with its six-arched entranceway, the jailhouse that could hold more prisoners than any other in the land, the hospital which could care for the sailors of an entire fleet of ships at the same time. I pointed through the lot of them at the cathedral. It was as big as several galleons under full sail. Its windows boasted coloured glass and the walls of the nave were adorned with rich stone embossings of the Stations of the Cross. From inside, its central cupola depicted angels leaping between the sun and the moon and the five planets. It was exquisite.

"A wise choice, my son. Religion *makes* civilisation. Ten years ago I watched this village become a true city. It was when the relics of the venerable Saint Sebastian came. We paraded them in a boat decorated with flowers and candles around the bay. Our guards let fly volleys of artillery and the military band a trumpet serenade. We paraded to the church with singing and dancing and everyone wept. We Portugals. The traders. The Savages. Everyone. We had a purpose then. We had something to fall back on however tough times became – united by the sweet blood of a martyr who knew faith in Jesus Christ alone could save us. Oh my son," he suddenly embraced me, "if only I could talk to Martin as I can talk to you!"

There is a reason why, Salvador Correia de Sá. I let you. I lead you on.

But I recognised there were other reasons. I appreciated his love because of his antipathy towards most. I respected his severe authority as much as I understood it would not hesitate to send me back to the *engenho* or worse should his version of justice dictate. His son drifted in and out of causes but Salvador Correia de Sá latched on to one like a leopard to a hart and held on until he grappled it to the ground. And that – I confess – struck a chord with me.

Yet his talk of Catholic virtue was repugnant to me: not for its content alone, but because I knew he would use it as a stick to beat me with if necessary. My passion could, I allow, boil over if I knew the other in the conversation was wrong. So to sycophantically smile as my master spoke about Catholicism lighting up the world required all my restraint. Why should one man in Rome govern beliefs? If English nobility supported their Queen that was to the credit of their lineage. They should not be put down because they preferred to address God directly rather than have the vassals of some Vatican misers do it for them. The good Lord was more than a little hard of hearing when you shouted right at him, so what chance did you stand if you let a fat old stranger in a cassock in Rome pray on your behalf? Catholicism epitomised what I believe in Latin they call the status quo; my master had the status quo flowing through his veins and I had the counter-current in mine. We both had to follow what we believed to be just and those paths could never be ultimately reconciled, even if they kept clashing together.

Only a few more days of the sycophantic smiles, I told myself. Because the Dutch ship was in; I had clandestinely met the captain and in return for a share he had taken on board my treasure; I was bailing out with my loot.

"Your son and heir, master, is much enthused over a different purpose. He talks of channelling the energies of the Jesuits into the field of education."

The Governor looked pained.

"His school. I gave him leave to pursue the scheme. But we do not have so many priests that we can divert them from God's work to tutor in... mathematics!"

"And history, master. And literature. And, I believe, astronomy."

"Astronomy!" The Governor's face looked thunderous. "And he has De Sousa's backing no doubt?"

It amused me how my master never called De Sousa by his true title which was Governor-General of all Brazil but went a paler shade of pale were he not addressed with his own.

"He claims so master."

"Which is why he wishes to send you for more slaves?"

"Indeed master."

"Anchieta advises me to curb our enslavement of the savages. It makes them harder to convert."

"Therein, master, lies the problem."

"My son and heir sees God as a thing he can trample through." The Governor sighed, leaning heavily on his stick. "Young men do have ideas... but you cannot trample through God."

He clapped his hand on my shoulder which I realised he was placing there because he needed the support; we strolled on, two equals, around the ramparts of the fort and below us I could make out the gangs of Indians - black specks in the green - hacking thanklessly at the *massape* in the evening shadow of Sugarloaf Mountain.

Sugar cane did look strangely beautiful when you looked upon it from above.

TWENTY-THREE

If I desired to be close to him, my master said, then close to him I should be. He needed a man to take charge of procuring fish to make oil for the *engenho*. I would be turning the cogs of Brazil, he said, and all the country would thank me for it. I found out later this was the worst job in the whole colony outside of the *engenho* itself, but I was not in this game for advancement anymore. My master did not realise this. He was a God in his kingdom and did not imagine a man could desire to do anything but strive to please him. But I did not believe in God. So I could go out at any hour of the day or night, clubbing and gutting my catch, bottling and delivering the oil, smeared in the excreta of dead fish — and I could secretly smile. My chests glimmered with enough of this colony's gold to get all Charlton sparkling, and sparkle it soon should.

But if Salvador Correia de Sá had under-estimated me I had under-estimated the drought. It had taken hold of the land. Doing my master's bidding I was engaged on an overnight fishing trip across the other side of Guanabara Bay from the River of January. It was a big trip. My master had donated several Indians for the task, and I was in charge of all of them. But when in the morning we were returning overloaded with fish, our keel stuck fast on the bed of the tributary into which we had rowed. The waters had retreated rapidly; we were stranded. There was nothing for it but to walk back around the bay and by the time I arrived at the River of January's dock the Dutch ship was gone, and with it my treasure from the land of the *pories*.

Yes, Kathy, before you is a sailor so destined for ill fortune he loses his toes from frostbite in summertime, and gets trapped by a drought in a tropical forest normally so swimming with water that the firmest ground squelches under your feet. A sailor who addresses his betrothed even though she said she would not wait for him, and frolics with some Stephan or other without a thought for him – a sailor who embarked on this voyage with visions of pearls to put round your neck but who no longer thinks of you three-dimensionally, only flatly, like a picture, you cannot hanker after a picture, not if you are an adventurer in Brazil with nothing to show for his adventures.

My master glanced up from his papers. His eyes were over-shadowed by the impenetrable thicket of his eyebrows, but I knew something was amiss. The Governor of the River of January, who could with his gaze alone swat anyone who displeased him, did not appear the least concerned about the loss of his daily catch of fish or the abandonment of his principal fishing vessel in such an inconvenient location. I bowed and left quickly, thinking myself fortunate to have evaded my master's wrath. Then I read deeper into his reaction. Had it not in fact been quiet satisfaction? Had he known he was sending me on a sleeveless errand, instructing me to fish in those particular waters? Had he guessed I would make a run for it with the Dutch?

"Englishman!"

Manoel was bounding up the steps of the assembly rooms. I had last seen him the summer before last as he delivered me into slavery; the intervening months had filled him out somewhat and further improved his clothes. I briefly entertained the thought of how things might have been for me had those dastardly Portugals not got me into a scrape and ended my prospects of advancement under him. My instinct was to embrace him and tell him everything – my escape into the wilderness, my time with Ubi and my encounter with his sister, how one tribe of Indians thought me a God and another tantamount to a king, how I had risen so high and secreted enough treasure to transform my station in life only for the de Sá's to wrest it from me – but of course I could not. The most decent Portugal in the colony had his first loyalty to the Governor and would sacrifice me like a pawn for that cause. I felt lonely; lonely and most of all wretched, and unable to tell a soul of my wretchedness. For squirrelling away treasure that belonged by decree to the Governor warrants hanging by Portugal law, even if such riches were rightful recompense for my services. Catholics can be more bloodthirsty than Cannibals. And cannibals are more generous with their fortunes. Come to that, cannibals are more desirable company generally.

"I heard of your crusades," smiled Manoel. "I had little doubt this jungle would fail to finish you. I bestow my congratulations: one obstinate rascal who refuses to meet his maker to another! So tell me, why so down-mouthed?"

Knights, I thought bitterly, at least had armour and a horse and – almost assuredly – a castle.

"I have not glimpsed my homeland in over two years. I should be returning by now with something to show for my toils."

"Bettering yourself takes time. Look at me. I was once trussed in the hold of your ship with little save death to dream of." He showed off his new clothes as if I had not already noticed them; the exquisitely cut doublet looked like it heralded from the same haberdashers used by Martin de Sá. You needed a certain figure to wear such a doublet; a figure fed on fine European food – wines, cheeses – yet toned from gentlemanly exercise such as riding a horse. But Manoel was a Catholic in a land increasingly dominated by the breed. What chance did I have of bettering myself? The Governor would sooner surround himself by rogues, illiterates and sycophantic cowards than he would place any of his important affairs in the hands of an Englishman. I felt beneath my shirt, not for the first time, Kathy, and clutched it – should I reveal it; the one thing that could have saved me? But I did not. The Knivet name mattered here too; you can tell my father that when you see him. Betray your name and you are nothing.

"And as for returning?" I asked quietly.

"It is no longer so simple." He hesitated awkwardly; he wanted to be rid of me but could not find the means. "You know too much of our ways here. I thought you understood, Englishman. The Governor can never let you leave Brazil."

I saw plainly how it was. The Governor wanted me on a leash. He wanted me to obey him like a dog and please him like a dog and keep me outside in a kennel like a dog too. He would never let me in. How could he treat me so? How could he call me 'son' knowing what that meant to me, how could he let me dream of a place at his side in his Brazil when his only intention was to keep me at his feet? I would have fought for him! I would have been his translator! I would have been his cook!

Find yourself on a leash and there are but two options: submit or tug back. The tide was on the turn. It was to be another fishing trip. I took the same Indians as before. I took the same boat. We made for a place two days' sail south where I had assured the Governor there were better supplies of oily fish than anywhere else in his captaincy. The latest trade I had turned my hand to up had given me knowledge about the comings and goings of more vessels besides that treacherous Dutch captain's. This was Brazil! Ha, this was the new land of opportunity. A quarter of the fleet of Europe had interests on these shores and I had found cause to be on just that part of the coast where boats anchored to take water after the long crossing from Europe; especially those not friendly with the Iberian Union. I watched and waited. Several days later I spied the most welcome sail of all. I recognised the colours of Queen Bess when I saw them. The ship was that of Sir Richard Hawkins – one of those who get far on their father's coat tails, and when your father was Sir John, founder of our English navy, that meant far indeed. I cared little for him as he was bent on trading for Indian slaves, but getting on board his ship was a way out and quite likely a profitable one.

"Seek provisions for our meal," I commanded the *wayanasses* with me. "And get us cassava. If we are to please the Governor and row back with all this fish we will need our strength."

I cared nothing for cassava, but it grew a way back from the shore, and demanded some digging. And I needed a decoy.

I assured myself Hawkins would take the chance to water at Ihla San Sebastian, the island just off shore, that night; any decent commander would. The evening was fair; the wind was fair. I simply needed to make that island. I started rowing. The Indians called out from shore for me to desist: I was crazy if I imagined I could escape the Governor. I laughed, and waved, and whooped. Adios, you lackeys! Prostrate yourselves to the Portugals if you will but we Knivets serve no one but each other, and the Queen, and justice, and – it goes without saying – the dignity of helpless maidens. The wind changed around then. It must have been the fiercest, most unprecedented wind to blow that January, and it whipped up from nothing in the half hour I was heaving oars for the island. I was a strong rower but this wind was too much; I found myself driven instead against the ugly little sister of the Ihla San Sebastian, a series of sharp reefs. My whoops became wails; panic gripped me; the panic of one who sees the void looming and suddenly finds the mad useless energy to fight it. I took on water: first in the boat then in my lungs. Anything else but drowning – a quick passage that gave you no time to think; a slow one that gave you hope you could elude it – but not an end that allotted you just enough time to experience every twist of the desperate horror of death. The rocks were rushing up, the rocks were there; they ripped into my hull, I was flung from the boat and that… that should have been it. There was a colour in the water that did not belong there. It was a bluish orange, the colour of an unripe mandarin, it was my blood but who had blood that colour?

Perhaps I really was immortal; a God or a man who traded his soul with a devil and deprived himself of the right to die.

It was not easy swimming with chainmail on. My father's house was unsalvageable; the water was up around the gables and chimney tops. The other voices had stopped, their screams gurgling away, all but one. My father was still calling for me. He was sitting astride the ridge of the roof humming an old tune from his fighting days about English glory outlasting everything.

"I am here now father; here for you."

"I am not your father." My father's plump, pink face had become leaner, paler, sterner – the face of the Governor. "My son, it is time to bequeath all I have to you" intoned my master. "And here it is." He gestured out at the view from the rooftop but of course it was not the old walled garden and the lawns and the orchards and the oakwoods; all was submerged. All was grey ocean welling around my eyes and ears. It was so cold. Death was so cold.

TWENTY-FOUR

Next time I awoke it was days later. I was in the rather more watertight location of the River of January's jailhouse; *wayanasses* had got word to the Portugals of how I had beguiled them and they had sent men to fetch me from the reefs where I had lain wrecked and half-dead. My feet were fixed to huge hoops of iron and I had a cell emitting no daylight. I could only guess at the passing of time by the knife of hunger in my belly. Every so often a grill was thrust back and a pitcher of water thrust in, but nothing more. It was a reasonable assumption that my master was angry with me.

The inquisition was in the River of January at that time and I conjectured my master would want me tried there. The Portugals embraced the inquisition with more fervour than Rome. A century on from Tordesillas[1] their mission was still to convert as many to the Catholic Faith as they might, and what with the Indians and the Huguenots and the Jews in Salvador and

---

[1] In the Treaty of Tordesillas (1494) Pope Alexander VI divided the New World between Spain and Portugal. The longitudinal divide was, somewhat unspecifically, agreed as 360 leagues west of the Cape Verde Islands. According to the treaty only the easternmost part of Brazil was Portugal's, but the Portuguese soon claimed all lands falling between the mouths of the Amazon and Río de la Plata rivers.

the English sailors more or less everywhere there was such ripe potential for conversion these warped trials ran continuously. There was a theatrical finality in their sham officialdom too. It was a stage established to legitimise imprisoning Jewish sugar merchants whose only crime was their success at the expense of Portugal businesses. It was a stage that drew attention away from the miserable poverty of the majority of colonists to the savages and the English that had been thorns in Portugal's side for many a moon, and who could now be dispensed with as they had not conformed to blinkered Catholic rhetoric. Most were given opportunity to convert rather than be hanged, but some double-dealing Portugals would still then execute those that complied.

The case against me was convincing: plenty could testify as to my speeches which not only conflicted with the teachings of the Catholic church but in some cases vociferously ridiculed them, and then there was the small matter of my being a runaway. I would be a criminal, certainly, but I would above all be a heathen criminal.

On the grime of my cell wall I readied arguments for my defence. Not all the world was Catholic; there were other beliefs and those that subscribed to them should be allowed to live their lives just as there was varying types of fish in the sea – some fabulous, some wretched; Queen Bess did not hate the Iberian kingdom; she had acted as she had only to save her throne and what leader would not try to do that; in England the nobility naturally followed their monarch's inclination to protect their loved ones which was an omnipresent theme in every book of the Bible and when it came down to it most conceded Portugal's fortified wine tasted better than claret; Englishmen universally admired Portugal food – and I spoke as one well-schooled in the art of cooking – not to mention Portugal dress; only a few dirty English pirates – the rogues – gave the rest of our nation a bad reputation; the only principles I had followed when trying to escape were duty to family, duty to Crown, duty to country; I doubted there was a man in the room who did not follow the same principles and if there was they were the traitors, not me;

I had never in two years of loyal service to the Governor – two years, mark, of endeavours in which I had risked my life countless times and so done without one treasure by way of thanks – never once exhibited malice to any Portugal. Were we not – I thought my argument might have this conclusion – all brothers in this Brazil, trying to make the best of it that we could?

"Knivet." The grill opened and a man with no neck and thinning hair that was either very greasy or intentionally dampened appeared; he pronounced my name 'Nee-vay' and I corrected him, which displeased him. I got another pitcher of water, but this time to wash with – this was the great new Brazil and Portugals did not want townspeople thinking they treated their prisoners like dogs when they paraded them through the streets. Well, I was getting out of my cell, and that it was to the inquisition did not matter to me. There would be holy men observing my walk to the assembly rooms which was where the trials were held; the route passed right by the College of Jesus. Some would certainly be historians and I did not wish them to be recording unworthy descriptions of any Knivet in the chronicles. I asked for a razor; the jailor said there was no time; I asked for at least a mirror; the jailor handed me his own and I marvelled that this unkempt man could possess such a fetching item for grooming. There was my face, the scars of the new world deep upon it. I was not a quarter of a century old, but I was born before Portugal even secured Brazil for herself, and already she was content to rule it with justice as iron as if she had been here as long as the jungle had. I positioned my curls; walked out with my pride in tact even if my clothes were in shreds. I would outdo them all with words even if they found me guilty. I do not deny that as the clamour of the hecklers outside hit me I fingered, not for the first time, what lay beneath my shirt, and very near drew it out. That would show them how wrong they were about me.

"Antoinne Nee-vay," the jailor proclaimed, to all who asked him and to many who did not, as he led me down the street like a mule. Nothing – not a church service nor an invasion – drew out the residents of the River of January in such numbers as a trial.

It was like they had been idling around their festering quarters waiting for some unfortunate to be mistreated for a diversion. "There goes the English traitor," the crowds bawled. "Runaway! Protestant pansy!" These blood-hungry knaves pelted me with old vegetables and what with the iron hoops still hanging from my feet and the various wounds inflicted upon me by those damnable sharp rocks during my escape attempt it was hard to retain any semblance of elegance.

The jailor, the old fool, was so busy telling the crowd my crimes that he overlooked the fact we were passing the assembly rooms.

"Why are we not stopping?"

The jailor cackled; he had a high-pitched laugh that lingered in the air after it had finished. He pointed on down the hill.

"That's where you're bound."

Down passed the College of Jesus, down the Slope of Mercy, out beyond the old town gate, a gibbet had been erected.

"Am I to receive no trial, *senhor*?"

"You *senhor* me now when you see your death in sight! Keep your words for your last ones, for they're not far off!"

An old woman, an Indian, tottered towards me, she was bent under a basket piled with wood and followed by two smartly-dressed men for whom she appeared to be working. The load was too much for her and the road was steep. One smartly-dressed man made a quip; the other sniggered; they sauntered along with their thumbs in their belt loops. As our eyes met, she with her wood and me dragging my shackles, she fell. She tried to get up again but could not. The men shouted at her to pick up their wood. She made some monumental final effort, then collapsed again. The men set to her with their boots. Their kicks hit bone, for there was nothing else to her. It was not a loud sound in a crowd, bone splintering, but it was distinct enough. The force of my jailor pulling in front and the mob closing behind lost her from sight.

I was going to hang. It was the last fibre of the rope suspending me over the abyss and it was about to be severed. What relief. No more creatures snapping at me, no more Portugals sniping at me. No more fighting back from the brink.

I looked for my master in the throng to congratulate him on being the severer – on putting me out of my misery. I was facing the masses, my neck was through the noose, my back to the sea, would they not allow me at least to be hanged facing the sea? Where was my master? I could not see him, just the crowd chanting "Nee-vay, Nee-vay!" – followed by some other words it would be uncouth to repeat. Was he not going to make a ceremony out of it? Would there not be some Catholic pomp with the occasion! My master only dealt with papers; with nice crisp white things – not with blood, not with dirt. He could dispense the justice just fine but could not stomach overseeing its conclusion. No follow-through. My father's militiamen had taught me when I was eleven years old: you must have a follow-through with your stroke if it is to prove a decisive one. My father would have taught me how to fight himself, he fought in the wars against the French and was much commended, he simply never had the time, of course, running an estate as he did. As it was, we never even got started on the toy soldiers. But there my master was, up on the parapet, high above the town! I knew it was him because of the dark cloak about his shoulders which fanned out in the breeze. He looked hewn from the stone itself. He had come. He could not let one as dear to him as me go without a goodbye – how could I think otherwise of him? Our faces were very far apart and at different elevations but I knew, somehow, that Salvador Correia de Sá, Governor of the River of January, Brazil's second-most important man, was looking up to me. There goes Anthony Knivet! There goes Anthony Knivet! *Alma minha gentil, que te partiste, tão cedo desta vida descontente*, gentle spirit, who has departed, so early of this life in discontent…[2] My master raised his arm. A wave. They kicked

---

[2] Luís de Camões, *Alma Minha Gentil*

the block from under my feet. I was swinging; swimming; far out at sea and unable to kick back to shore.

But traitors, as in the most despicable kind, did not get hanged in the captaincy of Salvador Correia de Sá. They got hanged, drawn and quartered. I found this out only as some water fouler than the bilges of the Roebuck was thrown over me and gasping I came round from the unconsciousness the noose had induced. Hands dragged me to the next device – I could not believe I had not observed it before – a rack not unlike our English variety, only with the board they strapped you on lengthways so it was the arms that got pulled apart from the body rather than the arms and legs in unison. I guessed there was sufficient sensation in my body to feel one last wrench of pain, or maybe three. My wrists were bound. It might take two or three turns for your arms to dislocate and several more for the limbs to detach or for the heart to give out. Oh, the crowds! All the way up the Slope of Mercy they went, which was twice the length of Charlton's main street, and many times grander on account of its elevation. Turn one. Shots of pain up both arms but nothing too severe; ha; you could look upon this rack as a parable for all of it – my father pulling in one direction and my mother in the other, Brazil and its riches in one direction and England and my birth right in the other, my life. My executor did not keep turning. They never did. They paused to allow the victim to truly feel the pain. And in this pause something changed.

The crowd – so thirsty for the blood that would make their own sorry lives seem more worthwhile – turned their heads. The rack allowed me a view of my executor. He was shrugging his shoulders; he had moved away from my little podium. And towards us sped a posse of black – no less than twenty priests from the College of Jesus – and now I heard their cries, "free Nee-vay, free Nee-vay!"

I was cut down and revived with cachaça from the priests' own hands. The crowd did not want to go against these cassock wearers for fear of being strung up as well but some of the bolder ones were questioning the priests' motivation. I was curious myself, and more curious how long frail holy men could stave off a rabble indignant at being cheated of their entertainment, even if God was on their side. Nevertheless these audacious Jesuits formed a protective wall about me, with one rubbing ointment on my neck. Another openly begged my forgiveness. It did not take the Governor long to arrive; he cut through the crowd like an impatient farmer through a crop field and did not hesitate to use his staff on anyone who got in his way.

"What is the meaning of this?" His shadow fell across us.

"We might ask the same of you," said the priests. "We devote our lives to converting souls in your name to the Catholic Faith, yet here is a Catholic you would kill."

I thought these good holy men might have become sun-addled out in the wilds doing their converting and my master evidently thought the same, but the priest who had massaged the ointment into my neck gently helped me sit upright.

The rack had pulled the shirt half off my shoulders and there for all to see was the rosary around my neck.

"As you can see this poor soul is a Catholic. Are you not?" the massaging priest entreated me.

I spluttered to find words to speak; it is a challenge when you believed yourself to have said everything you might in this life and had your next words prepared for God or the Devil or whatever you imagined awaited you afterwards, even if that was the maggots in the soil; in terms of conversation the Devil would be preferential to God or the maggots and if you are going to spend eternity somewhere I imagined it would be better to do so with *some* entertainment.

The lines on the face of the Governor were forked into the familiar frown that held Brazil together. The lines on the priest's face heavy under the eyelids, like he was only just managing to remain awake. I could not hear the crowd.

"Well?" my master demanded.

* * *

I had been out late fetching flour from the miller; when I got back to the bakery no candle was burning and I presumed my mother to have retired for the night. I had a mind to put the flour in storage then do the same for I needed to be up betimes that next morning. Our cellar was small, sufficient for stacking flour but with little standing room besides. So inconvenient was it for a person to descend that often I would simply lie on the hall floor and lower the sack of flour in from there. A baker's life is a tough one and I was usually so tired by this time of day I scarce thought about my actions. I opened the cellar hatch. I heard movement but supposed it to be rats. As I lowered in the first sack someone wrested it from my hands and yanked my arm so hard I tumbled straight into the cellar after the flour. I landed on my back, bruised and staring up in shock at my mother – although how she had fitted her portly posterior through the hatch was a miracle – and a dwarf I had never seen before. Both were covered in grime and clutching spades.

"Many more like that," said the dwarf, "and we would have no space for digging in!"

"What are you digging – in our cellar?"

My mother, who was doing most of the digging because the dwarf found it difficult to wield a normal-sized spade, sighed exasperatedly.

"*My* cellar, little man. And what are you doing back so soon?"

"I have a right to know what this strange man is doing here, mother." I substituted 'man' for 'dwarf' at the last moment not out of courtesy to the short fellow, who was, I noted in near disbelief, wearing a cassock, but because he was directly above me, and in possession of a sharp implement.

"We are digging a hole. Take the spade from Brother Owen[3] here, for he is tired, and I will tell you."

"A strange man down here with you at this hour, mother!" I was already a hot-headed young man in those times. "I ought to string him up!"

"You are not alone in wanting my neck," the dwarf intervened. "Many across England desire it. But heed your mother, for you are my accomplices and at this moment face the same punishment if we are caught."

The black look I gave him then persuaded him to clamber directly out of our cellar and retreat to a safe distance.

"Caught! What does he mean mother? What is this hole for?"

"Little man, there are many things in this world you know nothing of. When the good Queen Mary was reigning there were many families who supported her…"

"Bloody Mary!" I shouted. "Why do you refer to her as good, when she killed good Protestants!"

"It was a different time. She took her religion quite rightly from her mother. King Hal thought he could wipe out the Catholics but he could not. Many families survived…" she wiped her nose; I remembered that; it was the last gesture she made before my world collapsed. "We survived, little man. Even when Queen Bess came along they could not get rid of us. We just kept ourselves more hidden."

"The Spaniards that tried to capture England were Catholics." My voice quavered. "I am no Catholic."

"There is no need to deny it, little man." My mother reached out to ruffle my hair but I flinched back, as she had wiped her nose on her hand.

---

[3] Nicholas Owen (1562-1606) was behind the construction of numerous 'Priest Holes', or hiding places for known practitioners of Catholicism, during the late 16th and early 17th centuries in Protestant-controlled England.

The dwarf returned to the cellar hatch with some almond milk; he had made it wonderfully, generous with the honey, but he had also found the ingredients in our kitchen with suspect speed, as if he was accustomed to doing so.

"For the workers."

I did not like his attempt to be jovial.

"You would make me a traitor to my country," I said. "A traitor to my father."

"As your mother says, you cannot deny what you are. You were born a Catholic…"

"Do not tell me what I was born as!"

The dwarf smiled sadly.

"We are just digging, little man," my mother said soothingly but she was trying too hard to be kind and she was looking at the dwarf as she spoke. "Brother Owen believes, and I do too, that Catholics deserve a place in this land. That is what we are making here. A safe house for Catholics…"

"He would have taken us in!" I cried. "Father would have let us stay with him were it not for your religion!"

My mother's face darkened but perhaps on account of the dwarf's presence she did not say what she had been about to, although I have long speculated since on what her words might have been.

"Would that that were so, little man."

I sipped the almond milk, utterly dispirited it was so delicious. "Bastard, he's a bastard!" – the voices of the village boys chimed down the years. *I* was the reason. I was the reason my father had not taken us in. And somehow it made me love him all the more.

I picked up the spade and began digging. I dug ferociously, to blot out the image manifesting in my head of this Catholic dwarf pinning my mother down in the cellar dark and feeding her spoonful's of almond milk, I tried to believe that he was forcing her but the longer the image festered the more I suspected she was enjoying it.

"I will help you because you are my mother," I said. "But I am no Catholic."

"There, there, little man." My mother ruffled my hair. The dwarf sipped his almond milk smugly. He was so small he needed to hold the cup in both hands.

Next morning I was retrieving the damson scones from the oven when she came up behind me.

"You are all grown up, little man. I daresay you will be going away now, and leaving your poor mother all alone."

Evading her I took the scones to the shop window; arranged them; rearranged them; a sullen and pointless action because the bakery was not even open yet and scones are scones; however you present them you cannot change what they are.

"You're not far off twenty-one. Your father should send for you then; the Lord knows he should after the sorrows he inflicted upon me. But we cannot bank upon the eventuality. You might have to go away one day – perhaps as far as Malmesbury – to make money to help your poor old mother. And if you do I want you to wear this."

She gave me the rosary. I kept my back to her.

"Let's not have any trouble, little man. You've caused me enough trouble."

Oh, why could she not have said she wanted me to have it to remember her by, or something conciliatory at least, for this was surely the moment? But she never could entreat. She could only demand.

"My duty is to you, mother," I said meekly. And I dully fingered the beads, thinking in dismay of the Spaniards and Portugals doing the same before they gathered in their Armada to come after our noble English ships.

* * *

"Well?" My master's voice hung in the thick morning air of the River of January.

"I am Catholic," I said, and wept bitterly inside.

TWENTY-FIVE

"I grew desperate and carelesse what I did to end my life."

Anthony Knivet, *Admirable Adventures and Strange Fortunes*

You could call it murder, but I do not think that is quite fair.

Each day after my faith saved me from death was more miserable than the last. Faustus at least knew where his soul was bound but mine seemed tied to any number of unquantifiable evils and not least of these was the factor of Cidade do Governador. If he had used me terribly as a slave, and disrespectfully as the man in charge of his sugar boat, now this overfed man with his ill-fitting clothes was able to truly unleash his hatred on me, for I was a proven traitor. I was given the meanest work: the cutting of the cane during the midday heat and kettling in the night-time, which was work hotter than Hellfire as you were boiling vats of cane juice to rid it of impurities, and relentlessly too for if you tarried the sugar spoiled and you would be whipped for your oversight. We produced the whitest sugar, us *engenho* slaves, but we rotted inside at about the same rate. I was not a man any longer but an automaton. When in the dead of night I slunk to my bed I could barely fall into my fitful sleep plagued by nightmares of furnaces before I was shaken awake to go cutting cane again.

"*À terceira é de vez,*" the factor kept taunting me, which means that the third time is the time. I understood. Twice he had tried to finish me and twice he had failed – and being thwarted by an Englishman was not a thing he relished.

I marked the days then the months above my hammock in the hut; the summer turned into a remarkably cold winter and the difference between the scalding boiling house and the outside chill took its toll on my bones. I developed a fever but did not dare stop working; my arms and legs shook with the malady and the only way to remedy it was to warm my limbs by the boiling house furnace.

It had to happen, I suppose, for what other respite was there from my torment? The factor caught me as I was huddled in my one moment of rest, picked up one of the withies I used to bundle together his firewood for him, and struck me like one possessed, with such viciousness I did think he had broken all the bones of my body. I started up, and seeing him about to second his malice with another blow I grabbed his arms and locked in an embrace we tottered around the room. I had resolved not to get into fights with men bigger and heavier than myself, but unfortunately this was just the sort that loved to beat me most. To redress the discrepancy I got the great knife I had for my slave's labours and hurt him in the arm, and in the back, and in the side. On this third lunge he slumped to the floor. He screamed – pathetically childish now he was in the novel position of being the victim – that the English traitor had slain him, and seeing the blood leaking out of him I did not doubt that was the case.

"*À terceira é de vez*," I whispered, and stole hastily away.

* * *

Treat a man like a villain and a villain he becomes.

I knew not where I ran that night, except that it was into the thickest forest. I had been there before of course. But forest changes. It fools you like you can fool a child into believing a fable, and there were no paths, no landmarks, no light; the forest where I had met Katawa was gone – two years of forests had come and gone in that time.

I knew now that if the Governor got me again I should endure the most extreme torture ever invented for man, while an encounter with the *tomomynos*, Brazil's most notoriously savage tribe who dominated the wild part of this island would not be pleasant and my only possible allies the *tamoyes* were on last report still undecided if they wanted to worship me or devour me.

All of the above made me uneasy. In the back of my mind was the knowledge the higher ground on the island had been safer and less frequented by cannibals. But it was dark, and impossible to tell which way was up, and, panicking, I tripped. The fall was not great but it was soft; too soft. I was in a bog, and sinking. The mud was not deep enough to drown me but it had me stuck fast. And I was not alone. On the far side of the bog were lizards, beautiful ones, with glowing bellies. There were hundreds. We regarded each other; them calm; me scrabbling in futility to get away from them. One at the rear climbed onto the backs of the others and crawled to the front of the group so that it was the foremost lizard there. In majestic ponderousness it slithered into the bog towards me and instantly, by some sorcery, stabs of shock flew through the water and through my body. My eyes bulged. It had put a spell on me, the damned serpent, I could not move. The lizard reared up. It was wearing a purple travelling cloak and it put a strange horn-like instrument to its lips and began to play, *'Come o'er the burn Bessie, my pretty little Bessie, come o'er the burn to me!'* and when it was done it added, pointedly, so I could not have mistaken a word: "We are destined to do great things, you and I."

Daylight arrived. The lizards were gone. I pulled myself from the bog and lay gasping, spent with the effort. The lizard had been the quack from my childhood whom I had met after my father's duel; of that I was certain. But what had his message meant?

I did not have time to ponder it, then. Every minute I lay there the sounds I started to hear brought back my old paranoia. Whisperings in the trees... Movements just beyond my vision... Flashes that could be some trick of light but were almost certainly something more. Indians. And an instinct told me they did not mean well. I started running. I ran like a madman. Every now and again I paused and listened to see if the sounds followed me. They did. I was weak and I was up against people who knew these woods like their own hands. There was no possibility to outrun them. Ahead of me I espied a giant tree that soared up above the surrounding trees. It was difficult to climb but I was desperate. I got into that and waited. Within moments one of the *tomomynos* appeared beneath me. He was terrifying to behold, a colossus of an Indian. His eyes burned white in a face newly daubed in tar and blood, and he sniffed like an animal with huge twitching nostrils around the tree where I was. Then he beckoned to some others and they also came snuffling and soon all were looking at my tree. I did not understand how they could know this was my refuge when I was screened by the thick leaves, but they peered up into the branches with their white eyes in their red-black faces like there was nothing hiding me from them at all. I did not dare move, neither to climb higher nor to throw my knife at one, for either scenario would reveal my location precisely and even if my knife found its mark that would still leave four of them against one of me.

The tree was swarming with ants. A hoard was crawling towards me from a nearby branch. I held my breath. The ants were red and black too. Each was the size of a child's fist and their jaws twitched.

The *tomomynos* kept staring into the tree. Then the first one let loose a blood-curdling trilling similar sound to that I had observed before when I had overseen their kind sacrificing tamoyes; it was more the sound of a bird of prey than that of a human.

It went like this: "Yeeeeaiiiiiiii, yeeeeaiiiiiiii!" It was one of the worst sounds you could hear in this Brazil. It was a call to action – a call to arms.

The ants closed in. They looked like they could bite hard.

"*Lovas eyave pomombana!*" howled the *tomomynos*, and a moment after that the arrows came. In a rain of shafts they embedded around me; one pierced the skin between the thumb and index finger of my right hand but the others somehow missed. They did not have many: clearly this was a foraging party that had decided on whim to chase me; I was lucky they had not been in greater numbers or with deadlier intent for if so I would be scalped and half-roasted by now. Their arrows used up without any bellow of pain in reply, they seemed satisfied and moved off through the trees.

I moved my hand as the first of the ants began crawling upon it. I was shaking, whether this was the malady I had contracted in the *engenho* or fear I could not say, but I stayed in that tree two days and only came down when hunger forced me.

A few hours of slicing through undergrowth got me to the shore. I caught some fish – paltry but temporarily sustaining – and when rational thought returned to me I decided two things. One was that I needed to leave this island as soon as possible. The other was that I would not do so without Katawa. Her people needed saving from the *tomomynos*; I would be their protector and in return they would be my friends.

The problem was that I did not know where to look. I remembered glimpsing *tamoyes* villages when I had been living in the wilderness here before, but it seemed *tomomynos* had multiplied here in the intermittent years, whilst *tamoyes* had diminished. After several hours' search I thought I had found the beach where I had seen the *tamoyes* being sacrificed but when I studied it hard I had to concede there were many such steeply shelving beaches hereabouts. I cut a trail inland and made the high ground, but this was karst country and there were many caves and none, truth be told, had a clearing in front quite like the one where I remembered playing *peteca* that afternoon long ago. And what if I could find my cave, would I sit there and wait for her and Ubi to appear again? I did not know where their village was – if it still existed – for I had never, even in my stint as a God to these people, been invited there. I did not know if Katawa was dead or if she had finally journeyed to join the rest of their people in the interior. But I had a profound sense that she was not here. Eventually I did find what I was convinced was my old gourd tree; I went as far as hollowing out a gourd for a Ma-rrrah y kûá but forced myself to stop, for what was the point if no Ubi would come and no Katawa would come to fetch him?

Despondency or hope drove me again to the water's edge. I spied three Angolan slaves sleeping there. Beside them there lay bows, and arrows, and roots, I helped myself to what I deemed best and returned to the trees, noiselessly. It would take a wily Indian to take me unawares now. The Thing was returning back to me, it coursed through my veins and whilst I remained in this land so would I let it course, to Hell with the Governor, to Hell with his son, to Hell with the Portugals and their pretences at civilisation. They thought themselves so educated, yet they stumbled around hungry and lost in the forest, they knew nothing of its food or paths and this trajectory of thought was what sewed the seeds of the idea. I walked the lonely shore of the good Governor's Island, and I saw a much better way to draw the attention of him, of the captaincy, of the whole of Brazil. Yes, I thought. The whole of Brazil shall hear of it!

I continued around the island until I saw the promontory I judged to be closest to the mainland shore. As I drew closer I saw a canoe upturned on the sand, and another black slave besides it, once more asleep. I could not believe my eyes. Had luck at last deigned to smile on me? Eagerly I moved the boat towards the water; the sleeping man stirred not. It looked under a league to the mainland, which by my calculations would land me somewhere on the north side of Guanabara Bay. And then? Why, the interior of course: for the execution of my plan necessitated going there.

"Do you take me for a fool, Anthony Knivet? Do you think I'd be lying here if I thought there was a chance that there boat could get me off this damned island, yah?"

I started round in shock, for I knew who the speaker must be.

"That there boat be riddled with holes," said Quarasips Juca.

I went to embrace my old friend.

"What brings you here, Quarasips?"

"I killed me a man. And you?"

"The same."

We laughed.

"This mighty Brazil have a couple of right jesters up against it, yah!"

I was not comfortable with the word 'jester' but let it go.

"How did it happen?" I asked.

"All my life I keep my head down and work on that *engenho*. But the other day, this fellow with nowt better to do than spread rumours tell the supervisor some plan I be hatching to overthrow him… can you imagine? So I challenge the man, thinking to teach him a lesson, but it seem I done no more than touch his neck with my two hands here than he was swooning before me."

Actually it was easy to imagine Quarasips Juca as the leader of a revolt, and the size of his hands and frame made it still easier to believe he could inadvertently strangle someone, for he had all but crushed the life from me with his hug.

I told him of my own sorry state of affairs, and said that given my past offences against the Portugals my predicament was ten times worse than his.

"Do you have a notion what place can we go to save both our lives, Quarasips?"

"My only thought be to get off this island, for Lord knows our lives stand the best chance of ending if we remain!"

"So if this boat has holes we must build another. The only others lie fast to the *engenho*, which for sure the Portugals are guarding like hawks."

"We don't have time, yah. These shores be crawling with *tomomynos*, and the Portugals be a-coming for us."

"What then?" I looked out at the league's worth of ocean standing in our way.

"We swim," said Quarasips Juca.

"We would never make it."

They say Greek warriors in the heyday of their empire could swim three leagues, but that was hearsay and I did not fancy staking my life on hearsay.

"I got me enough strength for the two of us."

Quarasips was a great man; in his country, Angola, his father had been a village leader and had obtained the honour through bravery. He led men against the Portugals when they came ransoming for slaves and would have been executed but for his strength, which made him indispensable. He had the dubious distinction, Quarasips believed, of being in the first shipment of Angolans ever to arrive in the New World, and quite possibly the Angolan to have the first union with a tribeswoman from Brazil. She had been of noble birth too, he thought, his father had almost certainly told him so, but she was raped to death by a Portugal before he was old enough to remember his memories. Not many years later his father, despite his immense strength, had succumbed to the barbarity of *engenho* life, although Quarasips owned it could also have been sadness, immense sadness at falling from prince to slave, from paradise to Hell. One morning Quarasips shook his father to wake him and realised his spirit had departed. That would have broken many a child but the quality of the blood flowing through Quarasips rendered him stronger even than his father. He had known nothing but slavery and evolved to endure its hardships. He could pull a plough if no horse was available, he could cut cane twice as fast as the next strongest slave and with half the sustenance.

He told me of this as we swam; I never knew him to be more talkative than during that Herculean crossing. Perhaps there is some need to tell your story when you fear you could be silenced without having told it, the same thing motivated me to tell mine, and I suspected Quarasips, although he cut through that water with arms like oars, to have doubts about whether we would, in fact, make it.

The first part was easy, which should have been a warning for this Brazil was rarely what it seemed. Then we were out of the lee of the island and the waves picked up. Quarasips kept the pace like his body had no more feeling than a boat's keel but I lagged behind, he waited, and in the interim we were buffeted off course. My limbs felt like rotten wood. I swallowed my first water soon after that and the waves that had looked azure calm before were dark and swelling, and cresting just one of them sapped my strength. Then Quarasips, true to his word, carried me, like an ox of the water he pulled me, but soon I could not even assist him, this angered me, I kicked but it was with desperation not with strength, it was useless, the whole thing was useless, it was over and this body of water was the Styx, Quarasips Charon, he was delivering me to the underworld. A deep tranquillity descended. There on the shore a girl with a dark mane of hair and green eyes and red markings on her face like a cat's whiskers was waving to me. The thing was I did not know if the shore she stood on was the shore I had left, life, or the shore I was being hauled towards, namely Hell, and this lack of certainty filled me with indignation. I had to know. And so I was back, I was kicking back and carrying myself and the mighty Quarasips Juca fuelled by little more than my own need to know, which was for sure what saved us from drowning that day. We landed, very feeble, dragged ourselves out of sight from the sea and did not move for some hours.

"There was a time back there," said Quarasips Juca later, "when I was sure you be dead. The life went from you, I could not feel your pulse."

"It was not my time."

"Yah? And when be your time, Anthony Knivet?"

"Who knows? But there is something I mean to do before it comes."

"What?"

"An idea. I will tell you - on the way. For we have a long way to go."

Quarasips Juca began to chuckle.

"Are we free, Anthony Knivet?"

"I believe so."

He got up, and pulled me up, and gave me one of his crushing embraces.

"I never been free before," he said.

TWENTY-SIX

"We chose rather to fall into the pawes of a Lion, and the clawes of the Serpent, than into the bloudie hands of the Portugall."

Anthony Knivet, *Admirable Adventures and Strange Fortunes*

So what idea, asked Quarasips Juca.

Well, I replied, as we walked out into the great green nothing of Brazil, were we not two of the least valued individuals this land ever saw? Did he not have noble blood, was his father not a leader of men and his mother not from one of the most revered families of the *tamoyes*, Brazil's proudest tribe? Did I not myself hail from one of the most prominent families in South-West England, faithful servants to the Crown for centuries, was my ancestor not Master of the Horse to King Hal and my uncle not currently sitting on the Privy Chamber[1]?

The way we had chosen was tough, and our navigation based more or less on the sun alone which we could not always see whilst the dense foliage persisted. I hacked a path with a knife and Quarasips used his hands, which were a better tool than most men's blades. It was dire work. Formless bugs fell on us from

---

[1] Whilst Anthony Knivet was away in Brazil propagating the family name, his uncle Sir Thomas Knyvett was doing his own little bit in England – rising through the ranks at court, acquiring lands, getting knighted and, most famously, uncovering the Gunpowder Plot of 1605 – boasts Anthony would have no doubt added here had he known of them.

the branches we disturbed. Quarasips got bitten by a venomous spider on his jaw, the right side of his face swelled and I told him he could be glad of his size, for a slighter man might have been floored. After midday when the heat was most merciless the walls of vegetation acted like a slow-cooking oven and creepers and thorns clawed you until your skin was raw and yet more invitation for the odious insects. Sweat streamed off our bodies and that together with the limited space made wielding a knife with enough power to cut what was in front of you difficult, even were we not daubed in festering sores, which we were. Quarasips asked me through puffed-up lips if I was sure of our route, I replied that I was, more or less, for I knew that the terrain should be familiar to me, after all Martin de Sá had sent me trafficking for slaves in this region not a year before. The disadvantage of the River of January is that it has no rivers; only in Brazil would they name a place 'river' when in fact none was there. To reach the interior one must trek up over the surrounding hills then descend to link up with the network of rivers that get you about those mighty forest flatlands. When I had ventured that way before to the land of the *pories* I owned I had had a bunch of *wayanasses* to get me to there. So we were heading up, which was the best to be hoped for in the absence of such guides, and whilst our freshwater supplies were limited I knew enough of the forest by now to survive – I could siphon water from a bamboo tree or dredge it from a bog – and many trees we passed were well hung with fruits. It was not easy. But to a man that knew – to a man with the Thing – it was possible to get by. Those who come in years to come should know that if this Brazil is to their liking it is because of the likes of us. Never did more blood or sweat go into making a land than what our generation gave this nebulous nation. If those who come like the roads their carriages trundle on, it is because we cut them; if they like taking sweet cakes on their terrace in afternoon, it is because we extracted the sugar for them; if they like to be attended in the evening by a slave, it is because we *were* those slaves - in the beginning, we *were* them - and somehow we got by.

Well, I said to Quarasips Juca, could the Portugals not have used him in a manner more fitting to his true station in life? Could they not have furnished him with some post in recognition of his lifetime of service, some supervisory role perhaps? Take me, for example, who had demonstrated clear prowess in baking and in translation, who had gone where no Portugal had dared to expand Portugal's sphere of trading with the Indians – did such acts not warrant some elevation, to Captain or Governor or at least to the Governor's personal cook? Of course they did, but the Portugals were blind and they were greedy too. They owned all of vast Brazil as well as significant parts of the African continent and all from a tiny kingdom tacked on to the edge of Europe. It was hardly as if they needed the space. And what, I asked of Quarasips Juca, did we have? We had nothing but the clothes we stood in, which were soiled, and some few weapons, which were stolen and therefore not really ours, and a couple of coconuts. Did he see the disparity? He did. And was it justice that, after such services, we should be rewarded so scantly we were jubilant just to obtain our freedom, and that the Portugals begrudged us even that? Quarasips Juca guessed it was not justice, not at all.

In the evenings we were so exhausted we could have fallen asleep standing. I cooked cassava for us with a little coconut milk or some creature if we had energy to catch one and Quarasips would, were he not seized by one of his spates of melancholy, tell me tales of Angola that his father had told him in exchange for stories of England. I told him of the woods around Charlton – how they had majesty but felt somehow safe, how the peels of church bells hung in them sometimes, how there was manicured paths through them that people used for leisure, which startled him very much. I told him of the festival season we had in the village each autumn, how on holiday days at this time the Lord of the Manor became a commoner and the rest of the village chose one person to become Lord – and once they elected me. I had to order everyone about whilst reclining on a bed made of garlands and they had to obey me, whoever they were. Four youths carried me around and the parish was mine: mine! I could decide who did what and when. The problem of course was the bells. I had to wear them on my hose as part of the costume, and no one took my orders seriously as a result, so I became disillusioned and resigned the office. Quarasips told me of how, in certain provinces of Angola, people had disliked the taxes the Portugals began to impose, so had started delivering the money to the tax collector in the mouth of a many-toothed lizard. "There are the taxes, every penny and more!" the villagers cried to the tax collector, but the tax collector was too frightened to put his hand inside the lizard's jaws, and so he opted not to collect the taxes any more. But the melancholic periods of Quarasips grew. He needed regular signs of good-times-to-be in order to be cheerful, and we had soon gone a lengthy time without any portent of good times.

Well, I entreated Quarasips Juca, was he not half an Indian, half a native of this land? Did he not possess the strength of two, or more, had he not survived longer in slavery than anyone else he knew? Were the two of us not surviving, and none too miserably (I jested) in this hostile jungle – jungle anyone but the tribes therein would have perished in before now? Could I not speak more than passable Tupi, had I not such renown as an emissary that Sir Thomas Cavendish, celebrated General, and Martin de Sá, son of the second-most powerful man in Brazil, had sent me to commune with the Indians because I was the one who was best at doing so?

The day starts bright in the jungle, a sharp orange light cracks the night apart and for some privileged moments everything emits a heavenly glow. It is like a truce has been agreed. No insects bite you, the sun is warm but not scalding, the rain will most likely not arrive until afternoon, light seems to hit even the dankest darkest hole. In such a light one morning I got up whilst Quarasips snored and went for a scout. I saw that the forest soon ended completely. We had reached a plateau. Hills still reared above but not so dominantly because of the height we had gained. I looked at the sun. It was still rising direct behind me. I saw we had come west just as I planned; we had avoided the River of January and the populated coast route. And – yes – there when I looked inland were the watersheds, the ribbon-like tributaries of the great Paraná for which we were aiming; they did not look any further in front than the sea was behind. Barren, open ground lay before me. But its openness gave me hope, even if it laid bare the brutal truth of how far we had to go, because hacking your way forward in jungle is like fighting the demon you cannot see. I called Quarasips to tell him the news and he embraced me, calling me his dear friend, for it was, really, the two of us at this point against the rest of Brazil. And Quarasips wanted to know: now what?

Well, I said to Quarasips Juca, did he not imagine the Indians of this land might feel a little persecuted too? The Portugals treated them no better than they treated us, and it was more of an ignominy since this land had been theirs for centuries, millennia, forever, in a sense the Indians were part of the land, they owned each other and helped each other, their relationship was symbiotic as opposed to the Europeans who seemed bent on wreaking destruction everywhere. Did this not tell us something about Brazil, I asked Quarasips Juca? He rubbed his eyes and confessed it did not tell him very much whatsoever but he was sure I would enlighten him.

What we had taken for barren plateau was in part an area of felled trees. The *engenhos* along the coast sent *wayanasses* up here to chop firewood for their insatiable fires. It was an ugly place – blackened stumps and blanched branches – but once it had been the proudest forest, for the wood here was the hardwood which burned best and longest on Portugal furnaces. If I had cursed the jungle for its impenetrability not a day hence I was more appalled at this. Fires still smoked where vegetation had been burned: the colonists' revenge for how the forest had hurt them or hindered them. The sun beat down here unabated and the ground crunched under our feet into ash. I bid Quarasips take heed, as lackeys of the Portugals could be close by. I picked up a stick and began carving it. I am marking each day, I explained, because then we will know how many days we will have taken to make this trip in relation to how many we should be taking. How many days should we be taking, asked Quarasips. I told him: less than we will take.

I said to Quarasips Juca that there were many tribes in this Brazil and most of them seemed to hate each other about as much as they hated the Portugals, but their hatreds of each other were often trivial and their hatred of Portugals universal and deep-rooted. Can you conceive, I put it to him, of a Brazil where there were no inter-tribal rivalries? How much more impervious would be the armour of the Indians then, and how much more vulnerable their oppressors!

We struck out across this wasteland. Ten notches I carved in my stick, the felled trees fell by the wayside and it was a desert we were traipsing through. Twenty notches and there were bones, bones of animals, bones of people; something had picked them clean, something with big paws that we glimpsed prints of in the dirt, something that made us clasp our weapons tight. Thirty notches, and we were coated in dust, and weakened through surviving only on pine nuts or the odd snake, which were the only things that flourished here. The days and the landscape were become so relentlessly uniform that I pondered whether it was yesterday morning I had carved the preceding notch, or in fact the day before, or another day longer ago, or whether in fact I was a ghost of myself going through these motions, with my body already decomposing somewhere, another victim amongst this desert's many victims.

It was the day of the thirty-third notch. There was a squelching under our feet; it went bfffphhh, I got Quarasips to step on it and it went bfffffphhhhhh. We followed the trail of this loamier soil and there it was. The tributary! Ha, the outer tentacle of the Paraná, the beginning of the easy going, what the road of silk was to Eurasia so this great waterway was to the jungle. And when

I laid eyes on it I believed the interior closer, I believed Katawa closer. For of course I was not just doing all this for me or for Quarasips or for the betterment of the tribes of Brazil. I cradled a kernel of hope that she lived yet, that her people had journeyed to the interior as she had once told me they would and that she was out there, somewhere, in the trees. Well, we fell in a gorging frenzy upon that river water, and after our thirsts were slaked Quarasips wanted to know if we were almost there, or rather he sighed the words as if he did not really believe we would ever get there and I, not wishing him to guess just how close we had come to not making it, slapped him on his broad, dejected shoulders and bid him ready for a feast for that was what we should presently have.

There were, I said to Quarasips Juca, tribes of Indians in the interior that I could personally vouch were ready for change, there was a gunpowder stash of anger against the Portugals spread across this jungle and the fuse was there to be ignited. We will be the igniters, I said. We will lead the Indians against the Portugals. If we get some on our side, others will follow, it was like dominoes, did he ever play that game? You stood the dominoes in some formation, say a circle, knock the first into the second and the second knocks the third and so forth not by your action directly but by the momentum the first generates. Quarasips Juca owned he did not know what dominoes were but there was one big problem as he saw it, what if the first and the second dominoes were so far apart that the first just fell over by itself?

I did not have time to address his question for the tributary we were travelling beside had led us into a fertile, marshy land – a land I recognised. Not too far distant the smoke of campfires ascended into the afternoon sky.

"We are here," I said.

TWENTY-SEVEN

The King of the *pories* was having his face painted by two of the brazen hussies I had encountered before. He looked pleased with my return and as was customary asked us if we would like to rest a-while and have two of his women pleasure us. I declined; Quarasips asked if I would then be happy to let him have both; I nodded and off they went.

"So, white man! Come to fill your pockets with treasure once more?"

Un-daubed by his tribal hues the King resembled one of those wily market stall-holders you see at fayres in small English towns, the type that try to convince gentlemen to tarry and part with extra coins for merchandise they do not need.

"Sire I return to your kingdom, having endured many hardships to do so – fatigue, thirst, dense jungle, savage beasts…"

"And you find us open, as you see." The King spread his hands, his tone was pleasant but perfunctory, my obsequious flattery was not having quite the same effect as before.

"You may recall, Sire, the trade I was honoured to conduct with you."

"I gave you seventy men, and many jewels."

"In return for a selection of the best hatchets and blades in Brazil, Sire."

"And now, no doubt, your proposition is different. For you come overland, and not upriver as you would if the Portugals had sent you, and I see you carry no merchandise, unless it is the pine nuts you took from our trees."

"I apologise about the pine nuts, Sire."

"No matter!" cried the King. "You are my friend! You have my permission!

"That means a lot, Sire. In fact, myself and my friend…"

"I trust he is happy with my women? They are my best – and used only by me."

"Most happy, Sire, I have no doubt."

"It is their pleasure to lie with him, for I tell them: it is *business* – you please he who comes with good intent and kill he who comes with bad." He smiled and his teeth looked very little and white for an old Indian – perhaps on account of his preference for vegetables at dinner rather than human flesh.

"Then it is as well we are friends come in good faith," I said. "And with a proposition for you far better than hatchets."

He smiled broadly, and embraced me. This called for a festival, he said.

That night, after we had drained supplies of the *pories'* potent ceremonial brew and the village women chewed and spat cassava pulp to finish fermenting a second batch; after the King's fire dancers performed their daredevil antics and the tobacco pipe was passed around the revellers, and nostalgia broke out on the faces of the old men rocking on their haunches near the embers and stories of old were told, and I had given a performance on a Marrrah y kûá which I had imagined, correctly, would amaze the *pories* and additionally ease the passage towards them accepting my proposal; I asked leave of the king to explain my plan before all his village that next morning – all would become clear, I promised.

That night, I dreamed of buttocks, the swinging brown buttocks of the *pories* women that had pleasured Quarasips Juca began it but they had soon become a shade paler, crescent moons, my Katawa's buttocks as she had walked away from me some two years before, such buttocks could not be forever moving away from me, I wanted to hold them stroke them squeeze them. What was the point to advancement if there was no beauty to go with it? She had the sort of beauty you could wear at your side, like knights wear colours on their lance arms. I had to get to her. Somehow I had to get to the *tamoyes* and to do that I needed the *pories* on my side.

"They be gathering," Quarasips informed me, on the morning of my speech.

"How many?" It was a stupid question but it was important to me.

"Hundreds, a thousand maybe."

"More than the entire population of Charlton," I said. "At least, I doubt the population has increased so much in my absence... on account of the famines, you know. That is the thing Quarasips. Let us not forget things are far from perfect in our homelands. Here and now might be the best chance we ever have to better ourselves."

"And you think your grand words will win them over, yah?"

I did not know. The truth was that these Indians set upon each other with barely any pretext whatsoever. But they had never made a stand against the Portugals since the great confederation of the coastal tribes over thirty years previous[1], an uprising which just as it threatened the Portugals most was dissipated by some false Catholic promises from Anchieta, no less. And the *pories* had never been part of that alliance, they were their own people, their wealth gave them autonomy, they did what it suited them to do, they were an unknown quantity.

---

[1] The *Confederação dos Tamoios* of the mid-1550s. Several indigenous tribes joined forces to rise against the Portuguese: aided by arms from the French who were developing their own interests in Brazil at the same time. The uprising was unsuccessful.

I went out into the middle of the circle of huts, and the *pories* whooped, and when the applause had quietened I said unto them the following:

"I have journeyed far, with one purpose, and that is to tell you that you are not alone. The Portugals use your people cruelly, and make them bond-slaves, and I have been used cruelly by the Portugals, and as a slave in their terrible *engenhos*. Yet the English adventurers to this land have ever used you well; Drake has, Raleigh has, I have. And I say to you that the time has come to rise up, to defend yourselves against such tyrants! I will stand with you, along with my friend here (Quarasips Juca smiled sheepishly), for I have killed a Portugal, an *engenho* owner no less, and my head is wanted along the seaboard of Brazil for this crime and others. For our part we are determined to end our lives with you, if you swear to defend yourselves and us from Portugal tyranny…"

A great roar went up from those assembled; many there embraced me; the King himself embraced me longest of all. Quarasips Juca did not embrace me. Ending our lives with them was a serious undertaking, he muttered, however much he liked *pories* girls or pine nuts, I bid him hush, it sounded better if I said it thus, had he not heard of rhetoric?

Buoyed by this enthusiastic reception I continued:

"And you may say to me that Indians have tried making a stand before, and believe me I am all too aware of those noble attempts. Those attempts failed, I grant you, but only because of Portugal's superior numbers, Portugal's superior weapons[2]. The Indian spirit stood strong then and even in the face of adversity came close to sending your conquerors crawling back to their ugly king in Europe. I call on you to show that same spirit once again. For there are many more of you than there are Portugals. Not in this tribe alone, perhaps, but when you total the other *pories*

---

[2] A smallpox epidemic and internal rifts were likely more significant factors.

in other places, and the other tribes, the *mariquites*, the *petivaries*, the *topinaques*, the *topinabazes*, the *waymores*, the *waytaquazes*, the *tamoyes*, then, my friends," I paused and outstretched my arms, "we would have an army to make those Portugals quake!"

But there were no more whoops reverberating around the circle of huts, there was silence, and then there were uneasy mutterings, and soon not altogether complementary words were being shouted.

"Just when it were going so well," said Quarasips Juca.

Then the King stood up, he was not tall, but everyone sensed immediately when he had arisen and ceased their clamour.

"As long as our lives last," he cried, "and while our bows break not, we will do just that, and fight tyranny, and defend ourselves and you against it."

I took a deep breath. He was an intelligent man, the King of the *pories*. The dissent reverted into whoops again.

"A change of heart," muttered Quarasips Juca to me, "don't take these *pories* long."

The time that followed was one of the most sumptuous parties the King of the *pories*, who was known for his lavishness, had ever thrown: of roasted fowl or pig stuffed with acai or beans or custard apples, with gourd or ungurahui, with palm hearts, with pupunha, with tapioca and with turtle eggs. Whichever philanthropists say that Indians lead rude lives, poor lives, humble lives – they have never been hosted by the *pories* for our bellies and brains could scarce recover from the food and drink before more was thrust upon us.

"Something don't be right," Quarasips complained to me one morning, spent from his days of over-eating and his nights of over-exertion with inexhaustible supplies of willing girls arriving at his bedside with the King's compliments.

"I thought, Sire, that tomorrow I might with your permission take some good men and set forth on a call to arms as far and wide as this very forest. For if word gets back to the Portugals that the

Indians of this land are raising an army against them, it would be wise to add credence to the rumour" I said one afternoon to the King.

"White man," sighed the King, chomping on some tobacco or gambolling with his latest woman or counting then re-counting his stash of precious stones, "you lead life at a ferocious pace."

"He could be losing his mind," said Quarasips, from his hammock, one huge arm around each of his tiny *pories*. "He be an old man. Maybe he been ruling too long, yah."

"These things take planning, white man," said the King to me, selecting which jewel to wear for that day in his lip or on his ears, or having his markings re-painted.

"But the time to move is now!" I replied, thinking of the Portugals with a crystal ball, aware of our uprising somehow and pointing into the glass and laughing at the idea of it, at anyone who could entertain a hope of ousting them.

"The time to move is after the rainy season," said the King, and I saw that this did have a certain logic as the paths would now be waterlogged and the going, to those other kingdoms we would need to visit to muster our army, much more arduous. But I also saw that he spoke as if he were not all there, which was strange for a man who in my experience had always been so attentive.

"He is not losing his mind," I reported back to Quarasips, who had gone from being a big man to an immense man these last weeks and also, perhaps, to a lethargic man, a man who enjoyed the good things in life and was granted them almost before his brain had processed the thought that it desired them. "He is distracted."

"Perhaps we should wait like the man says, yah," slurred Quarasips Juca as he slurped coconut milk, as he poured it over his concubines, as they, tittering, rubbed it back into his back. "It be raining out there and here we are, dry and not wanting for food. Have yourself a girl, Anthony Knivet, and relax. God strike me down if we don't be due a little relaxation."

"The rains are over Sire, and with your permission…" I said to the King, thinking of the itinerant *tamoyes*, my friends, venturing further and further away.

"I discovered a new jewel this morning, red as blood, suddenly there in the soil, where I walk every day," the King said as he oversaw the seasonal turtle harvest, as he directed which should be flipped, and captured, and have their eggs extracted. "What do you make of that, white man, is it a sign, does it confirm my wealth or tell me it is threatened or perhaps the message lies in the colour, red, an indication of blood to be spilt – and if so whose blood, mine, white man, or yours?"

"The question is," I said to Quarasips, "what is he distracted by? What is he not telling us? My eyes scanned the room where we reclined, in the finest hut in the village and with the remnants of the finest food we had ever eaten, but unlike Quarasips I had no qualms about doubting the King, nothing in this Brazil was what it seemed, nothing, and my eyes alighted on the women lying beside him. "Who do you tell your hopes and fears to, Quarasips? You confide them to the women you lie with" I got one of the women and shook her and Quarasips bid me to desist, it was me who was not myself, he shouted, it was me losing my mind. But I held on to the strumpet: "what do you know, what has the King told you, what is his plan?" And just when it seemed her screams might bring others running she succumbed, for I had her arm twisted so hard I would have broken it. "The Portugals are coming, that is the plan."

"He has set us up." I fell back, panting. "Two overfed fools we are, waiting here whilst the King plays us off against the Portugals, waiting to see who offers him the best deal."

"He probably be thinking he can get a high price for us," Quarasips looked serious, finally, for the first time in months, "because there be little doubt who offer him the best deal, yah. What would you choose, Anthony Knivet, if you had the two options? A load of riches for a simple handover, or a high chance of a miserable death in return for months of tramping these here forests raising an army?"

"We must leave," I said. "Tonight. As to where I will work out the particulars. We do not know when these Portugals might arrive; the King has been acting strangely for weeks so my guess is he has known about their coming just as long."

I thought of the words of the *pories* warrior who would have killed me, Waynembuth, once I had overcome him and had him banished.

"The King sniffs prosperity on you, but when the scent is gone…"

To maintain secrecy we sent word to the King that the women he had given Quarasips had pleasured him so well we wanted to keep them; we could also easily accrue food and water supplies and pretend we were doing nothing more than proceeding with our usual cycle of gluttony. More difficult, however, was knowing where we should go. I was not familiar with the forest much beyond the domain of the *pories* and had no idea where the *tamoyes* might be. We could not go back to the River of January. We could hardly stay.

"Ready?" I came to get Quarasips that evening.

"We got us a problem Anthony Knivet."

"Which one are you referring to specifically?"

"I just heard me some voices. And they weren't speaking Tupi."

"Let us go," I whispered fiercely.

We crept out of the hut. I knew south was the way we had arrived and there was no cover there; I gestured north where the undergrowth was thicker. We crept to the village edge passed the enclosure where the *pories* kept their turtle farm, they gazed at us with their wizened faces, they judged us, it seemed to me, with their deep eyes, whatever you do now is not important for it is but a butterfly wing-beat when you compare it to our time on this Earth, you can come and go and we will still be here, we can be mastered here and now because your mastery over us is fleeting.

"There be someone there," Quarasips nudged me, "back from the treeline."

"We will go back; try another part of the boundary."

We stole along the back of the turtle enclosure, clockwise around the perimeter of the village, keeping cover in the grass.

"Try here."

We approached the trees again but Quarasips was right, those perimeter branches twiched, only infinitesimally but it was enough for our well-accustomed eyes, I knew when I was being watched in this jungle. My foot hit something and I fell: a damned pile of logs. Quarasips pulled me up immediately but the noise had triggered something. The trees parted and out came the Portugals and their lackeys the *wayanasses*, silently, muskets and bows raised. There was a circle of them as wide as the circle of the village; I counted twenty then gave up; twenty to two was about the limit of the odds I was prepared to gamble on in a skirmish if I represented the minority party.

"I was passing by," said Martin de Sá, impeccably dressed despite the hour and isolated location. He cut such a contrast with his malevolently silent henchmen it would have been comical had I not known with cold certainty what his apprehending me must mean for my chances of future happiness. "What a coincidence, Anthony Knivet, that our paths should cross like this."

He came over as nonchalantly as if he were strutting to one of his fine Lisbon haberdashers.

"It is a great pity," he grabbed both my cheeks in his gloved hands, "that you will come to such a sorry end as you are likely to come to."

TWENTY-EIGHT
(The Governor's Heir)

"A strange thing happened recently," said Martin de Sá. "I had spent the night with my good wife Maria, and next day travelled out of town to visit Lourdes – my savage lover," he reminded me unnecessarily, "a body like a Madonna, as, ha ha, the Italian painters *generously* portray Her but with none of the inhibitions, I assure you of that! The problem is the garments for our European women – so tedious to get off – with Lourdes the nakedness is immediate. It overwhelms you but it allows you to concentrate, let us say, less on the undressing. The following morning business called me back to the River of January and naturally I stayed in my quarters there with my wife overnight. But being called back so abruptly from Lourdes vexed me deeply, I set off next day to return to her and we resumed our pleasure where we had left it. The subsequent day was an official function, I think some inspection of the guard, and you will appreciate I could hardly go with a savage – my father would die from the shock – I was duty bound to go with Maria and she is in any case, I will grant you this, good at these ceremonies. And there are formalities to bear: the Captain of the Guard engages us in conversation; we dine together afterward. And this – I arrive at the crux of the matter – was the problem: the Captain of the Guard was asking me the usual pleasantries and my mind was suddenly blank, I simply could not think at that moment which woman I was with. He was asking me, perhaps, about my wife's happiness and to me his enquiry was ludicrous, my wife was very happy in the jungle in her hut, I thought indignantly, and told him as much. Then there was an awkward pause. I managed to laugh it off, I meant figuratively I told them, but then it happened again. My wife's back was turned and from behind, in my defence, she looks a little like Lourdes – it is only from the front that her view underwhelms. And I grabbed her breasts, Anthony Knivet, in public I grabbed her and murmured how I would like to toss her down and take her there and then! But I do not really know why I am telling you this," he concluded, and then with a naïve smile: "perhaps it is because you are different, you do not live by the rigorous rules of my father, indeed you openly defy him – ingenious! But you must know how it is with savage maids," he added, confidentially, as from one man suffering from man's most infamous weakness to another. "I doubt, ha ha, it is only me finding them such a temptation!"

"I beg you," I entreated. "Consider what services I have done you and your father. Think how unreasonably the factor used me such a long time, and how he attacked me on the night of the said crime for which you have here pursued me. You have it in your power, *senhor*, to save me."

"But of course." He beamed his engaging smile; his hat was always at that slight tilt, it was not the jungle that had dislodged it, he had purposely dislodged it, he knew the fashion and he tilted his hat at it and he kept that hat at a could-not-care-less tilt on the other side of the world. "We have endured much side by side. What are we now but two comrades that have the need of the other?" He was tapping his nose, and I knew what that meant, one of his bright ideas was what that meant. "The *engenhos* still need more slaves… go trading for me, once more. And I will settle the matter of your crime with my father.[1]"

"Would it not be possible to end my days with the Indians? I would go so far from you into the interior that you would never hear from me or think of me."

"The *engenhos,*" he said more firmly, "do need more slaves."

"Very well," I replied. My heart was sinking. What of Katawa I was thinking, what of my friends the *tamoyes*? But, as I again found myself in the position of having little choice, I forced myself to seem very willing to do the bidding of my master's son – even though I would have been very content never to lay eyes on him again.

"And now," he clapped me on the shoulders like we were the best of friends, like we were brothers, like he was my younger naughtier brother. "What think you of, ha ha, my little dilemma?"

"You must make the choice, *senhor*, between the one you are with by law and the one you would break all laws to be with. For you cannot be pulled in opposite directions. You will lose your mind. And eventually it will be the death of you."

---

[1] After several days on the verge of death, the factor began to make a slow recovery from the wounds inflicted on him by Knivet. He was, however, unfit to return to his position in charge of the Governor's *engenho*, was deployed in a meaningless administrative position for some years, became disillusioned with Brazil and died in obscurity in a small village in Galicia no one remembers the name of now. Knivet, therefore, is not – at this stage in the novel – a murderer.

TWENTY-NINE
(The Governor)

"When I sentenced you to death," said my master Salvador Correia de Sá, regarding me soberly from under his eyebrows about a year later, "it was what any man in my position would have done. My son, a society must live by laws if it is to flourish. There is not one law for you and one for others. There is one law. One doctrine. I would sentence my son and heir as I sentenced you."

"I understand master," I said, but I did not understand at all, for if what he said were true would he not have condemned Martin de Sá for his fornication, or chastised him for embarking on his numerous hare-brained schemes? If I had really been his son he would have shown me some special favour. If he had really been my father he would have let me show him what I was capable of. And all Brazil could have been the better for it.

"You do not understand." He wrung his hands, like he was washing them in invisible soap. "I am the dispenser of the law, and in the absence of the Pope I am the dispenser of doctrine. But the priests of the College of Jesus save you from hanging – the only men I would have deferred to and the last I would have thought would champion you – and for the first time in my governorship I am obliged to retract my decree. How does that make me look? How does that make this nation look? I should have listened to Manoel. He told me you had a habit of avoiding death. But no, I thought, even a man who can cheat death cannot evade me. Do you know why I like the written word, my son? I like words because they are black and white. Irrefutable. And I ruled this captaincy blackly, whitely, irrefutably, until you were saved from execution without even opening your mouth. Now I look indecisive. I look grey. This captaincy looks grey. And now my son and heir tells me you have again defied death, and returned from far-flung locations in this nation with slaves, more than it could be hoped for and which – God save them – can now become Catholics. So I wonder what to do with you my son. For the first time in my governorship I wonder what to do. I weigh up your merit against your mayhem, your helping this nation against your hindering it. And then it came to me. I will give you a job. A decent job. A job better than many Portugals here have. I will give you a house, a decent house. I will give you a salary. And that will be your fate. You will become grey, my son. You will do this job every day, forevermore. I will have people watch to see that you do it forevermore and report back to me if you deviate. And if you deviate just once, then I will come after you as you know I am capable of and I will throttle you myself. I am immensely interested," my master peered at me, "to know whether this is not in fact a greater punishment for you than anything else. No heroics; no one so much as breathing your name – for, after all, you will no longer do anything notable to prompt anyone into breathing it – nothing. Averageness, my son. And of course," he rummaged amongst his papers and produced a ream of parchment which I recognised, I recognised each stain of blood and mud, I recognised where the pages had got damp on the Roebuck, I recognised how the writing changed from well-formed characters in periods where I had been otherwise unengaged to deviant scrawl in moments of haste, or desperation, or danger – the account of my adventures that somehow, I could not think how, he had got his hands on, "of course this will be burned."

"You would do that?" I said, and my master knew he had got to me with this, it was clearly displayed upon my face for whilst I could prevent it from showing physical pain I could not prevent it contorting into rage at the first sign of outright injustice. "You, a man of words, would destroy that?"

"Bear in mind that I could have destroyed you."

"But you did not," I said. "You could not."

"No. I never knew how, before."

THIRTY

The hollering could be heard the length of Brazil: José de Anchieta was dead; the pacifier of the Indians was dead, and his death could not have come at a worse time[1]. Two *wayanasses*, bearing marks of extreme torture, had that same week stumbled into the Fort of San Sebastian, malnourished and raving. When some sense had been got from them they babbled that they were the only survivors of a large party the Portugals had deployed to the interior for tree-felling and had been set upon by merciless Indians that came out of nowhere, like vengeful spirits, and massacred the lot of them. Something must be done, they cried, or the vengeful spirits would destroy all Brazil in similar fashion. Something certainly had to be done. Portugal relations with even their closest Indian allies were strained with Anchieta gone, and suddenly Brazil faced its most major uprising in thirty years. I was not surprised when the Governor sent for me.

"Naturally," he said, "we will crush the rebellion. Word has

---

[1] Many did see this as the end of an era. Anchieta was an integral part of the establishment of Portuguese Brazil. His ability to communicate with many indigenous tribes was instrumental to Portugal securing "peace" in their new colony. A fragile peace, of course, and one that could not last…

gone out to all the captaincies to send every last infantryman to me here. We will show these savages the fist of this nation reaches out to its remotest forest if there are dissenters to be found there."

"Remotest forest, master?"

"Rumour has it the rebels fled deep into the interior – deeper than any of us have ever ventured. The way after them lies through much hostile territory. And in Anchieta's absence we need a man who speaks the language of these heathens."

"And what of my labours here, master?"

"Do this for me, my son," he sighed, "and I will give your freedom and passage on a ship back to England with enough riches to buy yourself an estate, or whatever it is you want."

"I shall get my things together," I said.

THIRTY-ONE

We left as soon as the rains were gone; Martin de Sá led us and his half-brother Gonzalo was second-in-command. We were almost 3,000 strong, with two thirds of us Indians – mostly *wayanasses*, because they were known to be loyal and *tomomynos*, because they were known to be brutal.

There were a few familiar faces among the ranks.

Manoel gave me a wink as we readied the canoes for departure; he went as chief lieutenant of the entire company, now only one rank below the de Sás and not significantly less well-dressed, with a brigandine clearly plated in Potosi silver and a rather striking scarlet sash.

"Glad to have you with us, Englishman. We will need the most resolute soldiers, and I know you to be of that calibre."

Give us all armour like that and food half as good as what you officers will be getting, I thought as I returned his greeting, and the survival rates of the entire company will improve.

I found myself loading up supplies with Quarasips Juca.

"Just don't speak to me, Anthony Knivet," said he gloomily. "I don't be wanting to hear about how this trip is gonna be the making of us, or yield untold treasures, or anything like that. I'm through with that, yah. I'm here because the factor promise me my freedom if I make it back alive."

"In truth I would not know what to promise you, Quarasips. Your guess is as good as mine where this adventure will lead for us."

"Whatever are you talking about Anthony?" a voice rang out. My blood brother emerged from the group checking our gunpowder; he had tried growing a beard since I had seen him last but it hung off his chin in a dribble of hair; it was like the fluff young birds have before they can fly yet or at least, when they have undertaken no more than a few blundering flaps in the vicinity of the nest. "We go to get those *tamoyes*!"

"*Tamoyes*?" I felt my heart pick up its pace. And I gripped Barrawell by his collar. "What are you talking about?"

"Come, Anthony, everyone knows that is the enemy we are going to root out." Barrawell laughed nervously. "Is that not so?" he addressed a few of the other men in his lamentable Portugal.

Yes, they corroborated, it was so, they were the violent spirits that massacred the tree-felling party, they were the most formidable enemy the Portugals now had remaining, thousands had mustered in the interior and it would be a grave challenge for Brazil because these savages were far from unorganised, that was the worrying thing, they had cohesion and that was indicative of an adversary worth taking seriously.

Something surged within me. I imagined *Peteca*, Ubi serving and me stretching to meet his shot, stumbling on that stump. I screwed shut my eyes and recreated hers with the red cat's whisker markings fanning out from the corners – "*why do you stare at me?*" – oh, why indeed, with your green irises and your ubiquitous hair and – dare I say – your oval buttocks and your coyness as if I was the first man ever to look upon you! That was it, I had made my own way to her, we had found our way to that clearing in the woods of our own accord, what we had was wholly ours and no one else could claim a part in it. Of course, I remembered, she might be dead. She might have been butchered by *tomomynos*, or washed away in a river as her people retreated, or dead from childbirth, but that beauty, that kindness, that *"why do you stare at me"* was what I preferred to think about. Why had the General not told me it was the *tamoyes* we were going to fight? In a heartbeat I would have readied myself. And then I thought: it is because he does not trust me. He trusts me less than any other infantryman, and even less than the lowliest slave. To the Portugals I was nothing. And yet they needed me. Well, nothing likes to be appreciated. Treat nothing well, or nothing becomes something. Ha, nothing rises up.

THIRTY-TWO

Things began badly. A storm that was not supposed to blow up blew up, and dissipated our army's fleet not a day's sail out of the River of January.

Martin de Sá laughed the misfortune off but Gonzalo Correia de Sá was not like his half-brother.

"The one father tried to hang, he is a smug one," I heard him snarl as our forces re-gathered, soaked through and with some provisions already lost, on the beach at Paraty, which was the point where we planned to beat our way inland. "What reason does he have for happiness, I want to know!"

It did seem that now I knew about the *tamoyes* I could not keep the smile off my face – an expression that had hardly been characteristic for me of late.

"God is smiling on you, Anthony."

"It is not God, Barrawell. It is the dominoes. Remember before we were captured, when I was telling you how, if you position a set of them in a shape just so, the first will knock the rest of them and you shall have that shape drawn out before you? They're falling, ha, they're falling!"

I was the only man there who cared not for being wet to the bone; the only man there who was, far from giving something up, returning to something he thought he had lost; the only man who did not mind in the least that he was embarking on one of the most dangerous voyages ever undertaken by white men in Brazil. Indians did far worse all the time, of course, but they did not count.

"Why do you stare at me, maker of the Ma-rrrah y kûá, why do you...?"

"You damned savage," growled Gonzalo Correia de Sá, interrupting my reverie. "Give me your hammock."

I woke up and looked, from close up for the first time, at Martin de Sá's half-brother Gonzalo, the Governor's bastard son. His was not the kind of face you wanted to wake up seeing. The circumstances of his birth were the worst-kept secret in Brazil. Really, our incorruptible Governor, surely he could not have any indiscretion outside of the institution of marriage he prized so highly, not when he stepped up alongside the priest to speak about it in the church on Sundays? But oh, he could, Gonzalo was the proof. And in his face, without being ugly, Gonzalo had an ugliness, the ugliness of the illegitimate, the year-upon-year accumulation of being, unfairly in his eyes, overlooked. The Governor's indiscretion, Gonzalo's mother, had also been, if not of absolute Indian stock, then at the least a mestizo, meaning Gonzalo had two generations of white men's indiscretions with Indians flowing through his blood. It showed, although he tried hiding it. His applied a paste each morning to make his dark skin paler, and cut his hair close to the scalp so it would appear less black than it was.

"We have new men joining us," he said. "A tribe from hereabouts. And even if they are savages, at least they are giving themselves to the cause of their own free will. We all know who and what you are, you are a traitor, you even lived with the *tamoyes* and your skin is as dark as one, who knows what coup you are planning, if I had my way I would run you through with my sword, you stinking savage, give up your hammock I say!"

His speech had woken several of the other men and after he

had my hammock and was gone off to give it to the leader of the party of Indians joining our forces, I remarked to a few of them how wrongly this man treated me.

"Englishman," said a Portugal by the name of John de Sousa, "there is reason for that. This voyage is a test for all of our mettles. Success is imperative to the Governor, Brazil depends upon it, he told us, and everyone here knows what their chances for advancement are if they distinguish themselves – Gonzalo Correia de Sá included. And I overheard the Governor speak to his sons about you before we began this journey."

"What did he say?"

"He said he would not be sorry if you did not return. Use him, he said, just so long as he is useful."

"God's will be done," I said, "for those of us, at least, that believe God is the one who determines things around here."

"What other will could have a say?

"The Indians, for example, believe he who wields the ceremonial rattle speaks the word of not just one God but all their many Gods. The spirits inside the shaken rattle clamour for the flesh of the Indians' enemies, and the wielder of the rattle is the mouthpiece for these spirits when they choose to speak."

"Damned heathens," cried the other Portugals near me. "Thank the Lord we are going to silence them once and for all!"

I said nothing, but rocked on my haunches. The Governor would not be sorry if I did not return, eh? I would *show* him. I would lead his sons and his men into the jungle just like they wanted. And when they were there I would kill them.

* * *

We lasted about a fortnight before we started dying.

The first death was an Indian. We had been toiling several days up the belt of mountains that stand guard over the interior, with our Indians hacking a path through the foliage as Quarasips Juca and I had done. But we were carrying many more supplies and in the extreme heat that hits once the rains end, we made slow progress and exhausted much of our food. When we were done, we came out into vast dry grasslands that appeared lush but contained nothing to eat but pine nuts and snakes. The men tired of the pine nuts and started on the snakes. But the snakes did not just lay down and die for us, they fought back, and they had venom on their side, although we did not know it until one Indian, one of our foremost guides, got bitten. He foamed at the mouth; within minutes blood spurted from his eyes and his nails, and so he died. We were more reticent to kill the snakes after that. And because men in unfamiliar territory rapidly become superstitious, mutterings commenced about whether we were cursed and whether this death was the sorcery of the vengeful spirits we were pursuing, punishing us for following them. To a man who knew Brazil's wilderness somewhat, such mutterings were laughable. If we were dying it was because we did not know the creatures of these wild lands nor the food that grew within them, it was because we were taking this mission on with no more knowledge of our undertaking than a circus troupe would have of a battle campaign – and a troupe, presumably, would at least offer humorous diversion. But I saw no harm in nurturing these first seeds of mutiny. It suited my purpose very well.

The second time, death hit us harder. A group of Portugals had, with some jubilation, found roots and, such was their hunger, began eating them immediately and secretively, so as not to have to divide their discovery amongst the others. We were only alerted to this when we heard their screams. The Indians and myself shook our heads when we saw them. Cassava is not a root you can just eat. You must boil it and purge it to rid it of the poison it contains.

"There is nothing we can do now," I said to Martin de Sá as we watched them collapsing, and vomiting, and expiring.

"You knew about this poisonous root," said Gonzalo Correia

de Sá, "and said nothing? More evidence of your treacherous inclinations, savage!"

"Easy," Martin de Sá calmed his brother. "These men should have shared their findings. They did not, and therefore they were the dishonest ones. Let this be a lesson to stick together!" he cried to the company. "We are marching against a foe who know how to stick together and we must do the same ourselves."

"If I had known you did not know," I told the de Sás, to exonerate myself, "I would have said."

Martin patted me on the back. Gonzalo glared at me like he knew the falseness of my words.

The rains came back belatedly to lash us. Day upon day it rained. Our clothes were damp, our souls were damp. The fiercest fire, if we could source wood dry enough to light one, could not banish the dampness from our clothes overnight and so we began again next day with the previous day's deluge still upon us. Men fell ill. There was increasingly less food. The ground got boggier and with the weight of the weaponry we carried we sunk up to our knees in bog – if we stood a chance of catching game before, that chance was gone, for any animal aside from a turtle could hear our fatigued steps long in advance, and evade us accordingly. If no tribes attacked us it was only because of our numbers. But our numbers became less of a consolation. The men grew nervous on the night watches. They were hearing the ominous sounds of the forest, I thought; for many it was their first time out of their closeted little townships. I knew what it was to hear such sounds for the first time. I knew how the whisperings and hootings of the unseen watchers could chill you more than any rain; how you could look around at your fellows and see the same misgivings in them; how they suddenly seemed like men who caught diseases and pissed their pants, men you could not count on being able to save you should it come down to it.

One day Martin de Sá called us to halt just after luncheon, the going was so bad. I went up into the hills above the plain where we were camped to fetch wood for a shelter. Going to cut boughs, my sword fell out of my hand, and I slumped beside the trunk where I was, with no energy to move. And there I would have stayed, the next death in a long series of deaths, had it not been for Barrawell, who alone observed my absence at the campfires and came searching for me.

"Anthony! Good Christ, you are cold." His boyish face loomed out of the mist. I could not tell if the mist was the weather or the mist they say fogs your vision just before the very end. Then again 'they' were the scribes, the writers of the ballads, those fancifuls who had probably idled their whole lives at court and never known true hardship, show me a writer who has known true hardship and I will read him.

"Barrawell – you find me… indisposed."

"You will be fine, Anthony, I will not leave you. We swore an oath to each other – like the knights of old, remember?"

And somehow it was this chit of a fellow and not any of the men there present that got me onto his back and back to the fire and laid me down there.

"You are a man, Barrawell. I have seen Brazil turn you into a man better than any of them," I managed.

"Hush. Do not throw me complements because I did what any Christian would and saved you."

"You are the only Christian in this Brazil I would trust to do that, Barrawell. I would trust any Indian above these Portugals."

"I know you blame me," Barrawell was close to me suddenly; his ridiculous wispy beard tickled my face. "For sending you to the *engenho* that first time. But I only m…meant to defend your good name, Anthony."

"I do not blame you," I smiled. "Without that, other things would not have happened and we would not be here now. And I would not swap being here with you now for anything."

"Nor I." Barrawell was moved.

"Two stupid knights together, hey Barrawell?" The fire was already having a welcome effect on me.

"You are changed, these last weeks." My blood brother peered at me. "It is not just happiness. It is peace. It is as if you have found God, but I know you do not believe in God."

"Oh, He is there alright." I looked up at the rain. "He has always been there, pulling me this way and that. I have found a way to tug back, that is all."

* * *

Once we were over the mountains the Portugals called the Serro do Mar, we were in swampy ground, swamps that would have been swamps even without the cursed rain and as it was were almost impassable. We began to see squat men observing us with hair shaven on top but mighty unkempt at the sides; they would venture quite close and wordlessly hold out their hands for shiny things. I advised our men to comply. Such offerings had often saved my own skin. I knew them to be *pories* and told Martin de Sá no less. He said that he thought their territory, which we had both visited, lay to the north; I said that it was a vast domain the *pories* possessed and it was likely these ones lived on the other side of the kingdom to that which we had visited before; he instructed me to go and speak to them for we could not go on much longer without a town to re-victual at; I might also ask them where we were whilst I was at it for he was damned if he knew.

"*Senhor*, I consent, but I must ask you something, it is about a rumour, I am sure a vile untruth, that some of the men have been spreading."

"Name it!" cried Martin de Sá.

"They say your father said expressly to you and Gonzalo Correia de Sá that he did not want to see me return from this expedition. And veiled insinuations from your half-brother's own lips would appear to support that view."

With that he laughed gaily and bid me walk with him a way.

"Anthony Knivet, do you remember when I told you once

about how I have a good side and a bad side, a white and a black? Gonzalo is all black. He is a bad man. But you need not fear, for I am in charge and he answers to me."

But I remembered too how he had lied to me before.

The army pulled up before a rain-swollen river and there made camp, for no one saw any value to continuing until I returned with news. I, meanwhile, made for the place upstream where I had last glimpsed the *pories* heading.

Before long I was in a kind of scrub where tobacco was being cultivated and then, around a bend, in the middle of a muddy clearing surrounded by many huts, I came upon maybe a hundred *pories* regarding me with a mixture of fascination and probably fright. The pause lasted longer than it should have done. I had been expecting to run into a handful of Indians not a village-full, and I must have shocked them for I had abandoned my white man's clothes at camp in favour of the loin cloth the Indians wear and carried a bow and arrows as well as a musket. The pause passed, and a number of spears were aimed in a flash at various parts of my anatomy.

I delicately set down my knife and fishing hooks and smiled as charmingly as I knew how.

"Gifts!" I told them.

They brought me before a dwelling where a man with many scars sat cross-legged eating something brown and unidentifiable out of a gourd. Five women squatted watching him, whom the man might have found off-putting, were it not for the fact that he was blind. He stared straight ahead and sometimes the food spilt a little. When this happened one of the women would dart forward to clear the spillage but as quickly he would thrust her back, grope around for the food on the floor, methodically wipe it up with his finger, lick it, then continue with his meal. He bid me sit and eat with him, which I did; the meal was bitter, chewy but not entirely disagreeable. I had not been opposite him a few seconds before I became uneasy – not on account of the vigilant women but because the man was identical, aside from the scars, to the King of the *pories* Quarasips Juca and I had lived with three years previously.

"When we have finished, they may start," the scarred man explained in fluent Portugal. "We do not have much food at this time but you are our guest so you eat before them."

We ate in silence. The rest of the villagers came and squatted in a semi-circle outside the hut, also watching us.

"Forgive me," I said, "but you seem familiar."

"And you to me," the scarred man replied.

"There is a king, far to the north of here, who has in his possession a mountain of jewels. He has to walk but softly on that mountain for new jewels to uncover themselves. He holds lavish parties almost nightly, with every delicacy you can conceive of to eat, and his women pierce their nipples with fabulous green stones."

"What of it?"

"Is it to him that you answer?"

"We acknowledge his existence."

"But you are *pories*, are you not?"

"Why? Are you curious to know if we have the same policy regarding abstinence from human flesh?" The scarred man translated these words into a thick dialect of Tupi that I could scarcely follow, and a ripple of laughter went up from the assembled Indians. The scarred man came no closer to laughing than baring his teeth, which were uneven but unblemished.

"I am curious to know why you look the very image of him."

The scarred man translated this, too, but a little more uneasily.

"I am his twin," he said finally.

"Then why the disparity in your kingdoms? Why do your people want for food, and come begging for trinkets, when that king encourages gluttony and has more treasure than he knows how to use?"

"I will tell you," said the scarred man, gazing straight at me despite his blindness. "If you will tell me why there was a foreign man, a *karaíba* just like you, who once came to persuade us *pories* to rise up with him and other Indians against the Portugals, of whom nothing more was heard until his very image appears right here in my village, only now seemingly on the side of the Portugals, and against those same Indians."

I smiled and nodded. He was every bit as astute as his twin, this scarred man.

"We have much to talk about," I said.

We talked for so long that his villagers in desperation begged leave to start eating. They finished, did their afternoon's activities and were again returned and turning meat on their fires at dusk before we were done.

The kingdom of the *pories*, the scarred man told me, was left to his brother, who was able to prove through the testimony of a soothsayer that he was some minutes older. His people listened to soothsayers, the scarred man lamented, just like Portugals listen to priests; their status alone is sufficient persuasion even if their use of the status is suspect. I could not agree more, I said. His brother, continued the scarred man, was notoriously greedy. He himself was allotted the sorriest lands in the kingdom, and at the same time his twin rapidly established himself as so superior in military might that a battle would have been futile. In some ways, the scarred man said, it was not so bad. He was glad to have many forests and hills separating him from his brother and the Portugals both, for it was difficult to say whom he cared for least. Instead he forged his alliances with whom he could, he said, call him a turncoat but you had to look out for yourself. Think of it like a river festooned with lizards, the lizards presented stepping stones across the river for those who wanted to get to the far side but of course some lizards moved and some lizards tried biting you when you used them to step on, you had to pick your lizards carefully, in the middle of the river when one wrong step could send you plunging to your death. We see eye to eye, I told him. Yet his brother and him had rarely seen eye to eye, said the scarred man. He had heard the news about the *karaíba* and his call to arms and had been all for joining him, indeed it was as if he had been waiting his whole life for such a sign; he would have taken the chance of failure because his people stood to gain better lands, lands they had no hope of taking by themselves, but he had to defer to his brother's will in such matters – which was of course against anything which did not have increased quantities of treasure as an immediate consequence. I am that same karaíba, I said, and my call to arms has lain dormant but is not dead. I told him of what had befallen me these last years, of his brother's betrayal of me and of the circumstances that led to me being camped with an army of lost and starving Portugals not two hours' walk hence – a force, I added meaningfully, comprising of Portugals' foremost fighting men. The scarred man had a glint in his eye just like his brother when he sensed a beneficial trajectory to the conversation.

When the two of us parted several hours later I had directions to a larger nearby settlement where our forces might be fed, and, more pertinently, we had ourselves an agreement.

THIRTY-THREE

"...wee travelled at least a moneth... the Portugals beganne to dispaire, and threw away their Peeces, being not able to carrie their clothes."

Anthony Knivet, *Admirable Adventures and Strange Fortunes*

Back at camp, our Indians were dying, and this time no one knew why. They had sweats, they were always drowsy, their skin became infested with blotches and pustules that swelled so that they were more red than brown, they began raving and had even less ability to direct us than before.

With my direction we managed to gain the town the scarred man had told me of, the foremost settlement of the *wamawa-waanasons*. If the de Sás hoped for a respite from their bad luck here they were to be disappointed. Nothing could prevent our Indians from expiring in such quantities that our entire army was soon half what it had started out as — that is, not much above 1,000 men — and these survivors in such low spirits they even lacked the inclination for fornication.

But this township was prepared for our visit: the scarred leader of the *pories* had sent advance warning. They welcomed us in the usual fashion, whooping and dancing before us in red and blue body paint; the main difference was that it was old men doing the dancing rather than young maids, which made the Portugals less appreciative of the entertainment. Indeed in this village there seemed very few people besides the very old and the very young; yet when the de Sás questioned them they evasively answered that they had successfully defended the town against the *tamoyes*, who by now were far away.

"It seems an unlikely story," murmured Martin de Sá to his half-brother. "For we have been hearing of nothing but the destructive trail the *tamoyes* have been forging; they trounced our troops, who were several score strong, and yet this village of some few old men fends them off?"

Yet the sprightly old leader of this village, by the name of Carywason, furnished our men with good food and offered to guide us to where he knew the *tamoyes* to be, and this offer was too generous to turn down. Beggars cannot be choosers and the de Sás were, like the rest of us, becoming more like the beggars.

"You are the one my friend told me of." Carywason came to me that night as the others slept. I knew he was referring to the scarred man and nodded.

"I am he."

"This plan of yours. How came you upon it?"

"Originally? A lizard told me in a dream."

"Why do you desire such a perilous path? What have you against the Portugals?"

"I will happily relate the long version in due course. But for now suffice it to say that they humiliated me. And I do not like being humiliated."

"It is a most unusual arrangement," said Carywason. "I never heard the like."

"White men stood as brothers with Indians before. The rewards for us both are significant."

"Yes. But to orchestrate this effectively we need many weeks."

"So be it. I am not immensely pressed for time."

"I have seen where this Brazil is headed." Carywason looked at me with clear, calm eyes. "What you are proposing will not be possible in a few years' time. It must be now if it is to be at all."

"My thoughts exactly," I said.

We beat west, and then north, and then, I was almost sure, east again. No one questioned Carywason's guidance; few had energy for voicing anything whatsoever, for it was simpler to traipse, head bent; half-starved; thoughts firmly fixed on food-to-be. We went for forty days, which was thirty more than Carywason had told the de Sás we would need and tramped so far we traced a river from a width wider than the Thames at the point of Carywason's village up to its very source. This meant it was five months all told since we had departed the River of January. Martin de Sá began to worry how his father would manage with such reduced forces to protect Brazil against attack and decided to return with half of our company, leaving the remainder under his half-brother's captaincy.

"Do you desire to be dogs all your days?" Gonzalo Correia de Sá strode amongst the several hundreds of us fated to remain. "For you shall you be if we do not come back to the Governor bearing news of the death of each of these *tamoyes* savages. Kill for me, God give you strength, and wealth and rank awaits you."

But he was seizing the reins of a flogged horse. We leaned heavy on our swords and gazed at him in exhausted despondency, the same men his half-brother could have spurred on with little more than a wisecrack and a pat on the back. We had no idea how many *tamoyes* were in store for us, but by now they must be many more than us. The firearms, our other main asset, were heavy, and we carried them weakened and in weather that had switched from relentless rain to the severest sun anyone there had ever experienced. As the weak or diseased cast down their weapons in despair Gonzalo Correia de Sá bestowed their loads upon the strongest and he took particular pleasure in singling me out for other tasks besides; cooking his meals; cleaning his musket; washing his clothes; on one occasion even trimming his beard in a style he claimed to dislike although I saw him admiring it in a looking glass later.

"How well-contented you seem, savage, when other men have hunger gnawing at their bellies."

You are nothing but a vessel, I fumed inwardly, oh if you could comprehend that you and your blundering men are like the unseemly chrysalises the butterfly hides within whilst it so requires then abandons when it spreads its wings; you are only here because I need you here and soon, chrysalis, you will break.

It infuriated him that he could not break me - or the smiling deference I somehow managed to maintain in his presence. Well, the occasional exchange of glances with Carywason reassured me we were getting close, not as close as he was telling the Portugals we were, but close - and I merely had to conjure the ebony of Katawa's hair before me to summon the powers of endurance I needed.

We had been a fortnight crossing a great savannah, and with nothing to eat save the same poisonous snakes as before. Ahead were orange mountains with precipitous gouged sides, like an ogre had scraped his nails along them. Carywason promised us that once we crossed them there would be ample water; Gonzalo Correia de Sá said that the issue would be crossing them at all in the state we were in. He bid us all place every edible thing we had before us on the cow's skins we carried our possessions in. We did so, and it was pitifully obvious we did not have sufficient for everyone there to partake of even one more decent meal. Our good leader took the best of what there was, and divided it amongst himself and his officers; he then commanded us to boil up the skins and eat the broth.

"And how it would be," said Quarasips Juca bitterly, "if the *tamoyes* chanced upon us now?"

"Whose side would you take Quarasips, if it came to a battle?" I asked quietly.

"The side most likely to give me meat, yah. And you Anthony Knivet?"

I thought about telling him what had passed between the scarred man and me but decided to keep it to myself, for now.

"I am not sure it will ever come down to a battle," I said.

Barrawell did not participate in the discussion. He was sick. His constitution, always weak, had succumbed to fever, and if one saving grace was that it was not the same malady that had decimated the Indians in our party, he was getting worse, and I was sorry for it because I had pledged to look after him, come what may, when we began this whole damned thing.

As we chewed our boiled skins to somehow lend us the sustenance to scale the mountains a couple of the *tomomynos* still with us began shivering, although the weather was far from being cold. We guessed it to be some sickness but it was not. One after the other of them, *tomomynos* and *wayanasses* both, started doing the same and no disease spreads as quickly. It was a kind of fit; they banged every part of their body on the rocks like they had lost control.

"What is it?" we demanded of Carywason and his men, who seemed the only Indians unaffected.

"Curupira," they replied. "There is nothing we can do for them now but bind them with their own bow-strings, and hope the evil spirits inside of them depart.

"Evil spirits!" cried Gonzalo Correia de Sá. "What tomfoolery! They are savages, they are accustomed to this country, they should not be dying like this when we have greater need of them than ever!"

Carywason went and faced our captain. The old man was only five feet to Gonzalo Correia de Sá's six, and he never raised his voice or betrayed a flicker of emotion, but he silenced that bastard son of the Governor more effectively than his half-brother. He should take heed, said Carywason. When Curupira appeared, it was the worse for all of us. Curupira was what the forest sent when she felt threatened. It was a sign we had gone too far. A man in the forest should take what he needs and no more, Curupira came to punish he who took too much. Curupira's feet are bent backwards, Carywason said, so you cannot track him down. When he attacks there is nothing to be done but succumb to the torment and accept it is equal to the torment you have caused to the land. Curupira struck these men down because they were doing Portugal bidding, Carywason added menacingly, and it would not be long before Portugals became seized by the same fits. Gonzalo Correia de Sá, cowed, asked is there was anything to be done to save them. Carywason replied that the only remedy was to leave this place immediately. Our De Sá, no doubt apprehensive now of this spirit with the backward-facing feet, wanted to know if he meant to press onward or to press back. Onward, said Carywason, every man that could still stand, we were too far in to go back and would just have to call upon the benevolence of whatever God we believed in to help us evade Curupira's attention.

Without further ado we dragged ourselves to our feet and began the climb into the mountains. We came upon a land of vast ramparts of stone, of cliffs that towered before us like jagged waves frozen on the cusp of breaking. Many men did not make it. Driven on at a pace by Carywason, their bodies or their minds gave up the fight and surely found respite in a Hell less harsh than this one. Of course it was Carywason's intention that they should be dying thus but I did think that he was relishing his role a little too much and told him so. He replied that he was doing nothing but what I had proposed and that I was accustomed to such savage terrain, so would survive these hardships even when every other Portugal there expired. But the Curupira, I cried, really, was that not taking it all too far? No, said Carywason solemnly, he thought it had been entirely necessary to mention the Curupira, because the Curupira was real.

The mountains were so high we could not see what lay below on the other side. It seemed, as we peered over the edge of the precipice before us, to be a flat land, moist like Carywason had described, for thick mist clung over it. There was no discernable path to descend so we made ropes out of the withies that thrived in these lofty altitudes and lowered ourselves down, inch by inch, through the clouds.

We saw nothing but heard lots of things, shriekings or shufflings, birds and lizards, the sounds of creatures never before seen by man, augmented by the mist.

"You do lead us around and about to break us" moaned the Portugals, for the most terrible thing about this new land we had reached was that you could not see more than a few feet in front of you, and the effect on the mind was to despair that there was no landmark, no goal, nothing but a featureless purgatory.

They were, of course, mighty close to the mark, and Carywason raised an eyebrow at me, which a couple of the men saw.

"We will gain our destination in two days," he said. "Cut off my head if we do not."

Closely examined, this was a rather superfluous promise, for we would do less well with a headless guide than one in full possession of his extremities.

"Christ, I see things." Quarasips Juca stared into the mist, like others stare at a fire and make shapes from the flames. "This be a land of mischief, Anthony Knivet."

"Have I died?" Barrawell would whimper intermittently. "Is this Heaven?"

"Not yet, Barrawell. For I would not be carrying you if it were."

"I see my village!" breathed Quarasips. There's sun, and baobab trees, and my father..."

"Do not dream." I slapped him, but I was dreaming too because that was what deprivation did; as you approached the point where it killed you it made you hallucinate.

The mist did not clear but Carywason marched on determinedly; those of us that could followed him and those that could not lay down to die. Maybe it was two days and maybe it was more but at last we pulled up by a riverbank. Carywason said this river took its headwater from Potosi in Upper Peru and that there was silver and gold to be found upon its bed. Upon hearing this news many men, despite their depleted state, dived directly into the water to search for it and it was a sorry sight to see: the current was strong, and many got swept away.

"I should tell you," said Carywason, far later than he should have, "that this is also where you shall find the *tamoyes*."

"Why did you not say so before my men jumped in the river?" Gonzalo Correia de Sá exploded.

"I am not their keeper," Carywason contemptuously replied.

"I should cut off your head as you invited me to do."

"Perhaps you should," said Carywason. "Depending on whether you trust the Curupira to spare you for I notice…" he looked emotionlessly into the de Sá's face, "…yes, the first signs of fever. Curupira's punishment for going against what is natural, perhaps."

Our captain's breath was ragged; his skin enflamed: disease was not concerned with rank.

"Go across the river," he growled. "Take him" – he pointed at me – "and him" - he pointed at one of his henchmen. "Tell me what sign there is of the *tamoyes* and report back.

We fashioned a rude raft out of logs and set off. It was unfortunate the captain should want a Portugal to accompany us; unfortunate particularly for the Portugal. When we reached the far bank Carywason called to the man that he wanted to show him some precious stones by the waterside, and when his back was turned smote him on the head with a rock.

"Has there not been enough death?" I cried as he held the bleeding body under the water to make sure, then cast it out into the fastest part of the current.

"We cannot afford to have the plan compromised," Carywason tightly replied.

Focus on the past, the green and pleasant past. The gourd rattles, the gourd shakes, it is the sound of the sea – not an approximation but an exact replica – mud and soft shells for the approaching waves, larger stones for when they break. "Ma-rrrah y kûá." Ubi serves. The sun shafts down on the clearing but the trees are high enough for shade. I fall back. The clouds are rolled back; right to the horizon; it is a clean sky; swept clean; you would pause, had you been sweeping clean that sky, and admire your handiwork. There are the tops of the trees, and there they are rushing down at me and it is hair, of course, not leaves or branches, and it brushes me a little. "*Why do you stare at me, why do you…*"

The mist fell back. I saw stakes hammered into a circular perimeter wall. The *tamoyes* always built their villages thus. We had arrived.

"Why do we not hear them?" Carywason asked in a low voice and I realised he was frightened too, for he was not a natural ally of the *tamoyes*. Neither of us were. We had both arrived in this place with a Portugal army the *tamoyes* must know by now was marching against them. They could kill us, these Indians we had been seeking, before we had opportunity to explain.

"I only hear frogs," I whispered. Indeed it was the only disruption to this sodden, mist-cloaked land, the sound was everywhere, it was like the Earth had summoned spirits to laugh at us, "wa-wa-i-i-i-i-i-i-, waa-i-i-i-waa-i-i-i…"

"They must be here." Carywason touched one of the outer posts, gingerly, as if it might spring into life. I peered through the gap in the stockade and saw huts within but no people.

"Wa-wa-i-i-i-i-i-i-, waa-i-i-i-waa-i-i-i…"

"Where are they?" said Carywason through clenched teeth and he banged the post in frustration. Something fell down: a human head, somewhat decomposed.

Her hair in the clearing all those years ago is like black lava, how I imagine lava to be, flowing over everything. It freezes me although I am warm, it stupefies me yet I am in full possession of my faculties.

"Wa-wa-i-i-i-i-i-i…"

Before the old man could restrain me I forced back one of

the stakes until it yielded sufficiently for me to squeeze through and ran into the camp. "Ubi," I cried. "Katawa." And the frogs retorted: "wa-wa-wa-wa-i-i-i-i-i-i..."

I saw fires still smoking, I saw a pot filled with cassava but half-cooked, I saw grain in a storehouse, I saw hammocks that they had not even had time to untie in their huts, I saw a turkey hopping about the camp and suddenly remembering my hunger I chased it and broke its neck and plucked it furiously and stoked up the fire. Carywason squatted opposite me.

"They were here, and recently."

"It was easy enough to guide you here," said Carywason, "for they had this for their base some time. Now it is more difficult. Now they have gone on the move again. And in this mist even my most skilled tracker could not follow them. It would be like chasing the wind."

"Wa-wa-i-i-i-i-i-i..."

"I must get my kinsmen and leave. I have led you around and around, as we agreed, in order that those Portugals lose their will to live, as now they have. Your captain will not take kindly to the *tamoyes* being gone. Whilst he still breathes he may yet fancy my head."

"Those damned frogs," I said.

Carywason got up.

"The *tamoyes* will continue waging their wars without us. We have at least the consolation that the greatest army our mutual oppressors could muster was unable to thwart them. If you should ever find them..."

"Oh, I will. I will find them!"

"...tell them the *wamawa-waanasons* would have stood with them against the Portugals."

I broke off a piece of turkey. I crammed it into my mouth, this tough and fatty bird, so much I could hardly chew, and secreted as much of the rest of it as I could about my person to take to Barrawell. Then I felt my way back through the mist.

And just ahead of me she walks, with her head half-turned and her hair flowing over her like lava. *"Would you not let me come with you?"* *"Look after yourself, maker of the Ma-rrrah y kûá."* Katawa-wa-wa-i-i-i-i-i-i, wa-wa...

THIRTY-FOUR

"…There be white men with beards a-coming along the road to my father's village, yah. Portugals. They want to know why we don't pay them taxes. My father, he be explaining to them: that don't be how things get decided. What right you have, he ask them, to be here, on the land my people have for centuries, it don't be right, not even natural. My father was a king, understand. And they knock the crown from his head, yah. They knock the good man's crown clean off his head…"

"…My[1] son – did you know I have a son, Anthony? A maid of my master's. They're standing on one cliff and I am standing on another and in-between is the sea. And they are saying something to me but I do not know what, the wind is snatching their words away, 'we are going, are you coming', something like that. I am replying, 'wait, wait' but they cannot hear that either, so I jump off the cliff and start swimming. But it is a rough sea and a long crossing and I am not a strong swimmer…"

"The captain wants to see you, Englishman."

Manoel. It seemed he was one of the few left with a steady head.

I nodded.

---

[1] Fever dispensed with Barrawell's speech impediment.

"He is raving, like the rest of them. He is in a bad way."

"We are all in a bad way."

"…I am being handed the governorship from my father. But as I bow before the priest to get his blessing I feel something on my face. First it is a tickling but then they are all over me – maggots – crawling on my skin and into my nose. I breathe maggots. I am a seething mass of maggots… tell me what it means, Knivet."

He who had once abused me and called me savage, suddenly calling me by name and with puppy eyes! The rash had spread; the vomiting was constant. He could keep no food down but he kept retching. He passed in and out of consciousness.

"The Indians told me something of their dreams," I said after consideration. "If they dream they are eating others, that is a good sign and things will go well for them. If they dream they are being eaten, the opposite applies. It is an omen. And your dream, *senhor*, is about being consumed."

"I am taking over command." Manoel took me to one side. "He bid me do that, in a moment of lucidity. All men are to be given a choice about whether they go on or return. I will command those who choose to continue."

"Command of whom? Which of us would choose to go on?"

"You will, Englishman." He winked at me.

"There are not enough of us," I said, "to bury our dead."

"Think of Orellana. He took fifty men and without knowing what lay in front of him traversed the mighty Amazon itself, headwaters to mouth. He faced the most terrible tribes known in Brazil, skies dark with flights of poisoned arrows, riverbanks lined with savage warriors shouting for his scalp. But he rallied his men against them, even when they swarmed in their thousands. He repelled the mighty Amazons themselves. And still when he was half-starved and had not slept in days, he bid the savages he encountered accept Christ as their Lord and the King of Spain as sovereign. And however gruelling the journey, I will go and do the same with the *tamoyes*, and win glory for Portugal. I will beat their heathen Gods out of their brains. I will bring back heads. They will be subjugated. Not because it is right or wrong, Englishman, not because I am maliciously inclined. It is them or us and I am the 'us', I am a Portugal and I serve my Governor and my King and through them the Catholic Faith."

"I am an Englishman. You cannot think I could have such motivation."

"The Governor's son told me something about when he brought you back from your time with the *tamoyes* and with the *pories*. He said you begged him leave to spend the rest of your days with the savages. Is that true?" he carried on keenly when I did not reply, grasping me by the shoulders. "I do not intend to decimate the *tamoyes*. That would be foolish – we need them for the *engenhos*. My aim is subjugation, no more. I will kill their leaders and as for the rest?" He shrugged. "They can keep a low profile, and where is the harm if there is one more of them? You cut my bonds once, Englishman, and let me disappear. Help me find the *tamoyes* and I shall return the favour."

"Wa-wa-i-i-i-i-i-i…"

"Those frogs. It is like the plague in the bible."

"Let those who choose go forth to the Promised Land" smiled Manoel.

"I am going."

"To the promised land, Englishman?"

"To catch some damned frogs."

I liked catching frogs. There was a practical reason for it: we were hungry and they were an abundant supply of food. But that was not why I liked catching them. It was their eyes – their little red impudent eyes glowing at me out of the night. While everyone else slept I slunk off with my bow and arrow and went to where the croak was most cacophonous, to take aim at those satanic eyes. A musket might have hit one but would have scattered the others; it had to be bow and arrow. I enjoyed the wet 'pht' as it hit its target and I enjoyed the respite from the misery of our camp too.

Sleep thinly veiled the misery. You could not tell who was dying quite so easily. We tarried at that camp days, then weeks. The pretext for this was that each man should ready himself for a return journey or an onward journey, according to his will, but no one was readying themselves. They were cowering in this wilderness from the inevitable, from the known horrors of going back and the unknown horrors of pressing on.

One could ask why I did not make a break for it: as I had attempted in Santos from Cavendish and at Ihla San Sebastian from the Governor. But it was not the time. I was not going to act too soon and jeopardise it all. I needed Portugals to pull oars with me to the last.

So I caught frogs and waited to see what would pass. The Portugals mocked me for being part savage to hunt thus and I suggested to them that maybe that was what they needed to become. I very much doubted any one of them had the Thing.

One night I was bagging frogs when I heard something large rustling in the reeds. A snake, I thought, and levelled an arrow to send it to its maker. But it was far bigger than any serpent I had taken on before in this Brazil, and frisky too. It went for me before I was prepared and I was obliged to dodge its venomous teeth at the last moment to strike it from the side. We tussled some minutes. At one point I was holding its large flat head in my hands and squeezing it with excruciating slowness towards death. When it finally lay still I saw it was many yards long. It might be a nice gesture, I thought, to take it to camp to give to Gonzalo Correia de Sáand the other sick.

I was in the midst of so doing when a group of those Portugals who had accrued the greatest hatred of me over these last days cornered me and at gunpoint told me that I had gone too far this time, this time I really would be hanged as I should have been hanged many times before. I demanded an explanation; they said that I had forsaken my watch, and dragged me before the captain. Certain men including Quarasips Juca came to my defence and proclaimed my innocence and I was released, for no one had

called me for the watch – it was all a vile ruse fabricated by
trouble-makers. Once freed I went direct to the ringleaders and
demanded of them why they conspired against me so, I had saved
the entire company several times over and they well knew it. We
do not like you, Englishman, they answered; there is something
sinister about you. We have it on good account that you survived
the gallows when you should have died, and survived the *engenho*
when you should have died, and survived amongst cannibals,
when anyone else would have died. You are our bad luck. Then
they called me heretic, which I was prepared to let go, and then
one called me bastard. White rage gripped me. I dealt that man
such a blow that he sunk before me, and did not get up again.
There was much commotion in the camp. Some men held that my
heckler had deserved it but the majority howled that an English
dog should not get away with violating one of them so. I was back
immediately before the captain, and unfortunately for me he was
enjoying one of his lucid moments.

"I have good reason to end your life, savage, as you have
killed one of my men, your superior. What have you to say for
yourself?"

"He called me a bastard." I looked at him levelly. "You can
appreciate, *senhor*, how much that wounded me."

The fever was burning him up. His own sweat had wiped off
the paste he used to pale his face; he looked his true colour at last
on his deathbed, him calling me a savage on account of my sun-
browned skin was ridiculous for he was darker than me. We were
two dark bastards, fighting to prove ourselves as bastards have had
to do since the beginning of time.

""I never liked you, savage. None of my men like you."

"Few Portugals do, it seems *senhor*," I said. "Except Manoel
your lieutenant. And he…"

"He is not in command while I still draw breath! And he is
not here to save you now, savage! He is gone to scout out just
what district of Hell we are camped in. He will not return until
tomorrow afternoon and by then, so help me God, you will be

swinging from the nearest tree. You *flagelo* - you scourge! I have watched you thrive in this wilderness whilst my men flail, I have watched you sap the fortune from this enterprise."

And you have watched your own command slip from your fingers, I thought.

"Take the savage away," the de Sá instructed his henchmen. "If I go by God's good grace I will see him go first, if it is the last thing I do I will see him go!"

My hands were bound, my feet were bound, and all four of them unjustly. I was not sure if Gonzalo Correia de Sá realised this was what the Governor and his half-brother had done to me on many occasions, and ultimately with ineffectiveness. I was tied so tight about a tree I could hardly breathe; I was flayed; I was given no water. And did I think I was going to die? Not really. I had never died before.

At ten next morning two Portugals came to read me my crimes from a hastily drawn-up parchment and bid me prepare for death. I laughed and replied that I had, many times over, that fate had spared me then and I knew for what, and it was not for this day. At eleven a friar visited me and urged me to confess, for God would then look more kindly upon me. God would, would he? Ha! I replied that God knew the secrets of all men's hearts, his as well as mine, and that if I looked into mine I could say truly there was no blemish there, no stain of fornication or hypocrisy, could he say the same? In the afternoon they led me to the place of execution. They carried Gonzalo Correia de Sá on a platform to a suitable vantage point. He was gibbering about maggots again. Most other able-bodied Portugals were gathered, all except Manoel, all except the one who could save me. The friar asked me if I had any last words. What could I say, really, in summation? Disinherit me, drown me, I will rise; exile me, execute me, I will rise. Tell me I am nothing and I will show you that I am something.

"Wa-wa-i-i-i-i-i-i..."

"Cut him loose!" Manoel's voice rang through the mist.

"Well timed," I told Manoel, rubbing my throat where the noose had dug into it. "For I had really given my last words insufficient thought."

"I think it is high time we continued this damned journey," Manoel winked.

"Directly," I replied. "But let me make one goodbye first."

"Anthony," Barrawell muttered, when I was holding his head in my arms. "Did I drown or did I make it to the other side?"

"Neither," I said softly.

"You have something to say to me, Anthony. I can sense it. You never could keep quiet… not when you had something to say."

"I have to leave you, Barrawell. You will return with the others. You will be better cared for with them."

My blood brother nodded weakly. He looked like he knew that was not true.

"Tell me." He squeezed my hand, feeble as a child. "Is it love?"

"Is what love?"

"The change in you. Your peace."

"Save your energy Barrawell." His pulse was very faint.

"Tell me at least what she looks like."

I looked up. Manoel was calling. He had got together a group of twelve and they were waiting for me, those last men standing of that great army the Portugals had mustered, above the slumped shapes of the others that had succumbed to Brazil.

"Like the jungle night," I said. "She looks like the jungle night."

THIRTY-FIVE

"He was like a brother to me," I confessed, after five days, as the thirteen of us paddled downriver. The trail had gone cold. We knew that we had strength only to go with the current and could but hope the same had applied for the *tamoyes*; we had to believe that for if it were otherwise this was an aimless wandering, a convoluted route towards death.

"Since we set sail from England seven years ago he was my blood brother. They say seven is lucky but it is not for me – no respect, no wealth, no notoriety, no love, and now not even a brother."

"We desire most what we can never have," sighed Francisco Tavares, after ten days, as we crouched in the mean canoe we had fashioned, because we lacked the energy to stand, because we saw no point in standing, either way our horizon was the muddy meanders of a river we did not know and the direction of which we could not be sure of, the meanders seemed like circles, circles of Hell, it could have been any of them but we hazarded one of the lower; the bottom, the uttermost bottom could not be far off, Dante might have thought it was ice encasing Satan's lair but Dante had never been to Brazil. Dante had never been to Brazil...

"We had a nice, white house in the vineyards," reminisced Antonio and Gonzalo Fernández, fifteen days in, as our mud-brown river met another still vaster one. In our desperate lethargy this was a good omen, as if there would suddenly be life on this new waterway, as if this was a cart-track joining a highway in some place like Europe, some place with people. But there was no new life. There was nothing, which was odd because the ground was fertile – we had encountered far more barren spots that had veritably teemed with Indians. Now the trees dissipated, now there was savannah; surely in those long grasses waited tribes, kindly tribes, with cassava meal or baked fish at the ready. "We used to find it oppressive, the orderliness of the vineyards and the cosiness of our little white house. But it is better than chaos. This is chaos. It is in our brains now. It is eating us up: the cicadas, all those jabbering screeching birds, the hollering of savages lusting after our flesh…"

"Ah Christ, I see now this be Hell," whispered Quarasips Juca, after twenty days, when we had left our boat at another village, as abandoned as the previous one and the one before that but like the previous ones bearing traces of the *tamoyes*, long-ago traces, traces so old it was in fact probably us willing them to be traces. Other canoes were moored here, which indicated the *tamoyes* – if it was them, and we had to believe that it was – had left the water to seek higher ground: for defence, we reasoned, for bloody-mindedness, we supposed, for a change from this jungle that yielded nothing but mud and blood, perhaps. In the huts of this village we found things that gave us hope; fishing hooks and pots rimmed in silver, stones that were green as grass and white as winter snow, which we took to be emeralds and crystals, but other stones, blue and red, wondrous fine to behold, and nuggets of gold as big as hazelnuts. And so we realised we could not be far from the mountain of metals, the jewel in the crown of the Spaniards' empire and the place of their colonial mint that forged coins for Patagonia, Panama, Valparaiso, Veracruz. Potosi. It was from Potosi alone that such splendour could originate. "In his kingdom, my father tell me, they have deserts – sand, far as a man might see. People often die crossing these deserts, and you know what they see, when the sun addles their minds, and they be ready to die? They see visions, yah. Floating on the sand. They see what they want to see, right at the end. And they try to get to them – to their pools of water and their pretty maids and their palaces and the Lord knows what else they thought they glimpsed, they have them this last burst of strength and stretch out their hands like this," Quarasips held out his own arms, quivering, "and they grab just hot air and more sand. And that be how they die, yah. Not thirst, not starvation: false hope."

"We have reached the end of Brazil, and the end of ourselves," whispered Luis de Pino, after twenty-five days, as we toiled towards the ridges of mountains which we knew must demarcate the beginning of Peru, as the ground thrust up from the hot belly of the jungle and the temperature crashed down and we shivered during the night, and not solely from the cold.

"All hail the great Manoel Caldeira," snarled Pedro de Casta, about day number thirty, after we had ascended above the thickest trees, onto upland grasses where even the timid deer that noticed us fled not, for they understood we were no threat, we could not run, we could barely walk. And as little as a week before the man might have meant the words genuinely, for Manoel was well liked. But deprivation turns men against men, devotion into spite, and our open grassland had ended in a rock face as insurmountable as a passage to Heaven for Portugals, no way over, no way around. And Pedro de Casta, an officer only one below Manoel in rank, who had begun this journey plump, now leaned his emaciated frame against the rock and banged his head against it. "*Apeia-te ô cavalheiro, que haveis de merendar*" he sang bitterly between bangs, and we gawped as the stone reddened with blood, too far departed from sanity ourselves to restrain him from his madness. "Get down from your horse knight," his words translated, "it is time for you to eat... and the sun will soon be setting across the mountain."

"And what if we can find means to cross it?" wondered John

de Sousa, and John de Silvesa, and Luís Loello, and Mateus de Galo, and Tomas Delvare as we wandered, sunrise to sundown to sunrise, in a daze along this strip of grassland above the forest below the mountain, tapping the rock feebly as if a miracle might open it up for us. "Spaniards must await on the other side. You do not stray into their territory, not if you value the join your head has with your body. What Brazil has done to us is enough, what the savages might try to do to us is more than enough, but taking on the Spaniards too will break us."

Soon after that we heard the sound of rushing water. Manoel heard it first, he asked us if this was his hallucination or no and some of us answered supportively that we could hear the water too whilst others scoffed and said death sounded like that, or the moments leading to it, it was for sure death shuffling up to his door and knocking.

The stoutest of us, John de Sousa and myself, volunteered to push on and ascertain what might lie ahead. We went in near delirium. It had been yesterday morning since we last ate and days more since we had come across anything to lift our morale. When a man is reduced to the stage to which we had been eroded, every tree seems an enemy sent to thwart you; every monkey hoot part of some macabre all-consuming fantasy in which you are pitted against the world, the worst of it, any and every evil it can conjure up. So when we saw the river we were mindful of Quarasips Juca's words about the spent travellers in the desert, reaching out to what they imagined to be their salvation and finding only sand. But a river it was – although we did have to stare awhile to believe our eyes. It was not flowing down into the forest, as we might have expected, but in the opposite direction – into the mountain. It was a way through.

"Now gather round, men," said Manoel, after he too had peered into the depths of this river as it pounded into the cavern, frothing like a mad dog's jowls, as the last light waned and throngs of vampire bats soared up from the within, screeching, for their nightly feed. "We have two choices before us and it is the same choice we have ever had before us in Brazil: onward or back. You, my farmers of Minho, my miners of the Algarve, my fishermen of Lisboa, my kinsmen, my brothers – you never chose backward before. You chose Brazil. Before us lies glory. If we crush these *tamoyes* there will not be one group of savages capable of standing against us in this land.

"Think of Túpac Amaru. He was the last King of the Incas. The Spaniards came after Túpac Amaru to his stronghold, deep into Peru, where the mountains meet the forest. They captured all the subjects but Túpac Amaru escaped. He fled further into the jungle with his wife. The Spaniards were already at the limits of their endurance; the journey had taken its toll on them and all seemed lost, for how can white men of Europe track a savage in the forest? But one amongst them volunteered to continue the pursuit. He carried on downriver for days, for weeks. He caught that Túpac Amaru and brought him back. And on the Plaza de Armas in Cuzco they beheaded that savage and the Incas were no more."

Manoel's once shiny Potosi-wrought armour had rusted. His hose had rotted. He was barefoot, having already donated his boots to be boiled for the broth that would be our only food that evening. His eyes might still have sparked but from out of a gaunt face lacerated by jungle thorns and swollen from insect bites – yet still he looked the best of us.

Antonio and Gonzalo Fernández objected that setting forth down a river so fast-flowing would be foolhardy, for it would be impossible to return against the current if danger should arise. Mateus de Galo reiterated danger was certain to arise should they make the other side, by a mountain as significant as this, Spaniards if not savages, and how could we defend ourselves, thirteen shoeless men?

"My brothers, this is our quest, and these are our savages to bring to justice. If it be Spaniards on the other side we can say truthfully that we come into their territory from necessity, and by rights. If it be savages, it makes no sense to fear them, for after all it is savages we seek."

Seeing the way the wind was blowing with Manoel's persuasions I deemed it strategic to voice my own thoughts.

"Friends, we may as well adventure our lives now as we have before in many places. Going back would kill us as getting here very near did. So doubtless we may live here like wild beasts, as long as it pleases God, without credit, or name, or religion, wherefore I think our best way is to go through if we can. God has hitherto delivered us from dangers infinite and there is no reason to suppose He will forsake us now. Questionless, if we reach the other side we shall find Indians, Spaniards, or both – for as we know we are now within the sphere of influence of the great mountain of silver and gold, Potosi, and might descry it from atop these very rocks. And Indians and Spaniards will be guarding that mountain as they would guard their own lives. But it seems to me if the aim of our quest is to hunt down Indians, Indians we must encounter, and if we want wealth – by which I mean truly fabulous riches, and notoriety, and to return to our families[1] in carriages lined with exotic bird's feathers – Spaniards must we take it from."

Mouths dropped open at my speech, as had been the desired effect, for I had used the Lord's name twice within as many breaths – when my ambivalence towards religion was known – and, so it seemed, quite genuinely. But I knew the carrots with which to bait these donkeys. And because they were ashamed it was an Englishman that had jumped to their leader's defence the protesters acquiesced.

---

[1] It would have been around this time (June 1598) that Sir Henry Knyvett – who preferred spelling his name with a "y" and an extra "t" for reasons that shall perhaps forever remain obscured and who was, although he chose to veil the fact, Knivet's father – died. Whilst his life seems to have been illustrious enough, and certainly one Knivet would have fancied for himself, not nearly as much is now known about Sir Henry Knyvett as about his illegitimate son.

We boiled up our boots with herbs and a lame monkey John de Sousa had caught: everything we could scrape together for one final repast. We contemplated the river, its current augmented by the caverns above it into a sound that must have seemed sinister to the Portugals, for all of them save Manoel began uttering prayers. But I did not share their fear. On the contrary, I saw possibility in the unseen rapids and jagged rocks. Call it an instinct, if you will, that something was about to change – and irrefutably.

"And might I add that we should all take our rosaries and give thanks to God for full protection in this ordeal ahead," I said, and made a big show of taking mine off upon which the Portugals, moved, did the same.

"…*He descended into Hell; the third day he arose again from the dead…*" I knew each word of the rigmarole; my mother had ensured that. And if the Portugals were surprised at my sudden show of devotion I was confident they would never guess the plan I was hatching. Only Quarasips Juca might have had an inkling something was afoot and he was rocking on his haunches, back turned on the rest of us and head bowed. Brazil had broken the strongest man I ever knew.

"*Glory be to the Father, and to the Son, and to the Holy Spirit. As it was in the beginning, is now, and ever shall be, world without end. Amen…*" It was a surreal sight, eleven Portugals being led in prayer by an Englishman, and an Angolan-Indian hunched disconsolately on the side-lines like he despaired of the lot of us, by the entrance to an underground river the forest and the mountain would probably prevent any adventurer from ever finding again.

Twelve disciples, in a room somewhere on the edge of Jerusalem, all partaking of a feast, it is not much but there is bread, probably fish, a carafe of wine to wash it down with. Jesus makes a speech. You are no longer servants, he says, you are friends. Fine words. The dinner guests relax, their feet are washed and that wine no doubt is going straight to their heads. And then comes the revelation: one of you is going to betray me. What? Who? The blustering Simon Peter? Matthew - that tax collector – well, men in his profession hardly had a history of trustworthiness, did they? Ah yes, Judas. He was a strange one; gloomy; sullen even; no, the guests would go further, the man appeared downright conceited on occasion. He was ever on the periphery of their group – but treachery? He was still one of them. He had broken bread with them. Surely he would not be capable of treachery...

After we launched our canoe out into the river late that following afternoon, the dying sun would alight on a solitary rosary, left, as if by accident, on the bank behind us.

THIRTY-SIX

"I am he that hath killed many of thy nation, and will kill thee."

Anthony Knivet, *Admirable Adventures and Strange Fortunes*

The huts were hard fast to the cavern mouth where we emerged, blinking, in the sudden sharp light. They flanked both banks in an unbroken wall, maybe five rows deep and continuing as far downriver as we could discern.

"Gunpowder, my brothers?" whispered Manoel hoarsely.

"Wet."

"Arrows?"

"Ready."

"So await my word. Heed me, my brothers, and…" Manoel paused as we saw the Indians come out of their huts, lithe cinnamon-coloured women with limbs like willows, naked from their lips to their nipples and vaginas, precious sights we men had to tear our eyes from for the women were preparing their menfolk, fastening their thongs, arranging their feathers, the russet of the hoatzin, the blue of the parrot, toucan-yellow, egret-white, repainting their salient markings – the outlines of animals – snakes, alligators, jaguars. "Make sure each finds its target twice over brothers. Do not miss. Upon your lives do not miss."

If each of our arrows had felled two Indians or two-hundred it would have made small in-roads into the numbers massing on the banks. Besides, I had seen the paint on these Indians' faces. The last thing I wanted was any one of them getting hurt – for they were *tamoyes*.

"Might I interject?" I asked.

"A 'no' never stopped you before, Englishman."

"Attack is futile. They would kill us all."

"You have a better plan?"

Cries ricocheted bank to bank, more cries that a wood full of carrion. Around the bend we came, and into their midst. They had blocked the river off with canoes. In each canoe was a posse of archers, bows drawn. There were trumpeters and drummers adding to the furore and warriors standing in lines going back at least as ar back as the huts had, banging spears on the shore in a manner which – if it was intended as intimidating – worked. As we watched the warriors parted to let through to the river's edge two men, one on each bank. *Paygi*. Black magicians. These newcomers were daubed head to foot in white ash and carried aloft large elaborately decorated gourd rattles: Ma-rrrah y kûá, no less. When they spoke, everyone listened. It was a repeat of the warriors' chant but these *paygi* were more theatrical with the delivery. They were inciting their people to battle. They pointed to the warriors, the warriors repeated the chant, they pointed to us and shook their gourds, the warriors chanted again. Some brought dried plants and set light to them. Smoke, like incense only more acrid, spread in a fog across the river. We could see nothing. Our eyes smarted. "The spirit of war is here," the men with the Ma-rrrah y kûá screamed, and their warriors chorused back, "let the spirit out!"

"Yes. Why not be nice to them?"

"Nice," Maneol repeated dully.

"And let us decide," I added, "what story we will tell them for questionless, they will examine who we are, and from whence we came."

"If this is our strategy then I will be nothing but honest with them," Manoel said. "I am a Portugal, and proud of it."

The other Portugals agreed; they would admit what they

were.

"Quarasips. You are part *tamoyes*. Tell them. That could help us, or at least save you."

"In blood perhaps, Anthony Knivet. But as to all my waking life I been Portugal. And if they be wanting to kill us, yah, I doubt even the grandest words will stop them."

"As you wish. I will say that I am a Frenchman. *Je suis Française, mes frères! Et vous? Vous êtes bêtes, vous tous.*"

We were bound around our wrists and midriffs and dragged through their settlement to the largest of their huts. There was a fire outside, a big pot on the embers and a broth simmering away within. A girl, perhaps seven, was stirring it. The child was so small she needed both hands to stir. She could barely see over the rim. The hut and the pot were elaborate. The hut had parrot feathers around the entranceway; I guessed at least ten birds must have been plucked bare for the decoration. The thirteen of us, eyes still streaming, had our bonds fastened to stakes hammered into the earth, in a bedraggled line along the front of the hut. We were left alone with the girl. This was not as foolish as it sounded on the part of our captors. Even if we had freed ourselves, where would we have run? We could see little on account of the damnable smoke the Ma-rrrah y kûá wielders had waved everywhere. It was more open country this side of the mountain too, and I knew full well the *tamoyes* were good marksmen – and dipped their arrows in poison.

"Well, Englishman, yet again it seems fate has declined to send us to our makers," Manoel muttered. "If they meant to kill us they would hardly have brought us to their principal dwelling and cooked breakfast for us!"

"How is it possible you Portugals could live so long around these people yet not know their ways whatsoever?"

The more I looked at the pot's contents, the more I doubted whether it was our breakfast.

But he did not have time to ask me what I meant. Three men

came out of the hut, one wiry and uncharacteristically small for a *tamoyes*, the other two taller and looking rather less amenable. The wiry one was evidently the leader. He walked in the middle of the three and had the most white feathers on his head. The *tamoyes* prized white like all these forest Indians; there was precious little white in hot green Brazil. Only the most revered of these tribesmen wore white.

"*Mamoyguápa ende?*" he asked each of us, and the Portugals, not comprehending, said nothing or mumbled prayers in their own tongue. This earned them a kicking from one of the tall *tamoyes*. Then they got stripped of their clothes, and they looked pathetic, their rosaries sparkling in the sunlight as they hastened to cover their modesty. Their rosaries were taken, and they were kicked again.

"*Mamoyguápa ende?*"

"I am from France," I said in Tupi, looking at him levelly. He had the grave intonation of a priest reading late rites. There was not an inch of unnecessary flesh on him – not an inch! But I was relieved to note he had dimples. You feel, somehow, that a man with dimples will not treat you unfairly. "These long-beard Portugals captured me not a week ago. Save me from them I beg you."

"When *tamoyes* learn the language of the *Karaíba* it is to help us beat them in war, or when they enslave us and we have no choice. Why do you learn our language?"

"Because I desire to be your friend. Because I would live amongst you, and share my fortunes with you; go to war *with* you against your oppressors. Because…"

At the leader's gesture, his henchman approached, got his hands around the rotting remains of my shirt collar and tore. There, bared for all to see was my torso, and I braced myself for a kicking and a stripping like the others. But nothing happened. An expression flashed over the leader's face like something had relieved him slightly, and the three moved onto Manoel.

Because I was one of you once, my King – if King be how you

command me to call you. I was one of you, and this is no chance encounter in the mountains. I want to be one of you again.

"*Mamoyguápa ende?*"

"Portugal," Manoel had the presence of mind to reply. "We… come to do you great service. Tell them, Englishman!"

Manoel always hesitated when he lied.

"He and his men will kill all of us," I said to the *tamoyes*. "Unless you kill them."

A woman had taken over from the little girl at the pot. I smelt aji, and guizador[1]. The woman had a carving hanging between her breasts fashioned from vine and wood. The vine was bent into a spiral with nine coils, held in place by interlocking sticks. The woman whispered something to the girl who squealed with laughter and ran off, away from the huts, up a gently rising pasture, ridiculously gentle, given the sheer-faced mountain we had passed under to get here. In the pasture, more women tilled earth. These women had children too, who joined the little girl and scurried on as a mass, squealing the whole while, somersaulting, standing on their heads, laying down and pretending to be dead and then leaping up again shrieking all the louder.

Manoel had his bonds cut. The *tamoyes* were gesturing him to follow them.

"No hard feelings, Englishman. It seems they have taken to me. That is the error these stupid savages make. They let you in like silly dogs."

I do not know at what moment Manoel realised he was not going to be taken to, or let in – or indeed even have breakfast served to him. It was not so many more steps that he took. I did not see from which direction the youth came up, but he smote that Portugal lieutenant on the head so quickly the many-feathered club could have been a jungle bird, a fusion of the most brilliant hues of every bird in that forest, swooping in for a landing. The

---

[1] Seasonings for cooking meat.

youth struck cleanly, signalling he was ready for more – and along went the Fernández brothers, Tomas Delvare, Luís Loello, Luís de Pino, John de Silvesa, Pedro de Casta, Mateus de Galo, Francisco Tavares, John de Sousa.

"What are you doing?" I cried out as the twelfth, my dear friend Quarasips Juca, was herded before the executioner. The space between the huts was already red. One of the Portugals in the mounting pile was not quite dead. Pink bubbles frothed in his mouth. Get up, I willed, if you only got up now it would confirm none of this was actually happening. Most of the *tamoyes* were no longer watching the macabre spectacle and the wiry old leader, whilst still officiating, looked embarrassed; even disgusted. "This man is *tamoyes!* He is one of you!"

The executioner kicked away the bodies of the Portugals to give himself room. He swung the club. Swoop. Quarasips went to his knees but did not fall. This irritated the youth and he brought the club crashing down again, and then again, and sunk to the floor himself from the exertion of having killed my last true friend in Brazil.

"If they are a threat, they must die," he panted, heaving himself up and coming over to me. He looked at me intently. I could hardly discern his battle paint under all that Portugal blood. "As you well know… Jaci."

Ubi. My old *peteca* partner, brother of the lady I had been searching Brazil for. I had last seen him with big child's eyes being pulled away from me by my Katawa five years before. Now no one could have pulled him. He had grown up fast – and hard.

"And me? Am I a threat, Ubi?"

He pointed to my neck, and then to the heap of bodies, which the wiry old man with the dimples was overseeing the cleaning up of. The corpses were not being removed, I noticed, but stacked.

"You are evidently not one of them, for you do not wear the strange beads they do. Our King says you must be from some other land. But your chances of survival are in doubt, for none of us see how you can be our friend as you claim when you arrived here in a boat with our foes."

"You know I am your friend!" I cried. "You watched me make Ma-rrrah y kûá for your people!"

"That was long ago, when we lived on the island. It was a different time. We are a different people now."

"You grew up quickly."

"They bound me and attached ants to my body, as is the *tamoyes* way to decide who among our young is fit to become a man. Many boys die, for the ants eat through them before they can free themselves. I nearly died. I lay in the wilderness fifteen days on the edge of death. I did not die because I was not meant to die. I was meant to help lead my people against the *karaiba*."

"A noble story," I said. "So mark my words. I almost drowned in the oceans, froze to death in the ice of the Far South, got executed by the Portugals thrice over, and I too survived – and I know what for. For the same cause, Ubi! I have seen the wrong people colonising this Brazil and its true people beaten back. Let me help you lead your people against those that have wronged us both."

"We will see," Ubi said curtly. "Now there is work to do. Later we will examine you."

"*Why do you stare at me?*" her voice tinkled, from down the years, from across the forests. "*Maker of the Ma-rrrah y kûa.*" "I would gladly go with you," I mouthed the words again, "as your peoples' friend, would you not let me come?" I had never seen another human being with so much hair... And what of your sister, I wanted to ask Ubi, did she make it, in your journey from the sea, how is she, which hut is hers, is she married, or promised as you say in your language, is she promised to one of your tribe or still free?

But I was weak and all hands save my tied ones were engaged in cutting up the Portugals. That was the work to be done, and in a sense it seemed a theatre for me alone, for I was the only onlooker, fixed in position as I was and unable to avert my eyes. With the tooth of some wild animal the outer skins were removed, the fire stoked and the bodies lowered over the flames. The colour drained out just as it does from chicken, and when the flesh was white and just a little charred, and the heads had been removed along with the arms and legs, in short long after they had ceased to be Portugals, I was still hoping that perhaps they would reassemble, that Luís Loello or Mateus de Galo would laughingly appear from around the corner, reattaching their heads, climbing back into their skin, assuring me this vision was but a symptom of my madness. Only it was not; it was more a test of my mettle; I was sure now that this was a test. One woman said to me how sad I must be to see my friends thus roasted. No, I replied with an effort, I had said already that they were not my friends. Oh, but was it not a pity, for young men like these to end their days as cooked meat on a fire in a forest far from their homes? No pity, I said faintly, they were my enemies, what did I care for them? They extracted the guts and gave them to the women. The roast meat they divided so that there was a portion for every hut, and representatives of each hut came; gave thanks; took away their flesh with considerable ceremony. The trumpeters and the drummers started up. Those that had been cooking or carving formed a circle around the fire, held hands, moved clockwise around it, tapping the broth pot with sticks as they went so that a clanging got going like cowbells. I sat for hours as they danced. Occasionally one of the women bounded over to me and told me how the meat of the *karaiba* would be eaten that night, would I not like to partake, just a little bit, a leg or an arm or a cut from nearer the middle? I was ravenous. I had not eaten decently in days and then it had been boiled leather, as I recollected. That was one thing you could say about my mother. I never wanted for food under her roof. There was always damson scones, or bread with purslane or rosemary – my mother mixed herbs with the dough, and mingled more with a butter to glaze the tops once just baked; this was why her loaves were so irresistible. Strange that I had gone away from there to make something of myself yet here I was, years later, in the place I should have been making it, starving and with no food to eat except human flesh. I swayed. My bonds lashed tight to the stake were all that stopped me falling. Clank, the Indians hit the cooking pot. Dearest father, I think you remember the orange cakes mother made, the Halloween your own son got made Lord of Misrule. Charlton certainly remembers them. The villagers never had oranges before, and then she gave them more than they knew what to do with, how she got her hands on them I may never now know but bakers do that, they dazzle and delight, in this regard it is a most wonderful profession – and by no means dishonourable. Do you remember how I lay there, on the bed of garlands? I wanted you so badly to notice me. But everyone was laughing at me because of the bells I had to wear on my hose when they should have been obeying me, because I was the Lord. Lord for a day perhaps, but still Lord. The sweet cloying taste of the orange cakes that day became for me part of my mortification, but what would I give for it now? Clank. The representatives were returning with the roast meat. They went naked but bore the meat on the most intricate ceramics. Each deposited his meat in the pot of broth and now the smell enveloped me, ghastly, like smallpox, like the orlop deck of the Roebuck after weeks at sea. Manoel Caldeira and his men were meeting their maker from a cooking pot – at least the fumes from their flesh were rising skyward to where Heaven is generally perceived to be – and I guessed few others around me spoke the Iberian tongues adeptly enough to appreciate the irony that Caldeira means cooking pot in Portugal. Like name, like demise, Manoel my bold lieutenant. And what if my name should hold the clue to the manner in which I should go? Take the 'v' and the 'e' out and replace them with a 'g' and an 'h', ha, I would go out like a knight not fizzle out in a cooking pot, and Brazil was where the annals would say I won my spurs. Clank. Here Lies Anthony Knivet… but the memorial slab was blank, there was nothing to write yet, and what if the few who had known me then came and took advantage and wrote, in unlovely scrawl in the blank space, 'bastard', 'flesh-eating bastard', 'accomplished nothing but the lowest thing a man can which is to eat his fellow men'.

"Eat!" commanded the wiry old King of the *tamoyes,* holding out a bowl of the broth of Portugal flesh. He was marked like a jaguar. Then, as was customary, there were the separate markings to indicate the men he had killed in battle, a commemorative cemetery of gravestones right there on his face, which disfigured the jaguar quite terribly. Ubi stood at his side. He had washed. He was marked like a capybara. Together, it seemed it was Ubi, with his Pharaoh's gaze, that was the ruler, and the King his wry advisor.

"I... thank you but... I am not hungry."

"You are faint from hunger." Ubi frowned. "And our King offers you broth from his own hands!

The odorous brew was a hand's span from my nostrils.

"Why would you not eat, *karaiba*? Unless you mourn the death of your comrades, in which case you must be in league with them and against us."

"Very well. A little, then."

When you eat your enemy, you become like him, only a better version of him. When you eat your enemy, you have one less enemy and by that token your enemy's people are diminished, and you are elevated. I slurped the contents of the bowl the King proffered, trying to think of fresh-baked damson scones and praying I would not retch the meal back up again over the most powerful Indian in South America.

I sensed the eyes of the most senior *tamoyes* analysing me – who was I, why was I here? It was a lengthy story, for I was a baker, a gentleman, a man of words and a man of arms, a sailor, a slave, misunderstood regardless and on a journey many times skewed by fate. But I felt I should be candid, so I told them, all of it, from being shipwrecked to coming through the caverns there into their kingdom. My only untruth was that I was steadfast in my French-ness. Huguenots helped the *tamoyes* when they warred against the

Portugals in the 1550s, and if I was not going to be eaten I needed to summon together every favourable fact – with every shred of ingenuity us Knivets ever did possess. By the time I arrived at the part where I had defeated an entire army of Portugals by gradual demoralisation they were breaking into smiles.

"The long-beard *karaiba* cannot survive longer than babies in the forest!"

"Maybe those beards weigh them down."

"And they are quite fat – that cannot help."

"Can I eat it?" One of the King's henchmen picked up a rock and mimed a Portugal biting it. "Ooh, what a tough fruit!"

"It seems we owe you a debt, *karaiba*, for ridding us of those who would come to take our land." The King wore an expression on his face that could have been grudging magnanimity or just-disguised rage. "And all may be true as you say. But we *tamoyes* have a custom when strangers enter our midst. We each tell the other a secret – the *utmost* secret – something we never told anyone else. So come, drink cassava brew with me and tell me – what is your secret?"

I thought of the best things I had done and realised I had already related them all; I thought of the terrible things and realised none would impress this venerable veteran. My bonds were cut and it was an effort to steady myself. We squatted. The sun dipped below the mountains. I could see ridges soaring up – like in those fanciful paintings where some saint journeys into the wilderness to discover something fundamental, and the artist strives to make the background inhospitable because that makes the saint's endeavours worthier – progressively higher as the river stabbed between them.

Be humble, it suddenly occurred to me. Show him you think him greater than you, which at this moment he is.

"Do you recall in my story where I first met your people – on the Ihla do Gobernador?"

"Its true name was Paranapuã." The King of the *tamoyes* smiled without revealing his teeth. "Before the Portugals built

Hell there."

"I became one of you, then, when I lived with you. I discarded my *karaiba* clothes; I daubed myself in the purple of acai and the yellow of the jungle clay; I wailed louder even than the *tomomynos*, whose wailing abilities are well documented. And I went hunting with bow and arrow. I caught lizards; I caught a jaguar despite the fact it was running at full speed. But then my arrows failed me – or rather I did disservice to my arrows. There was one thing I could not bring myself to do."

"What thing?" The King handed me the pitcher of cassava brew and waited expectantly until I had drunk, which I thirstily did, to erase the taste of Manoel Caldeira from my tongue if nothing else.

"I could not kill the deer. I had a buck in my sights, time and time again. But I could not shoot him."

The King nodded. He wore his crown of feathers with such ease. Not because he was a wealthy man, like Thomas Cavendish, or a man that liked to impose his authority, like Salvador Correia de Sá. No. He wore it because he should. The flames were still high. From that river bank there wound into the night sky a thousand other *tamoyes* fires just like it. Lights swum, the King's head split in two, even as he keenly watched me, and subdivided, and for a moment many kings were watching me, from all angles, upside-down and back to front. Then I was sinking – away from the fires, into true darkness – and this time I could not stop myself.

THIRTY-SEVEN

The floods subsided eventually, of course, and he climbed down from the tops of the trees where he had hidden, this survivor, into a new land that glistened. It seemed to be that around the time he had clung there on the gables of his family estate, as he had valiantly tried to save everyone that had mattered to him and failed, he must have screwed his eyes shut as forcefully as he could, and then opened them again, to wake up, as it were, and that the gables had been branches all along, with that tidy prospect of scythed lawns and walled gardens and neat woods in fact the canopy of an unfathomable forest. It was like all that water had been necessary – to give everything a good scrubbing. How rich the soil was now! How replete the rivers! He walked along the forest floor, this survivor, as one walks one's first steps in the world, like a faun, with buckling legs and wide eyes.

"He wakes!" exclaimed a voice. "The afterlife has not claimed him yet!"

It was like stained glass – as I tried to open my eyes it was as if I was trapped inside the stained glass like a fly, and around me were the rich reds and blues of this or that holy man's garb, or the white of a holy man's flesh. Then I dimly became aware of reassuring jungle green just beyond – framed by what appeared to be a doorway – and the other colours when I focused upon them were parrot feathers, those that fluttered above the thresh-hold of the principal hut of the *tamoyes* as someone strode under them and in to where I lay.

"It was the drink," I said.

"No matter." Ubi knelt crisply beside me. His warriors' markings were painted with care over the pockmarks of adolescence; if I understood them correctly he had killed ten already, this half-boy-half-man, not bad given he could be no more than seventeen or not good, of course, if you judged by the standards of England – which I no longer did. "You had travelled far. The King hopes you are recovering."

That was a notable improvement, I thought, since the other day he was sorely tempted to eat me. But then I imagined me as the eked-out death, the slowly plumped up *karaiba*, stuffed by their finest food so that I might go to the very same cooking pot fat and happy and tasty: and this vision kept me from lapsing into complacency.

"There are things I have to tell him," I said hurriedly, suddenly eager to prove my usefulness. "Things regarding our enemies the Portugals."

"They can wait," Ubi placated me. "I have a task for you."

"Name it."

"We are preparing the cassava today for eating. You are to assist."

It was an odd request; humiliating even. Cleaning cassava was women's work. They could have consulted me on the whereabouts of hostile tribes, had me demonstrate how gunpowder worked or set up a forge to melt metal into usable weapons. And they wanted me to scrub tubers? But I was not in a position to be choosy about my responsibilities.

"Another thing. I found this ring. Is it yours, Jaci?"

I held out my hand. It was gold. An emerald in the rim. I turned it over. Yes. 'S.C de Sá'. It must have fallen from Manoel's finger.

"You will see we *tamoyes* are not concerned with gold. For us land is gold."

"*A symbol of all that is great about colonisation of these barbarous lands...*" I heard Manoel chuckling, all those years ago. Oh misguided Manoel; you bet on the wrong horse, you did not see he who rose up from the very back as the one to place your faith in but look where you are now, dead, look where the Portugal army is now, a wounded beast with numbered days, look where I am now... I put the ring on. It still fitted. I turned my index finger up first one way then the other; see-saw; see-saw. Ha! To the victor the spoils, ha ha!

"It is mine," I said.

A gathering group of children followed me as I walked downriver through the village to where the cassava plants grew. It was like I was some pied piper. They clapped their hands in time to my steps and giggled whenever I turned around. That is why I liked children[1]. They were the best mirrors to hold up to yourself. This was also why I disliked them in equal measure[2]. The adults were more reserved. They stopped doing whatever it was they had been doing, standing up if they had been sitting or bowing if they had been standing; tight polite gestures. If I was a circus attraction to these *tamoyes* the audience was far from universally enthralled.

It was not a camp, nor was it a village, I saw as I walked. It was a town of clear and precise industry; no man or woman was idle. I knew these people could not have been living here more than a few months, and to construct any such settlement so soon was

---

[1] Knivet's flights of fancy rarely extend to thinking of himself as a family man but here is a rare example of him getting – dare it be said – broody. It is not recorded whether or not he did eventually have children, but he was illegitimate, so there is actually no Earthly reason why anyone should have recorded anything.

[2] It does seem as if Knivet retreated into an almost self-righteous celibacy at times. Then again, so – in Arthurian legend – did Sir Galahad.

impressive, but I had arrived here after weeks of nothingness, and looked upon the ordered rows of huts with awe. Young maids crushed annatto seeds for war paint, youths sharpened arrows or opened up poison frogs to dip them in, mothers with a child on each teat still found a way to pluck parrots for feathers or break wood into tinder or shell tortoises for shields, old women chewed roots in their cheeks like rabbits to ferment the brew these Indians drunk for any and every occasion, and in quantities which would have finished me but seemed not to affect even the weakest of them. The men were mostly on the river where the turtle farm was; some baited the turtles with things turtles like to eat into pens; the nimbler ones fastened the gates to trap them; the cunning ones flipped them onto their backs so they could not swim away; the strong ones knocked holes in the shells and trussed them in rope to tow to shore. Food was everywhere; baked fish, fried larvae, anaconda, ant-eater, chilies, coconuts, papaya, plantain, and so was sound; there was always a drum beating, a rhythm to work by, a hint of wilder times to come once work was done.

Near where the huts ended a man finally did approach me. I recognised him as one of the exuberant fellows who had been smeared in white ash during our somewhat hostile reception and sure enough he took me to a hut that could have housed four families but which had nothing save a gourd rattle on a dais in the middle, surrounded by what looked like offerings and a strong smell of incense.

"Ma-rrrah y kûá," said the man, proudly.

"Yes." I peered at it. "It is one of mine. I made it."

The man looked from me, to the gourd, to me, and appeared too astonished to continue the conversation, so I bid him good day.

I proceeded through a meadow peppered by flowers of an unusually bright red. Soon enough I saw the cassava plants on the drier ground above the river where the mountains closed in. I had imagined cassava preparation would be a large-scale activity, but it seemed that even though the *tamoyes* had several athletic young men flipping turtles on their backs, the harvesting of their entire cassava crop was being overseen by just one girl. She sat on a boulder on the riverbank, washing the roots in the shallows. I adjusted my loincloth and approached. She must have heard me for my steps were loud but she did not turn round; again odd.

"I have been sent to assist you with these tubers."

"Why do you not sit, maker of the Ma-rrrah y kûá?"

THIRTY-EIGHT

"Katawa. I did not know… I would never have guessed…"

"But you dreamed, did you not?"

"I suppose I did dream. But I would not have come if I had known."

"Known that I would be here alone? You do not want to see me?"

"I waited five years to see you. But decency…"

"We do not have a word for decency."

"May I borrow this stick?"

I took it and wrote my name in the mud.

"I want to show you what decency is. This is my name: K-N-I-V-E-T."

"You *karaiba* write your words. How strange."

"Only those few of us who place a value on words. You say a word and it blows away in the wind. Write it, and that word stays for longer in the world."

"I do not understand."

I smoothed over the "v" and the "e"; "g" I wrote instead, "h".

"You have made a new word?"

"Knight."

"Night when the moon comes? When *jaci* comes? My brother calls you Jaci, you know."

"I speak of something else. Knights were good men who once lived in the land I come from. They lived for honour and love. They lived for overcoming evil even when it seemed it would crush them – unless of course they were bad knights, and in the legends those always die in the end. They were gentlemen. They represented decency."

"We do not have a word for gentlemen."

"No matter. Know that there are not many in this forest. There are not many of them at all any more."

"Decency." When she said the word, hesitantly, from under her eyebrows, it was lovelier than poetry. "I suppose I should be grateful to you, maker of the Ma-rrrah y kûá, for being this... decency."

"No!" I seized her hand and kissed her fingers, God, no gloves, no undergarments, there was nothing to stop my kisses continuing over her wrists and up her forearms as I had imagined them doing many a time whilst hacking through that jungle. Martin de Sá had said uninhibited nakedness got the heart racing and other base fellows told me similar things. Why stop, they argued, if there is no frock to stop you. Decency. That was why. "You! Grateful to me! Never! That is not what I meant."

"I would be grateful" – she withdrew her hand; it was clear no one ever kissed her the way I just had and as for my part my heart raced faster than ever it did at those times too numerous to name over the last five years when my very life had been in jeopardy – "to anyone who acted in kindness. And you are kind, I believe that."

I knelt before her in the mud, went to seize her fingers a second time but stopped myself by clasping my own hands together in something akin to prayer; farcical; I never prayed.

"Katawa – forgive me – may I call you that? Your words mean more to me than any others, I can endure abuse from gentlemen, from generals, perhaps even from kings but not from you, never from you, you do not understand, it is as if..."

It was as if I had been on trial my whole life and now the trial was over.

"We have many cassava to clean," she observed. She had eyelashes like a doe.

And you can say to me 'kneel', you can say to me 'clean cassava' and I do not feel demeaned, only elevated.

It is a very important task, preparing cassava, it is no mere potato and therefore you cannot compare the act to, say, a scullery maid scouring potatoes. Cassava is deadly. Foolish foreigners pull up the plants, devouring the roots immediately like gannets, and are within the hour laid low, within two writhing, hallucinating, dying. For cassava contains badness. Indians say the badness is in fact a spirit there to remind them that they are futile before the greatness of nature. The *tamoyes* depend upon this foodstuff utterly. They smoke it, they pound it into crumbs, they eat it in cakes, they concoct brews from it. And so extracting the badness is a ritual. First you clean and peel the cassava so the flesh is fully exposed. Then you pummel it. You pummel it against a board studded with the teeth of wild animals. Then you leach it. You leach the pummelled pomace in a basket with a rock and finally the bad juices go away.

I believed Katawa liked my action with the cassava very well, that day and those just after that it merged into. We always found ways to be alone, even when there were others on cassava duty. There were many spots on the river where we could clean unseen. We bathed there too sometimes; once the evening cool came and the other cassava preparers had gone home. The cassava plants grew up to the base of the mountains; here in the hidden valleys I picked fruits for her and derived immense pleasure from watching her eat them. She would say to me again: "why do you stare at me?" and ask me many times: "did you really come here for me?" We carved out a little world within the big world. She would smile as I gave her my hand to help her over boulders or, on one occasion, made a carpet of ferns for her to sit on. And I would smile for, in evenings when the cassava was done, the King would send for me with increasing frequency to hear from my lips about the Portugals and the devious tricks they had been playing – tricks involving generous gifts of fortified Portugal wine to coerce other tribes into fighting for them – and Ubi with the King's other henchmen would squat with smouldering eyes, waiting to see if I showed any sign of treachery, whereupon I would emphasise that I was with them, now and for all time, but that a cloud was forming beyond the mountain that we must ride out and meet if we did not want it to grow blacker and smother us. Talk of black clouds seemed at odds with the clement river valley where we lived but the most prominent men of Brazil's most prominent tribe listened to me, Anthony Knivet, in respectful silence and with growing rapture, and as I walked back out into the town the children scurried at my side and the men and women were not so hostile as they had been.

Katawa and I had come far, I reflected, as I fashioned her a crown of red meadow flowers, as she laughed at me trying and failing to catch a fish then impaled it herself in just one stab, as I showed her how to skim stones and she marvelled at how I could make them travel right across the river, whispering that I must be a little like a God if I could turn stones into fishes. We had journeyed across Brazil to be here. We had known death along the way – her of her parents and me of my only friends. We deserved this respite.

"There," I proclaimed with mock solemnity. "We are the queen and king of the cassava."

"You are always making jests," she laughed, embarrassed.

"But how? I am not a funny person."

"I do not know anyone else like you."

There was restlessness in the town. People were wondering if the rumours they had heard were true. They went about their duties distractedly, or abandoned them altogether in favour of conspiratorial exchanges, and no one was there to ease the unrest for the King and his advisors were increasingly ensconced in the hut with the parrot feathers, themselves in heated debate. Maybe the people suspected the *karaiba* within their midst was the cause, but maybe they thought his call to arms was what was needed. Maybe they thought it time their King stopped procrastinating and the *tamoyes* stopped running – and rose against the enemies that had pushed them from their lands.

One afternoon we were on opposite sides of the board with the wild animal teeth, scraping this way and that when the inevitable happened; our hands slipped on the pulp and touched, our upper arms too, her face veering close.

"Did you really come here for me?" she murmured.

Your lips are open; I have never seen them thus; your tongue is pressed against your bottom teeth; you keep swallowing even though you are not eating anything. I can smell the sour cherries I picked you for luncheon on your breath.

"You command the attention of many, Katawa, the King included."

"He treats me like he would his own daughter."

I imagined her lashes like jungle creepers, pulling back each and finally finding a way through into some idyllic clearing like the one where we had first met.

"So tell him to listen to me. Tell him the *tamoyes* must strike now against the Portugals. With me at your side you cannot lose. I know where they are weakest."

"And all will be well, if we listen to you." She stood up, with all of her natural reserve tumbling back down like a barricade between us. "Why are you always looking one step beyond what is right in front of you? Why can you not find peace?"

My demure doe was suddenly wild; I did not understand; I was her people's friend – did she not see that all paths, in my life, in her life, in the lives of her people had converged here by this canyon for a reason, namely for me to lead them against the Portugals and reclaim their greatness?

And – I jest not – as she strode away from me there was a rumbling in the sky and as if from nothing it began raining for the first time in weeks.

"Katawa!" I shouted after her as the clouds came down.

I cursed and set off in pursuit, taking the container of cassava pulp with me, but my going was slow – what with the load and the wet – I would not catch her before she got back to the village unless she waited for me. And then I fancied I did see her again, crouching facing me on the other side of the meadow with the red flowers; it was hard to see through the deluge but there was definitely someone there.

"Katawa!" I called again, miserably.

But it was not her. It was a man, and I knew him. His old markings were long gone. But I knew that look – full of a malice no one else, Englishman or Portugal or Indian, could muster. It had stayed with me since our last encounter, five years before, and now here he was once more: that former warrior of the *pories*, Waynembuth, the man I should have killed in battle long ago but had spared instead.

His last words had stayed with me too.

"Maybe, fiend, we will meet again upon the field."

THIRTY-NINE
(The King)

"They were dead men; so they seemed to me as I saw them the first time; white; gaunt; bleeding. They came out of the mist early one morning. My father restrained his people from attacking. He had seen all this before in a dream, he said. Our Gods had sent these men as a test, he believed, maybe they were in fact Gods. The men wanted food, and shelter, and directions. Of course we found that strange. The forest is full of food. The trees are shelter. The river and the sun and stars point the way. But we gave them what they wanted and hoped they would go. We wanted merely to fulfil this terrible test our Gods had sent us, in order that the crops would grow tall and strong and our children would be tall and strong, stronger at least than the enemies we would need to overcome. We thought of these newcomers as spirits to appease for the sake of our land. But they wanted more; more food than we had, our best people as guides. They were insatiable. At first they ridiculed our beliefs. Then they told us our beliefs were wrong. We must believe in their beliefs, they commanded. My father said their Gods did not incline him towards worship; these white men were tired and sad; their Gods must be displeased with them. Gods, cried the white men, there is only one true God! That was when we knew their words were lies. They must be desperate people from a cursed land, to have journeyed all the way here to try taking over another. It was not just us that turned against them; it was the forest too – which convinced us turning against them was right. The forest attempted to dispel them. She sent creatures to attack them. She deprived them of the food she happily provided for us. The white men responded by burning the forest, but there was more forest than they had fire. They kept dying, and we peoples of the forest worked with her to fuel their misery. Yet they did not give up. They used magic against us – weapons that killed in one puff of smoke – and we were weakened, and conceded we should give them the coast, which was all they seemed to crave. The interior was large, my father said, the *karaiba* would never come here. But the *karaiba* did come, you came, you said a black cloud was forming and that we must ride out and meet that cloud or it would smother us. The clouds are here. What do we do?"

As the King lapsed into silence, the rain pounding down outside the hut with the parrot feathers became the primary sound, as if reminding us some action were now necessary. The King looked like he already knew everything there was to know about the world but still, he was looking at me expectantly. So was Ubi, so were the King's foremost henchmen Abousanga and Moyagunga, so were the tribe's two magic men. It was not just expectancy. I do believe it was awe.

The King wore his authority effortlessly; to have 20,000 people under you as he did was quite something; as one of his foremost advisors I would have a significant percentage of those directly answerable to me; if all of us here assembled descended as one on those scattered Portugals we could not fail to topple them and 20,000 could become twice that, more, we would be an unstoppable river and sweep all before us in our wake. I hardly felt it appropriate to say that I had intended my words about dark clouds forming figuratively. If this was what it took to make them heed me, so be it.

"We ride out and meet them," I said. "Every last foe standing in our way: Portugals, Portugal lackeys, anyone who resists. And we do not stop until this land is as red with our enemy's blood as it is green and you, my King, control all of it.

FORTY

*"...they all lay downe in their beds, like men
without lives or soules..."*

Anthony Knivet, *Admirable Adventures and Strange Fortunes*

One day on the way south I stole away from the *tamoyes* just after
we had made camp and dusk was falling. I could not tell anyone
why I was going for in truth I did not know why, not really.

We had been heading down along the bare ridges of the
Andes; risking a foray into Spaniard territory in return for a
speedier passage to the coast of Brazil, aiming for the province
of Tucuman and from there east to Santos – where we would
raise our standard, there and at each Portugal settlement, pushing
them until they gave us fealty. And all of us agreed that there was
no time to lose; eighteen hours of marching per day, we agreed;
six for sleep. But in so doing we had ventured into the hotbed
of Spain's domain in the New World: Potosi. The mountain of
metals. Where Spaniard wealth was concentrated in vaster sums
than anywhere else and where their armies were concentrated
in greater numbers, too. So why was I creeping away from my
Indian brothers when they needed my leadership most?

Something was niggling me. The King had been asking the
last days if we should not attack the Spaniards too while we were
at it; I had told him no; at this time they were not our battle; first
our lands back I told him, first Brazil, then – if he desired – the
continent. But I hated myself for saying such things for I hated
the Spaniards like any respectable young man hailing from the
good country of England who grew up with the Armada, I knew

anything southwest of the Pyrenees was bad news. And here we were – 20,000 warriors – we could have taken the Titicaca Lake, or Nuestra Señora de La Paz! The Potosi furnaces had been staining our horizon for days, goading us with their wealth. Oh, they would not escape unscathed, why should they when others suffered on their behalf without a single *real* of recompense. Upon my family's honour, I would give them a tickling they would remember – and I would do it right in the midst of their precious Potosi.

More than any other tribe, the *tamoyes* knew how to become part of the land even when they were many in number, and pass through it unseen. Thus had we been moving; staying away from settlement; staying out of trouble. But now I was alone I felt more exposed somehow. As I neared the mountain of metals and saw more people, the Indians forced to mine the ore or the Spaniards forcing them, I worried my appearance might be too singular not to attract gossip. When I passed on the slopes those uncouth Spaniard long-beards, partaking of Andean *aguardiente* the Indians had procured them, the liquor scarcely going in their mouths so much as down their overly hairy chins, draped in cloaks to protect their pallid skin and dozing with guns for pillows, I saw I was not white like them, but an off-brown hue enhanced by the fact I was wearing nothing save a thong decorated with feathers and the markings the *tamoyes* had painted on my face, I did not move like them but crept like a phantom, I did not even arm myself like them. But as I passed the Indians slumbering where they had fallen at the end of their days' work, sometimes still bound, at the mouths of the filthy holes they were digging, I realised I was no more like any of them, I was paler, I was taller, there was hair on my face although I tried to pluck it like other t*amoyes* men, I might have moved like a wind compared to a Spaniard but besides an Indian I was still an avalanche, would I not always be an avalanche?

I guessed I was making for the very top. From a distance this mountain which the smug Spaniards called *cerro rico*, or rich hill, looked like a volcano, spouting plumes of manmade fire. But the fire came from the miners' tunnels its sides were riddled with, and the summit was still, a still dark desert of boulders. The Spaniards had erected a cross here – quite a marvellous one – and two men sat below it smoking.

"…I was getting the headache all the time before… now nothing."

"Now that she is dead?"

"Yes, now I feel better than ever…"

"Jesus, Mary and the saints… what is that?"

'That' was me and I stood before them with an arrow in my bow and the string pulled taut.

"Give me your guns."

They gave me their guns. They were too surprised to be afraid at first.

"What do you want?"

"Read what it says on the cross."

"Behold, for this land is the King of Spain's."

"Now," I commanded, "wipe out the words."

They did not dare disobey. With sharp stones they hacked away until the letters were sufficiently defaced.

"Now I could kill you or I could show mercy and bind you. Will I regret it if I bind you?"

They held out their wrists, trembling, and I fastened them hard around the base of that cross.

"Wait," one ventured. "There must be something we can do to remedy this."

"Remedy, knaves? Do you think there is anything *you* can do for me? There is only one man that can give me what I want and he lives on the other side of a rather large ocean. But he will give me what I want, when he sees what I did this night, and what I will soon do, on nights yet to be, when he sees our family name…"

"Please. Don't leave us here. We will die in this cold."

"Death." I said the word slowly. "The likelihood of it gets easier to deal with, that I can vouch for. Did you ever play dominoes, long-beard rogues? Well did you?"

They shook their heads, genuinely frightened by me it seemed for they were trembling.

"You can stand them on end." I bid them crouch low and, excusing myself, stood on their shoulders. The extra elevation was perfect. I could now reach the lofty cross-arms with ease. "You can arrange them any which way; in the prettiest formations; idea being you knock the first and then it bangs right into the second, and so on." I got my knife and carved in big letters that spanned the width of the cross: 'THE QUEEN OF ENGLAND'S' – and then, in smaller writing underneath, 'A.K'. "But even with a line of dominoes, even if you have planned it perfectly, you do not really know how they will fall. That is the thing. None of us know. We must all of us make a mark in this filthy mire of a Brazil when we get the chance, would you not agree?"

I stepped off the Spaniards, stood back to survey my handiwork, took a hearty puff of their tobacco and went on my way.

I was back at camp well before dawn, and thought I had got away with my night's activities undetected. But I was wrong.

"Hark the mighty leader, with his face painted like our faces."

The words were said with bitterness; they could only be from one person.

"Katawa! I have missed you these last days on the road. I wanted to explain..."

"Where have you been? To betray us to the Spaniards?"

"I am one of you. I would not betray you."

"No." Her comely face was closer to mine than it had ever been yet defiantly further away than ever too. "You are one. You are alone. You always will be."

"You do not mean that. I journeyed five years through Brazil for you."

"You journeyed five years for yourself."

Abousanga cleared his throat behind us.

"The King is asking for you."

He was a good man, Abousanga.

Imagine it – 20,000 men and women on the bare brown Andes. The King goes first; the feathers on his head are white; he creeps close to the ground and moves swiftly. He is no pompous target like these generals of Europe, nor will he sit back in battle whilst those under him sacrifice themselves. The steps that he takes, everyone takes, as surely as one wave on the oceans is followed by the next. The King's foremost men deploy themselves throughout the army at intervals: they must keep spirits high during the toughest parts of the march and when enemies come, they must drive the warriors to victory. The women, the young and the old come near the rear but can move as speedily as the men, and carry on their backs everything this mighty force might need – arrows, poison frogs, tortoiseshells for shields, clubs for when the arrows run out, cassava meal – and little more besides. Then there are the musicians, and they can be as intimidating as the most formidable fighter for they provide the deadly beat – gourd rattles; Ma-rrrah y kûá – they too are found throughout the force and the sound when they choose to make it resonates from everywhere all at once like an earthquake. And when you behold this 20,000 from above it is a little like beholding a raging river that has burst its banks and cascades across the land in flecks of – ha! – white, vermillion, cobalt, which are of course the feathers of the birds the men wear in their hair... swooping... unstoppable.

Down we went into the dry and desolate land of Tucuman, in the rocks of which lay, somewhere, the divide between Spaniard territory and Portugal territory. Here everyone fought with everyone, Spain with Portugal, Indian with Indian. It was a lawless place even by the lawless standards of South America. But it was beautiful too. We turned east, making for lower, lusher ground; and between the crags appeared many lakes of an extraordinary blue. I found the openness of these lands agreeable for by association, when the way is clear your path in life has the semblance of clarity.

Our scouts found the corpses soon after that. They were pygmies, the stunted peaceable souls that were the natural inhabitants of the region and who would oblige you with anything within their power to give. They were oases in this hostile place and there was no cause to kill them unless you had a passion for butchery. I guessed the culprits, therefore, before the scouts showed us the sinister confirmation: charred hoops of vines and feathers. *Just like this shall you be consumed.* I recalled the frightened face of the sailor on his deathbed, relating how eighty of the fleet that brought me here all those years before had been set upon by red and black devils and massacred; I recalled the brutes I had once seen cutting up the *tamoyes* and anointing themselves in the juices. *Tomomynos.*

We met at a fissure between two hills; the setting was dramatic but there was none of the pomp I had imagined might go with open battle. There was a fleeting moment, maybe, when they were suddenly frozen there opposite us – our mirror image you could say for of course once they were us; their roots were the same; it was in a sense like attacking one's own reflection. But the red on their faces was blood.

Our men started pouring down the slopes, two rivers bent on meeting, and I was at the King's side in the melee. Indians use bows relentlessly – even in close combat when there is barely time or space to draw them. But their arrows run dry soon enough, and if you survive that first hail of the things – ha - that means it is not your day to die. No shaft could touch me, and we were onto the clubs, the self same clubs my dear deceased friend Quarasips Juca and the other Portugals had been sacrificed with. If you are the swinger it is a challenge to raise one from the ground, let alone rotate it with sufficient impetus to slay your fast-approaching foe. If you are the swung-upon the clubs are so heavily studded in sharp stones and shells that if you are struck once it will likely be the end. We were an efficient fighting force, us tamoyes, but how to compete against a people that so relished war? They breathed war, these *tomomynos*, with their twitching nostrils they inhaled it like it was a fine-smelling stew, and with the squelch of stone or steel in flesh came on the stronger. Meanwhile, we had charged down the hill to meet them too eagerly; we were all in the river at the valley bottom whilst many of them were still coming down on top of us. In an uphill battle against *tomomynos* you will be punished whoever you are. Too many of our boys and old men had taken up the arms of the fallen. The water was red with largely our blood.

"Forgive me," I cried to the King, and without waiting for his consent shouted to the *tamoyes* to fall back, which they did, as my voice sounded like the King's.

"What treachery is this *karaiba? Tamoyes* never run from their enemies!"

"Trust in me, my King. Take half of those we have left back over the hill. I will stave off any pursuers then flee along the river the league or so until it empties into that lake down there. They will follow us. When we are at the lake a-battling you will come upon them from behind and the victory, mark my words, will be ours."

I commanded my men to throw the vilest insults they could muster at the *tomomyno*s alongside their most valiant blows; my mind, I admit, went blank but Abousanga, who stayed with me, thought up some exquisite slander. It worked. The *tomomynos* were so provoked that they attacked us like mad dogs while the King and his share of our forces escaped. "Fight dirtily!" I rallied my troops. "Now, run!"

The running was simple enough but when we reached the edge of the lake we had to hold them, we had to fend off a pack of riled hounds that sensed blood, our blood, blood they would dearly love to ornament their gruesome facial decorations with.

We were hemmed in with the lake behind us and there were no more steps back we could take.

When you hold your breath underwater the only sound you hear is the water, just an otherworldly rumbling, when you come up for air you hear the other unwelcome sounds of reality and they are more unwelcome on account of your having been in that underworld quiet, you dip back under, the sounds are drowned out. I was under. I chopped wood to light the oven in the bakery in Charlton, candied flowers, batch on batch of them, the fragrance of the woods of Wiltshire. I was up. Bloody, tarry faces, snuffling nostrils, screams, sweat, shit. I re-immersed myself and chopped more wood. The plunge into the void would not be so bad if I thought of Charlton.

The King heeded my words. His men did what the *tamoyes* do so well, becoming part of the land, and stealing up behind those *tomomynos* so close they did not notice until the clubs came down upon their skulls. Our enemies did not know which way to turn. They had never encountered strategy.

Nor had the King. We met in the middle when he had hacked in from behind and I had kept hacking in from the front, and we were suddenly facing each other, clubs raised, like we could not believe there were no more to kill. He tossed down his weapon and embraced me.

"You bring our people to new glories," he said. "Name what you want, and it shall be yours."

I was destined for great things, the quack had told me so, and here was a king offering me whatever I wanted.

"This is our battle, but the war is not yet won. When you are installed on the throne of Brazil, my King, and no more dare rise against you, if I am still fortunate enough to be at your side you may ask that question again."

"Come. I know there is one thing you would like, *karaiba*. Say it. There is no shame in it. We are men, are we not? We need women, and the sister of Ubirajara is a good choice. She is like a daughter to me. It would be my pleasure."

But would it be mine? Now I stood on the field triumphant but if I took her, ran my mouth up from her toes to her thighs, down from her shoulders to her belly and then – *that* place - would I not be distracted by the King and Ubi observing my performance – and what if my touch inspired derision and not pleasure at all?

"It is not the time, my King. But if the time comes, and it is your pleasure, then of course it will be my pleasure as well."

I wondered if any of this was right, looking about me at the bodies, sometimes mere boys, strewn on the plateau above the lake scarlet with Indian blood on the edge of Brazil. Is this what we set sail for from Plymouth, from Cadiz, from Lisbon?

The virtuous man goes out into the wilderness and is tempted by the devil, but what is succumbing to temptation, really, and what is not succumbing? If you take a flake of gold from the ground, are you compromised, if you feel lust for a woman there, are you compromised, if you do battle in a land to regain it for its rightful owners, are you compromised, if in the process you kill a man who would have tried to kill you, are you compromised? Or have you in fact become the true you? Have you not become defined by the pull between what is wrong and what is right?

The red colour did not fade from the lake for many days. I suppose our blood had nowhere left to flow. The battle had taken its toll on us. We stayed by the water, dressing our wounds. The magic men said incantations over the dying, which perhaps had as much effect as Catholics calling for God's mercy might. I fished. There is not a lot else to do when you are stuck for a long time by a lake. I was not good at fishing. I could have sorely used Katawa's talent for it, but she did not come to find me. The fish I pulled from the water were brown at first. But after about a week I caught one that was bright red. The blood of the *tamoyes* had stained the very creatures of Brazil. Then I had a moment of enlightenment. I had been contemplating, privately, how we could possibly go on to defeat the Portugals and their arsenal, when the *tomomynos* had laid us so low with clubs and arrows. Now I knew. The French! We had been making for Santos. But below the southernmost Portugal settlements, and above the Río de la Plata that lay in the hands of Spaniards, there was a patch of coast dominated by traders and farmers, and free from the clutches of any Iberians whatsoever. These traders and farmers were almost all Frenchmen. There would be scores of men sympathetic to our cause there, for Frenchmen were our old allies and had fought with us against the Portugals before. And they would have weapons. They could be our cutting edge – ha – they could be the teeth with which we could rip open those Portugal flanks and bleed them dry. Brandishing the bloody fish, I went among the *tamoyes* and held it aloft as a sign. A great cheer went up. And on we went.

* * *

I blinked in disbelief to see the sea again. Some *tamoyes* there had never seen it.

"You *karaiba* concern yourselves with silver and gold," said the King. "But this is brighter than all the treasure in the world."

"This is what the Portugals took from you. Let us go and retrieve it."

It was a fertile land we had descended into, there were low green hills, and well-tilled fields below the hills, and streams meandering down to yellow bays where small houses sat with smoke rising from their chimneys.

I asked at the first dwelling where I might find their leader. They regarded me with confusion and dread and directed me to the water's edge. Here there was a wooden pier, and a man dressed in black standing at the end. His hands were clasped behind his back and he was looking out at the ocean.

"With your good leave," I approached him, "I come to ask for your help."

"*Mon ami*" the man turned; he had a cane; when he spread his arms the gesture therefore seemed overly dramatic. "You have many men under your command. Why do you not take whatever it is you want?"

"Do you know who we are?"

"Is it important to you that I know?"

"We are the *tamoyes*, your old allies. You fought with us once against the Portugals. We march to fight them again, and to put and end to their tyranny for good. Come. March with us."

"No. *They* are the *tamoyes*." The man pointed at our army, scattered across the fields around the village. Several of them were gingerly stroking a foal chained to one of the houses, and deriving amusement from its whinnies. "Who are you?"

"I am… one who would lead."

"Your guardedness tells me all I need to know." The man looked back out to sea. "The thing is that they will not follow you – not all the way. I speak from experience. We had the upper hand before when we fought with them, and then the Portugals split them, using no more guile than a priest who spoke the Indian tongue to turn them on each other. And thus dichotomised…" he shrugged. "That was the end of the last true threat the Portugals faced in Brazil. There will not be another."

"This time your people could be the difference between success and failure." I gripped his shoulder but he brushed me away.

"You could take every able man here and in every village hereabouts. You could take all our weapons – which total some few old guns, no more. You could take the last things we have and it would not be enough for we are talking about the Portugals who have enough firearms in just one of their garrisons to obliterate your forces. Do not bring that upon yourself. I would not willingly bring it upon my people."

"We could kill you!" I cried, impatient with his protestations.

"You do not need more enemies. And you do not want to rile me, I think. For I know you are not who you say – at least not what you have told these people you are."

"You know nothing about me."

"I would wager these good Indians think you are French, yes? Oh, they think of us as some sort of salvation because we once did them the kindness of standing with them in battle. But we are clinging on here ourselves!" He raised his voice for the first time.

"I will not risk what we have left for such a doomed enterprise as yours. And you, you faux General, you will be clinging on to your leadership or whatever grand word you use for it if I tell them that you are not French, that you have been misleading them all this time!"

"You would not…" I began hotly, then sighed. "What is it that you want?"

"I want you to leave."

We went. The *tamoyes* did not seem too concerned about the Frenchman's refusal of help. Arrived at the seaside they were like lambs in spring grasses. They kept bringing me shells as presents like they were the finest gifts on Earth. The King himself went around with a big open smile on his face. And as I observed their happiness I wondered why I felt none of it myself. I wondered if I could ever feel it.

"Something troubles you, *karaiba*? For I assure you it need not. We *tamoyes* have never been more ready for battle."

I was troubled. I was thinking of the day the storm broke, back in the cassava fields where Katawa had run away from me. But I was not thinking of her. I was thinking of the crouching figure I had seen through the deluge. Waynembuth.

"If you once do a man wrong," I asked the King, "is it right to fear that they will one day take their revenge?"

"We *tamoyes* have an easy answer, *karaiba*," chuckled the King. "Kill those you fear will do you wrong. It is a rule we always lived by. But fear not. If it is just one man you speak of, what can he do against 20,000 of us?"

Our scouts reported the land ahead was changing. The fertile farming country was gone. Swamp had replaced it. There was a terrible smell on the air – worse than excrement, they said – and swarms of flies everywhere that gave you a terrible bite.

"Santos," I murmured.

"You have been here before, *karaiba*?"

"Once. Long ago."

When our army got to within a couple of headlands the King

bid us all gather and listen to me. I told them Santos was an island; that in itself it was a sorry place, but a strategic one, for it was the Portugals' principal port in this Brazil, and their southernmost town, and that the taking of it would give the so-called invincible armour of these Iberians a denting they would never forget. I proposed to lead the first attack but Ubi came forward to stop me.

"Let me go," he said determinedly.

"Save yourself for another day. I know the town."

"You know everything, Jaci," he retaliated bitterly. "But you are not in command here."

"Two of my finest young warriors, both wanting to claim glory for the *tamoyes!*" The King smiled. "Why do you not both go?"

"As you wish. But who will be in charge?"

There was a tense pause.

"You will, *karaiba.*"

Ubi looked thunderous. I could barely contain my delight.

We took a hundred men and paddled across the muddy estuary an hour before dawn, which Cavendish had found a most effective time for attack all those years previously. The moon was not full this time, but it was enough to see by, and hopefully not enough to be seen. We somehow kept ourselves from retching at the foulness of the air and made the first of the wide streets that led to the centre. The houses were all dark. That could have been because the inhabitants were sleeping of course, but something did not seem right to me, so I bid some men knock down a few doors. Nothing. And again, nothing. No one was inside.

"Where are they all, Jaci?"

I pointed to the *praça*, the central square where the slipshod builders of Santos had made some attempt to bring the town dignity. I guessed they would be there if anywhere. I was right. As we reached the square the arrows started raining out of the College of Jesus; thick; fast; pinning us back to the side streets for some minutes. But even at their worst I calculated there could be no more than a score doing the shooting. Just after the thickest flurry of arrows fifteen men emerged, a few Portugals and their lackeys the *cariihos*, covering themselves with pistol fire, and scampering off in the direction of the pier. Half of us gave chase whilst half secured the building, but the defenders of Santos escaped, and there were no more to be found. The town was ours.

"What nation defends such an important port with fifteen men?" Ubi asked me coldly.

"We have the port," I answered. "That is the important thing."

The *tamoyes* – the King included - thought that was indeed the important thing. A whoop went up when the rest of our forces heard the news. We poured into Santos in our thousands and despite having had no sleep that last night and a long march before that we filled the wide stinking streets with revelry, dancing and drumming and sucking on tobacco pipes for sustenance whenever the revelry seemed to tire us. But Ubi was right. Who did defend a port they valued with just fifteen men?

I took plenty of puffs of the tobacco, as I wanted to stay awake too – but not for festivities. I prowled the streets nervously, opening every door of every house and searching for weapons. Cavendish had made the error of not defending Santos effectively seven years before and I was not about to make the same mistake. I got together some swords, gunpowder and even one or two muskets, then put them under lock and key in the College of Jesus. I paced some more, and finally, deciding there was nothing to be done for tonight except partaking of the party – which I was disinclined to do – I went down to the pier, where I could at least be sure of some small amount of peace.

The tree with the oranges was still there. I squatted; peeled one; it was unripe; I ate it anyway.

"You are not celebrating with the others?"

Katawa.

"Why do you not sit?"

She did so, most demurely, on the other side of the pier from me. The moon shone on certain parts of her body – her knees and shoulders – and on other parts not at all. She had her arms folded in her lap and was bending forward, as if to look into my face better from around an obstacle that was not even there.

"There is nothing to celebrate. Not until the Portugals are defeated."

"You really do want to help our people," she observed, curiously.

"Of course. What else could I want, having fought for you these last months?"

"I do not know. Back in the cassava fields, I did think you wanted me."

"Forgive me. I have been preoccupied…"

"Your only preoccupation is yourself," she said, sadly.

Do you see those marks in the sand, I wanted to say to her, those patterns that the worms make when the tide is low and get immersed again when the tide is high? I want not to be like a worm. I want not to be washed away. That is what I want and you cannot give it to me.

"I came to tell you something, maker of the Ma-rrrah y kûá."

"Do not call me that," I said stiffly. "My name is Anthony Knivet."

"I am promised to Abousanga. Ubi approves of it. Abousanga is a good man. And he is one of us."

I laughed, probably too shrilly, I nodded several times.

"Yes, yes, he is a good man – ha – one of the best."

"Very well. That is all… I should go."

"You should. You should go to him."

She stood up. She walked back down the pier. It did not even creak under her weight. She really was beautiful. And yet again she was making her way away from me.

"But stay," I cried on an impulse. "Have an orange, I have one peeled…"

"*Why do you stare at me, maker of the Ma-rrrah y kûá?*"

The arrow hit her cleanly, in that soft area just below the throat. It came from the side; from somewhere out in the darkness. I got to her just as she fell. I knew I did not have long. I picked her up and ran back towards the merry-makers in the square. They laughed at me when I came, like I must be acting out some terrible drama, like what I was doing could only be an act.

"They are coming!" I screamed.

"What have you done?" they screamed back, sobering, realising, snatching Katawa from me.

We were borne away from each other, in two separate tides of Indians. They blamed me, which hurt me. But of course I blamed myself – that was the irony of it.

The arrows were raining in our midst. More men fell, but we could still not see clearly from where we were being attacked. Each shaft made a wet 'pht'; it was ridiculous such a sound could represent the termination of a life like that.

"To the College of Jesus!" I tried to rally my troops and somehow we made it; we were in utter disorder and for the most part utterly intoxicated but there – a good solid wall behind us – that was something.

"K*araiba*," gasped the King, but he could not even hold his bow and arrow straight, none of them could.

So there we were, us 20,000, an army that did not care a tuppence for God protected by the Godliest building around. A very elegant building. Marble. A spiral staircase. An old painting at the top of some noble, young and determined looking with fair hair curling out from under his visor atop a steed of the purest white.

We had the door barricaded. It was dark. Not enough of a moon.

"What do you see?" I cried to the archers I had posted at the windows looking out onto the square.

"Just one man. He has no weapon. Shall we finish him?"

"On no account! Make way, imbeciles!"

I tore one of the *tamoyes* from his post. The window was small, but enough to get a gun through, which I did, letting in the hot sour air of Santos and the bizarre sight of an Indian, clad in

Portugal armour, walking across the square towards the steps of the College of Jesus as casually as if he was going to sit down on them and take in the view.

"Is that your gun barrel I see, fiend?"

"Waynembuth! When was it you decided to renounce your own people and side with the Portugals?"

"As I recall, fiend, it was you bid me walk away from my own people! Now I come with a message from the Portugals, and that is to lay down your bows and arrows and not stir, for if you disobey you will all be put to the sword."

"Never!" We are the *tam…*"

The first canon blasted away the door and the ten or so *tamoyes* huddling closest to it. I had never seen a blaze like it and the Indians certainly had not. They lay down, whimpering and blocking their ears with their hands. If they did not do so through fear then they did so because of the liquor they had consumed. The second canon ripped into the upper balcony. Down crashed the masonry but the picture of the nobleman, I noticed, stayed hanging there imperiously.

After that the Portugals appeared to realise there was no need to waste any more of their gunpowder. They came in, ruthlessly, some of us they bound, some of us they killed, there did not seem to be any logic to it. It was reminiscent of the day we Englishmen captured the Portugals at Christmas mass at the church seven years previous, I heard Stafford's tuneless rendition of 'Greensleeves', *if you intend to thus disdain, it does the more enrapture me, and even so I still remain your lover in captivity*, he had known all the words but the notes had come out gargled, he could turn anything beautiful into something ugly, Stafford, and it seemed that was a knack I had also.

The College of Jesus was emptying. Why had they not killed me yet? I was ready for it.

"Come, villains!" I pointed to my heart. "Put your blades there if you dare!"

But they were avoiding me, skirting around me and taking the *tamoyes* and leaving me alone in the debris of this house of God.

"Take me you knaves! Why will you not take me?"

The door reopened. It was Martin de Sá, future governor of the River of January, looking fine as ever – how did he manage to stay looking so fine? He took off his capotain hat. He twirled it. He tossed it up. He caught it. He leaned against the gap where the door had been as if finding me thus had always been part of the plan.

"Anthony Knivet! Whatever are you doing here, naked and quailing and with deer markings on your face? And with my father's ring upon your finger? What on Earth were you thinking?

"My father…" I struggled, trying to explain. "The General… You… The Governor…"

"I do believe," Martin de Sá said, tenderly, "that you thought you could rise to the very top. But look at you." His hand was on the hilt of his sword. "Look at you."

"Take me," I beseeched him. "You have a blade. Here: through my heart. Make sure of it for plenty tried sending me to my maker, and none yet had a firm enough hand."

"I told you before that I have two sides. A white one and a black one – and this night, Anthony Knivet, I suppose I am showing you my white."

The painting at the top of the spiral staircase chose that moment to fall. Perhaps only a thread had been holding it. It tumbled some way, over and over down the steps, that young noble, the expression on his face never changing, breaking up into fragments which made me suspect that, in fact, the whole thing had probably been made of an inferior material.

I looked at the sword of Martin de Sá. It was still in its sheath but his hand continued to clasp it, as if he was erring between dispatching the fatal blow and suspending the death sentence a little longer. What did white mean for this man? Killing me cleanly? Imprisoning me? Exonerating me? Up to now life had always dragged me down the sorriest of the ways that branch off from the crossroads, and I did not see a reason for it to suddenly become more benevolent, so I closed my eyes, ready for the worst. And I waited. I felt the pulling again. The old feeling. The rack, if you like, tearing me between… well, why find other words for it at this late stage… white and black. But it is never as simple as white being right and black being wrong. All you can say in life – and put this on my gravestone, if I get one, although the devils might overlook even that – is that you are pulled, sometimes to the other side of the world and sometimes? Sometimes you are pulled right back again to where you began it all.

I was back in the woods above my father's estate, but not as Lord of the manor, oh no. I was who I had always been; still dusted with bakery flour. Below me they were hunting: all the gallant young gentlemen. The buck sped through the trees ahead of them. Would they bring it down? Well, what of it? There was a comfrey pie in my hands. And the pastry – if I said so myself – did taste rather good.

ROEBUCK

COMFREY PIES

Take your meat (swan is good, but most game birds can suffice)
and gut it, and wash it, and season it liberally in nutmeg, and salt,
and pepper, and divide it amongst the number of pie bases you
have prepared. Distribute around the meat ample quantities of
clary (you may instead use sage), hyssop (you may instead use
mint) and galingale, which is necessary to achieve the desired
pungency. Liberally sprinkle the comfrey roots (split open to
allow their regenerative juices to flow somewhat) over the meat
and other herbs, and also place butter and shallots in the pie bases.
Close the pies up, and bake them well with more butter. Serve
them cold with honey and mustard and just a little more butter.

AUTHOR'S NOTE

Roebuck – Tales of an Admirable Adventurer is – at least in part – a true story. Anthony Knivet really did exist, and the original account of his adventures was published in 1625 in Samuel Purchas' huge volume of explorers' tales, *Purchas his Pilgrimes*, under the title *the Admirable Adventures and Strange Fortunes of Master Anthony Knivet, which went with Thomas Candish Upon his Second Voyage to the South Sea. 1591.*

It was "at sea" or rather engaged on adventures that Knivet remained for most of the next ten years (this novel concerns itself with the years 1591 to 1598, but there are many more colourful episodes to the man's escapades in the New World besides). Nevertheless, the original account is published almost 25 years later, and questions have to be asked about its validity as a historical resource – indeed they have been by the scattering of historians over the years who have shown an interest in Knivet's story.

Were his memories faded, or at least slightly skewed, when recounting his adventures a quarter of a century afterwards? Possibly. Even if his memories were crystal clear, can Samuel Purchas as an editor be deemed trustworthy? Probably not: his margin notes often seem to be exaggerating Knivet into a figure of fun. Why is so much of the juicy detail we would have loved to see in Knivet's account – the brutality of life upon a privateering vessel; the customs of the tribes that then populated the fledgling colony of Brazil – absent?

This story follows the 1625 account as published by Purchas – and as far as it is possible. Beyond that, it follows what could have happened – but what has not been proven to.

Knivet was the illegitimate son of a Wiltshire aristocrat, but he didn't necessarily have delusions of grandeur that he would one day inherit his father's estates. He is not proven to have possessed any talent as a baker. He never makes a mention of Katawa – or any love affair – in his original account, but perhaps there were good reasons for that.

But he did indeed embark from Plymouth with the already famous explorer Sir Thomas Cavendish, on Cavendish's second circumnavigation of the globe. Harry Barrawell and William Waldren did sail in the same expedition. The fleet did run into difficulties after exactly the chain of events described, and Knivet did end up being set on shore. He did end up fending for himself for the following decade in a country that would have seemed every bit as hostile to Elizabethan sailors as it comes across in this book. And for a significant chunk of that decade, he was living with, or travelling with, or fighting alongside tribes that would soon die out completely – decimated by smallpox or slavery or European bullets in battles they could never hope to prevail in. Indeed, the amount of time he spent with South America's indigenous peoples is calculated to have eclipsed any other *karaiba* (foreigner) until the 20th century – even that of Hans Staden, whose encounters with cannibalistic Brazilian tribespeople are far better known.

Anthony Kivet's story really was a riveting one – of that there can be little doubt.

ABOUT THE AUTHOR

A Creative Writing graduate from the UK's University of East Anglia, Luke has written for publications including the BBC, the Independent, the Telegraph, the Guardian and travel publishers Lonely Planet, for whom he has specialised in telling the world about the Amazon Basin – present and past – for the last seven years. One could infer from this that he is overly obsessed with rainforests. But the truth is that he adores the outdoors anywhere: as long as it is in the middle of nowhere.

Urbane Publications is dedicated to
developing new author voices, and publishing
fiction and non-fiction that challenges, thrills and
fascinates. From page-turning novels to innovative
reference books, our goal is to publish what
YOU want to read.

Find out more at

urbanepublications.com